AN.

In Denial

ALSO BY ANNE REDMON

Emily Stone

Music and Silence

Second Sight

The Genius of the Sea

The Judgement of Solomon

The Head of Dionysos

ANNE REDMON

In Denial

Published in 2003 by

The Maia Press Limited
82 Forest Road
London E8 3BH
www.maiapress.com

ISBN 1 9045590 1 8

A CIP catalogue record for this book is available
from the British Library

Printed and bound in Great Britain by Thanet Press

I would like to thank Cambridge University Press for allowing me to quote from *A History of the Crusades* by Sir Stephen Runciman; the Rev. Anthony Meredith SJ, and David Widdowson, who patiently answered my questions about prison protocol. Any mistakes I have made are my own. In addition, I would like to express my gratitude to the many prisoners with whom I have worked since 1990 for all that they have given me and for the kindness they have shown me. Above all, I owe my editor Maggie Hamand an acknowledgement that makes expressions of gratitude seem inadequate.

All of the characters in this book are fictional and the situations portrayed are imaginary.

AR

For Benedict as always,
and for my mother
Elizabeth Redmon

1

SENIOR OFFICER GOSFORTH stood on the Centre and looked down the length of J Wing. It was a sticky day in August, only 9 a.m. and already the sun blistered the landing floor through the high fortified windows of the Victorian prison. Damp from the thick walls, combined with male sweat and the steam from food trolleys, hung on the air in an ooze of humidity. S.O. Gosforth had bad news for Hythe and he did not want to deliver it.

Every morning, while the able-bodied inmates were out on exercise, Hythe, supported by a stick, took his solitary constitutional up and down the landing. A few old lags, elderly men with arthritis or heart disease, did the same, but they never spoke to Hythe, or he to them. Maybe they shunned him. Hythe might have committed mayhem for all Gosforth knew, but this was the unit for loners, so it was hard to tell. In any case, it didn't do to enquire too closely into the offences of these inmates. A baby-faced lad could have raped a woman taking a short cut home. An old codger with a smile like Santa Claus might have spent years molesting babies. There were scoutmasters, schoolmasters and care assistants, tax-payers and church-goers who looked as bewildered to be in prison as if they had never had anything more sinister planned for a sunny weekend but to dig the garden and wash the car. It was a strange preserve, the unit, where Dr Jekyll languished, all unknowing, for the sins of Mr Hyde.

Gosforth smiled at the thought process that had conjured up this literary analogy. It was not only the similarity of the villain's name, but the apparent harmlessness of the man. Hythe caused the regime no trouble. He was something of an enigma to Gosforth. He was quiet to the point of being invisible and never went anywhere but the prison library. He read voraciously and, when he was checked through his peephole, was often seen to be scribbling in large exercise books. In what manner Hythe was crippled, or even if he actually was, Gosforth was not sure. Inmates were endemically self-dramatising and worried endlessly about their health. Hythe, nevertheless, must have merited his single cell on the Twos where he had no need to tackle the long iron staircases.

It was hard to guess his age, though he seemed rather elderly, with a greasy lock of grey hair flopping on his forehead like an old rag. As for his social background, that was even more difficult to gauge. He was a small man with bandy legs, but, bloated perhaps on steroids, he looked ponderous with the weighty expression on his face of a judge. Well, Gosforth had heard about the judge they'd once had on the unit. They'd had a doctor, too, and a variety of civil servants. Somehow, Gosforth associated Hythe with this odd aristocracy, who bobbed about in the prison like souls in some medieval paradigm of hell. They had a perpetual look of indignation – astonished, perhaps, that they had to share the fiery lake with the cannon fodder of the prison population, those inmates who came from an underclass so deprived that their depravity seemed a foregone conclusion.

Senior Officer Gosforth was himself an educated man and was fond of classical allusion: he sometimes thought of the havoc Eros wreaked when he chose to dip his arrows in poison. Since he had come to work on the unit, he had tried to understand what it was that induced men to risk everything they had on an orgasm. They came in the gate, at which he now gazed, to be sequestered from the passions that had possessed them. At night, the gloomy rows of locked doors gave off the aura of a morgue with drawers and, save for the exceptional nocturnal howl of pain that sometimes went up, the occasional but all too frequent suicide, it was easy for Senior Officer Gosforth to imagine that he was guarding the vaults of a bank.

Gosforth held Hythe's message, a fax which had only a few moments ago been thrust into his hand. Just as he was about to take the necessary step of bellowing for the inmate, Hythe materialised as if by prestidigitation. He had been round the corner at the medics and was now shuffling his way towards the telephones, a prescription packet in his hand.

'Hythe? A word . . .' Gosforth said, leaving the nickel grating of the Centre, that protecting mandala where only officers were allowed to stand.

Hythe looked round, impassive. On closer inspection, Gosforth observed that he could not be more than fifty. His face was like a weather-beaten statue, one that would not have been out of place in a stately garden, an eroded Pan without pipes. Indeed, there was something elfin about him, the eternal child, and this was disquieting.

'I think we'd be better off in the office,' Gosforth said.

Hythe took in the flimsy bit of fax paper with a glance, but saying nothing to betray anxiety, nor indeed any other emotion, he slowly followed the officer.

From the high barred window, they could hear the incessant mutter of the men out in the yard. It was stuffy in the monastic white room and a heavy stillness lay between them.

'Look, I'm sorry, mate,' said Gosforth, 'but this came for you this morning. Do you want it or do you want me to read it to you? Not brilliant news, I'm afraid.'

Hythe paused and considered. 'Read it . . . please,' he added. 'My glasses are in my cell.'

'It's been sent through the Governor's office: "Re: Gerald Hythe," it says, and comes from a . . . Cassandra Hythe? Your sister?'

Hythe shook his head. 'My cousin,' he said.

Gosforth read aloud, '"I am writing in hope that someone will inform Gerald that Harriet Washington is dead."' There was another pause.

'At last!' Hythe said without clearing his throat; the sound came out like a gravedigger's spade on stones. He gave a mirthless laugh and for a moment Gosforth felt both relieved at not having to mop him up and unreasonably shocked by his coldness. But how could he judge? He didn't know. Some of these men had histories like compressed world wars. When he looked up, however, Hythe was quietly weeping. The great laconic stone of his habitual expression had collapsed and he sat with his two arms rigid on the chair clutching and unclutching the leatherette pads. If Hythe had been fit, he might, Gosforth sensed, have leapt up and banged out of the room, for he shot him that look of impersonal hostility from inmate to officer. But he was either too tired or too upset to move.

'What?' he asked at length. 'What did she die of?'

Gosforth cleared his throat. 'It says she had a stroke.'

'Like me,' Hythe said. His tears dried as quickly as they had come. 'She knew I had a stroke, but it didn't kill me. It only maimed.'

'Her funeral . . .' Gosforth paused.

'Don't worry,' Hythe interrupted. 'I shan't ask to be going.'

'Is today. Your cousin . . . Cassandra . . .'

Hythe leaned forward with a meaningful and steady eye.

'Is this something you'd like to talk about?' Gosforth asked. Someone as bottled up as Hythe could be at risk.

'You don't know who I really am, do you?'

The oddity of the question took Gosforth aback. 'No . . . Who?' He shook his head slowly, anticipating a Napoleon or Julius Caesar in reply.

'I used to be Gerry Carney,' Hythe said. 'Ring a bell?'

HMP Grisholme stands on the baleful outskirts of Peckham Rye. Although it looks grim with its crenellations and portcullis, it is of some architectural interest and a landmark in the history of penology, one of the earliest panopticons constructed. It is circular, the wings of the prison radiating like the spokes of a wheel from a hub whence it was thought easier to observe, control and reform the inmates. When the prison was built, the captives were urged to repent before God; now, they are persuaded into group therapy. From time to time, tales of brutality escape but Grisholme functions a fraction better than many other prisons, albeit on the shoestring allotted to it by the government. The old style of prison officer, the sort famous for the split peaks of their caps and their open admiration of Hitler, is being phased out and replaced by such as James Gosforth, who is sent on courses where he is taught the fundamental skills of cognitive therapy and man management. Unlike many, he has a degree, but he keeps quiet about it. He is also writing a novel in his spare time. The skinhead element that remains in the service sends a shudder down his spine. Gosforth is always delighted to see signs of progress and reform. As for sex offenders, he isn't sure they should be in prison at all . . . perhaps special hospitals, for he is not convinced that what they do is entirely of their own volition.

S.O. Gosforth is a closet idealist who entered the service with a wish to do some good. He keeps quiet about that, too. Although he is in his late thirties, he has not married because the right woman has to come along for him before he commits himself. He is wistful in this pursuit and has looked among the women officers with hopes that are continually dashed. It is difficult at Grisholme to ask someone out for a drink after work in the casual way that is easiest for a man naturally bashful with women, because the area around the prison emanates a haggard viciousness. Tower blocks range like pylons that hum with the restless energy of frustration, and often it is an easy and logical move to Grisholme for men whose families live virtually across the road in high-rise flats that share the ethos, if not the appearance, of the prison itself.

Gerry Carney (or Gerald Hythe) spent much of his childhood, not in a stately home, though he might have done, but on the thirteenth floor of a nearby estate. His mother, still living, never goes to see him, but she thinks of him . . . bitterly.

Even though Mary Carney gets hate mail and graffiti sprayed on her front door, the Council won't rehouse her. She is afraid to go out after dark down the long, concreted, ill-lit walkways, even to get a packet of fags if she has run out. A good by-blow of this, she tries to convince herself, is that she is giving up smoking. She misses it, though, and she misses, too, the high times of youth. Now and then she even thinks with nostalgia of Gerry's father. She appreciates more than ever now her cut of Hythe money, discreetly gained, discreetly squirrelled away. It certainly won't do Gerry any good where he is and where he will remain, she hopes, for ever. Mary spends her days watching television. Not into hard drugs any more, she has the odd spliff to calm her nerves. She is a prisoner too, she thinks, a prisoner of fate.

2

ASHDEAN PARISH CHURCH has a squat Norman tower, the sort that retired people, who have taken up watercolours, like to paint. From one angle, a row of Kentish village shops makes a delightful background for the church; from another point of view, orchards swollen with apples and fields dotted with oast-houses create the impression of a changeless English countryside. And then, of course, there is a perspective that includes the Elizabethan manor, with its walled garden. Sometime during the Second World War the blue clock in the church tower stopped at three but no one has yet got round to putting it right.

Cassandra Hythe might have lived in the manor if she'd liked, but a few years ago everyone agreed the house should be sold. There was an entailment and she had rights, but the moment she signed the papers waiving them, she experienced a relief that quite surprised her. Her childhood in Ashdean had been happy enough, but even now, at thirty-five, she could not articulate exactly why it was that she generally avoided the village, living as she did about ten miles from it. Perhaps it was because she was the only member of the family left in England, save her long-lost cousin Gerry Hythe, of course. Perhaps it was to do with Gerry himself and the murder of the boy. If murder it was . . .

But Cassie was an unconventional woman with an independent mind whose immunity to gossip stemmed from the time when, at twenty, she ran off with her tutor from art school. The village had wagged its collective finger then; tutted when she had borne him two sons; then shaken its head when he had run off with another woman. For a whole array of reasons, Ashdean was not for her, and she gave the matter little reflection.

She had nothing in common with the big house anymore, she told herself. Even Uncle Godfrey, who had epitomised what it was to be landed gentry, had had enough. Its Tudor chimneys caught her eye now as she crunched down the gravel churchyard path after Harriet Washington's coffin, borne by undertakers' men who outnumbered the mourners. Behind her, treading the unsure gait of people wearing nice shoes in the country, Averell, Harriet's ex-husband, supported Emma, their daughter, on his arm. Her mother was being buried in Ashdean at Emma's dreadful insistence.

Harriet, too, had disliked the village and had left it when the marriage broke down. Emma lived in New York, and when Averell remarried he had moved some thirty miles away so that he and his second wife Sally could join the Eridge Hunt. Once, the Washingtons and Hythes had been friends and neighbours, but the community had changed almost beyond recognition. Its sleepy, feudal certainties had been replaced by the precarious energy of market forces. Rich Australians owned the manor now, and who knew how long they would stay.

On the whole, Cassie supposed, there was no where else to *put* Harriet but Ashdean. This was why, although reluctant, she had lent the Hythe name and her efforts to the dismal project, ringing the vicar and arranging the plot. Emma was not going to have her mother cremated, nor was she about to see her buried in East Sheen. All of this would have been reasonable if she hadn't shouted orders down the phone to Cassie with tearful accusations. The whole sad enterprise seemed to be a question of decency to Emma, and nothing to do with the reality of the woman who had died.

Emma clearly had more in common with her father, though there were 'issues' here too, as she darkly told Cassie, whose best friend she had been in primary school. As far as Cassie could remember, Mr Washington, as she still found it hard not to call him, had indulged Emma, who had a pony and who was always first in the village to have the newest craze in toys. He travelled a lot, especially to the States, and brought back gizmos and baseball hats, almost as if he had wanted her to be a boy. None of Emma's efforts to be one appeared to be sufficient to save her parents' marriage. And, despite Emma's bad manners, Cassie felt a quirk of sympathy for the self-pitying woman she had become.

Averell, who now picked his way down the path after his ex-wife's coffin, was clearly experiencing the full martyrdom of his own guilt. From time to time, he patted Emma's hand, sighing and looking upwards. He was still a good-looking man, this ex-patriate American. With his high colour and hair cut en brosse, he resembled a venerable movie star. He and Harriet had once cut quite a picture as a couple. When they divorced, it surprised everyone and no one simultaneously. Their perfect house, perfect child and perfect parties were somehow too celluloid for a village like Ashdean to credit as real.

But it was Sally, Harriet's successful rival, who fared the worst, bringing up the rear behind the two stars of the show, and Cassie could not help feeling sorry for her. She had not aged well. She'd once been a jolly, horsey woman with a husky voice and a twinkle; Harriet's dead opposite. Since she had broken a hip and could no longer ride, she had shrivelled, looking now merely old. She plodded along with her stick, looking grim and miserable, the spectacle of a home-wrecker, and cause of so much pain. At least, that was Emma's rendering of her character and Cassie had no doubt that she had shared this frank assessment with her stepmother.

If there was anyone the band of Washingtons could agree to dislike, though, it was Cassie herself, and it had held them together through the funeral in London. It was not as if she had done too little for Harriet in her last illness; she had done far too much. At first, the family expressed an edgy gratitude to Cassie for her visits to the sick woman, but soon, in Emma's words, 'the gloves were off'. Another range of Emma's 'issues' came to the fore, such as Cassie's trips to Grisholme Prison to visit the man who had brought disgrace to Harriet. 'He as good as killed my mother!' Emma had shrieked. 'And you go to see him?'

Worst of all, Harriet had given Cassie a pearl necklace that should have gone to Emma. There was no outright accusation that Cassie had conned this pretty piece out of a dying woman, but she felt like a thief and would have given it back had it not been that she actually valued it. She had wept irrationally hot tears at the news of Harriet's death. A kind of sympathy had sprung up between them, a bond it was hard to quantify. But then, the Washingtons resisted outright any attempts to put the whole business of Gerry into a context that would leave Harriet with a shred of dignity. It never seemed to occur to them that Cassie too had been scarred by the death of the boy Vassilis, nor that she had a right to her own feelings. The trial, with its unclear verdict, had left not only Harriet in suspended animation. And it wasn't just a question of the justice or injustice of Gerry's sentence. To Cassie, the mystery of what had passed between Harriet and the man who was, after all, her own first cousin, was more profound than the simple logic of guilt or innocence. And the more Cassie investigated it, the more opaque that mystery became.

Much to her family's distaste, Harriet had become a Catholic, which seemed to provide her with some tools, at least, to find redemptive meaning in her suffering. In this, Cassie both envied her clarity and feared it. She had long ago lapsed, partly because she had never married the man she lived with, and partly because, in the first place, the world she had grown into lacked cognates with the faith drummed into her in childhood. Nevertheless, when the Washingtons were about to bypass Harriet's last wishes for a Requiem, Cassie found herself sounding off like a Redemptorist. She had ended up roping in both priest and vicar, who had ecumenically agreed on the Mass in London and the burial in Anglican soil. It would have been a beautiful funeral, had it not been for the tight-lipped Washingtons, born again, it appeared, into a Protestant faith they had never before observed, sitting like stones in the pew. And it was this interference by Cassie that made her villainy complete.

Why she had lent herself to the social impalement of this funeral, she could not now imagine. The coffin swayed and jolted round the wall of the Lady Chapel, under which ancestral Hythes were interred. As a child, Cassie had always hated the church, partly because her immediate family had brought her up to regard the Anglican faith of the Hythe mainstream as an aberration, and partly out of morbidity. The Crusader Hythe, with his crossed legs and sword, the Tudor Hythes with their ruffs and smug smiles, all seemed false euphemism for the spidery bones that lay beneath their effigies. Thinking of it now, she had never been to a wedding in the church, nor to a christening . . . only funerals. And then there was the matter of Uncle Edgar. What an irony it was, she thought, that Harriet's cortège was approaching the outlying vault where he was buried. Was there any sense in thinking about that now? Emma had been so keen to see her mother planted in Ashdean that she had quite forgotten that Edgar had been Gerry's father. But then the mausoleum, with its marmoreal Gothic fili-gree, was the repository for so many Hythes of the modern era, that perhaps the association had escaped her. Cassie looked away.

The vicar had met them at the lych-gate; together with the priest, who had come along behind the hearse with the family, he led the way down towards the grassy vale by the high wall that surrounded the manor. Only a few short hours to go, Cassie thought, before she could make good her escape. If now she were the lady of the manor, it would have meant arranging one of those awful wakes, where people in black wolf sandwiches and get quietly drunk. Cassie suppressed a laugh, the sort that is born out of strained nerves. Ashdean churchyard might have been stuffed with her DNA, but some curious loop had occurred in her, making her incapable of graciousness and opening bazaars. Perhaps it was because she wasn't fully English, she often thought. With her olive skin, dark hair and a certain bluntness, Cassie resembled her Greek mother. In more ways than one, Cassie often thought. As she grew older, she found the suffering of fools increasingly difficult. And a sheer bloody-mindedness had given her the strength to stand up to the nest of Washingtons.

The vicar slowed, the pallbearers shuddered to a halt, making the tendrils of freesias and lilies tremble on the coffin lid. They had arrived at the grave, with its surrounding carpet of plastic grass. The sun, this August day, shone like brass, and rivers of sweat escaped from Cassie's only funeral hat, a felt cloche from Accessorize she had unearthed from the depths of a cupboard. God knew when she'd bought it or last worn it!

She could not help but think of Gerry now. She wondered if he had received her fax. Cassie stopped, and aligned herself by the grave, standing a little apart from the Washingtons.

Throughout the Requiem in London, in the cortège through the heat and dreadful traffic, and down the long gravel walk to this final place, she had been aware that something was missing. So strong was this impression that she had looked round several times during the service to see who or what it was. Of course, Emma had seen fit to leave Tom, Harriet's grandson, in New York. Someone called Boo, Harriet's only friend as far as Cassie could see, was meant to come and then did not, owing to ill health. But it was Gerry who was missing, of course it was! Not in body, because he was likely to be in prison for a very long time, but in spirit. Cassie imagined he would treat the news with that lack of engagement with anything real that seemed to typify him. It was beyond her to conceive that he would be glad that Harriet was dead.

She put together the heels of her black patent leather shoes and squeezed her hands in something approximating prayer. The priest was asking for perpetual light to be shone on Harriet. The vicar intoned something from the Book of Job. One would have thought it was for Harriet to forgive Gerry, to put it mildly! She saw him now in her mind's eye, his palms flat on the linoleum table in the Visitors' Room in Grisholme, his pallid face set against all of Cassie's intercession and her pleading. 'Look, Gerry, the poor woman is dying!' she had said. 'What would it cost you to write her just one letter?' She had visited him at Harriet's request, and more than once, this man who had done so much damage.

But then, as they said these days, Gerry was 'in denial'.

It was not until Cassie managed her escape that she realised how upset she was. As soon as she had driven a mile or two from Ashdean she slowed her wheezy Renault and stopped. The wake in the village pub, now an antiseptic den with horse brasses and faux French cooking, seemed to provide yet another incongruity with the Harriet she knew. Averell and Sally had drunk whiskies in rapid succession; Emma, in her slick black New York suit, had stuck to Perrier and wrinkled her nose at boozing smokers nearby. They hardly seemed to notice when Cassie pleaded children waiting to be collected from her neighbour, bathed and fed. She decided that, despite the quarrels and resentment and the rudeness, the Washingtons had little real animus against her. Her final vision of them as she left the dark pub for the sunlight was how they seemed to blur into each other as they sat at the polished table near the unlit fire. It was as if Sally and Averell and Emma had interchangeable limbs, heads that proceeded from one mass of torso. Harriet's death had united the disunited, obliterating the distinction between them.

She opened the car window and drew deep breaths of air. She could almost smell the sea. Before her lay the wide expanse of Romney Marsh, with its dykes and reeds and criss-crossed fields and its odd Saxon churches with their clean white interiors, their unusual spires and towers. Her house lay in the lea of the wind from the Channel, a former smuggler's cottage. Her boys would be wondering where she'd got to. Tomorrow the men were coming to install the printing press in the barn. She had the new cards for her Christmas collection already designed, and had found enough markets up in London to expand. Cassie concentrated on how thrilling this was and told herself she couldn't wait.

She was glad that she had foregone the glass of pub Chardonnay she'd been tempted to down. When she got home, she'd give herself a treat, open a nice half-bottle of claret, then have a good soak and early bed.

But she arrived to find her elderly spaniel had wet the sea grass matting in the kitchen, and the firm delivering the press had left a message on the machine saying that they could not come till Thursday. What was more, her mother's voice, sailing out from Greece across the miles that divided them, complained that she had not heard from her for over a week.

Cassie hadn't had the heart to tell her parents about Harriet's funeral. They had strong feelings, and who was to blame them? Her father's health had declined badly; the shock of Vassilis's death was to blame. She'd ring her mother tomorrow, when she was sufficiently rested to disguise her voice into the perky, positive tone she knew worked best. She tried to put it out of her mind while she made supper for the boys and listened to their day. Having heard Grandma's voice, though, they wanted to know when they were going back to Greece. Could they go back in the half term? The sea was still warm in Naxos in October. They'd hardly been swimming at all, not all summer!

It rattled round in her head, displacing Harriet, the way she attempted to keep her children and her parents important to each other. She dandled them in front of each other, making trips, promising trips, sending photographs. It was as if the hole created by the boy's death needed constant filling and replenishing. It was a way, too, of restoring Naxos to the purity she remembered it by from her own childhood, for she had spent every holiday there. As for her parents, it seemed such an awful irony that Gerry had emerged into their lives just when they were basking in their retirement, content at last in the lovely old house that had been her mother's legacy.

Although she found it difficult, every time she visited the island Cassie got old Manolis to drive her out to Vassilis's grave. She kept this from her parents and her children, and made the clandestine pilgrimage as a mark of respect to the community. It was greatly appreciated.

Her parents had spared no expense on the child's tomb, which was erected to the highest expectations of Greek funerary taste. Cassie's father, once an architect, had designed it himself, a small shrine of Naxian marble in the classical style with a porch where the boy's father could sit and grieve. One day he would be buried there himself, beside his son.

The path to this grave was also strewn with gravel, green marble chips. The tomb glared white in the Greek sun. For the benefit of Manolis, she told herself, she always made the sign of the cross. He doffed his cap and did the same. Each year she brought white roses, which she placed in a waiting stone vase. There was a permanent bunch of plastic flowers, but now and then people brought fresh, and when they saw this she and Manolis would exchange a smile. The child's death had shocked the whole island and it was good to see him still remembered. The part of this ritual Cassie particularly disliked was having to look at Vassilis's photograph, which was preserved in stone behind a glass case along with a watch light and an icon of St Basil, his patron. The great Doctor of the Church in his stylised bishop's robes had faded somewhat with time but looked sternly on. Vassilis, his namesake, grinned out from the hazy blown-up snapshot annealed against the marble. His tow hair grazed the spectacles he wore, a gift her father had given him as a reward for high marks in school. His expression was, perhaps, of pride in the gift.

Cassie had never met the dead boy, but each time she saw his picture, she had a fresh sense that not only a life but an intellect had been snuffed. Above the child's grin, his deep-set eyes were shadowed by thought. How flies got into the glassed-in niche she could not tell, but a few always lay dead by the olive oil bottle set there to nourish the watch light. If she could have felt rage for the abomination of this death it would have helped, but she could not; it was, rather, a queasy horror that infused her every time. Now she had met Gerry, the horror had metastasised into something altogether worse. She found that she could feel nothing.

There was something so unnatural about Gerry, something so perplexing that anger seemed a futile response. It was more as if the child's smiling photograph conveyed a sombre enigma, binding Gerry like a magic spell that could never be undone.

Despite Cassie's half-bottle of claret and the sleeping pill she took, she lay staring at the ceiling well into the early hours of the morning. With Harriet gone, she would never really know the truth, unless, of course, she gritted her teeth and went back to visit Gerry.

This she knew she was bound to do. She knew too that it was not entirely because of his secrets, nor with the blood tie that, astonishingly, bound them.

Cassie's sterner friends often told her that pity was her weakness. And it was true that it often compelled her, collapsing her will and interfering with her better judgement.

After her boys' father left, she thought she had excised it from her character, but it crept back. As a case in point, she hired a skip to dispose of the big abstracts he could never sell, paintings with no merit, but in the end she found herself incapable of this cruelty. So, still, they cluttered up the barn.

It had been a barely conscious pity in the first place that had drugged her into setting up house with him, a lonely, divorced man, conscious of his failure, and pity that had kept her from deserting him when he took that failure out on her.

And, despite her revulsion, it was pity that drove her up the motorway to the gates of Grisholme, where her cousin, with his flabby dewlaps, awaited her with trusting, needy eyes.

3

THAT NIGHT, GERRY DREAMED about his father. His pounding heart woke him with a jerk, and he was relieved to see the shadow the moon cast through the grille of his cell window. He knew the time without looking. It was midnight (this was invariably the hour when the nightmares woke him) and sweltering hot. Although most inmates found Christmas the worst, for Gerry it was August. The door seemed cemented shut and the silence on the landings was absolute.

Sweat ran down his whole body and drenched the rough sheet. If he got up to splash some water in his face, he'd never get back to sleep. Moving these days meant a painful flexing of his muscles, one group after another. Getting to sleep was a process of slowly disconnecting clenched fibres, easing them so that they would not cramp, then finding eroded patches on his hard mattress, that bed of nails, where his stricken left side did not protest all night.

Carefully he reached out for his plastic mug and gulped some water. Gerry had devised a list of things to think about as an antidote to nightmares, but he still struggled in this one, one of the worst. In the dream, he was always very small, as if he were trapped in the body of a tiny child and couldn't get out. He was playing in a muddy pit next to a river that flowed in an endless torrent. There was something he had to do, make strange little mud figures, but it gave him no pleasure. He kept putting sticks in their sides for arms and the sticks kept falling off. Edgar always came up quietly, his hulking form crouched unnaturally as if entering Gerry's little kingdom were intensely difficult and painful. As soon as Gerry realised that the obscured form was his father, he became paralysed with fear and was unable to move for the few crucial seconds it would take to escape. He always ended up clambering up the slithering mud wall, desperately scrabbling at the sides that collapsed in large brown mucilaginous slabs around him. Sometimes he woke screaming, even peeing himself. This time, however, he had escaped that indignity.

He debated with himself if it was worth the struggle to see if he had any more tobacco in his tin. He fumbled for it. There was just enough if he was to go without his breakfast fag. He made the roll-up. He could get some burn off the weirdo in the next cell who owed him for certain matters Gerry had been willing to over-look. His hands shook as he lit up, but the acrid smoke punched his lungs like a hit and calmed his nerves somewhat.

So Harriet was dead. Maybe he should add this to the list of small triumphs to contemplate, but the clods that fell on her fell on him – death frightened him and he could hear the grating shovel heave the soil on her coffin with a horrible empathy. Gerry was no Daniel, but it struck him now that the muddy pit of soil in which he and his father were immured in his dream might just as well be a grave for its narrowness and its loneliness. Harriet had written him letters after the trial trying to explain her actions, and he had torn them up in a rage, but he had somehow always expected to see her again, although how, as he had sent her no Visiting Order, he could not have said.

He tried to think of Cassie. Cassie would come to see him now. She said so in the fax and if she promised a thing she did it. Mind, she had never given him the picture of herself and the kids as he requested. He couldn't look at her photo, so he had to imag-ine her. Each time she visited, seldom enough, she seemed to have altered radically. This was because in his mind her features became finer and purer with time and distance. After each visit, he had to reinvent her.

It was not as if she had ever promised to have him to live with her when he left Grisholme, but he dreamed of this felicity all the same. She would have a huge house, like the manor their grandparents once owned. That was sold now. Cassie had mentioned it casually one day as if it happened to be any old house, not one that had stayed in the family for eight hundred years. Although Gerry knew in his mind it was unrealistic, he'd entertained a fantasy that when he got out of prison he'd be asked to the manor, maybe for tea. His uncle Godfrey, only a shadow on his mind, would be there, lord of the manor. Courtly and erect, he would give Gerry a guided tour of the property. Gerry would see the hall with its minstrels' gallery, his grandfather's study, the nursery, rooms that Edgar had talked about. Gerry had his own intuitive map of the house, but after the visit, he would be able to fix the truth of it in his mind, saying to himself, 'This is what I came from and where I belong; this is what it really looked like.'

Thus it had been a blow, hearing that the place was now occupied by Australians.

He didn't know if everything had been auctioned off after the sale, but somehow he thought that Cassie would have retained bits and pieces. In his best fantasy, she had a deer park. He'd walk up her drive lined with poplars, his duffel bag over his shoulder like a sailor home from the sea. She'd be so eager to please, rushing out of the door, kissing him on both cheeks. Inside, there would be oil portraits, like her father, his uncle Michael, had in Naxos, of long-dead Hythes, some of whom had played a part in shaping world history; even his father had told him that, even Edgar had a pride in the family's high destiny. Although Gerry had no evidence for this, it pleased him to imagine that Cassie would own a suit of armour, pigeon-breasted and polished up to a mirror shine. After all, one of their ancestors had been a Crusader.

Gerry could spend literally hours in this daydream: Cassie would take his arm and speak encouragement to him as they walked down a long gallery. Sometimes a soft rain pattered on the roof and at other times she wore mystical garments, flowing robes with heavy sleeves. In whatever dress, ancient or modern, Cassie always trusted him with her kids and sometimes he imagined taking them swimming off the Kent coast, giving them a great day out, giving Cassie a break. In the evening they would sit by a huge log fire drinking whisky and Gerry would tell her all of the pains he had suffered at the hands of his father, her uncle. And, being his cousin, she would be able to illuminate the tale of his struggles, filling in the vital bits of family history that were missing. He would be so eager to learn.

Gerry had done a calligraphy course in another prison many years ago and had been deeply impressed with the pictures of medieval manuscripts where a whole story could be contained in the frame of an initial letter, scrolled and embellished with gold so that you could see the essence of what the words conveyed simply by looking at the picture. Cassie was the letter 'C', curved and protective. She was the sole repository of a whole chronicle – his own. Gerry read nothing but history these days. Partly because of his time in Naxos, the seat of those ancient Venetian dukes who had assisted in the fall of Constantinople, he was into the Crusades now and he was especially drawn to Richard Coeur de Lion.

'There were grave flaws in Richard's character. Physically, he was superb, tall, long-limbed and strong, with red-gold hair and handsome features and he had inherited from his mother not only the good looks of the House of Poitou, but its charm of manner, its courage and its taste for poetry and romance. His friends and servants followed him with devotion and awe. From both his parents, he derived a hot temper and a passionate self-will . . . He had been brought up in an atmosphere of family quarrels and family treachery. As his mother's favourite, he had hated his father . . .'

If Gerry was grateful to anyone, it was the prison librarian, a lover of history herself. She had noted his interest and was good at recommending books, sometimes very difficult ones that he only half understood, but he was proud of their weight, their gravity. Because of her, he had read Sir Stephen Runciman, and he had copied this passage on Richard from his *History of the Crusades*. He knew it by heart now and could recite it in the dark. Sometimes he could think himself into the shoes of the king. Gerry was oblivious to the sad truth, that he had run to fat, a consequence of prison stodge and the inaction following his stroke. Once, his face had been his fortune, as it were, and he still imagined that he was handsome. He yearned to see Richard in his dreams: to catch a glimpse of him, the dull gleam of chain mail.

None of these techniques helped him this night, however. As in life, his father in death appeared at random and at will. Over the years, Gerry noticed that a catastrophe was often the result of these apparitions, as if Edgar were one of those banshees he'd heard about from a cellmate once. He nervously consoled himself with the thought that the nightmare had something to do Harriet's death . . . but then that had already happened. Gerry told himself not to be superstitious. It was only a dream and if he could get rid of it everything would be all right.

Gerry had always appreciated a quiet life, even as a small child. Too much excitement worked him up, his mother had liked to say. Then she would be cursing and screaming. No matter how quiet he was, she could never seem to cope with him for long and he was put into care as often as not, particularly when the school holidays came round.

Gerry had been a beautiful child. At least everyone agreed on that. But he'd once considered cutting his face so that he wouldn't be. Even now, the vestiges of what had been ethereal about him clung round his temples. He looked like his father, a point his mother often brought up in his disfavour. Gerry hated the sight of himself in the mirror.

A solution arose when, at seven or eight, he saw *The Invisible Man* on the telly. His mother never minded what he watched as long as it kept him quiet. The man who had to cover himself in bandages to become visible was a revelation to Gerry. He would have given anything to be able to vanish at will and after he saw the film he tried to do it, squeezing his eyes shut and wishing with all his might. To reduce himself to pure spirit became, from that time, the task of his childhood. In the end, he became quite successful. Often as not he managed to be vacant, a notional boy with no cravings nor tastes. He got into building models in his room and later into ham radio.

However unpredictable his mother's moods, though, Gerry learned to forecast the outcome for himself with some accuracy. The fluctuations of her strenuous love life indicated his comings and goings. A new man generally meant a new set of foster parents for a while and Gerry could resign himself to this; in fact, he came to derive a perverse pleasure from being turfed out of their flat so that she could 'make some money by taking in a lodger'. When she lied, she was always vulnerable to a silent kind of blackmail. Transactions between them became more subtle as time went by and her guilt often paid him the substantial sums of her permissiveness.

There had been nothing his absence of being could do to avoid his father, though. And as for guilt, his father didn't feel it. He might arrive at the flat at any time demanding to see Gerry. Or he would descend on foster families, or he would be outside the school gates. There was no telling. At one point, nearly a year went by without him and Gerry believed he was rid of his torment. Not so.

Edgar Hythe always made a good impression. Like Gerry, he was slender and slightly built; like Gerry too, his features were finely moulded and sensitive except for his full mouth with its heavy, over-developed lower lip. He had a dreamy look that appealed to women. In fact, one could say he was almost chivalrous to them, especially Gerry's teachers, foster mothers and social workers. Although he did nothing to emphasise his social background, it was implicit in everything he did and said. He was distinguished by the marks of a gentility that had fallen on hard times. His collars might be frayed but the shirts came from Jermyn Street; his hair, which touched the collars, had none the less been cut by a good barber. His scuffed shoes were finely stitched and he had an address in Pimlico. No one questioned his right to see Gerry. In fact, the vague consensus was that contact brought positive benefits to the child. This had been at a time when illegitimacy still had pejorative connotations. The expensive presents Edgar gave Gerry – his own telly, a record player, a bicycle – provided a sense of his generosity in acknowledging the child in difficult circumstances (considering the mother).

Edgar put it about that he had a rare bookshop in the King's Road. Indeed, he sometimes minded this place for some old geezer, but it did not belong to him. There were shelves of heavy volumes in leather bindings and Gerry would have liked to have a look. Instead, Edgar kept a collection of erotica under lock and key and he guided Gerry's reading in that direction in order to give him clues as to how he could be pleasing. So he'd had a classical education of sorts. Edgar admired Gerry's beauty extremely, and his favourite volume had prints in it of Greek vases showing men 'sporting' (as he put it) with boys at drinking parties. The book provided ocular proof that what Edgar liked to do was okay, 'quite natural', he used to say. Gerry wasn't sure it was natural to do things like that to your own son.

Edgar liked to play the part of a languid intellectual, well heeled but Bohemian. Sometimes he wore a thick corduroy jacket, which gave him the impression of being an artist. People sometimes thought he was an artist. He was 'working' on a book of 'verse', he called it. He admired a poet called Baudelaire and he would sometimes recite the poems in French to Gerry who could not understand them. He never visited the same school or foster family twice and, whenever he did turn up, those whose business it was to protect Gerry readily released him to Edgar's care for the day. Edgar would complain to those in charge of his long trips abroad, how his business had taken him out of the country. He would shake his head sadly at Gerry's plight, as if he had nothing to do with it. For some reason everyone believed that this was true. The powers that dictated Gerry's young life always seemed cautiously hopeful that Edgar would soon settle, take Gerry on permanently and away from the chaos that was Mary Carney.

When discussing his son with caring professionals, which he did with furrowed brow and rapt attention, Edgar had the dignified manner of a member of the minor nobility. He might have been a Russian prince saddened by exile. But the day trips, taken to 'get to know' Gerry better, were never to the zoo. They involved afternoons at Edgar's flat in Pimlico. As for Gerry's mother, she kept on thinking that Hythe money would come her way if she complied with Edgar's wish to see the boy, but Gerry believed this would never come to pass. If Edgar wanted family funds it was to support an expensive habit he had picked up during the war, and to introduce Gerry to his relations would have been to lose the advantage he had in having a little boy to hand whenever the need for one struck him.

Gerry often wondered why none of this had come out at the trial. He'd sketched it in for the Greek psychiatrist, the sort of things he'd been through, but she wasn't very sympathetic. Maybe her English wasn't as good as it sounded. Instead, the courts threw his reputation to the dogs and the papers branded him a monster. Of course they dragged the family in, all right, but that was just the English papers that wanted to have a go at the class thing, something about landed gentry spawning a paedophile. A bit rich considering that, except Edgar, he'd never met any of his family until Harriet had effected the introduction. And by that time, Gerry had just turned forty! Not that he looked it, of course.

Oh, it had all been taken up in a big way. Once he was in gaol, there had been no bridling the press, which catalogued his every crime since puberty. The case had stimulated the retrospective (and thus more comfortable) outrage of a nation that had once released imprisoned sex offenders to go scot-free, the better to indulge their bestial desires. Gerry sometimes wondered who Scot was and how free it was to be Scot, but because of him the civil liberties campaigners who challenged the hounding of paedophiles were now truly routed. According to the tabloids, Gerry, bent on his evil purposes, had scuttled off to Greece through the loophole a judicious parliament had since plugged. One thing had pleased him, though. The press had branded Harriet Washington too. How often he had relished it, the portrait they had painted of her, a sex-starved crone who, indulging a kinky passion for her convict toy boy, had set up the victim as sure as any pander.

He shifted on the hard pallet. His roll-up had gone out and now he had started thinking about the trial he knew he would not sleep until unlocking. No sense in thrashing about. No sense in tossing and turning even though his pulses were jumping in anger. He had never touched the boy! At least everyone was agreed there was no forensic on that. And if it hadn't been for previous, the worst they could have done him for was a few years for accidental death when even that was hard to prove! Tears started in his eyes. His brief thought he was so clever at getting him the Greek equivalent of 'involuntary manslaughter'. 'Better than murder,' he'd sneered when Gerry objected.

Well, whatever happened that day he spent with Vassilis, there was nothing 'involuntary' about it. Everything, except for the death, had been willed and meant, the climb up the hill, the bright sky expecting eagles, the summit of breath-catching perfection. It was as if a moment of transubstantiation had been granted him, a period of grace in which his desires had become pure and right: if he could have died in Vassilis's stead, he would gladly have done so.

The boy's image came to him now, as it often did, almost tenderly, as if he were visiting Gerry to encourage and forgive him. He was not anywhere near that well where he'd drowned, but was sitting cross-legged as they shared their picnic of bread, cheese and Sprite. Gerry always remembered it this way, the way they had been sitting on a flat stone together after their long walk in the heat, the way they had been all breathless and sweaty. The boy was taking his shirt off, his shoulders wiry with a nascent muscular development, his lengthening flanks beneath the shorts glinting with sweat as if he had been oiled for games played long ago. His face was like one of Edgar's vase paintings come alive. Except that he was blond, his deep-set eyes with their enigmatic expression made him like a kouros of old. He was laughing. For Chrissake, they had been laughing! Gerry forgot what the joke was.

How could he have harmed Vassilis in any way? Gerry would have kissed the boy's feet if he could, worshipped this icon of unmixed beauty. Even now he wanted to weep with gratitude that he had been granted this quintessential experience of acceptance. The boy had chosen him as a fit companion. Gerry's only memory was of a child surrounded by light, a light that made painted haloes look superficial.

Why, he might just as well have murdered Jesus!

Or, irony of ironies, a being from one of those Greek myths Edgar was so keen on, heroes that Gerry had been made to pretend to be. Vassilis could have been Ganymede whirled up by a god, Adonis or Narcissus, his father's favourite, who had drowned in a pool, ravished by his own sublimity.

Well, Harriet was dead now too. Fitting, he thought, and just.

In fact, it struck him now how just it was.

And so he hoped her end had been painful. Very painful.

For Harriet had not simply destroyed Gerry's life by exposing his secrets: she had defiled it.

4

DURING THE LAST FEW WEEKS of Harriet Washington's life, she indulged in what she knew was an escapist fantasy. It was not that she deluded herself that she would recover. Her body told her the truth. Nor did she very much fear death. As she neared it, things simplified. Indeed, she surprised herself at the matter-of-fact way in which she tackled the business of dying. It was a bit like moving house after Averell had left her. She had made her peace with God, now it seemed important to make peace with those around her. It was a process of packing, tidying and getting rid of rubbish.

It didn't seem wrong, therefore, to get through the lonely nights in hospital with an imaginative release from the cramping pain she suffered. In one fantasy, Gerry would respond to Cassie Hythe's visit and write, telling her he understood why she had taken action after the death of Vassilis. It seemed important to her that he should accept that her unconditional love for him included the truth.

In the years that followed the dreadful events in Greece, Harriet had gradually given up hope that she would ever know exactly what had happened between Gerry and the boy, and so her wildest dreams did not include an explanation. All the same, she longed for some sign that one day he would find it in himself to face out whatever mad and dreadful thing he had done. Whenever she prayed, she prayed for Gerry. She could not bear to think of the torments of guilt he must suffer, and she yearned for his liberation. When time went by and no letter came, she tried to resolve the matter by imagining it had gone astray, or had somehow been censored by the prison regime.

An easier scenario for Harriet to imagine was her own funeral. Where her soul was headed she did not dare guess, but the thought sustained her that her body would be taken to the pretty church in Cadogan Street to stay the night before her Requiem. Her coffin would be draped with a pall, the pall bedecked with white roses and lilies, her favourite flowers. How peaceful it would be in the dark with only the light in the sanctuary lamp dancing and flickering, the solitary, concentrated illumination a metaphor for the singleness of purpose her life had so long lacked!

How he was expected to get there, especially alone and particularly at night, she left to poetic licence; but out of the darkness of the scene, both sombre and filled with an air of spiritual simplicity, Gerry would emerge, swimming into her consciousness like a figure in a dream. Harriet would watch mesmerised as he unfolded before her mind's eye. First blurred in shadow, then strangely refulgent, he was revealed as quite beautiful, almost like an angel as he tiptoed up the nave to her coffin. On seeing it, his resistance would melt. Unable to help himself, he would kneel, awkwardly making a sign of the cross he had never accepted as redemptive. The climax of this imagined moment was one of emotional deliverance for Harriet; Gerry would find the grace to pray and, like a charm, this would unlock the twisted bonds that had united and fettered them both.

Short bursts of this daydream were as good for Harriet as morphine. When her daughter Emma arrived from New York only to throw her weight around, bossing the nurses, shouting at the doctor, excluding first Cassie, then Averell, then the chaplain, Harriet took refuge in what became the drift of a coma. The phantasm of her reconciliation with Gerry wove like a gleaming shuttle through all that was stark and undignified in reality, the worst aspect being for Harriet the way her daughter hung back, terrified of her slurred voice, her frozen face. A vision of Gerry would interpose itself: Gerry laughing with pleasure at one of her cheerful, silly stories; Gerry beaming at his smartness in the fine clothes she'd bought him after his release; Gerry's wan face lighting at the sight of her in the Visitors' Room at Grisholme. As the fantasy progressed, she saw him standing by her grave, the chief mourner, sobbing as he strewed earth on her coffin. That she would be buried in Ashdean among the Hythes never entered her mind as it thinned and faded and furled out. And whether she noticed or cared what Gerry actually said on hearing the news of her death is a matter for metaphysical conjecture.

Harriet would have been astonished at the warm words Father Luke spoke about her in his eulogy. The text he chose would have moved her:

"'Come, O blessed of my Father, inherit the kingdom prepared for you from the foundation of the world; for I was hungry and you gave me food, I was thirsty and you gave me drink, I was a stranger and you welcomed me, I was naked and you clothed me, I was sick and you visited me, I was in prison and you came to see me." Then the righteous will answer him, "Lord, when did we see thee hungry and feed thee or thirsty and give thee drink? And when did we see thee a stranger and welcome thee or naked and clothe thee? And when did we see thee sick or in prison and visit thee?" And the King will answer them, "Truly, I say to you, as you did it to the least of my brethren, you did it unto me.'"

Eight years before her death and a few months after her decree absolute, Harriet decided it was about time to take a firm hand on her destiny, and steer her life out of the doldrums where she had lain passive for so long. Averell was gone, leaving her embarrassed to be single in Ashdean, where her life had been one long round of couples and dinner parties. It took her some strength to muster the sale of the grange, which had been part of her divorce settlement, but the property was in superb order, and it went quickly. Harriet resolved to move to London. Until then, her fifty-nine years had been as neatly upholstered as the Victorian chairs that flanked the ornamental logs of her gas fire, which she had installed as a matter of priority in her new Chelsea home.

The flat occupied the upper storeys of a Georgian house renovated by a firm of interior decorators below her. They had sold it to her at an exorbitant price on a long lease. At her age, she had not thought she would live to the year 2150 unless she became bionic, but the negative equity, as it soon became, did mean that she was stuck there.

Harriet had hesitated over the move for Emma's sake, even writing to New York to consult her. Her daughter had made it painfully clear that she had no interest whatever in Harriet's plans, so she had felt justified in buying the extravagant flat. The very day she moved in, however, she found a scathing letter from Emma on the dusty mat. Harriet had been selfish after all in selling the grange, which was Emma's childhood home. It was the sort of place Tom might have come to stay in future. The clear inference Harriet drew from this was that her daughter's trips to England would be even fewer and farther between. As for her grandson, she had only twice met him. Dear little boy, he might indeed have liked staying with her in Ashdean! She could imagine him joyously running down the garden to Emma's old tree house. And now the grange was gone for ever. Harriet had wept at that. She could never understand Emma's alienation from her. What had she done that was so terrible? Something to do with giving her dolls for Christmas and dressing her up in frocks. Emma, who was a successful journalist, had done more than all right in life, but it was never enough, and she had enlisted the aid of a New York analyst, it seemed, in order to punish Harriet more effectively.

Although it was probably not the main reason for her move, it had been in Harriet's mind to spend a cultural old age. Years with Averell had worn her down; and, although she might at any time have taken the train from Ashdean to London to spend a day contemplating the Vermeers in the National Gallery, she had become too apathetic to do this. There was music in London too, but above all the theatre, her first and neglected love. Harriet had once been an actress and had trained at RADA. She planned an assault on the Barbican and the South Bank. Maybe she would make friends, the sort she, not Averell, would like to have to supper, possibly after the theatre. She could imagine a pool of mellow light on the table while autumn rains lashed outside, a warming cassoulet or possibly something lighter. She would assemble her own salon where she would generate discussions about books and acting.

Above all, she wanted to get away from gardening. She wanted nothing whatever to do with trugs and slugs and mulch. When Averell, wracked with guilt in the drawing room she had created to his specifications, had announced his intention to leave her because he was 'in love', her eyes hit upon a vase of lilies she had grown herself, and it was the first thing that occurred to her. In a moment's calm before the storm of emotion hit her, she had seen clearly that she would never have to arrange anything for anyone else again, flowers, dinner parties, furniture.

But from her first day in Chelsea she had been miserable, and the misery only intensified. London had beckoned so theatrically from Kent. She had expected a gold-tasselled curtain to rise on a new life. Harriet tried not to mind getting older; she was determined not to stoop to any Joan Collins vulgarity. She tried to remember the wintry distinction of Peggy Ashcroft, and, although she had abandoned the thought of going back to her early career, she still thought of making entrances and of being creative in some way. She had visions of stylish luncheons at restaurants she had only read about where waiters would wonder if she were royal or famous. She had vague notions of assignations in little-visited rooms of large galleries, an elderly but handsome swain, a widower perhaps, who would approach her with a trumped-up question about Alma Tadema only to treat her later to poached quenelles, perhaps, and champagne. A bittersweet friendship, savoured the more for the knowledge that time was running out for both of them, would be the poignant result.

As Harriet Stiffert, her gifts as an actress had lent themselves to parts where upper-class ingénues trilled blithely and were fetchingly married off. Sadly, this talent was rendered horribly bourgeois in the new wave of drama, which would have required her to stand at a kitchen sink. Harriet, the only child of smart, wealthy parents who had lived in Tunbridge Wells, had only the sketchiest notion of what a kitchen sink was for.

Averell had been one of Harriet's fans, which seemed romantic at the time, especially for the red roses backstage, the suppers at Rules. He had been 'nuts' about her act, her tact, her cut-glass voice. He had only recently arrived in London from New York and went to the theatre because he was lonely. Harriet epitomised everything he imagined England to be. Averell was a successful businessman, who took pride in always being a jump ahead of European muddle, but he also glorified his somewhat dubious connection to George Washington whose family, he never tired of telling her, had been every bit as squirish as any old Hythes. The night he proposed, he asked Harriet, without quite as much irony as he intended, to become his 'First Lady'. The kitchen was the last place Averell had ever wanted to see his wife, so Harriet had sailed through the audition and got the part.

Harriet soon discovered, once in London, that there was no audience for her. In the beginning, she bought single tickets to everything recommended by the *Sunday Telegraph*, which Averell had accustomed her to reading. It had been bad enough during their marriage whenever she had dragged him to plays; sitting next to him while he nodded off had driven her close to tears. To be by herself, however, only exposed the dull and almost unendurable pain of abandonment.

She soon stopped going. Her brave plans were, ironically, defeated by a Peter Hall production of *Othello*, which had moved to the Haymarket after resounding critical acclaim on tour. Harriet had fought for a first night ticket and decided to honour the occasion by dressing to the nines. This was Shakespeare, not *Look Back in Anger*. Press cameras flashed, autograph hounds clustered round the foyer, wowsing at the famous. Critics bustled and the more important theatre types came in smart mufti, not to be confused with the drab of lucky tourists who had managed to squeeze themselves in. Harriet was mortified. In her taffeta, she might as well have been in drag. She knew no one, and did not even recognise the stars who pretended to snub the cameras with their best profiles averted.

As the archetypal tale of jealousy unfolded, she became aware of its sad lack of application to her own situation. She deeply resented Averell for humiliating her, but she had never had enough passion for him to want to throttle him.

At the interval, however, Harriet made her way to the crush bar and, on impulse, bought not one but two glasses of champagne. 'For my husband . . .' she murmured to the indifferent barman as she paid. In the throng of theatre people, who hailed and kissed each other, Harriet consumed both glasses surreptitiously. All the while, she pretended to look anxiously in the direction of the men's loo, as if a husband who adored her would soon emerge and join her.

After that, she had gone home and got seriously drunk on the malt she kept for visitors who never came: that had been the first and only time. She could not sink that low again.

Harriet found herself arranging flowers as before, only she bought and did not grow them. Her drawing room was full of silver boxes and bits of porcelain she had inherited. Sometimes she thought she would scream in order to hear a human voice, and if it had not been for the television, she was sure she would have gone mad.

It was on a Sunday morning three months into her new life that Harriet found herself, almost by incorporeal means, inside the church that stood almost across the road from her flat. Thinking about it later, she could not actually remember having decided to go in. She had been out to buy a newspaper, something like that.

Harriet had almost forgotten that in her early youth she had briefly converted to Catholicism. Although her parents had sent her to a convent school, it horrified them to see her going over to Rome. The Latin Mass, as it had been then, had seemed grand and theatrical to Harriet, full of mystery and medieval romance. She could see herself taking the veil or becoming a saint. Although even in the 1950s it was becoming an aberration, Harriet had always had an inclination to chastity. The way her friends in the theatre carried on privately scandalised her. And so the Church's stringent rules on sex had protected her, a beautiful young girl, from predators. It was always easy, she discovered, for a Catholic to say no. But Averell, a convinced WASP, had worn her down over this as well. Out of relief, her parents spent a fortune on the wedding; Harriet's reward for apostasy had been a white satin dress by Norman Hartnell.

Harriet sometimes wondered if she had found sanctuary in St Mary's because she had the vague idea that Rome would regard her failed marriage as invalid, this being her own jaundiced view. More accurately, she had been forced to return with an empty belly like the prodigal. Luckily for her, the parable kept its original shape. The intelligent parish priest received her back after nearly a lifetime's lapse. Of course, she was unable to marry again, but that was the last thing on her mind and she soon found herself attending Mass every evening.

It was one such evening when Harriet first met Boo McAuley. Boo sometimes did the readings, booming psalms and epistles in the authoritative voice Harriet associated with her mother's friends in Tunbridge Wells. Boo always sat near the front and on all the committees. She called the priest by his Christian name. She was an indefinable age, solid and pugnacious, and reminded Harriet of school. Boo would have been a good back half on the hockey field or even Head Girl. Harriet would have envied Boo her complete lack of self-doubt had she not been so consistently pleasant. She actually smiled and even nodded to acknowledge Harriet.

That evening, just as Harriet was rising from her knees in preparation to leave the church and return to her Marks and

Spencer baked potato, Boo strode down the aisle and accosted her. Harriet was new to the parish. How nice. Would she be interested in the prayer group? They chatted, and to Harriet's embarrassment everything she said revealed her unmoored state. But, not surprisingly, given the evident generosity of her nature, Boo asked Harriet to lunch. No actor or intellectual had made this simple effort and Harriet, overwhelmed with nerves, went the next day clutching a bunch of freesias for her hostess.

Boo, a widow, occupied a mews house nearby rather like a general in a field hut. Mr McAuley's departure from life seemed only to have given her the benefit of more room for an ancient Labrador, box files, a computer and masses of papers heaped on bookshelves and stacked on the floor. It looked as if she were running a campaign – as it turned out she was. Boo, in frightful trousers, shoved the flowers in a jam jar, lit a cigarette, poured Harriet a vast G&T, and set about reforming her life.

They ate late, cold salads from plastic tubs. Harriet, slightly drunk with gin and the wonderful unconventionality of Boo, poured out her story, even to details. Boo hooted with derision when Harriet told her she had been her husband's 'First Lady', and Harriet laughed too, at last finding it funny. Quite without meaning to, she went on to disclose the episode at the Haymarket, and suddenly it seemed not so bad once shared. By the time they had sobered up on coffee, Harriet felt that, far from being deserted, she had had the shackles struck from her legs; and by the time she went home, she had agreed to visit Gerry Carney in Grisholme Prison.

Prisons, it emerged, were the object of Boo's formidable concern. She was the scourge of Home Secretaries, the friend of all charities for penal reform. Harriet would have taken her for an unquestioning Tory, and Boo admitted that she had once been one. In fact, she had been a magistrate in Dulwich where she and her husband had raised their numerous family. When invited to inspect the remand facilities in Grisholme, she had formed a poor opinion of them, to such an extent that she had resigned her post in order to work for the betterment of those she had once sentenced. Boo had many irons in the penology fire, and one of her many projects was a Visitors' Scheme in Grisholme, 'Grisly-hole' as she called it. Inmates without family or friends could apply to be seen by volunteers. Would Harriet like to visit one of them? She had a man in mind and her other visitors were fully stretched.

'Carney', as she called him, had come to her notice through one of the 'good' prison officers who was concerned that he was depressed. He had no contact with the outside world. He refused to work or have anything to do with the educational facilities. He lay all day in his cell and shunned the other inmates. Recently, he had been eating less and less. He had no truck with the chaplains or with the psychologists. Boo and the officer had seen it all before. This was the sort of behaviour that often foreshadowed a suicide attempt. In cases like this, a regular visitor could help, someone who had nothing to do with the regime. Boo was sure he was desperate.

Put like this, it was hard to refuse; yet Harriet demurred. As she stirred her coffee, a sharp instinct for danger arose in her. It was a new sensation and she found it both attractive and repellent. And yet, as she listened to Boo, she felt a pull towards the exotic, sequestered world from which her conscientious life had divided her. It seemed extreme and Dante-esque to do what Boo suggested, and that day she imagined conversations with this 'Carney' as being almost like a communication with the spirit world where the dead spoke riddles and gave tongue to inscrutable knowledge.

Harriet wasn't sure she could do it. Boo was sure, very sure! Harriet asked . . . well, wouldn't the class thing matter? Boo told her just to be herself. It only showed how demoralised she'd become because of her divorce. Carney was sure to be thrilled with her. Boo knew. She had an intuition.

When Harriet first met Gerry she had just passed, but not celebrated, her sixtieth birthday. It was a raw October day and the prison was a long way from Cadogan Street, a matter of six miles. The journey entailed a series of complex changes of transport: the tube, the train and then a bus that lurched through awful traffic south of the river. The deeper she went down the Old Kent Road towards Peckham, the more she wished she had not sold her car when she had packed up and left for London. Although when she left the flat, the sun was bleakly shining, cold rain started coming down in needles and Harriet was insufficiently protected from the weather in her Jaeger coat and skirt, an old tweed outfit she had worn to lunches of medium grandeur in Ashdean. Boo had told her that the 239 stopped almost outside the gates of the prison and Harriet clutched a map in her hand, reading it time and again for reassurance. The bus ploughed on, depositing the better-dressed passengers and picking up shabbier and rougher ones as it jerked from one fare stage to another. In the end, she was squeezed between a Rastafarian and a fat girl with greasy hair who hauled off and slapped a tiny child whom she held in a vice between her cold and unclad knees.

Harriet had never seen a prison before, not even from the road. In fact, until she had met Boo, she had never given prisons a second thought. The scene of urban devastation along the route that unfolded outside the steamed and splattered window bewildered Harriet as much as if she had been transported to Beirut. Huge estates that lined the road seemed like gigantic supermarket shelves with tenants stacked in rows like so many tins of sardines. Store-front churches with placards proffered invitations to Jesus so minatory that they would have been difficult to refuse had anyone paid attention to them, and the Asian shops offered blurred bunches of strange herbs and vegetables in seedy racks. But the only reality of which Harriet was sensible that day was the horrid jam of cars around her, battling for supremacy. She was in a panic lest she were late. Boo had told her that she had known visitors to come from as far away as Yorkshire only to be turned away if they had not managed to arrive on time.

Harriet might have jumped off and tried to catch a taxi back into town if there had been one. And she was so frightened of meeting Gerry Carney that she found it difficult to move at all. An animal terror possessed her. She'd had no sleep the night before. In theory she had agreed to do some prison visiting, a respectable activity for Christian gentry, but now she was on the way to her first assignment the prospect of meeting an actual criminal appalled her. Why had she not thought of this before? A criminal was a person who came through the bedroom window or one who made the tell-tale noise in the dark at the foot of the stairs or who left in his wake the shock of the rifled drawers, the overturned furniture, the smashed vase and the excrement smeared on the carpet. Criminals murdered old ladies for their pensions; or raped them then murdered them. At best, they were dishonest; they cheated, lied, stole, conned and bullied. Why should anyone try to make them feel better when they should feel ashamed? Boo McAuley had simply overpowered her. Harriet had always been weak-minded. Sometimes she thought Averell had bound her feet like a Chinese princess; at other times she wondered if she had provided him the bandages herself! All anyone ever had to do was to speak with self-assurance to Harriet and she knuckled under. She had spent her entire life doing what others expected of her and, now that she had the peace of a little freedom at long last, she was repeating the pattern. This man, Gerry Carney, would probably laugh at her in any case. She was wearing the wrong clothes for a start . . . that she could see by the clientèle of the bus. Well, she could invent an excuse for not making other visits – illness, say. And maybe she really was going to be too late to see the man. That would be an end to it!

By the time the walls of Grisholme stood plainly before her, she had talked herself into such a state that it took a supreme effort to get off the bus. A whimper of fear came from her throat so audible that the driver stared at her as she descended. She was, in fact, on time, and so she made her way up a blackened flight of steps into a door marked 'Visitors' that stood ajar beneath a crenellated tower.

Harriet held her kid handbag close to her. The Rasta man, who shot her a nervous smile, and the fat girl had also descended at Grisholme and again they flanked her on the hard bench in a room overheated and humid from the wet clothing of people who generally did not wash. Alone in a corner sat a woman in a mink coat, her hair bleached and teased, her pockmarked skin heavy with foundation. Gold chains surrounded her plump neck and she surveyed the entire company with disdain. Some thin children in tracksuits and anoraks sat alert and strained as whippets next to a defeated-looking mother in polyester trousers. Everyone was staring at Harriet. She was overwhelmed with shame. She looked the very picture of the county lady she had ceased to be and this Carney was going to despise her.

Ordinarily, Harriet knew that, at sixty, she was still a handsome woman. She took pride in her height, her slender figure and pure white hair which she wore in a French knot sculpted close to her head. In the antechamber of the Visitors' Room her tweeds were lustrous with subtle shades of red and green and brown picked out nicely by the rollneck jumper, soft in its combination of lambswool and cashmere. Her skin, creamy white, owed its perfection to the great care she took of it, and she wore a tasteful minimum of make-up, just lipstick and a little mascara. She held the Visiting Order in one gloved hand and, though she did not tell the beads, she clutched a rosary, a new acquisition, in the other which she thrust deep in her pocket. Instead, she recited like a mantra the 'contract' Boo had made her sign.

'Take nothing in. Take nothing out.

'Do not reveal where you live.

'Do not reveal any personal details.

'No social contact with an inmate's friends or family is allowed.

'Any connection with an inmate, his friends or his family,

must be revealed to the prison authorities.

'Politely refuse to make any phone calls on the inmate's behalf.

'You may buy the inmate a cup of tea, but he is not allowed to handle any money.

'Anything you bring for an inmate must be handed in so that it can be checked through Security before he is allowed to claim it.

'You may not bring in mobile telephones, cameras or tape recorders.

'You may be searched.'

Harriet quivered at this last, imagining that some contraband had wriggled into her handbag on the bus, but at last the officer on duty called the visitors to order and, to be fair, they were courteous in their searching. It was really only like an airport with its X-ray machine, though Harriet observed that the Rastafarian, last in the queue, was taken off somewhere, presumably for a more thorough investigation of his person. As for herself, she showed the letter Boo had written on her behalf and she was nodded on in a friendly way.

Hours seemed to pass, but they were minutes extended as if by witchcraft. A mousy woman who looked like a social worker told her the inmates were being fetched. At last Harriet's number was called, and she squared her shoulders, marching through the gate as if it led to a scaffold. Ahead of her there stood two gates of iron bars, one behind the other, and both were fitted with substantial locks. Two large, heavy-set officers flanked this entrance to the prison itself and in the background Harriet could hear the echo of male voices shouting orders and the clang of barred doors, the jangle of keys perpetually locking and unlocking – a cold, deadly sound.

She knew nothing about Gerry Carney except that no one ever came to see him. She did not know what crime he had committed, what he looked like, or even if he really wanted to see her. Fits of terror seized her spasmodically. She expected him to be very rough and imagined him tall, perhaps with a shaven head, coarse and cynical.

She looked around the room, made more dismal by pictures from a local primary school; there, seated at dingy lino tables, were rows of subdued men dressed identically in blue sweatshirts and baggy trousers. As they spotted their wives or girlfriends, their mothers, their friends or their children, their faces lit. It was like the prisoners' chorus from *Fidelio* where men see sunlight for the first time in years, Harriet thought. Even though she was afraid, she found this moving.

In fact, she was so busy with these new and startling impressions that it took her a few moments to register that Gerry Carney stood before her on the other side of the table where she was guided. Until she died, she never forgot this first sight of him, though as time went by the memory became embellished and deepened with first one meaning, then another, until a complex picture emerged rather like a Cubist painting where the angles rather than the flesh itself dig out the essence of the features.

It was hard to gauge Gerry's age. When later she discovered that he was forty, it seemed, like so many other things, disjunctive, for she had assumed he was somewhere in his late twenties. He was small but his well-proportioned limbs made him look taller. His dark hair grew in a wavy, boyish lock over a high forehead and he had large green eyes with long dark lashes. If his teeth hadn't been stained by nicotine, his mouth would have been attractive with its bee-stung underlip. He was desperately thin and even in the stuffy room he shivered as he acknowledged her presence with a flicker of his eyes. He might have been handsome but for the look of ingrained poverty that hung about his features, as if his childhood diet had consisted of chips and tea.

For whatever reason, he had been reduced to the sort of man no one would notice in a crowd. On a train, he might have been going to work or coming from it. In a doctor's surgery, he might have had a bad back, but nothing more serious. Neighbours would never have thought to ask him to water their geraniums, and in a pub no one would imagine that he was waiting for a friend. He looked as if he dried his smalls in an all-night launderette, as if maybe he worked for some council in a vague, ancillary way, as if he spent Sundays under the duvet. She had never seen anyone who looked so completely harmless.

He had been studying her, she realised, all the time she had been looking for him and, when their eyes met, he smiled.

'Are you Mrs Washington?' he asked.

There was something almost too courteous in the way he greeted her. She might have been a teacher and he a pupil with a bad label new to her class. Her voice stuck in her throat, but she nodded.

'I'm Carney, but you can call me Gerry if you like.'

She still said nothing. She noticed that he had nicked himself shaving.

'Do sit down,' he said, oddly in command. It was his home after all, she supposed.

'Of course! I'm so sorry,' she murmured, cringing into the folding chair.

He sat, his eyes the tone of a leaden sea, his hands flat on the table. Even then he looked familiar, though it was not till months later that she made the connection with the Hythes.

'Are you frightened?' he asked.

The question caught her off balance. 'Yes,' she replied. 'I've never been in a prison before.' She looked up. 'I feel awful saying that.'

'I've never been in one before either,' said Gerry. 'It *is* "awful", as you put it – being banged up in here, I mean.'

Harriet could smell rank sweat as it oozed from her armpits in the artificial heat. 'What . . .'

'What did I do to get here?'

She blushed, squeezing her eyes shut. 'I didn't mean to ask that.' Boo had told her that it wasn't etiquette. She kept even her-

50

self deliberately in the dark. Inmates had a right to their privacy like anyone else.

'I don't mind telling you. My ex-girlfriend – ' here he gave a contemptuous snort of laughter – 'was giving me a hard time. I got drunk . . . sorry . . . and I smashed a brick through a jeweller's window . . . to get her a ring, you see. I got two years for that.' His voice was otherwise expressionless.

'How dreadful!' Harriet cried. Her sleepless night, the long journey, the unfamiliar surroundings made her feel light-headed and suddenly irrationally angry at the guards at the gate who stood like two giaours, arms akimbo, keen-eyed.

'I meant to ask you,' she continued, 'what you did before you got here, your job, that sort of thing.'

'Oh, that! I worked for the Parks Commission . . . Lambeth . . . That's where I live . . . or did live until last month. But all I did was garden.'

'I used to have a garden,' Harriet said. 'I ended up hating it,' she added. She had the urge to confide in Gerry, a stranger after all. He was stripped of everything, she thought. He was reduced to nothing.

'I hate the mud,' he said. 'They won't even let you have a pot plant here, though. That's in case we grow cannabis or something.'

Harriet laughed. She'd had a puff of cannabis back in the 1970s. One of Averell's less boring friends had brought it to an Ashdean dinner party. Everyone had giggled and had a go. 'I tried it once but didn't like it,' she said. 'It made me sick.'

'I don't do drugs,' Gerry said severely and so abruptly that she was tempted to apologise again.

'Do you do tea?' she asked. She couldn't remember when she had last made a joke. 'Boo McAuley said I might offer you a cup.'

Gerry's dull eyes flashed with a moment of humour and he smiled. 'Tongue's hanging out!' he said. 'Mind, it's diesel. That's what we call it, anyhow.'

He was right. The tea was revolting. Fifteen minutes later, however, by the time this and a packet of biscuits had been consumed between them, Harriet believed she had found her métier. It was crazy, paradoxical, but as she warmed to the slight, anonymous man in his convict's drab she felt the liberation of an instinct she did not know she possessed. Hard to name it, but for the first time in her life she felt she knew exactly what to say. It was like a triumphant dinner party where everything had gone right or a dance where an unknown partner applied such exact and subtle pressure that she and he flew together over the polished floor. In fact, if it hadn't been for his accent, she would have thought from his manners that Carney came from the same social background as she did. And when it came time for her to go, she flushed with pleasure when he asked her to return.

'Of course,' she said. 'Is there anything I can bring you?'

'You don't smoke, do you?' he said sadly.

'Well, I'll bring you some cigarettes.'

'I'm not even sure it's allowed unless you offer me one here and you're smoking too. You see, I don't ever have visitors.'

'Well, I'll puff away then, Gerry!' She was moved by the thought of his isolation.

And he grinned, his sad, dull eyes truly lighting at her genuine gaiety.

Harriet made the return journey in a trance, not feeling the cold nor minding the rush hour bus and train and tube. She rang Boo, burbling, and that night, again unable to sleep, she wept: at the horror of Grisholme, where the smallest sign of life seemed crushed by the grim mathematics of control.

5

SENIOR OFFICER GOSFORTH was asking Chloe the librarian a little bit about Hythe, just chatting, when Hythe himself came into the library, and so the gear of the conversation changed without the hiatus of embarrassment that would have occurred outside the prison walls. Two halves of one disjointed sentence fitted together without a seam. Of course, it never fooled Hythe, but he too behaved as if the officer and the librarian were not discussing him. He shuffled in at the door under the weight of two volumes he was returning.

'Your book's come,' she said, lifting a paperback from a pile on her desk. Its sober cover made it look like an academic work, something to do with the Sack of Constantinople. 'I ordered it months ago,' she told Gosforth. He observed, perhaps because he was writing a novel, that her dark eyes looked ineffably tired.

Gosforth had a heroine in mind, a beautiful nun working for the chaplaincy and she fell in love with, well, an officer. Sometimes he wondered if he shouldn't make her a probation officer, as he knew very little about nuns, but he wanted obstacles. The larger plan of the book had to do with a riot . . . sympathetic characters getting caught in the crossfire. Gosforth had thought of a more literary theme but rejected it in favour of a thriller, which he thought might be easier to write. Now he wasn't so sure.

From an artistic point of view, Chloe's air of resignation interested him. It was almost like a scent worn by civilian women who worked in the prison. Maybe they dispensed it in the ladies' cloakroom, a fragrant, indefinable sadness that female officers did not share as a rule. Trying to deepen the image, as his creative writing manual recommended, he thought it had something to do with an ulterior call on their femininity. The prison was largely a place where men dominated other men who had dominated some victim. Women could sometimes open the tomb of a mind, but it cost them.

Gosforth had accompanied prisoners to trial and had heard victims grilled in the dock by barristers seeking to mitigate loathsome crimes. It was a salutary experience for any Utopian and he had to develop strategies to cope with the revulsion and indignation he felt, emotions that took him by surprise. Numbing horror with drink was a route all too many officers took and, though he was alarmed by his increasing intake of alcohol, he was determined not to let it get out of hand. He hoped he would never allow such a dumbing down of himself. In theory, he thought it was more honest to live with contradictions rather than pretend they were not there. Most of the time, though, he tried not to connect the offender with the offence. There were men who had killed wives, mugged pensioners, supplied teenagers with heroin, buggered children, kidnapped, raped, deceived and embezzled. Once convicted and inside, the reasons they were there became blurred. Perhaps in order to get through each day without planting a fist in a face, he resorted, like most of Grisholme's staff, to euphemism. Somehow one never said 'bad' or 'crime' or 'evil' or 'punishment'. Instead, one talked about 'offenders' and 'behaviour patterns', 'sentence plans' and 'outcomes'.

And yet, for all of this, Gosforth had a moral sense like a naked bulb; it lit things in a plain way to him as it had since childhood. The prison service had attracted him partly for the very darkness that lay within its purlieu. By chance as a student he'd blundered into the wrong lecture, one given by a former prison governor with an inspirational cast of mind and an imaginative approach. Maybe it was because he had been recently persuaded to read *Crime and Punishment* by a girlfriend, but

Gosforth stayed to listen. If there were a grand design to villainy, then men and women of good will should not shirk the task of delivering those caught up in its meshes.

Gosforth did not respond to this challenge immediately. Instead, he cast about himself for some years after getting his degree in archaeology and anthropology, teaching for a while, then joining the civil service. At length, starved out by boredom, he gave way and made the radical choice. In his early thirties, he started training at HMP Brixton, moving quickly up the ranks. Soon he would take exams to qualify as Principal Officer; after that, he would join the bottom rung of the governors' ladder, at the end of which he hoped one day to be managing his own prison. He was a man of ability.

This might have divided him from his brother officers, and would have done had it not been for two things. First, in common with many, he had northern roots. Secondly, his inside knowledge of the forces helped him make a bond with the large number of ex-squaddies who manned the prison service. His father, a Yorkshireman, had been a captain in the Army, had served in Cyprus and later settled there. Gosforth rarely saw him but he remembered visiting the island as a boy and perhaps it was that place, with its alliance to ancient intensities, that informed his consciousness. 'The island of Venus', his mother had called it with an irony he only later fathomed from the severed bonds and visceral outrage of their divorce. Saddened in childhood, he could, as an adult, see both sides of most questions and his chief clarity was a secret pity he had for people who had nothing but themselves to blame.

Chloe had been saying how she thought it might do Hythe good to offer him a job as a library orderly. Gosforth agreed with her. He had spent a few days dipping in and out of Hythe's dossier. Not that he had many idle moments in which to do this kind of thing but, for reasons best known to himself, the inmate seemed to have taken to Gosforth, throwing him meaningful looks as he stood on the Centre, coming up behind him on the landing, clearing his throat as if about to speak. Gosforth found it unnerving, especially when he recalled the public fuss over Gerry Carney. How the inmate had managed to swing his reincarnation as 'Hythe' Gosforth couldn't tell, but he imagined there was some legal justification for it . . . a wise move considering the circumstances of the case. Whatever had prompted Hythe/Carney to break cover and reveal his identity to Gosforth, it seemed a striking thing to do. Inmates sometimes got fixations on prison staff. Maybe it was that.

And so Gosforth pulled his file.

To someone with a less practical grip on life, it might have provoked a crisis of ontological despair. Hythe's record showed that, from adolescence onward, it was as if one long arm of sexually expressed rage had ended in the fist of his last offence. Indecent assault followed indecent assault, false imprisonment, gross indecency. He was 'in denial', the psychologists said, which, in their terms, meant that he refused to partake in any programme that might help him 'address' his 'offending behaviour pattern'. More simply put, Hythe claimed innocence.

Gosforth had a theory about those who lived on the margins where good, evil, madness and sanity blurred into indistinguishable shapes in the fog they created around themselves. Such inmates seemed to have preternatural instincts, sharpened, prehensile. And as if some psychic tom-tom had activated him, alerting him to the officer's interest, Hythe cornered Gosforth the very moment he had finished with the file and put it away. It seemed an immense effort for Hythe to speak; he puffed with exertion, his eyes shifting, whether malign or fearful it was hard to say. He looked like a blowfish, its needles extended. Could they talk? he asked. In the wake of Harriet Washington's death, he needed someone to talk to. Gosforth said he would arrange for counselling. And Hythe had stormed away.

Gosforth trudged up the dark tower where the psychology department lived. Why was he doing this? he wondered. In the heat. It was quite legitimate to seek advice, especially as he was new to the unit and had not worked much with sex offenders in the past. They were famously manipulative and if Hythe wanted to talk Gosforth didn't want to be treading on Psychology's corns by listening in the wrong way. He did not want to get sucked into Hythe's maelstrom, or naively condone, or allow the man to justify his conduct. Gosforth thought all of this and meant most of it. With a part of himself, however, he had an unreasoning urge to explore Hythe, get to the bottom of him simply out of curiosity. Whether this was right or wrong he did not know, but it felt unprofessional.

He was met by Hedda Paget, a smart young woman with a cutting edge of diamond. The prison invested heavily in psychologists, and Hedda looked expensive with her sharp jacket and crisp vowels. There was something wrong with her eyes, though . . . a squint? She read out her notes on Hythe like Leporello singing out Don Giovanni's list to Donna Elvira. In Brighton, 'duecento quaranta'. And an account, too, of Hythe's failure to 'confront' his guilt. This was an inmate to whom prison was home. Although he'd been in and out of establishments around south-east England, Grisholme had been his most consistent address since his early youth. For a while, he had managed to sustain a kind of life in a high-rise council estate in Lambeth, but that hadn't lasted for very long. If ever he left prison this time, he was down as having no fixed address. This meant he would be released out on to the streets. At 48 and in ill health, it was unlikely that he would ever work again.

Hythe had been an itinerant gardener. Gosforth smiled at himself, realising that he had bought the illusion that the man, with his studious habits and supercilious air, was in some way illustrious. Gardening had given him access to prime spots for 'making friends' with children: parks, private homes and even a prep school. To do the prison service justice, it had tried, at various stages, to crack Hythe's code, and there was documentation, pieced together over years, as a testimony to this attempt.

He loved nothing better than kids . . . this was his line. He'd never do anything to 'harm' a child. As for their sexuality, it was a known fact, he liked to claim, that it was far more advanced than most people thought. Somewhere he'd picked it up that Dr Kinsey had scientifically 'proven' that kids enjoyed sex from an early age and sexualising them gently initiated them into a sort of 'learning curve' that meant they had no hang-ups as adults. This, Hedda said, was his myth.

His distinctive perversion, she told Gosforth, had to do with chocolate with which he lured his victims, smearing it later on their bodies. It was something to watch out for, images of chocolate – mud, excrement. After an hour's conversation, Hedda told Gosforth that, particularly as they had no available counsellors, he might as well have a go. Anyone at all who could get Hythe to talk might put him on the right track. She'd be there to supervise if he needed it. Would he be interested in some in-service training? Gosforth accepted the idea for a vague middle distance in the future.

As for the case of the Greek boy, there had been neither chocolate nor mud, however; nothing reported of Hythe's signature tune, as it were. Perhaps it had washed off. The child had fallen in a well. He had not been buggered, but then that had never been Hythe's style. It was thought he had died because he had resisted Hythe's advances. Equivocal evidence, some bruising consistent with either a struggle or an accidental fall, had let Hythe off a much more serious charge.

The inmate now shuffled towards Chloe's desk, but he looked at neither of them until he had unloaded his books on to the table. He glanced from one to the other. A casual observer would have seen no exchange between the three impassive faces. The volumes were the last two in Gibbon's *Decline and Fall of the Roman Empire*.

'A bit of light reading, eh, Hythe?' Gosforth joked clumsily. His own researches had been heavy. Had Hythe felt at home with the Vandals and Visigoths? he wondered. Perhaps he had found the excesses of late Roman emperors more congenial reading. He glanced at the inmate with the sort of scrutiny he might have given a piranha in a goldfish bowl. A sudden impulse to clutch the prisoner's throat, fell him and bang his head against the floor flashed into Gosforth's mind and then was gone. He flushed with shame, for he deplored any kind of brutality. Even to think of bashing Hythe was a danger sign, a descent to the man's level. Surely it would be far more painful for such an inmate to admit the truth, to acknowledge to himself what he had done, than to be hit by an officer.

'I found it gripping,' said Hythe, and Gosforth wondered where a jobbing gardener had acquired the faint air of mandarin disdain.

'Well, you'll enjoy this one,' Chloe said proffering the new book. 'It's a chronicle of outrages.'

Hythe took his spectacles from the case he held in his hand and pompously adjusted them on his nose. He opened the book and held it out with the mannered air of a pundit. 'One of my ancestors, *Sir* Aelric Hythe, assisted in the Sack,' he told them, 'or so I was informed.'

For some reason, it touched Gosforth, the bloated man in the nasty prison-issue shirt making this ridiculous boast. 'Well, history is a fascinating subject,' he said mildly. A clutch of inmates hungry for new thrillers entered the room and Chloe went to help them. 'It is,' said Hythe. 'It's my life now.' He stumped with his stick and specs and new book towards the door and Gosforth accompanied him back to the wing.

'Working on a project, then, are you?' Gosforth asked.

'I am working,' Hythe said grandly, 'on the mystery of myself.'

'*Your* history?'

Hythe paused and, evidently forgiving Gosforth for their last encounter, said, 'Where I fit in; I used to think I came from nowhere.'

'Everybody comes from somewhere.' But Gosforth knew what he meant.

'It was my alleged victim,' said Hythe, 'who showed me . . .

everything . . . in a flash. And *she* . . . Harriet Washington . . .
took it all away.'

Harriet was not able to visit Gerry more than once a fortnight; a
good thing too, she thought. As much as she anticipated seeing
him, she was drained when she went home and would sometimes
sleep for hours when she returned to Chelsea. She developed a
little eczema on her hands. Her nerves, too alert, took days to
wind down.

And yet, when her prison Wednesdays came round, she would
panic over what she was to wear, or if she would make the journey
on time to see Gerry. She ended up leaving the flat earlier and earlier so that she regularly became the first in the queue.

As for Gerry, he seemed no less eager to see her. She noticed
with a little flutter of pride that he'd generally had a haircut before
their meetings. In fact, he was immaculately groomed for one in
such circumstances. His fingernails were evenly cut and cleaned,
his shirt fresh, his face cleanly shaven. It was Harriet's intuition
that he liked to see her well turned out. Far from being ashamed
that his regular visitor was undeniably upper middle class, he
liked it, she noticed, and would look surreptitiously at the other
men, their wives or girlfriends, with an endearing pride, as if he
wanted to show her off. The dismal room with its boiling tea urn,
its dank and tarnished smells of sweat and clothes drying out
from the perpetual rain that winter, became for her a dazzling
Viennese café where ladies and gentlemen chattered, flattering
each other with harmless compliments.

Gerry was so young, she thought, twenty years younger than
herself, he had told her. She thought and thought about him.

They were never at a loss for conversation. Sometimes they
discussed gardens. Her method of growing difficult lilies interested him a great deal and he had plans for her window box when
summer came. Although she knew she should not reveal where
she lived, she found herself coming perilously close. He longed to
hear the smallest detail of her maisonette, how she decorated it.

As he had committed a burglary, under whatever understandable circumstances, Harriet was cautious about giving him full mental range of her antique furniture, but window boxes seemed harmless enough and he was well informed about the wide variety of plants she could choose, changing winter pansies for daisies or petunias with lots of trailing ivy. He'd brightened his one-bedroom council flat, stuck at the top of a tower block, with hanging baskets, full of geraniums, bright red.

But there was a nervous feeling about gardens; they both had it. Harriet found herself volunteering her resentment at Averell, who, she told him, had created a wife in his preferred image and likeness, a lady who would spend all day doing everything prettily. The garden, she said, had finally become a symbol of this. Gerry said he had an emotional thing about gardens too.

She discovered that he was peripatetically educated. This oddity seemed to go with his accent which shifted from South London to a curiously clipped BBC Standard and back again, as if cogs in his larynx slipped from time to time, re-meshing without conscious thought. Maybe there'd been an enlightened schoolmaster in his background. He seemed to have acquired chunks of knowledge that fitted into no larger scheme. He even mentioned *Les Fleurs du Mal* once, which astonished her. But other aspects of his mental field remained entirely untilled. She set about a programme of intellectual encouragement. He should read Shakespeare. As drama was offered at the prison, she tried to get him to join the group. He loved to hear her accounts of the stage, her own career. But, chiefly, he enjoyed science fiction, and though it bored Harriet to tears she made a study of it in order to improve his reading. Because of Harriet he joined an English class, and she felt after that a deep gratitude. However she had wasted her life, she had at least given one man the confidence to expand his mind.

He was a strange, heathenish boy, though, with odd beliefs. Harriet modestly tried to offer him the comforts of religion, the comforts she drew on now more than ever. He believed that Jesus and the Buddha had been aliens visiting this planet and that their intentions had not been entirely good. When touching on the lip of any philosophical thought, his face would darken and, despite her growing affection for him, she often carried home a misgiving that had the hidden energy of fear. And, of course, he was a man and no boy. She did not know why his after-image suggested an alternative to the reality she observed. It was almost as if his parallel universe theory were true. After only three meetings, she began to wish she had a photograph of Gerry, just to make sure she saw him accurately in her mind's eye.

By that Christmas, she had seen him on four separate occasions. In the darkest time of year, she found herself travelling home from Peckham shortly after teatime on Christmas Eve, the wet sleet shining on the road under infernally coloured sodium lamps, lost in the thought that her gift for him, *2001: A Space Odyssey*, had been confiscated for its silver wrapping paper, opened, then put aside to be given to him when it had been checked through. She had protested to an officer, who had laughed in her face. 'You don't get it, Madam, do you?' he said. The inmates used silver paper for drug-taking; who knew but the book could be pornography?

What, Gerry? The homeward bus ground towards Vauxhall. Harriet decided she would get out and walk. Tears were in her eyes. The inmates had their Christmas Eve meal at four o'clock. Every evening they ate their supper at four o'clock. They could not choose their socks, nor receive a simple gift from a simple friend. She walked across the bridge and studied the currents of the dark river. Gerry told her that most inmates spent Christmas day in bed with the covers over their ears. And she did wonder then how he knew, when he had told her he'd never been in prison before.

On Christmas morning, Harriet had no gifts to open. Even though she had sent Averell nothing, she had half expected something from him, a card at least. She had long ago posted gifts to Emma and little Tom, but she had nothing in return. In fact, the only people from her former life who remembered her were Cassie's parents, Michael and Helen Hythe, who had sent a card to her old address from their house in Greece. Gerry, of course, had given her a card, a robin whistling on a shovel in the snow. And Boo McAuley had sent her a Botticelli angel who benefited CAFOD. That she was invited to go home with Boo for Christmas lunch after Mass seemed to her that day so precious it was almost a grace.

Harriet made a resolution not to become maudlin, but she arranged her three cards on the mantelpiece with a gush of weeping. Memories of Helen came back, how Emma and Cassie had once romped about their knees as they had tea by the warm Aga in Helen's kitchen. How exceedingly kind, how delicate of Michael and Helen not to allude to her divorce! They had clearly heard of it because the card, though forwarded from Ashdean, was addressed to Harriet alone. How kind to think of her and how lonely she must be, when once her Christmas parties had been almost as sought after as those at the manor on New Year's Eve, when first old Mr and Mrs Hythe, and then, in feudal succession, Godfrey and Sophie, had given their definitive 'rout'.

Harriet firmly chose her claret jersey dress, pinned her diamond brooch to it and clasped big faux pearl earrings to her ears. A little twirl in the mirror gave her hope. This was, after all, the first Christmas she had spent away from Averell in decades. It was bound to be an ordeal. And look, she was already making a difference to Gerry; she had made a start, at least, on a constructive new life. As she crossed the rainy street to the church, she had a little laugh at herself. Next to the reality of Gerry in his plight, what were all the theatre suppers in the world but vanity?

And, when the organist was playing the congregation out with a grand and joyful fugue, and when Harriet knelt, dutiful before the manger, a sudden meaning came to her from the familiar scene. In one flash of vision she saw Gerry in the crib, the perpetual Infant, the promised birth. All the poor with whom she shared the visiting queue at Grisholme seemed to connect with him, herself, the ox, the ass and the shepherds in one exalted image of God, discovered quite by accident, in Grisholme Prison.

Lunch with Boo was the gayest occasion Harriet could honestly remember. The turkey breast from Marks and Sparks they shared tasted better than the dinde truffée she'd ritually cooked for Averell and Emma, a delicacy they had eaten with clenched and unclenched teeth. She and Boo pulled naff crackers, drank far too much good claret and exchanged gifts. Harriet gave Boo, who was thrilled with it, a cashmere scarf from Peter Jones and Boo gave Harriet a nice copy of an icon she had bought at Westminster Cathedral showing Abraham entertaining angels unaware. She'd also rustled up a picture of Nancy Reagan, First Lady, looking particularly silly and the two women roared with laughter, then talked prisons until Boo had to lurch into a taxi to have yet another Christmas meal at her son's house in Fulham, an occasion she secretly dreaded for the *awful* daughter-in-law.

With her new icon held tenderly, Harriet walked home. It was snowing lightly and each flake gilded in the lamplight seemed to stand out as an individual gem . . . like people . . . like every human being. Her heart was full. Boo had pulled out stops more than the organist. She told Harriet that Gerry Carney was making a spectacular recovery from the suicidal slide. He ate, he took interest, he washed and he had put his name down for several classes.

6

IN THE FEW DAYS following the news of Harriet's death, Gerry started having peculiar pains around his chest. Considering that Jonah a few cells down the landing had recently been taken to hospital following a heart attack, it made him wonder. Since his stroke, every day had been provisional, not seen as a gift by Gerry, but as an accident waiting to happen. A seismograph in the back of his mind jotted automatic readings; any change spelt peril and these pains were new.

Of course, if it hadn't been for the stroke he'd had several years into his sentence he would have been stuck in a Greek prison for the rest of his life. Gerry blanked out on all of that now, but the smell lingered with him, the harsh foreign language and the food . . . on Sundays a lump of boiled meat so hard and dried and cold that it became fibrous and stuck in his teeth. The stroke that nearly killed him saved him from something worse, he often thought. Although he knew he had been extradited due to Harriet's campaigning, even though he'd heard that she was ill, this made him even more angry at her, patronising bitch! He thought of her now with contempt: an absurd old woman. It was a word his father had often used, 'absurd'. He had applied it to life in general or to Gerry in particular when he cried. 'Don't be absurd,' Edgar Hythe would say.

Gerry was frightened enough of the mud dream. At least he did not dream of Harriet, but he was afraid it might come. He was pleased with his new library job; it got him out of his cell and, even though he coughed, the money was useful for more burn. He'd chanced on a National Geographic book on spiders, though. The cover showed a vast arachnid enclosing a fly with its spinnerets. Gerry had phobias, especially of rats, but in the past he had been able to remove spiders from the bath with his bare hands. After all, they were the gardener's friend, capturing and eating pernicious insects as they did. Now, ugly visions of the photograph came to him unbidden. In a flash of intuition, he saw Harriet translated into a monstrous eight-legged creature, now scuttling over his cell floor, now lurking in the ceiling ready to descend and wrap him in her smothering love, stinging him with paralytic juices, humming as she spun. These thoughts made him feel sick as if in a lift going down from the top of a very high building, a lurch to the stomach and a crawling sensation. Maybe this was the reason for his pains.

It could be nerves.

Gerry did not know what had possessed him to give his 'chronicle', as he called it, to S.O. Gosforth. A few days before, the officer had dropped into his cell, all friendly as if he hadn't tried to bully Gerry into seeing the shrinks. Fancy asking him if he wanted a counsellor to talk about Harriet's death! Before Gerry knew it, he'd have been manhandled into a Sex Offenders' Treatment Programme, playing mind games with a load of other cons who just wanted parole. They called it 'group therapy', but no way was it therapy! The shrinks set the inmates against each other, forcing them to admit their 'guilt'. Well, what if you were innocent, like Gerry? What then? It made him indignant just to think about it.

In Gerry's opinion, there was no good officer but a dead officer. Anything they did had a motive behind it, Mr Gosforth included. It was hardly as if he was dropping by just to pass the time of day. So Gerry had been bracing himself for the twist, waiting for the hard sell for 'therapy' that would be sandwiched somewhere in the seemingly casual conversation. But Mr Gosforth hadn't touched on anything to do with Harriet's death. Instead, he started chatting about a novel he was writing and, before he knew it, Gerry had handed him the wadge of exercise books. Although he had wanted to scream for them back the moment he had surrendered them, he did not.

Right now, it was making him anxious to think that Mr Gosforth might be reading his story, but more anxious to think that he hadn't bothered. He seemed an educated man, and Gerry couldn't spell. He also found punctuation difficult, even though he studied the books he read for the proper way to set things out. Words slipped and slithered out of his head on to the paper. It seemed hard to order them in any concrete way. Commas, full stops, queries all looked wrong because they made it seem as if each thought had borders. His own thoughts didn't work like that. They were unbounded.

Maybe Mr Gosforth had read it and hated it, because he had mentioned nothing about it even though Gerry had seen him several times since.

He wondered if he should have written down an explanation of the key to the story. Maybe Mr Gosforth wouldn't be able to get the point without knowing that Cassie had photocopied their family tree and given it to him as a Christmas present. It was the nicest gift he'd ever had. He couldn't think why she had no interest in it herself, seeing as she'd given it to him, but she explained that the genealogy had been drummed into her head too often by her – their – grandmother. Because he asked so many questions about the family, she'd got the genealogy copied to set the record straight. 'Batty Aunt Matty', as Cassie called her, had made the family tree a life's work, embellishing it with scrolls and heraldry. There was no sense why Gerry shouldn't have it. It was his heritage too.

Well, it was Gerry's life's work now, his inner consolation.

Born, married, deceased: the family history spiralled out in a rhythm he had lacked in life. Some of the Hythe nobility had rubbed off on him, he knew it. There was even a crest with quarterings! Gerry was rather proud when he discovered he should be 'bar sinister', a fact gleaned from a book. Cassie had written him in under Edgar, but Gerry supplied the left-hand slash. He could call himself Fitzhythe, he discovered. Maybe he'd do that when he got out.

What he had done with his story was to pretend he was in a time machine, a device he had used since his childhood to escape into the future or on to other planets. Now, with the help of the histories, he fled into the past and joined his ancestors, becoming at one with them in his imagination. A long time ago Gerry had a cellmate who had done some kind of regression therapy under hypnosis and was supposed to be Catherine the Great or something. Some queen he was, too! Gerry's story was a little like regression therapy only there was nothing haphazard about the connections with himself. Like someone doing a brass rubbing, he traced the outline of his double helix. From Ethelbert through Aelric down to and through his father Edgar, the genetic thumb-print marked Gerald, as Cassie had styled him on the family tree, a signature, a distinction and a doom.

A lot of other things surged up into the story, some feelings about his own predicament. What could Mr Gosforth expect with the sort of education he'd had, which was not much? Just when he got his feet under the table at one school, he'd be shoved off to another where the kids were learning something different. How should he know how to write a book? he thought angrily. He got teased and bullied for being so small, bad at games and 'weird', so how was he to get his head round books? Edgar had taught him some stuff, poetry. Once he'd even had a go at Latin, but he didn't have the patience. It was Gerry's fault for being 'thick'.

Gerry didn't want to give one inch to Harriet, but he grudg-ingly had to admit that she had helped him catch up on some schooling. She got him reading. You could say that for her. When they had been planning to go to Greece together, he had found himself thinking in a new way about the gods his father had told him about, especially when they'd studied the vases together. Maybe it was them . . . gods . . . who had been responsible for him. He liked the idea of the dark and special destiny they seemed to confer on the mortals 'they swatted like flies', Edgar told him Shakespeare had said. Yes, Harriet had made it different for a while, giving him a feeling like a god or the son of a god, someone who had been flung out of heaven, seeded in the womb of an unsuspecting girl, and nurtured in a wild place, perhaps by animals.

Gerry's chest ached when he thought like this: he was aware of an acute emptiness, as if someone had amputated a phantom limb or organ, something abstract that he did not even know he had possessed.

It was the intolerable idea that the boy was dead, wasn't it? The one and only boy he had ever really loved.

No one from the prison ever came back to Gosforth's flat. If challenged, he would say he was a bit of a hermit, and this was partly true. He did have friends whom he saw from time to time, but they were mostly from his university days and came less and less to East Dulwich. Some were married, some had partners, most had children. All had social aspirations and few understood why he had entered the prison service. As for his colleagues, he fitted in as Jim who would buy a round in the pub every so often. Sometimes Gosforth wondered if he would try his hand at something new, but he was too far up the ladder now, too near realising the ambition he'd started with. In the circumstances, it did him no good to be aloof, but for various reasons he was a very private man and he could not help himself.

Gosforth, a Scot on his mother's side and thrifty too, had scrimped to get a mortgage on his flat, this the first rung in another kind of ladder. It was modest, half of a Victorian cottage, and the other tenant was always away. The prison had given him much exercise with keys and his threshold was stoutly bounded. It was heaven to go home and bolt the door.

In summer his windows were a maze of potted plants, and in winter he drew floor-to-ceiling curtains the moment he came in.

The prison, both arduous and dangerous, made him want the stiff drink he invariably downed with censorious warnings to himself. This and switching on the stereo: Bach. He profoundly rejoiced in the order of baroque music, in which he had discovered an antidote to Grisholme.

He sat now in the chesterfield he had picked up at an auction and flipped for the third time through Hythe's exercise books. It had been an effort to bring them home, but they lay there in his sanctuary and he had promised the man he would read them.

Gosforth did not know what he had expected or even what he had wanted to know, but the chaos of the pages actually startled him. It was like reading a literal translation of cuneiform or Linear B. Although the individual words were English, many of them were virtually unrecognisable through the poor handwriting and bad spelling; but it was the sense of each sentence, if that was what you could call unpunctuated statements often without verbs, that eluded him. It seemed odd coming from an inmate who read thumping tomes for pleasure . . . and one so theatrically Brahmin. Maybe he was dyslexic. Inmates often were.

The scrawled notebooks were not without interest, however. Odd bits of meaning slipped through the net of Hythe's blotted, blunt writing, his cursory grammar. It was clear that someone somewhere had given him a family tree and he was painstakingly trying to fit his ancestors into historical context, surrounding them with such period details as he had been able to glean from books in the prison library. It seemed a desperate effort, somehow pitiful, this borrowed finery. It made Gosforth think of Americans who came to Scotland in search of a tartan. His mother, whose own clannishness left most competitors standing, despised these purchasers of Cairngorms and lineage, but Gosforth always had a sneaking sympathy for their sad attempts to counterbalance shopping malls and Disney with Black Watch plaid and a sense of continuity with the past. As for poor Hythe, he hadn't got very far. In an attempt to get Alfred the Great into the picture, he made elliptical leaps over facts; the Conquest, where he placed a Saxon ancestor called Ethelbert in the battlefield next to Harold, opposing a Norman Hythe next to William, didn't really come off. And yet, when he got to the Crusades for which he claimed Richard Coeur de Lion as royal companion to his extremely great grandsire, a shaft of touching lyricism emerged.

All of this would have been a good idea, well and good, even original, if the notebooks had not thrown up wild interpolations that seemed to have nothing to do with the focus of intention. In fact, if they had not been bound, Gosforth would have thought he had missed pages or that they were out of order. Great patches of bitter prose seeped out at intervals, most of them diatribes against the woman who had died, this Harriet Washington. A lot of it was mildly obscene, written in the form of unsent letters that intimately described her ageing flesh with loathing. There was something startling about this and it was very unpleasant to read. What could the woman have done to deserve this? The writing forced Gosforth, as if some subtle assault were taking place against himself, to imagine a large, voluptuous hag with hanging dugs, licking her lips while she disrobed an evil-smelling body to the prim and innocent Hythe.

Scrawled in the margin of one of these outbursts, there was a brief note about the great whore the Crusaders had seated on the Patriarch's throne in Constantinople. This seemed to be the link with the remaining text, but it was a faulty connection at best. It was as if Hythe's mind were basting in a stew of morbid sexuality. At times he'd be under control, then suddenly the dam would burst and his whole being would become flooded. Then he would resume the narrative as if nothing had happened . . . as if all his thoughts were sequential and built one upon another with the coldest kind of logic.

The book, if you could call it that, was dedicated to his cousin Cassandra whom he called 'Cassie' and there were little sentimental tributes to her throughout the text. She seemed to escape Hythe's swingeing view of womanhood. It made Gosforth curious about the Beatrice to such a Dante.

What on earth was he to say to Hythe? Try as he might, he could not glean enough sense from the argument to discuss it. Small clues to Hythe ended in cul-de-sacs and he would have to go back to the beginning. There was nothing about the dead boy, but one small passage caught his eye, a fragment, a shard. 'I know you understand you always knew me you were me but not me so important why cant you speak and tell them the truth because you come to me and comfort me.'

Gosforth did not know whether it was right to assume this was the victim. In his own lonely childhood he had played Sherlock Holmes for hours at a time, inventing a Watson with whom he had long conversations – mostly, it must be said, in an effort to understand his parents' hostility to each other. Inventing mysteries, he had used the dictionary magnifying glass and his mother's eyebrow tweezers to inspect the chilly house in Edinburgh where they had gone to live with his ailing grandmother after the divorce. As a child, Gosforth had wanted to join the police and be a detective, but this seemed to horrify his mother who, from as early as he could remember, pushed him towards university where she had wanted him to study law. In the weird plea bargaining system of families, he did his degree on the condition that he escape to London and read what had then interested him. It was perhaps a secret bond with his father, so contented now in Cyprus, that his chosen subject delved the ruins of the past.

With what archaeology he'd acquired in his course there had been some satisfaction of the Holmes in him, the rigorous sifting of clues to ancient rites. Flipping now as he did through Hythe's twisting prose, he laughed as he saw it. The scribbled notebooks were like a description of the Labyrinth written by the Minotaur. It was as if, sealed in and blinded by the dark, Hythe scooped away and butted his head, frustrated in the painful understanding of what only light could make manifest. Poor monster, he had revealed what he had been attempting to conceal, a brute – or maybe a brutalised – mind.

Gosforth put down the notebooks and looked at his watch. The sun had crossed the yard-arm and he felt like a drink. He made an excuse of the puzzle Hythe presented and poured himself a few fingers of malt.

What had really happened to the boy? An unwanted vision of the drowned child came to him, his hair floating, his eyes opened wide, face pallid and upturned in the narrow aperture, a grisly rebirth. What kind of accident could it have been when a romp in the countryside between a convicted paedophile and a boy had ended in death? He had the urge to kick the pile of exercise books from the coffee table with the heel of his boot. Gently, he put down the glass and vowed to go for a run rather than refill it.

Quickly and before he changed his mind, he got into his jogging gear, plugged his Walkman into his ears and ran in the August heat all the way to Dulwich to the tune of the B Minor Mass.

7

IN JANUARY, HARRIET WROTE a little note to Helen Hythe thanking her for remembering her at Christmas and giving her new address in London. 'As you may have heard,' she wrote, 'things didn't work out between Averell and me . . .' then stopped and sighed at the modern cliché. Too late. She had bought the pretty notelet at the V&A and couldn't spoil it now.

Harriet had always been rather nervous of Helen. It made little difference that they had shared school runs and that Emma and Cassie had been such friends. No one in Ashdean knew quite what to make of Helen. She was Greek yet she was a Hythe, which made her one of them and not one of them at the same time.

Somehow, Harriet and Helen never became the soulmates they seemed destined to be. They were always said 'to have so much in common'. This meant that they were both outsiders. Though they bravely battled on, attending village cricket matches and helping with the charity Christmas Fayre, they were known to follow that most occult of pursuits, the arts. Together they had even tried to get an amateur dramatic society going, but it failed. Whereas Helen (or 'Eleni' as she sometimes styled herself) was by nature histrionic and wanted to put on great tragedies in the village hall, Harriet took a professional approach and rejected even *Lady Windermere's Fan* as being too ambitious, much less Euripides. They were friends for want of anyone better around, and when Cassie and Emma came along, they played together nicely.

Helen's background was exotic. Her father had been George Bellini, a renowned plastic surgeon whose international success at giving noses a desirable classicism had taken him to London before the war. During it, he did marvellous work repairing damaged airmen in East Grinstead. Her mother had ties with an Anglo-Greek shipping family, and they saw out the war and its aftermath in Sussex, settling in England thereafter. The Bellinis were an oddity: Greek Catholics. Their family seat was in Naxos, an island in the Cyclades. Although their ancestors had come with the Venetian conquest of the island in the thirteenth century, the Bellinis' customs and language were Greek; indeed, they could never have been confused with any other nationality, and certainly not with Italians. But they had never succumbed to Orthodoxy, and this loyalty to Rome gave them an odd displacement in a Greece that covertly revered their ducal heritage and, at the same time, mistrusted them as 'Franks'.

George Bellini chose to spend most of his life in England, yet he owned and maintained the house his ancestors had built in the medieval Kastro of Naxos Town when they had been courtiers to the First Duke Marcos Sanudos. In addition to this, the Bellinis had a country estate on the island.

So when Helen Bellini married Michael Hythe she brought him a considerable dowry in the way of the Greek real estate she was to inherit. This was one point in her favour, especially considering that neither property carried outstanding debts. Certainly, this should have endeared her to Michael's father Aidan, who had the reputation for being a hard man when it came to money.

The second consideration that should have united Helen and Michael's mother was religion. Maeve Hythe was an intense Catholic. But the truth was that if Helen had been the Duchess of Alba and a living saint, she would never have been good enough for Maeve. Maeve adored Michael and favoured him over his brothers in a blind, unselfcritical way.

The question of religious allegiance amongst the Hythes was something that puzzled Ashdean greatly. A family like that should be Church of England, most thought. And, of the three brothers, Godfrey and Edgar were Anglican, in keeping with their father. Michael alone had been baptised and raised a Roman Catholic.

Out of curiosity, Harriet once asked Helen for an exegesis. Cassie's situation rather drew attention to it. If she spent Friday night with Emma, she had to have fish. If Saturday, she was always whipped off early Sunday morning to go to Mass some miles away. Michael, Helen and Maeve Hythe, unnecessarily grim and uneasy, would come to fetch her. They were a redoubt, they seemed to say, as proud of their faith as if they had been recusants. Harriet subtly envied them their assurance, and now and then it pricked her heart, remembering that she'd given it all up for Averell.

Helen was only too pleased to get in a crack at her mother-in-law, who had a high tone and wore a mantilla to church. But though it was a meaty story, full of gossip, Harriet had found it too convoluted to follow properly. Back in the fold herself, she strove to remember it now.

Maeve was Irish. How she'd met and married Aidan Hythe was a bit of a mystery, but dark reasons were cited, which meant that she must have been pregnant and the wedding had to happen in a hurry. A proud family the Hythes were too. Helen told Harriet that Aidan Hythe had forced Maeve's hand, making her choose between her faith and her child's legitimacy. And, sure enough, Godfrey had been 'premature', born seven months after the wedding. All seemed to go smoothly. She had a second child, Edgar. She must have resigned herself to the situation, for her two sons could not have had a more conventional English upbringing. It was when Edgar went off to prep school at six that Maeve gave birth to Michael.

Helen had told Harriet that she could never make sense of what then happened. Call it conversion, call it post-natal uproar, but Maeve insisted that her new baby had to be baptised and raised a Catholic: nothing would do but she must return to the Church. What surprised everyone was that Aidan gave in to this.

Harriet remembered him as a reclusive man, who had done little for the village when he was squire. Helen would not be drawn into talking about her father-in-law, except to say that he was very cold. And that could have meant anything, coming from her.

Maeve's uncle was a bishop, otherwise she would probably never have been forgiven the shotgun wedding. That's what Helen said, at any rate. The condition was that Aidan and Maeve had to agree to live 'as brother and sister', so it was for this reason, Helen conjectured, that her mother-in-law poured all of her energies into Michael, making him the centre of her life. There were all sorts of ramifications to this that did not ring true to Harriet, but it was Helen's story anyway.

Helen detested Maeve, and Maeve tolerated Helen with high martyrdom. If it hadn't been for the house on Naxos, Helen used to tell Harriet, she would have gone mad. Every year she and Michael would sweep up Cassie and go to stay with old George Bellini who had retired to his native island after the death of his wife. Later, Harriet remembered, they had invited Emma to go out and stay, but it fell through. Harriet would love to have seen it herself. How romantic it seemed, a crumbling Frankish palazzo on Naxos, the island of Ariadne!

Whatever Helen might have felt about Maeve, she stuck it out in Ashdean until she could move to Greece in good conscience. Initially, it had amused Harriet to hear Helen rant and rave about her in-laws, but then the Hythes had a few truly awful years and she rather clammed up. First of all, old Aidan Hythe died – of drink, some whispered, but there was little evidence to go on except the gossip of dailies. Harriet remembered the pompous funeral at which no one looked as if they were holding back tears. Then, not long after that, the black sheep Edgar, who had not found the time to attend his father's burial, died, also amid rumours – a great shock for the family, she recalled. As for Helen, she became moodier and less communicative.

After their 'anni horribiles' Helen and Michael started to spend more time on Naxos, presumably looking after old George

Bellini; Godfrey, as was fitting for the eldest son, took over the manor and the care of Maeve as dowager. As an architect, Michael was well placed to oversee the modernising of both the ancient palazzo in the Kastro and the Bellini farm in the island's interior that supplied them with fruit and vegetables, milk, cheese and Easter lamb. For many years, school holidays allowing, they commuted back and forth from Greece to England, smuggling home-grown olives, feta and sausage in their smalls. They threw Greek dinner parties in Ashdean. Helen, now calling herself Eleni, was at last a chatelaine in her own right, cocking a snook at the dull bankers and brokers and their duller wives who had made her feel 'like a wop' (her expression) when first she married Michael. Whether he enjoyed the change or not it was hard to tell, but he did say that reconstructing a Naxian palazzo was better than doing up oast-houses. Truth to tell, he was besotted with his dynamic wife, and would have followed her if she had whimsically decided to live in Borneo.

Helen had something wrong with her womb and it was a source of grief to her that soon after Cassandra's birth she had to have a hysterectomy. Harriet was privately grateful that she had not had to endure more than one pregnancy, but she never said so to Mother Earth. The deep affection between Helen and Cassie was, however, a source of smothered envy to Harriet who had found Emma awkward from birth.

Even though Harriet had always liked Cassie, she found it hard not to gloat when, at art school, she had scandalised everyone by running off with her tutor. It seemed to offset the appalling rows she was having with Emma. For a whole number of reasons, one of them being the death of Maeve, Michael and Eleni soon after sold their Georgian rectory to some people in advertising. They moved permanently to Naxos, leaving Godfrey in command of the manor, the sole remaining Hythe in Ashdean.

Harriet had rather missed them, not realising she would until they were gone. Helen had always said, 'You must come out,' but had left it vague and Harriet had not heard from them for years.

This was why their Christmas card, coming out of the blue, seemed such a gift. It was extremely pretty too, both elegant and spiritual, a modern Madonna enthroned with angels. Turning it over she saw that it was made by Cassie. Again, a little spine of jealousy pricked her heart; why this was she could not say, as Emma was publishing pieces in the *New York Times*, but she even mentioned it in her next confession.

Harriet wondered if Averell had received a card too and hoped that he had not. Although Michael and Helen had been on both of Harriet's dinner party lists (she kept one for the gentry and another for those she thought 'interesting'), she always felt that Averell was the stumbling block. With the years he had become almost aggressively the plain businessman who loved his golf; and with one whisky too many he came to affect boorishness, the loud American guy he most certainly was not by birth.

Harriet wondered now if it wouldn't be a good idea to throw in a word of praise for Cassie's card, make small reparation for her ungenerous thoughts. Wasn't it marvellous? she wrote, underscoring the word. Where could she order some for next Christmas? She was squeezing too much into the notelet, so she added a sheet of paper. She thought the Hythes might like to know that Emma was working in New York now and had a son. After that, it occurred to her that they might be interested to know that she had 'gone over to Rome'. She decided not to add that it was partly to do with their influence, because it wasn't true. Why ever had she been tempted to put this? Was she, without meaning to, angling for an invitation out to their Greek island? Harriet frowned, bit her lip and re-read what she had written several times over to see if it made her sound lonely or pathetic. She ended somewhat lamely by telling them she had taken up prison visiting. That sounded positive. No, she'd written a nice letter, a good letter. The picture on the card of an embroidered phoenix was both elegant and resonant of rising from the ashes of her divorce. She posted the letter but, in taking up with Gerry a week later, forgot all about it.

The New Year promised to be a good one for Harriet. Boo and she popped into each other's houses and Harriet even fed and walked Jolly, the fat Labrador, when Boo was 'off on a toot'. This meant she rushed off round the country lecturing. They chortled a lot. Harriet had never chortled in her life. They ate snack meals and went to Peter Jones and Harriet met the 'ghastly' daughter-in-law (whom she privately thought rather nice).

The great thrill came when Boo was mentioned in the New Year's Honours List. She had an OBE! And threw a big party with champagne. Harriet helped with the substantial nibbles. Prison worthies all jammed into the little mews house, the Governor of Grisholme, the local MP, the parish priest and whatnot. Even Lord Longford came, and a selection of ex-inmates made good who did not know how to behave or what to say and thus stood in the corner scoffing the canapés and getting drunk.

Harriet had an urge to nobble the Governor about Gerry, to intercede for him in some way. Gerry called him 'a right bastard', but when Harriet came to meet him he seemed quite civilised, with lines in his face that showed perpetual anxiety rather than cruelty. It came to the point and she said nothing, and thought it best not to mention to Gerry that she had met the man.

Harriet's life was bouncing back. A couple from the church asked her to a dinner party and she enjoyed it. And though Boo's taste in music ran to Hundred Best Tunes rather than Mozart, they took in a few concerts, though not the theatre, for Boo had to admit that she frankly loathed it.

Thus it came as a surprise to Harriet that her feelings for Gerry intensified.

Perhaps it was a little like being a therapist, she sometimes thought, this befriending of Gerry. She was startled to tears the first time he snapped at her then fell into a sullen silence; she anguished about it for a fortnight, even consulting Boo, who told her, 'These men!'

Harriet could not imagine what she had said wrong to him, and combed over every word. Boo told her to ignore it. Most of them were unstable. Since the closure of mental hospitals, prisons got inmates they weren't designed to treat. It was unfair to expect officers to be psychiatric nurses, she said.

Harriet had purchased two noisettes of filet mignon and made a Béarnaise sauce to go with them for Boo OBE. And a rather good burgundy from Waitrose. Boo admired Harriet's cooking, thought her flat 'exquisite' and loved her style. She had something nice to say each time she came. They sat on precious inlaid chairs Harriet had long ago snapped up from an antique shop in Rye. She always used linen napkins, even when alone, and she had lace table mats that looked as if they had been woven by spiders. They ate from translucent Dresden plates and drank from crystal goblets. Harriet wore her hostess caftan and Boo wanted to know where to get one to hide her lumps and bumps . . . not that Harriet had any! (She did not! A source of pride.) Her pure white hair, upswept in its perfect French knot, her fragile well-tended complexion in the candle light . . . 'Look at you, Harriet,' said Boo. 'Carney must have all sorts of conflicting feelings about you. Your interest in him must be a tremendous vindication for him, but it works both ways. You also represent what he is not; you have what he never had and probably never will have. It's an effect you have on people,' she added this last obscurely.

'Oh dear, I do make an effort not to look too grand!' Harriet cried.

'Darling,' (for they had reached that stage), 'if you wore sack-cloth and ashes you couldn't conceal the fact.'

Boo advised her that the rigours of prison made volatile men more volatile. She also gently suggested that Harriet needed someone else to visit, perhaps.

A cold thrill of fear ran through Harriet . . . the thought of losing Gerry. She concealed it first from Boo and then from herself with the offer of more wine. 'You mean I've stopped doing him good?' That really did bother her. She really did care.

'Not at all!' Boo gulped the wine. 'I simply mean to balance him out.' As ungainly as Boo was to look at, she had surprising délicatesse . . . like fat people who dance gracefully. 'One does get frightfully attached to them, but one mustn't. You see, it isn't fair to them. Many of them are in prison for the precise reason that they cannot form adequate relationships. To trust them is to expect too much from them as a rule. To love them, though, that's the trick, in the full knowledge that they can never love one in return and that one's best hopes for them will almost certainly be dashed.'

Harriet pondered this over the washing-up. As things worked out, she did visit another man from the segregated unit of the prison, a sex offender who gave her the creeps. But he was moved to another prison directly after her only visit. As for Gerry, one could never have guessed that he had snapped at Harriet, nor that he had shown her a sudden, cold disdain – a curious element that seemed to come from a deep source within. If the contrast to his normal behaviour had not been so marked, she would have decided she had been imagining things. It had been like catching a glimpse of the dark side of the moon, Harriet thought, on which light never shone. 'Well, we all have one,' she said to herself, cheerful and grateful for his restored good humour.

But that was not all. The rest was precious, a sign of his trust that she held close to her. On her last visit, they'd been chatting away about, of all things, how he had loved *Quatermass* as a boy. Suddenly, Gerry looked down at his hands, which were reflexively turning his tea mug round and round. It seemed very difficult for him to talk, but at last, in a painful effort, he confided to her that he had been terrified of his father. When his father had beaten him, he told her, he would pretend that he was in a spaceship looking down from another planet.

In her wildest imaginings, Harriet could not have thought that Gerry's father had been Edgar Hythe.

Lent came early that year, and a hard frost prevented even the snowdrops from showing themselves in Cadogan Gardens. In the past Harriet had eschewed chocolate, which she never ate anyway, but now, in an excess of fervour, she proposed to renounce meat altogether, and to do without her evening glass of white wine.

Because she intended to fast on Ash Wednesday, it flustered Harriet when she realised that she had engaged to slog all the way out to Grisholme that day. The prison made her ravenous, and when she returned she needed a drink. Nevertheless, she decided that breaking her promise to Gerry would hardly be in keeping with the spirit of the day, and so she went. Her chief concern was to conceal from him that she was fasting and she scrupled over whether or not it was a lie to tell him she had a tummy ache so as to avoid her share of tea and biscuits.

The problem, however, did not arise. Gerry was in a communicative mood. This was increasingly coming to mean that the question of his childhood would come up, and Harriet settled herself down to listen. As for the biscuits, he forgot all about asking for them.

Over the past few weeks, his story had unfolded of the most appalling background she had ever heard of. Incredible though it was to think that anyone had undergone such suffering in the twentieth century, Harriet believed him. What a shiftless, immoral mother! Wicked, actually. It shocked her to hear that, though she was presumably alive, she had washed her hands of Gerry. He didn't even know where she lived! A picture was emerging of a lonely little boy, rejected by one dysfunctional parent, rejected and battered by the other. Harriet had a mental image of Carney senior, a red-faced labourer who drank himself senseless every night and whacked his kid whenever. And to think of it! Gerry as an adult seemed so fragile. Imagine what he had been at ten! She could see the shivering child warding off blows from the ham fists of a towering brute.

Today he seemed more agitated than usual, she thought. He sat, legs twisted round one another, jiggling and pumping his foot under the table. His hands were knotted together, almost as if he were washing them, and his eyes were focused inwards, as though he were looking at his soul. Harriet was faint with hunger and with the overheated room, where the other tables spilled over with an unusual crowd of inmates and their visitors. The loud conversation next to them was between a man and his angry wife, who hissed some sort of accusation or other in a vehement stage whisper.

And so when Gerry revealed the identity of his father she was not sure that she had heard it in the first place, coming as it did after a long and obscure reminiscence of the man's habitual physical violence.

'You probably think this is wrong, Harriet, but I cheered when he died. Edgar! He never even let me call him "Dad".' Gerry gave a snort of contempt. 'I can see why now!'

'Edgar?' She wasn't sure she heard him.

'Oh, yeah. Edgar. He was a toff, don't you know. You don't believe me, do you?'

'Of course I believe you!' Harriet replied. 'Why shouldn't I believe you! I simply couldn't hear you.'

Gerry shot a look so hostile at his neighbour's wife that the woman went quite silent. He dashed the wavy lock of hair from his eyes, almost as if preparing for a fight. There was something very upsetting about all of this, and Harriet tried to re-engage Gerry's attention.

'Oh, yes, I have blue blood,' Gerry continued with a defensive pride. 'Not that I ever met his family.'

Somehow this touched Harriet with pity. She searched his face. Maybe he was inventing the whole thing, but she suddenly realised that his story explained several things that had puzzled her: the way his speech was peppered with odd references and, at times, strangely elevated diction. His manners, too, could take her by surprise. One might say he was often courtly. The situation looked more Victorian by the minute. She half-expected to hear that the mother had been a servant in a grand house, 'ruined' by the young master.

Gerry's eyes locked on to hers, certain now of her full attention. 'And you know, Harriet, I wasn't even asked to his funeral! I only heard he'd died after he was buried. I was fifteen years old.' He spoke with deep bitterness. 'I found out where his grave was, though. I once went to see it. It's in Kent, a village called Ashdean.'

'What!' Maybe it was his intensity, but the power of recognition made her jolt back in her chair.

'Do you know it?' He looked at her sharply, a fox guarding a wounded paw.

Harriet's promise to Boo that she would conceal all details of her personal life went out the window with the shock. 'Ashdean? *Know* it! I lived there for most of my adult life!'

They stared at each other in amazement.

'Edgar Hythe. Did you know Edgar Hythe?' he asked, breath trembling.

'Of course I knew him. I knew the whole family!'

Gerry and Harriet said nothing while it sank in. It was like guessing the whereabouts of the ace of spades in a deck of fifty-two or being discovered by a casting agent on Sunset Boulevard, a circumstance that extends the bounds of probability into grey areas where things seem fated. They were bound for a moment in that sort of astonishment which unites even complete strangers. They might have been witnesses to a traffic accident or a bank robbery, something sudden and calling on a common humanity to respond.

After a little while, Harriet noticed that Gerry's face had turned grey. He sat very still and his eyes blinked rapidly. 'You never!' he said.

'Oh, yes, I did . . . I did know him.' Harriet didn't know why she was so urgent to convince him, when the rational part of her knew it would be better to say she must have made a mistake.

Gerry looked down at his hands. 'What was he like?' he asked in a small voice. '. . . there, I mean, on his own home patch?'

She said nothing, but again he searched her face, demanding to know.

'I'll give you any odds he was . . . he could be really smooth,' he said with disgust.

Harriet did not like to tell him what she knew of Edgar. 'I didn't know him well. He didn't come often to Ashdean.'

A murderous look of irony came over Gerry's face. 'I'll bet he'd turn up when he was skint, though.'

Harriet looked at her lap.

'Look, Harriet, I'm under no illusions. He was a junkie. I know that, who better?'

Of course, all Ashdean knew that Edgar Hythe had been addicted to heroin. Many said it was the least unpleasant thing about him. At least it provided some excuse for his arrogant behaviour and the appalling way he had treated poor Maeve Hythe. Helen had often talked about it.

'You know how he died?'

Harriet shook her head. There had been rumours, but the best element in the village showed decency to the Hythes by refusing to gossip with the worst.

'They hid it from me until I kicked up such a ruck they had to tell me . . . social workers!' He nearly spat. 'Edgar died in the dustbins behind a Chinese restaurant in Soho . . . ODed on bad skag . . .' He smiled thinly at her puzzled face. 'Heroin . . . an *over*dose,' he added in a posh accent.

Harriet put up her hands to ward off his mockery, but she knew he wasn't really getting at her. To think that Edgar Hythe had beaten his son like a navvy! 'I had no idea,' she said.

'Do you know, they even had the nerve to lie to me at first! They told me that he died abroad and was cremated. Oh, he went "abroad", all right . . . "tripping", I'd call it, to wherever he could feed his habit. You name it, he took it – coke, smack, speed, puff . . . whatever.'

Harriet sat back in her chair. Gerry's temples were throbbing and the veins jumped in his neck. His pale face was red. The officer on duty caught her eye, but she signalled to him that she was all right.

'Gerry, dear, I had no idea! I'm so sorry!' She comforted him with a pat on the hand. He was crying.

'Do you know what he used to call me? His "little bastard". But he was the bastard, not me. The joke is I have a right to his name because my mum made him put it on my birth certificate . . . no way he'd marry my mum! But I use hers. I kept hers instead. You don't know the half of it, Harriet!'

This was so awful she held one hand to her mouth and the other on his, gently rocking herself back and forward. The officer broke it up as if they had been making love. Harriet wanted to attack him.

That evening she received the ashes on her forehead with a vow to offer mortifications for Gerry during Lent. Catching Boo after the service, she opened her mouth to tell her what had transpired that afternoon, then shut it again.

But she got through the evening without so much as a sip of white wine.

8

HYTHE REGARDED MR GOSFORTH with a cold, imperious eye
that yet asked a question. He surveyed the officer from head to
toe, taking in the neat figure he cut in his white, open-necked
shirt, pips smart on the strong, wiry shoulders. All very nice . . .
a jogger, Gerry reckoned from the thighs, the sort who pounded
past you on the pavement, forcing you into the gutter. He smiled
as he came into the library.

One minute screws were chatting with you, the next they
could spring into action at an alarm bell and ten of them would
appear and wrestle you down to the Block where you could be
stripped and searched and banged up in solitary on some
trumped-up charge. The S.O. was no taller than, say, five ten, but
he loomed over Gerry.

He'd be punished for his writing, he knew it. A cold fear
opened his nose and throat. Gerry fumbled with the stack
of books he was trying to re-shelve, Stephen King and James
Herbert. The officer was talking to Chloe. His head was etched in
silhouette by the murky sun that poured through the high barred
window, and the spiky ends of his scissored, wavy hair stood out
in fine detail, glorified in the motes that shone in the light.
Gosforth was quite a bit younger than Gerry, but Gerry sensed
him as older. Again he raked his memory for anything in the
manuscript that shouldn't be there. He was sure they'd come up
with something.

'Hythe?' Gosforth met him halfway but beckoned in that seigneurial way they had.

Gerry did what he was bidden, put the books gently down and approached.

'Thank you for your story. I've read it now.'

He had put the exercise books in a pink folder and he handed it to Gerry.

'What did you think?' Gerald, as he had been inscribed in his family tree, had not meant to show this weakness; Gerry invariably did show weakness.

'Very interesting,' the officer said noncommittally. 'I have a few minutes and Chloe says she can spare you. Would you like to talk about it? There were a few things I didn't understand.'

This sounded ominous. 'Like what?' he added, 'sir.' But the officer had spotted a reading table with a couple of chairs and he invited Gerry to sit. He sat himself and leaned back in a relaxed and confidential manner as if they had a pint between them or a cup of tea.

'Of course, it's very private sort of work, meant for your cousin's eyes? Sounds like a nice woman.'

Gerry shrugged. He'd been expecting a letter off her all week and was both frightened and angry that she hadn't written because he had sent her the Visiting Order.

'So she will be getting all the connections,' Gosforth continued, 'ones I can't make.'

Gerry said nothing.

'There aren't many of us who can trace our ancestors back to before the Conqueror.' The S.O. shook his head with apparent admiration. 'And what an original idea, to make each one interact with important figures of the time! Sort of brings history alive, doesn't it?'

'Did you like that?' Gerry, hungry, quested round the brown eyes of his interlocutor.

'It's a grand design!'

Gerry's veins beat against his temples in sheer relief, but he showed no expression. 'So what couldn't you get?'

The officer shrugged as if to indicate that it was of minor importance. 'Well, I hope you don't mind my saying this, but it's chiefly this woman, Harriet. I'm sure your cousin . . . Cassie? . . . will understand, but if you ever want to do something more with the story, it might be a good idea to write some extra bits to explain how a character who died just the other day fits in with these prominent ancestors of yours? Not, of course, that I know anything about it, but you did ask me if I thought it was publishable.'

Gerry frowned but he was pleased. 'She's the sort of woman who goes with any century,' he said. 'I don't know why I think that, but I do.'

'Ah, Potiphar's wife,' said the officer.

Gerry looked to see if this was a trap. 'Who?' To tell the truth, ear to the ground on the Wing, he'd heard nothing against Mr Gosforth and a few things for him as he'd helped Joe Smith get parole. He was supposed to be firm but fair. Mind, he hadn't been on the unit for very long.

'It's in the Bible. The bit about Joseph, the one with the coat of many colours. While he is in Egypt his boss's wife takes a fancy to him and accuses him of attempted rape when he turns her down.'

'"The Technicolor Dream-Coat",' said Gerry. He'd heard of that. 'So you did understand!'

'She tried to seduce you, then put the blame on you? My, but that *is* an old story,' the officer said equivocally.

Gerry looked sharp.

Mr Gosforth deeply contemplated the folder that lay between them. 'Of course, coming from Biblical times, that doesn't link up with the Middle Ages, does it?' He frowned in concentration. 'It's as if you're telling two stories at once, the medieval one and the one you were about to tell me when you said you wanted to talk with me about this Harriet.'

'It's her fault I'm here,' Gerry said, both pleased and alarmed at the officer's perception. His heart was beating fast. 'That's the point. I'm innocent.'

'That's what you wanted to tell me?'

'It was her! She . . .'

The officer silenced him with a hand. 'That's to discuss with your brief.'

Gerry had already had one appeal turned down. He looked at Gosforth for signs of mockery. 'I am. I'm innocent.'

'Let's get back to the story,' the officer sighed. 'You're saying, then, that Harriet isn't meant to fit into the medieval idea after all?'

Gerry was beginning to feel confused. People sometimes pointed out to him that things he said didn't mesh with each other and it upset him. At the time, it had seemed perfectly logical to lay slices of his feelings about Harriet on top of the chronicle, sort of like pickle on a burger, but now he began to panic. 'Inside me, it fits,' he replied. 'She took me out to Greece where it all happened, led me by the nose . . .'

'Where what happened?'

'The thing I'm accused of!' Gerry cried. 'Also, it's where I got to know about the Middle Ages and my ancestors.'

'So, if I get your meaning,' Gosforth lifted the folder from the table, 'she accuses you of rape and you get into all sorts of bother?'

He had gone too far. Gerry took the folder, opened it and checked through the pages to see if anything was missing.

'Okay, mate!' Gosforth raised an elegant hand. 'Don't mean to tread on corns. I just wanted to know how she fitted in, that's all.'

Gerry turned to wood.

'Maybe you could make her one of your historical characters and then she'd be part of the story. I liked the bit about Richard the Lion-Heart. You could add something there . . . make this Harriet a queen in some Frankish castle.'

'I've got to help Chloe,' Gerry said.

Gosforth made a compliant gesture and rose to go.

'She didn't accuse me of trying to rape her,' Gerry blurted out after him. 'She said I'd killed the boy when all along . . .'

'Put her in a Frankish castle,' Gosforth repeated. 'That's the advice I have for the book.'

'My aunt and uncle *live* in a Frankish castle!' Gerry said with a desperate pride. 'That's where we were staying, me and Harriet, with them!'

'Well, you have your plot, then, haven't you?' Gosforth said, then vanished, funnelled once more into his various duties.

Now how, Gerry wondered, for many days afterwards, had he come up with the idea of a 'Frankish castle' . . . in so many words, as it were? He was torn between two thoughts: one, that the S.O. had tracked down the newspaper stories of the case; two, that he was psychic.

Gerry read everything the papers had said about him. He always did, a bit like an actor reading reviews. He was sure none of the reports had mentioned the words 'Frankish' or 'castle'. He checked back on his cuttings, shaking his head at how wildly inaccurate they were in most respects. The property was called variously 'the Venetian palazzo of Michael and Eleni Hythe' and their 'Greek mansion'. It wasn't really either, just a big old house. So how did the officer know that 'Frankish' was a word (one that she deplored) sometimes used to describe his aunt's family? And that the house was part of a whole medieval complex, a citadel called 'the Kastro', meaning 'castle'? This led Gerry to conclude that Mr Gosforth was on a wavelength . . . maybe telepathic, maybe something more inscrutable.

Gerry considered the proposition of writing Harriet into his story rather than making her stand outside of it, but no matter how he tried, she didn't seem to go. All the same, as much as he wanted to hate the S.O., Gerry had to admit that he had made an effort. Given time, Mr Gosforth would reach the inevitable conclusion that Gerry was indeed innocent. In fact, he was nearly halfway there. Potiphar's wife! Gerry had looked it up in the Concordance kept in the library. Joseph had been a handsome man.

Well, Harriet had thought him handsome. Edgar too, in his own special way. What was more, Joseph had been wrongfully imprisoned. Gerry mused over the significance of the verses in which 'the keeper of the prison' had put Joseph in control over all the other prisoners, and wondered if being library orderly were not the first step in a series of career moves in Grisholme, but he sourly rejected the idea.

At night, when he closed his eyes, parts of his story would come to him. Now he had shown it to someone, his vision of it sharpened and became more complex. He hadn't thought of putting present-day characters in his time machine, but the idea was there now and he couldn't make it go away. Cassie could be a princess!

Suppose Richard Coeur de Lion had arrived on the scene, the actual scene! In fact, it took no real leap of imagination to see the gracious king, maybe on his return from the Holy Land, disembarking at Naxos harbour and mounting the flagged steps cut through steep, mountainous rock that led up to the Kastro. Blondel would be in train. Crowds appeared in Gerry's mind, as when the Queen was visiting a foreign country, and they would fall aside for Richard. And there was Gerry himself, Gerald now, standing at the citadel's narrow gate, flanked by its frowning keeps. Pennants fluttered in the stiff breeze. A gasp of surprise rippled through the crowd as the Plantagenet king greeted Gerry as an old friend. What a vindication!

Once inside the Kastro, they proceeded together up the final ascent (and never out of breath from the climb). He was taking Richard to meet Eleni. The king's brow would darken as Gerry filled him in. It was easy enough to picture *her* in medieval dress! He could see her in his mind's eye, haughtily expecting the royal visit. She'd have prepared a great feast, had a wild boar roasted, something like that, everything laid out in the saloni (her word for the vast lounge), a room larger than a good-sized barn with a huge high ceiling held up by original rafters, in place since 1200 AD. So, Gerry mused, Richard actually *could* have been there! Eleni would be wearing a conical hat with a veil. She'd sweep towards the king, delighted to have him in her home.

In Gerry's new imagining, he saw rushes on the floor and rush lights in sconces on the white walls as in a film. Proud Eleni in long sleeves would brush Gerry aside with a cold sneer, only to find Richard's face like a thunderclap. 'Kneel!' Richard would command. And she would be forced to apologise to Gerry! Maybe he'd even make her eat some dirt, something like that.

She had disliked him from day one.

If the BBC hadn't discovered Boo, Harriet might never have written to Michael and Helen Hythe to tell them about Gerry.

Boo was thrilled that she was to be the subject of a documentary. One of her ex-cons, a bright lad she had fished from some human dustbin or other, had gone on to make an astonishing career as a young director and, on reading of her OBE, had decided to make his gratitude manifest. His crime had been drug-related and he had already done a brilliant programme attacking Ecstasy. 'Meteoric' was the word for his rise from the pit of F Wing. He toured schools with grim warnings and the tale of his genuine reform was used on fliers distributed by Narcotics Anonymous.

At first, the programme was to be made in Grisholme, but Boo's rushes turned out to be so good that the idea was extended. And so, quite suddenly, she was whirled off 'to film' in Scotland, the first of her stopping points on a nationwide tour of prisons.

Harriet was *very* pleased for her. Well, she was a little hurt that, with her expertise in the theatre, Boo had not taken kindly to a few well-intended bits of advice. And she could have included Harriet just a bit in her hasty preparations. However, when Boo jetted off, Harriet took charge of the dog. This forced her to walk a good deal and while she walked, she thought.

She had intended to tell Boo about Edgar before she next went to see Gerry, but with all Boo's frantic phoning and arranging and working on a script, there didn't seem an appropriate time. She supposed it would all keep until Boo got back. It wasn't as if

Harriet had intended to infringe any rule. The whole thing had been such a shock that she needed to assemble her thoughts before she confided to anyone Gerry's story of the Hythes. Boo was a good egg, no doubt about it; but as Jolly Labrador watered the bushes and sniffed the pavements, Harriet wondered if her friend could grasp the complexity of this situation. What Gerry had told her had been in the nature of a confidence. For a man so untrusting, so wounded, what would be the effect on him if Boo were to pull the rug from under his feet just because Harriet happened to have some connection with his ghastly father? That was her chief consideration.

Besides, suppose Gerry's story were not true. She really ought to find out more about it before she laid the whole case before Boo. Of course, he might *believe* it was true, but this Mary Carney, this mother of his, sounded like, well, let's face it, a complete tart! She could have claimed Edgar out of many putative fathers.

An alternative she did not like to consider was that Gerry could have picked up information about the family somewhere, and was simply making the whole story up. By this time, Harriet was pretty sure that he had spent more of his life in prison than he wanted her to know. She even began to wonder if he had been a professional burglar. It was little things that he'd let slip into their conversations, and the things untold too. He had never, for instance, alluded to this girlfriend of his again – the one for whom he had allegedly stolen the ring. One would think he had room enough for bitterness against her, but his father seemed to have exclusive rights over Gerry's anger; and, whether this individual was Edgar Hythe or not, it did seem odd.

Harriet thought he should be angrier with his mother. Surely this Mary Carney person had failed in her responsibility to protect Gerry. She must have seen signs that Edgar had beaten Gerry. Why hadn't she stopped the visits? All he would say was that Edgar knew how to hide bruises and that the only time he'd tried to tell his mother she'd 'slugged' him too. Harriet pondered the possibility of finding this awful woman, checking on the story of Gerry's paternity, even giving her a piece of her mind, but when she looked in the telephone directory she was overwhelmed by the task of ringing each M. Carney listed. How would she start the conversation? 'Are you the Mrs Carney whose son is in prison?' Besides, Gerry said she'd probably moved from London. Then Harriet remembered he'd once told her he thought his mother was dead.

Usually, the time crept by between her prison Wednesdays, but this time it seemed to go only too quickly. The Monday before her scheduled visit was due, Harriet was dreading Gerry. She owed it to herself, to Boo, and to the Hythes to question his story. The more she steeled herself, however, to ask him pertinent questions about Edgar, the more she shrank from the prospect.

Alternatives and permutations turned round in her mind like some maddening Chinese puzzle. For one thing, Gerry certainly seemed to know how Edgar had died and with a detail she herself had not known. Also, his shock over her having lived in Ashdean was genuine enough, his hatred of Edgar so emphatic that there must have been some strong connection between them. Nevertheless, two great lacunae stood boldly in the centre of the story. Why, if Edgar acknowledged Gerry as his son, had the family in Ashdean never met him? Even if Godfrey and his wife Sophie were awful old sticks, Maeve Hythe was hardly the sort of woman who would have turned away a grandchild.

Despite Helen's quarrels with her mother-in-law, Harriet had always secretly liked Maeve. Her main achievement was the creation of an Elizabethan knot garden, which had taken decades of patient work. All of the manor grounds were lovely as a result of the constant love and attention she gave to anything that grew. Maeve was out in all weathers, a bit of an eccentric. Wrapping herself in a tatty cloak against the rain, she looked as if she had stepped from the pages of a Celtic fairy tale. She had sad eyes too. And Harriet, who privately knew the taste of defeat in these matters, always felt that Maeve had been unhappy in her marriage. In their different ways, they both struggled on.

In fact, thinking about it now, Harriet remembered a curious episode. Anyone in Ashdean who wanted to know anything about gardening consulted Maeve Hythe, and Harriet, ambitious to extend her herbaceous border, had one day taken Emma and Cassie over to the manor to get some cuttings. The girls had rushed out into the precious knot garden with some game about getting through the maze. Cassie was, after all (as everyone thought then) Maeve's only grandchild, but Harriet watched aghast as the two 'little horrors' rushed about, knocking off bits of box in the process. Maeve had stopped Harriet from calling out. 'I shall never have any more grandchildren,' she had said, 'and I always dreamed of having a whole tribe of them. It was my dearest wish that this garden should be full of them.' Her rumpled old face had become so wistful that it was necessary to look away.

Surely, whatever the nature of the conflict Edgar had with his mother, he would have known Gerry might receive a welcome from her at least. Well, maybe this Mary Carney, feeling threatened by the big house, had prevented any contact with Edgar's family. She sounded the sort who would make problems and obstructions.

This did not explain, however, the second hole in Gerry's story. From what Harriet had heard of Mary Carney, she was hardly proud. It was not as if she would have missed the opportunity to get her hands of some of the Hythe money, using Gerry as a little pawn. But Gerry had suffered a childhood grim with want . . . real need, Dickensian need, squalor, in fact. Surely Edgar was not such a reprobate nor Mary Carney such a slut as to see their only child suffer deprivation on such a scale. And Harriet's recollection of the Hythes was that, generally speaking, they were odd but honourable. It seemed unlikely that they would have refused material help to one of their own, no matter how misbegotten. They were good people, the Hythes, or so she had always thought.

But were they?

Harriet had to admit that what she meant by 'good' more often than not had meant 'respectable'. She thought now of the pretty manor house with its gables and mellow stone walls where pleached vines sunned themselves. It seemed to stand as an emblem of a social order hard to fault. Even if old Aidan had been a bit of a recluse, the Hythes collectively assumed their responsibilities to the community in the time-honoured way, doing everything that was expected of them.

If Harriet disliked Ashdean, she still trusted it. And though she barely admitted it to herself, the thought that Grisholme had any real connection with people with whom she had dined made her squeamish and uncomfortable. No, surely there was some mistake. Maeve and Aidan could not be Gerry's grandparents, nor Godfrey, the present incumbent of the manor, his uncle.

Harriet wondered if maybe she should write to Boo. No matter how fussy and bureaucratic it sounded, she was technically at fault if she did not inform the relevant authorities of any connection with an inmate extraneous to the visits she made under Boo's scheme. If she put it all on paper, she'd be able to explain everything, make a case for her continued visits to Gerry. That way, Boo wouldn't be able to bulldoze her until she had finished all that she had to say. A letter on Boo's mat on her return from Scotland would set things up so they could talk. There was more. Suppose something did go wrong. Were there legal implications? If so, it was probably a good idea to have something in writing. It lurked in the back of Harriet's mind that she had given her word.

And so she sharpened some pencils and sat at her desk trying to compose something in the nature of a report. She began first this way, then that. A pile of scrunched papers built up in her wastepaper basket with its flowered panels, and Jolly Labrador seemed to peer at her from the hearthrug, a totem of Boo and her avatar. Harriet looked at what she had written. What would she herself do if her situation with Boo were reversed? Well, she would get some prison psychologist on to it, wouldn't she? Harriet frowned. She'd heard Gerry's emphatic views on that sort of person! No, any revelation she made would be seen as a betrayal by him. And of all things she could not risk that.

She scrawled and doodled, squares and hearts, which she shadowed in, not even hearing Jolly's whimpers for a walk. She tapped the pencil. Suddenly, a third way presented itself to her. It was so brilliant she gave a little gasp. She would write to Michael and Helen Hythe! Before she leapt into any irretrievable action, she would check Gerry's story with the only people who would be likely to know if it were true. Well, why shouldn't she write to them? In a reply to her New Year's letter, Helen had sent a sweet note on the back of a postcard depicting a pretty, shell-pink, eighteenth-century Virgin. How sad about Averell! Wonderful that Harriet had embraced the Faith! Before Jolly wet her rug she took him out, and when she returned she was stuck all over again.

How did one say it? 'Dear Michael and Helen, I've discovered your long-lost nephew in gaol'? Just writing it down made it seem absurd and, if one thought the thing through, socially unforgivable. Should one draw attention to such a thing? Maybe they knew about Gerry already. Was she, as Boo would put it, opening 'a whole can of worms'? Suppose Gerry had been telling the truth and they did not know? What a shock!

By Tuesday evening, Harriet had given up in exasperation. Leaving several drafts of this new letter in her desk drawer, she went to see Gerry. The thaw had come, and it was one of those premature spring days when the weak sun touched the snow-drops, finally out, with a penumbra of silver light. The scent of moist earth was in the air even as the bus plunged down the Old Kent Road and a light fuzz of green clung to the few bare trees planted along the way. Maybe she would confront him. It might even be a good idea to confide in him, telling him about the prison rules, including him in any decision she made.

Gerry was straining to see her. She glimpsed him from the

queue, craning his neck from where he was seated. His eyes were wide with excitement and, when he spotted her, he popped up like a cork from a bottle and stood breathless with anticipation.

Harriet stood stock still for a moment in a shock of recognition, and had to be moved on by the pushy woman behind her. There it was, as simple as the optical illusion so loved by children in which a white chalice becomes two black faces in silhouette only when one is given the clue of where to look. Gerry was indubitably a Hythe. A memory of little Cassie came swimming into her mind's eye. How could she have missed this obvious family resemblance? In the moulded lower lip, the deep-set eyes, the delicate fragility of the brow, there were the imprints of a common ancestry. So that was the eerie feeling of familiarity she had, from the beginning, sensed in Gerry! Was this why she had liked him so quickly and instinctively? She had always enjoyed having the imaginative little Cassie to play with Emma. She shook her head, trying to rid herself of this proof of their consanguinity.

'Harriet!' he cried. And with this, all of her good intentions flew out of the high barred windows.

'Gerry, I've been so worried about you!' she said, without preliminaries. 'You were so upset last time . . . and they just *took* you away!'

He sat. His eyes, usually a cold sea-green, habitually took time to warm up, but they were alight at once now, seeing her. 'All along it was meant,' he said, 'you and I were meant to be.'

Harriet smiled graciously and passed over this remark, but later it reverberated. Had he said 'meant to be' or 'meant to meet'?

'What are the odds on knowing someone from Ashdean?' he said. 'It's fate!'

'Gerry, I've been thinking . . .' she began, but he went on, speeded up like an animated cartoon.

'You knew my grandparents! Tell me, tell me what they were like. Edgar hated them.'

Like a badly stubbed toe, Harriet felt the pain of her stupidity in not telling Boo. She would, though. She'd just see how this visit went. 'I liked old Mrs Hythe a lot,' she said cautiously. 'She came from an Irish family . . .'

'So did my mum,' Gerry said with disdain.

'Well, they had that in common then.' Harriet thought how little, in fact, that would have been. She searched around for something anodyne to say.

'Mrs Hythe', Harriet was scrupulous to avoid the word grandmother, 'was fond of gardening. In fact, her gardens, especially the Elizabethan knot garden, were so beautiful they were open to the public on Bank Holidays.'

'Gardens!' Gerry exclaimed.

Harriet had not thought about this, but supposed it was possible that green fingers were genetic. 'There you are!' she said weakly.

Gerry's face darkened. 'They must have known about me.'

Harriet was taken aback. There had been no transition between his excitement and the low snarl that came out of him.

'Edgar would not have missed an opportunity to screw more money out of them. A kid? With a mum like my mum? C'mon! The social workers nearly had me made a ward of court.'

Harriet said nothing.

'Just before he died, Edgar told me he was going to take me to meet his mum. He was fed up with me by then. That's what I thought anyway. In fact . . .' he rummaged in his pocket, 'I brought this for you to see.' He opened a sealed plastic bag from which he drew a yellowed envelope.

Harriet threw a glance at the officers.

'It's all right. I've cleared it.'

She fished out the paper within. It was a birth certificate, his parents Mary Carney and Edgar Hythe. Gerry had been born in Paddington. She looked up at him and saw him smiling thinly.

'You see? I'm not giving you the runaround.'

'I never said . . .'

'But you thought, Harriet, you thought.'

'I didn't know what to think,' she said, flushing at the truth. 'It was a shock to me too.'

Gerry scraped the chair forward and leaned on his elbows. His intensity forced her back. 'He got me the certificate because I was going to meet them. I was looking forward to it, see? Then I didn't hear nothing, and then he died. Don't tell me he didn't go down and pave the way first! They just said no and washed their hands of me. That's what happened, I reckon.'

Harriet gazed at the embossed paper, Gerry's parentage inscribed with a fountain pen in neat script by an official hand.

'All I know, Gerry, is that your grandmother wasn't that sort of person,' she said. 'If Edgar made you suffer, he made her suffer too. I think she would have loved you if she'd been given a chance.' Harriet thought she'd gone too far, but Gerry wasn't listening anyway.

'A knot garden!' he added. 'Perfect! A nice little maze an' all! And for me, for my mum, they did bugger all – excuse me, Harriet – and I say to hell with 'em!'

That night Boo rang from Scotland to ask after Jolly the Labrador. And still Harriet said nothing about Gerry. 'Well, what harm can it do?' she asked the dog when she had put down the telephone. 'Surely he has a right to know about his family!' Jolly looked mournfully up at her and thumped his tail.

9

'AS GALLING AS YOU may find it, Gerald,' Cassie said, 'Harriet Washington has left you rather a lot of money in her will.'

Gerry had been awake all night in expectation of her visit. Would she come after all? She'd let him down once because one of her boys was ill.

What would he say to her if she did come?

He'd been too excited to eat his lunch, dog food anyway with a pinch of curry powder. He must remember to put himself on the vegetarian diet. At least they got raw carrots and the like.

Gerry had a hundred million things to tell Cassie, the library job, how Mr Fairbrother had spun his cell . . . he always picked on Gerry . . . And he felt ill. The medics ignored his chest pains . . . gave him a paracetamol.

But mostly there was S.O. Gosforth and the book.

Gerry had copied out some of it to give Cassie so that maybe she'd get it typed up for him. With S.O. Gosforth's blessing, Security had passed it. He had it in his pink folder, sealed up in the official plastic bag.

The Visitors' Room was much more comfortable than it had been all those years ago when he met Harriet. There were leatherette chairs now. This time, of course, he was on the Rule, classed as a sex offender, so they had to sit in a special section away from the men from the main prison who'd been known to sling turds wrapped in bog paper over the partition. Now and then, the men on the Rule got a slow hand-clap, catcalls, 'Nonce,

nonce!' with murder behind the voices of those righteous barons of a sad kingdom: drug-dealers, car-thieves and armed robbers.

Unfortunately, murder happened all too often, especially when, for one reason or other, sex offenders got stranded on the Main. Gerry knew personally of one 'suicide' that had been nothing of the kind. It had been a case of screws leaving certain cell doors unlocked, then afterwards stringing up the strangled victim to make it look as if he'd topped himself. Usually, though, they just turned a blind eye at kicks and beatings meted out on exercise or in the showers. Well, that was what he'd heard, anyway.

When Gerry met Harriet all those years ago, that's where he'd been located, the Main. The irony was he really had been in for burglary that time, the only crime he'd ever committed in his life, to his way of thinking. And so he'd been thrown in with Jack-the-lad. Some of them were Mafia, even. The way they bragged and strutted made him sick, boasting about shooters and violence, which Gerry thought was wrong. Because at the time he'd been slight and slim he'd pretended he was a cat burglar, but he'd also had to act as if he shared their attitude about men like himself, in fear of his life if he didn't. Day after day it preyed on him, having to show contempt for his very self. Maybe what he did with boys and that was against the law but, like being gay, one day the world would see! Okay, maybe he'd hated Edgar, but in some ways he'd enjoyed it. In any case, it was incest and besides Edgar had been cruel and hurt him. Gerry had been kind and gentle to the boys he'd been with and basically they liked it.

The one time he'd stolen, that time they put him on the Main, there seemed to be no connection with his previous, but there was. Back then, he'd smashed in a shop window to grab a trendy Nintendo for some tyke he'd been melting over. Stupid thing to do, but he'd been in despair at having earlier overtures rejected, chocolate and sweets. In one way it was lucky they hadn't worked out what he'd been up to; in another, not. He'd been scared shitless his whole time on F Wing. Maybe it was paranoid, but he'd always suspected his allocation, back then, had to do with their wanting to get rid of him, erase a problem that wouldn't go away. His landing officer at the time had told him: one false move and he'd leak the knowledge of Gerry's form to the elite cons who worked out in the gym, Essex men with gangland skills. That's why he'd been so depressed, that's why the Visitors' Scheme sent Harriet to see him . . . not that any of them knew his real problem. But between her and the bull who fancied and protected him, he'd come through.

Cassie was frosty today, Gerry thought. She was always tight-lipped about Harriet. She was wearing a green dress with a long skirt, no make-up, and her heavy dark hair was caught up off her neck because of the heat. 'You'll be getting a letter from her solicitor,' she continued.

'I didn't ask for *nothing* . . . anything,' he corrected, hard now but cagey lest he put Cassie off.

'Well, Gerry . . .' she shook her head, 'that's obvious. Of course, you can always turn the legacy down. It'll go to charity if you do, though.' She looked down at a piece of paper. 'The National Association for the Resettlement of Offenders.'

'Not NACRO!' he groaned.

'One thing you'll love,' and she went on in a weary tone, just short of malice, 'Her daughter Emma's pissed as hell.'

This inelegant way of putting it made Gerry laugh despite himself, coming as it did from his cousin whose rule of dress was simplicity and whose gentle, gracious manner was the same to everyone alike. 'Ha! Emma! Harriet told me all about that little cow!'

Cassie had spent the better part of two hours battling up to Grisholme from the Marsh. Her Visiting Order had been challenged and a woman officer had frisked her. It was hard to know how to respond to Gerry at the best of times, but the sheer meanness he evinced today made her waspish. The humid heat slid off them both in beads of sweat. 'She thinks entirely of herself,' Cassie snapped.

'What did Harriet leave me, then, considering I'll never let it go to NACRO? They never did a damned thing for me.'

Cassie tried and succeeded not to laugh aloud at the irony he'd missed. It wasn't really funny. Gerry's egoism made Emma look like Mother Teresa. 'She left you £50,000.'

'What!'

'Five, zero, zero, zero, zero. The money is in trust contingent upon your release, though dividends may be added to your private money here as the prison sees fit. Harriet thought that the legacy would help you when you got out, you know, so that you'd have something to live on.' She waited for Gerry to say something, but he simply sat there. The left side of his face was slightly dragged down as the result of his stroke and this added to the impression it gave of a mask, an ancient museum piece, a totem.

'Emma and her grandson get the rest, quite a bit, really, considering she will also inherit from her father. There's a small bequest to Boo McAuley . . . and a little gift to Harriet's church. If you do not get out of prison in time to enjoy this bounty, at least you now have something to leave in your will.' Again she paused. Nothing.

'Oh, and she wanted you to have a personal memento, chosen from her things. She suggested her father's cufflinks. Her grandson Tom gets his gold watch.' Cassie enjoyed watching his eyes shift behind the rigid flesh.

'I don't know what to say.' Gerry mopped his brow with a tissue and blew his nose on it.

Cassie softened. Gerry with his heavy pallor . . . poor mooncalf . . . poor Caliban. He wasn't stupid. In fact, with the right chance he might have done well in life, but given his starting point, how could he have understood someone as complex as Harriet Washington? And, given her refinement, how on earth had Harriet thought to comprehend him? He looked genuinely bewildered by Harriet's generosity, the lavish extent of it, what it signified in terms of her turned cheek, her second mile, her longing for the prodigal's return to her love, even beyond death.

'You could start by trying to forgive her,' Cassie said quietly, then thought how priggish it sounded. She herself was nowhere near forgiving her ex-partner for the way he'd dumped her and the boys.

For a moment, she caught a glimpse of something in her cousin she had not yet seen. Was it genuine misery? Something of that order, but compounded with exhaustion, self-disgust. 'I don't know how,' he said; he flailed his good hand in the air, a poor swimmer caught out of his depth.

'Well, think about it, you know,' she said leaning back.

He frowned at the little table between them in a puzzled way for a few silent moments. 'Cassie!' he cried, changing the subject. 'This looks like being my week.'

'Oh, tell!' she replied a little too brightly.

'I'm writing a book!'

'Jolly good,' she said. 'About what?'

'It's on our family . . . from the tree you photocopied.'

Cassie smiled.

'I got Mr Gosforth to read it . . . he's an S.O. He thinks I should get it published! He says it's brilliant.'

Whenever she went to see her cousin, Cassie set a mental hourglass running. It was nearly over, very nearly over. She'd go home, bathe and have a stiff drink.

Every now and then, she saw the little boy in him. It cut her, his eyes so like her own. Except for her dash of Greek, he might have been taken for her older brother. She tried not to let that pre-occupy her, the resemblance. Maybe it wasn't as strong as she thought. He put his head to one side in an engaging manner. 'You wouldn't read it for me too?' he asked. 'Maybe get it typed? I can't spell and my punctuation isn't so hot either . . . but Mr Gosforth, he wants me to go on with it. And . . . guess what? I've got a job now, as a librarian.'

After Cassie left, Gerry went back to his cell hugging memories of the visit to himself. She could sometimes be a bit of a madam, but she was always pleased to see him and he could tell she thought the book idea was fantastic. He was mightily relieved, though, that he had left out all references to Harriet in the copy he had given Cassie. There was some bad language in it after all.

Harriet wondered what harm it would do just to find out. Well, did they know of Gerry's existence or didn't they? Now she was sure that he was genuinely Michael's and Helen's nephew, it might still be a good idea to write to them, asking what, if anything, they knew about him. Given that Gerry was so upset by this issue, she was in a unique position to resolve it for him once and for all. In any case, though Harriet would not have voiced this thought aloud, Michael and Helen were, well, the sort of people that one could trust. Just as she would never imagine them breaking a promise or telling anything but a white lie, if she wrote in confidence, she could expect that confidence to be kept. What she meant to say to herself was that the Hythes had a certain code. If things didn't work out, then Gerry need never know.

What was more, it flitted across her mind that the Hythe family ought to know about how she had made the slip about Ashdean. *The* slip? It had turned, she reddened to admit to herself, into a landslide. Each time she visited Gerry, he quizzed her. No detail was too small; he snatched at every scrap she gave him, turned it into evidence and spent the intervening fortnights building scenarios. He was obsessed with Edgar.

Harriet had not known what to do other than to let him talk about it. But it was supposed to be therapeutic, wasn't it? She ought to know. Averell had always accused her of not being very good at opening up about herself, but then he was an American, and she had been brought up to be reticent about her feelings. It was a class thing, she supposed.

As for her memories of Edgar, Harriet hardly liked to tell Gerry that she had always thought him a bit of a bounder, who sponged off his parents. She had met him only rarely and was thankful for it.

Harriet's sharpest memory of Edgar was, oddly enough, an encounter in the greengrocer's one funereal winter day when the brussels sprouts lay frozen in their bins and earth-encrusted potatoes seemed the only things on offer save cauliflower. Edgar bounced in, eyes unnaturally bright; he needed a pound of onions for his 'mum'. He hadn't shaved and his oily hair had marked the back of his corduroy jacket. He called Mrs Biggins 'Betsy' and squeezed her, to her evident distaste. Then, sucking up to Harriet, the local 'intellectual', he began a rambling monologue about a 'slim volume' he was 'thinking of publishing'. In a self-important way, he told her about the influence of Housman on his work.

Maeve was waiting in the car outside. Harriet had never seen eyes so despairing, cheeks so drawn. Averell, for all his disdain for the cultural life she craved, had obviously read *Jane Eyre*. He once called Edgar the Hythes' Mrs Rochester and said what a shame they couldn't chain him up.

Helen, whatever her quarrels with Maeve, pitied her for Edgar. (Mind you, she wasn't above making a little capital here on what a disastrous parent her mother-in-law had been.) Harsh though she was, Helen was essentially kind. Perhaps her Greek filial piety was offended that Edgar liked to humiliate his mother . . . calling her an 'Irish potato'. He mocked her religion too, jeering at its 'medieval' theology, guying her devotions. Edgar saw himself as a mutilated genius, an eagle who flew too high for earthbound beings. What was petty morality to him?

Remembering all this, it seemed no wonder that Gerry had become a thief, Harriet thought. A peccadillo on Edgar's scale of values! How could anyone have guessed that Edgar, for all his arrogance and profligacy, was capable of violence to a child? Gerry's stories of smackings and beatings bruised her as if she had been the recipient of the blows.

What to say to Gerry? What to do? Harriet carefully edited what she told him, but when he started questioning her about his uncles, it seemed cowardly to lie and ungenerous to refuse him the information he sought.

Harriet thought it very peculiar, but Edgar had, it seemed, refused to tell Gerry his uncles' names, mentioning only that he had two brothers. Maybe he was frightened that Gerry would ring them up and seek their protection. So it had seemed silly not to tell him they were called Godfrey and Michael. By and large, though, Harriet was quite pleased with herself. Gerry talked to her as he had talked to no one, or so he told her. She urged him to pour it all out, and she received it into herself, gladly, willingly. She was, she told herself, not really a prison visitor any more. She was Gerry's friend.

Just before Easter the balance of things, so carefully built up, changed. It was hardly surprising that Gerry should mention his release, but when he told her he was leaving Grisholme in September, it came to her as a wounding shock. He looked at her slyly, somehow gauging her reaction. Hadn't she known this was his release date? Gerry asked. In fact, once she thought about it, she was certain that she had known it. Why she had forgotten it? Gerry was her prisoner. It startled her to realise that she had never thought of him as being a free man.

Of course, she was thrilled for him. Delighted!

Later, though, the pain at her first hearing of the news spread and progressed through her. It seemed so soon, September. Must she and Gerry part for ever? She supposed they must. It was one thing to ignore Boo's instructions as she had been doing by discussing the Hythes with Gerry. That was the result of an extraordinary coincidence. It was altogether another thing to flout them deliberately. She could hardly make arrangements to see Gerry when he was out of prison. In fact, at some level the whole prospect frightened her.

It possessed her at night, how she had turned a blind eye to the very idea of his release and its possible consequences. Apart from anything else, the routine of her Wednesdays defined her life now as surely as if visiting Gerry were a job from which she was about to be made redundant. Well, she supposed she could take on another prisoner, but that didn't seem right to her, almost as if it were an infidelity to Gerry.

At night, she thrashed around trying to get comfortable, or would wake at four. At first she could coax herself back to sleep, but when it finally struck her that there were other ramifications to his being out of prison her mind turned on like a light switch. And she would lie awake, haggard, until dawn.

Suppose Gerry were to seek out Godfrey Hythe? He already knew that his uncle lived in Ashdean Manor. What was to prevent him from simply turning up and introducing himself? This had not occurred to Harriet before, but now it did with the impact of a heavy weight. Suppose he said, 'I'm a friend of Harriet Washington,' or something like that. She could see Godfrey's face if Gerry produced that birth certificate. And now she really thought it out, it would be humiliating to have her name bandied about. Godfrey was an utter blimp who thought the *Daily Telegraph* too left-wing. He was bound to think prisoners should be flogged. Harriet could see it now; the door slammed in Gerry's crushed face. Before long, it would be all over the village that Harriet was consorting with criminals. Averell would get wind of it and smile.

Maybe Godfrey would even have her prosecuted, though for what she couldn't say. Well, she could say. She had failed to inform Boo that she had discovered a connection with the inmate she was visiting. Was that a punishable offence? Harriet had grim visions of herself in Holloway. Worst of all, there was no telling what Gerry might do now he'd been talking about the family, brooding on them. He was so wounded, so angry.

Just how angry he was struck her now when she saw new and baleful significance in a story he'd told her only a few weeks before. At the time she heard it, she had been assuming he wasn't going anywhere. He was locked up in prison. Now, his tale of his one and only visit to Ashdean filled her with dread.

It seemed that several years ago, Gerry had decided on the spur of the moment to go down and see where his father was buried. He wanted to 'have a word', he told Harriet. With his father's dead body? She assumed he meant that he wanted to come to terms with Edgar, something like that. When he reached the village, he thought he'd 'suss out' the parish church first, take a load off his feet; he had walked from London.

'Walked!' It seemed an eccentric thing to do.

He shrugged. A middle-aged woman with permed grey hair and a thin, forbidding mouth had asked him brusquely what he wanted. 'Work,' he had told her. She was cleaning the church. She said there was no work until the hops were ripe.

Mrs Bakewell! Harriet stifled a shock of recognition.

Gerry had looked at the funerary wall dedicated to Hythes. There was a Sunday school corner, he said, with a picture of Jesus looking like a girl surrounded by kiddies. 'Suffer the little children and forbid them not,' was inscribed beneath it.

Harriet had always thought the vicar's wife a bit mimsy.

Gerry told her that Edgar often laughed at him for being like a girl. And then he added, in an almost conversational way, that the real reason for his trip to Ashdean was to desecrate Edgar's grave.

Harriet looked at him, for the first time openly appalled. It took her so by surprise, this bald statement unmitigated by any retrospective shame.

'What with the old bitch in the church it seemed too much bother,' he said, so he wandered into the churchyard. When he found where Edgar was buried, he had spat on the tombstone instead.

Well, what was Harriet to do now? She supposed it wasn't too late to tell Boo what she had got herself into. It had all been done in good faith, after all. Harriet felt wretched about being in so deep. She imagined Boo's round face, first collapsed with disappointment in Harriet, then bright with indignation. She would certainly prevent Harriet from seeing Gerry again. Maybe she would even call the police.

Oh, these were midnight thoughts! She mustn't get this out of proportion.

And indeed, things looked brighter in the morning.

Harriet was beginning to see little flaws in Boo. She had been too dazzled at first to think Boo through. Wasn't she just a little patronising to her vaunted prisoners? And she certainly dined out on them.

Harriet determined to invite Boo to lunch, test the waters, then judge if it were safe to plunge in to a full admission of the truth. That seemed the best idea. She needn't commit herself all at once. Maybe they could talk round the subject. But when she finally steeled herself to ring Boo, she appeared to have half the BBC at her mews house. They had some edits; the deadline was frantic. Boo didn't know when she'd be free. Harriet put down the telephone, her heart pounding with relief.

It was sort of a sign, wasn't it? In fact, now she thought about it, she was a little ashamed at doubting Gerry. Why should she imagine that he would do anything destructive when the bond between them had become so deep? Of course, he was angry, but now he had someone to confide in, his feelings would surely blow out to sea. They talked like old and dear friends. And there was a lot of time between April and September. Already he was making progress. He'd even gained some weight. By the time he was released, she was sure her listening to Gerry would have made a crucial difference. It struck Harriet that she was handling this herself. And that she was handling it well. If by August things had taken a turn for the worse, then she would tell Boo. In this way, she had the chance to do Gerry all the good that was in her power before his release. No, sharing his secrets with Boo had to be a last resort.

Once she had made this decision, Harriet felt better. Maybe it was a daring thing to go it alone like this, but a life without risk was hardly worth living, and since she had married Averell she had taken no risks at all. Making up her mind to this had been arduous, like doing a difficult sum. And, as with anything of this nature, she thought, there were always bound to be discrepancies. In this case, the only consideration that did not square with the course of action she planned was the question of the Hythes.

For a number of reasons, not least the small danger to Godfrey and Sophie that she had got so out of proportion, they really ought to know that she had discovered their long-lost relation, and in prison. It was all very well to take risks herself, but was it really fair to involve others without their knowledge and consent?

Well, what could be easier than ringing Godfrey? She had important news. Could she come down perhaps for tea some day? After all, he was head of the family.

Just thinking of it made Harriet laugh and shake her head. She could see them, Godfrey and Sophie, sitting as they did every afternoon on either side of the manorial hearth engraved above with its pompous crest. You could set your watch by them, Averell often said. At 4.30 precisely, they tottered into the drawing room, the tray set with Earl Grey, milk, no sugar, two slices of bread and butter and two translucent slices of fruitcake. No matter what the temperature, the fire was always laid but never lit between May and October, always lit between October and May.

'I met your nephew in Grisholme Prison,' she heard herself saying. How would she say it? What a line to deliver!

'*Neh-v-yew!*' he would pronounce it thus. 'Nephew! I haven't a nephew!'

Sophie was Godfrey's mirror, his moon, the pale reflection of his dim glory. She made ugly samplers to sell at exorbitant prices at church fêtes and worked them up at teatime. She would mouth the word, repeating it.

No, there was no sense in going down to Ashdean. It would only end in Sophie's locking up the teaspoons.

And then, of course, Godfrey might respond in such a way as to thrust Harriet into a situation that might get out of hand.

Well, what about the idea she'd had when she had been keen to verify Gerry's story? She had already made a start on a letter to Michael and Helen; she had even considered extending its original purpose in an effort to relieve Gerry's mind about whether the Hythes had known about him and turned their backs. Why not lay the whole case before them now? If Godfrey needed to be involved, surely it would be better coming from Michael than from her.

It was common knowledge that Godfrey didn't get on with his brother Michael. There had been murmurs about a family feud, something to do with money, she thought, but she wasn't quite sure. Still, whatever lay between the two brothers, there were advantages to resurrecting the letter she had drafted out weeks ago. First, Michael and Helen lived a long way away. There would be no need for them to become entangled with Gerry.

Secondly, if ever there was a safe pair of hands, they belonged to Michael Hythe. Courteous, reliable and gentle, it seemed highly unlikely that he would tell his brother about Gerry unless it was absolutely necessary. He was in a better position to judge what Godfrey might make of this news than she was. Michael was Godfrey's opposite, the sort of man who never made harsh judgements. If she made out a good enough case for Gerry, who knew but that her old friends might not try to help him? Yes, that was the solution. It covered all bases, as Averell had been wont to say.

Harriet sat down at her dining room table with a pad of paper. After four drafts, she thought she'd got it right.

She marked the letter 'Private and Confidential', and put it in the post before Mass that evening. Then, suddenly feeling very exhausted, she decided to give church a miss. Maybe she would go the next morning . . . that was if she finally got a good night's sleep.

10

MICHAEL HYTHE TOOK the airmail sheets from the envelope once more, four pages addressed to him and Eleni. Gerry Carney? In his agitation, the crisp paper rustled like dry leaves. Edgar had a son? Surely that was impossible, and yet Harriet Washington's carefully written letter left little room for doubt.

He shook his head from side to side, catching his breath in little gasps. When he had collected the post that morning from Naxos harbour, it had pleased him to see a letter; looking forward to something newsy, he had opened it with a little treat of coffee at the Rendezvous, his favourite waterside café. The moment he read its contents, the port scene, which never tired him with its moored boats rocked by the glittering water, vanished. He even forgot to pay the waiter Andreas, with whom he normally liked to chat. He had not known what to do and so, even though he knew he was in a state of shock, he risked driving out to the farm. He could ring Eleni from there. He'd think of some excuse.

The larger part of Michael was callused by the pain Edgar's miserable life had inflicted on everyone who had close dealings with him. It had formed a necessary buttress that normally would have defended the rest of him from the extraordinary vulnerability he now felt. But this was different. He was taken completely off guard.

As his wife most certainly would have said, even from the grave Edgar was, as he had always been, a master of random surprise. It was a technique he'd used in life, she'd often noted, the way he'd spring an upset, stage a catastrophe when it was least expected. Michael was aware of this, but as he made his way over the winding roads to the Sangri valley and the safety of the pyrgos it hardly seemed to matter. The mountains, an iridescent blue in the soft spring light, were his abiding pleasure, but he did not see them today. He drove blindly. Harriet's news had brought Michael close to tears.

Of course, long ago he had forgiven Edgar, but any loving of his brother had proved catastrophic for those he had enmeshed. And yet the shock of this letter revived feelings that he thought he had long ago put aside. Could no amount of suffering destroy the primal childhood connection? Michael had taken measured steps away as years went by, for Cassie's and Eleni's sakes, and for his own, it had to be admitted.

Edgar had a son! The sheer unreason of this feeling, gratitude, was such a worrying enigma that he actually put up his hand as if to ward it off. Maybe there was some way at last that his brother's awful death could be redeemed. That was all the sense he could make of his response to this extraordinary circumstance.

With age, Michael had grown thin, shrinking to his bones. His greying hair was scattered over his temples so that he resembled a ruminative, ancient Caesar bewildered by the throes of high office. He was bent to a question mark. His brow furrowed every now and then as if some revolutionary idea had occurred to him, and then it would relax as though he had thought the better of making the effort. He was not a lazy man, but one beset by uncertainty. He tested any hypothesis that entered his mind with such rigour that it ended up mangled by thought and worthless in his eyes.

He was happiest at the farm, especially in summertime. There, a mellow, crenellated tower, which the Greeks called a pyrgos, beetled over the Hythes' estate, which lay down a dirt track in the fertile interior of Naxos. The building could hardly be called a castle or even a fortress, having over the ages grown into a farmhouse. The land had been parcelled out to the Bellinis in the Middle Ages and was meant to supply the Kastro house in Naxos Town where his wife preferred to stay. On leaving Ashdean, Eleni had thrown herself into the coils of island society: she was related to half their friends and had become a little clannish. Michael kept right out of it with the same instinct that had not been entirely effective in preserving him from his own family in England.

April, this lovely time of year, usually swelled his chest with a longing to put on paper what he felt. He would have written a Georgic if he could to this happy place of exile. He liked to survey the rich fields that lay below a hillside of euphorbia that changed their green blooms for orange for yellow for red in all combinations like a kaleidoscope. Wild flowers of every kind, so many, so incalculable in number and variety, unfolded, a mass of colour that shifted subtly in the breeze. Michael loved the Greek word 'anoixei' which signifies both spring and opening. They had just eaten one of their own lambs, slaughtered for Easter.

This time, however, he had no inspiration to emulate Virgil. As he drew up inside the gate, the dogs barked welcome. Getting slowly out of the car, he gingerly patted Harriet's letter in his breast pocket, almost as if it were a bomb that needed to be defused before he showed it to Eleni and confronted her with his probable decision on what to do about it.

As good fortune would have it, this was the day she was hectically getting up her annual 'English' dinner party. He wished she would not go to such lengths, but he knew she did it largely for him. No matter how he tried to convince her that he was happy in Naxos, it was she who had demanded this radical uprooting to Greece and he knew she worried about it. They worried about each other, Michael and Eleni, most of the time for no real reason.

The first time he saw Naxos he fell in love with it, even from the boat that had chugged six hours from Athens to deposit them there for the last days of their honeymoon. Perhaps it had been the immortal prestige of Ariadne's abandonment and rescue there that charmed him; perhaps it was a romantic sense of Eleni herself, that his bride was in some fabulous way exotic. From the day they disembarked, he was possessed by the archaic mystery that hung about the island and soon found himself collecting snippets of history and pre-history. He had a vague plan one day to write an authoritative guide starting at Neolithic times and ending in 1850 when Naxos joined the Greek state, but, like other projects, most of it was stuffed away in a filing cabinet, the drawers of which he was unable now to close.

Eleni was a great one for theories. One of her favourites was that because his father Aidan Hythe had been an amateur of classical scholarship, the wings of Michael's interest in archaeology had been clipped in fear of some Oedipal form of competition. Never one for pondering psychological motives too deeply himself, he did sometimes wonder if his enthusiasm for ancient Greece wasn't a way of extracting something positive from an emotionally absent parent. When Eleni jollied and nagged him to write, he told her he lacked the confidence, at which point she would pull the father card and play it. His own theory was that he preferred to daydream, immersing himself in the past.

Often he would contemplate the old black-clad village women, who emerged from byres and shepherds' huts on summer evenings to warm themselves in the setting sun so fierce by day. To Michael, they looked as if they were simply waiting for western civilisation to go away, leaving them in peace to commune with the old deities of corn and fish and light.

Even though he had been settled in Naxos permanently for many years, Michael still made regular visits to the archaeological museum, high up in the Kastro. The antiquity of the crocks and shards there still had the effect of making his head spin. He could stand absorbed for hours wondering who had painted the serpentine arms of octopi on pot-bellied vases or what deity the marble votive offerings were meant to serve. Stick fishermen, drawn with squiggly hair, aeons old, cast nets round fishes on a terracotta krater. A square of beaten gold, once flaunted by some Neolithic personage, made him shiver when he thought of how it had been wrought and worn before the pharaohs.

The island could not have suited both of the Hythes better. It was large and varied enough to attract proper visitors, not just the tourists who came with backpacks and expected the plumbing to work. Eleni cultivated a small, select band of expatriates and it was a group of these who were coming that evening to be mingled with 'the Venetian crowd', as she called them. By this she meant her kindred, at least those she was talking to, all descended from the original administrators of the duchy. A sophisticated lot these ancestors must have been, a little bewildered to be so far from Venice, yet perhaps more comfortable in the colonies away from court, and safer too.

As for the way that Eleni of Naxos had all but routed Helen of Ashdean, it saddened him not a bit. Although he couldn't bring himself to tell her, he dreaded the annual 'English dinner party'. This year, however, he was heartily glad that her energies were diverted in a way that ordinarily would have maddened him. He need not excuse his absence from the Kastro, he realised, when she would have only snapped at him for being underfoot. As old Manolis, his farmer, rounded the corner of the house, surprised but pleased to see him, Michael felt an acute relief. The two men understood each other without words. When there was something on Michael's mind, Manolis sensed it, halving the burden with a rueful smile.

Michael had made the room at the top of the square pyrgos his summer study, where most of the time he simply did the accounts for the farm. Today, he made some pretence to Manolis that he was looking for something and said, no, he didn't need help getting the room ready. All the same, when he opened the shutters and the strong April sun illuminated the collected filth of winter, he laid about him, brushing and removing dustsheets from the heavy furniture and his drawing board. He could not deal with

Edgar or with Gerry Carney or, for that matter, with Harriet Washington until he had set the room to rights.

He stood and gazed out at the mountains from the window. Usually when his eyes browsed amongst the changing shadows, he was as content as his own sheep. Sometimes he took out a box of watercolours and tried to paint the scene, but increasingly he felt it was creativity enough to admire it. Let Cassie do the drawing! She was young. Today, though, he had an itch to paint, almost as if in getting the shape of the hills on paper he could draw on their strength. But there was no time for that. He sat at his desk, Harriet's letter in front of him, and sighed.

Because Eleni didn't like him brooding on them, Michael kept the photographs of his family at the farm. They'd quarrelled about this many years ago, his cache. Once, in a moment of fury, she had even threatened to burn it, sending Maeve and Aidan, Godfrey and Edgar spiralling up the chimney. But the two had grown more peaceful with age and now it was accepted: they kept parts of their lives separate.

Gerry Carney? Michael ironed out the letter on the table. Gerry Carney of HMP Grisholme. Back in England, Michael had passed the prison in the car dozens of times driving from Ashdean up to London on various commissions he had in town. He'd hardly glanced at it except in pity. Imagine losing one's freedom! Imagine being disgraced in such a way, feared and despised! Maybe some of prisoners were innocent; he'd often thought that.

He frowned and re-read Harriet's explanation. She had seen the birth certificate naming Edgar as the father. Maybe it was forged, perhaps the mother had been lying, but no benefit had come to Gerry, who seemed to know a great deal about Edgar and in such detail that banished at least her doubt. The family resemblance was striking. Did they know anything about Gerry? She hated to ask. After all, her letter might not be welcome. They could know and, for so many reasons, might have decided to leave well enough alone.

Know? Michael's fingers rummaged for the meagre file of Edgar's photographs and he fished them from his drawer. He sat with the clearest snapshot placed at precise right angles to the letter on his desk. When it came to his brother any knowledge was a jumbled arithmetic, never balancing, never coming out.

This Gerry person . . . fellow? Nephew! Harriet said he was forty. Edgar would be in his mid sixties if he had lived. How old would Gerry . . .? He turned over the photograph. In his draughtsman's handwriting he had dated it . . . yes, Gerry would have been a small child when this picture was taken. The colour in the photograph was faded. Edgar was bent low, scratching the head of their dog Tansy. One never saw his brother's eyes. What a foolish thing to think! Of course, one had! And yet the expression was always opaque.

It was as if Harriet had taken up a jigsaw always in place on a corner table in an old-fashioned parlour and thrown it up in the air. The more Michael tried to remember if Edgar had even hinted at a son's existence, the more hopeless the muddle seemed.

Surely, Edgar had been gay. That was the family assumption anyway, rarely discussed, except by Eleni who left nothing implicit. But gay people had children. Of course they did. Not Edgar, somehow, he kept thinking. But then the way the family had handled everything to do with Edgar's sexuality had been so fraught with deceit and euphemism that it was hard to make a rational judgement on the matter, even now.

When Michael had been at prep school, Edgar had come home from public school, sacked. He was in awe of his elder brother who smoked secretly in the garden and bribed Michael not to tell. He hadn't the slightest idea what Edgar had done and thought it probably had something to do with the cigarettes. Their father, usually such a remote figure, shook with a peculiar wrath, their mother was red-eyed; there had been shouting and sobbing behind closed doors and, at seventeen, Edgar had been sent to Malaya to work on a cousin's rubber plantation, from which he disappeared – funnelled, presumably, into the war. Edgar's bright and interesting mind had been treated like a diseased field, uprooted, burnt and left fallow. No one had mentioned homosexuality, though nobody did in those days. In fact, it was not until Michael had married Eleni that it had truly sunk in.

So Edgar's son was a burglar, a prisoner, poor boy!

Thinking about it now, which he had not done for a very long time, Michael wondered why the crisis of Edgar's sacking had not diminished with the years. Looking back, and with full knowledge of the facts in hand, adolescents' experiments with younger boys had not been completely unknown, even then. Surely his parents had terribly overreacted, setting what might have been a passing phase in stone. Edgar never seemed to get a chance to work out whether or not it had all been a sexual whim, not the way the family had come down on him. If his innate predilection had been for other men, there had been nothing of the acceptance that would have helped him lead a productive life.

And yet it struck Michael as curious that the memory of this painful episode, which had happened so long ago, seemed to sharpen rather than blur with time.

As a small child, Michael had taken his parents' muted unhappiness for granted. Until Edgar's sacking, it had never really occurred to him that they were unhappy. They never rowed; but the disgrace, as they called it, polarised them. As far as he could remember, they had never slept in the same room. After Edgar had been bundled off to the Far East, they took to living in separate parts of the house. But then it was the war, and everything seemed chaotic at that time.

Even Godfrey had been affected, though it took Michael a long time to work out why. He was in the Army, which should have given him an independent life, and yet, even now, he blamed Edgar for everything. The hopes that Edgar had distinguished himself in conflict were dashed, and fears that he might have been taken prisoner were put to rest, when he returned to England. Evasive though he was about his movements, one thing was for sure – he had developed a bottomless appetite for opium.

By this time, Michael was spotty and furtively lewd, in paroxysms at the sight of a bra through a thin blouse. He remembered how shocked he had been to see Edgar on his return. He'd lost weight and his skin was sallow. This time Michael was told that his brother had malaria, which was why he was being hustled off to a clinic in Switzerland.

It did no good. Nor did any of the other remedies applied. In the course of time, it became too evident to conceal that Edgar was a drug addict. Over the years that followed, the family pushed him into any and every possible occupation for a gentleman: the stock market, the wine trade, real estate . . . and, finally, antiquarian books.

His sexual orientation came to be only one of their many concerns. Although no one directly said it, a late telephone call or knock at the door could always have been the police informing the Hythes of Edgar's arrest.

As Edgar in prison was unthinkable, he had to be set up. Shares were sold, money was realised, a flat in Pimlico was bought outright. Godfrey, who was by then a solicitor with a grand London firm, masterminded the whole thing. Prudently, he insisted that the property was registered in their mother's name. This would become the source of an unending quarrel between her, Godfrey and Edgar, a hideous three-cornered struggle in which she vacillated and Godfrey insisted and Edgar wheedled.

In important respects, Michael had been sheltered from the full brunt of Edgar. His mother, who was fond of Dostoevsky, loved to call him her 'darling Alyosha' after the pacific Karamazov whose meek and affectionate heart undid powerful wrongs by love. Deep down, Michael always knew she wanted him to be a priest. He had adored her. Even up to her death, his pet name for her was 'Queen Maeve', after the Celtic heroine. He profoundly identified with her struggles, a kind of bravery she had. Yet even though he felt surreptitiously guilty at being her clear favourite, his innately beneficent nature sheltered him from taking much account of the resentment his brothers felt. He always thought the best of people.

To some extent, the family energies changed when Michael married Helen Bellini. He was quite taken aback that everyone blinked in surprise. Until then he had not realised to what extent he was supposed to remain Mummy's boy and she never quite recovered from this reversal of expectation. To his barely acknowledged relief, she responded to his marriage by turning the whole force of her formidable maternal energies into the salvation of Edgar. Even so, Michael and his mother remained intuitively fond of one another which, in turn, became Eleni's cross to bear.

Poor Queen Maeve! She'd trailed up to London often enough to clean Edgar's flat. She'd beaten a track up and down Harley Street, getting news of first this cure for his addiction, then that, from quack after quack. God alone knew her tears and prayers! The more she did the worse he became, vilifying her as he fell. Eleni took a dim view of Maeve's efforts. She once famously claimed, to everyone's horror at a family dinner, that Edgar only liked to manipulate the family into thinking he was a true addict. Michael's burden was being able to see every side of a question. He winced whenever he remembered how Helen had lived to regret making that remark.

Whatever he was or wasn't, however, Edgar wanted managing. With his lawyer's eye, Godfrey had formed a distinct if chilly view of a situation that could have been financially catastrophic. He made an airtight trust on which most people, even with expensive tastes, could have lived comfortably: not so Edgar. What could account for his profligacy but the drugs? No one knew how he got hold of them without being caught. At one point, they seriously thought of handing him over to the police. Thus the family dragged him from the forties to the sixties, which should have been his heyday, when he died.

But as for a son? One of the most depressing things about Edgar was a self-centredness that seemed to preclude any relationship whatever. That was it. He thought about it, struggling with it. Even now, Michael couldn't imagine Edgar finding time or energy for anything as outgoing as sex. Apart from his narcotic state, the whole erotic chore would have been too much of a distraction from his painful, narcissistic ego. This certainly went to support the view that he was dominated by his addiction. Well, the whole family would have become dominated by it as well if Eleni hadn't stood there as a bulwark against Queen Maeve's anguish. She had a marriage to protect, she cried.

And yet his wife was a moral woman, who did not enjoy causing pain. Repentant of her challenge to Maeve's role as suffering mother to a junkie, Eleni had tried to work up a more supportive thesis. A great friend of hers had been a Freudian analyst (who had – and Michael was thankful for small mercies – turned to Jung in later life). Together she and Eleni worked up a great symbolic scheme in which heroin took the part of badly sublimated sexual desire, the words 'heroin' and 'heroine' having an identical pronunciation. What was feminine was destructive to him. A needle was a phallus, and so forth. Michael always listened gravely and politely to his wife, but he never paid too much attention to her. Although she was a Catholic and shouldn't, she read her horoscope too.

He squared himself again for Harriet's letter, though by now he knew almost all of it by heart. On the second page she said she did not know if the boy's mother was still living, but her name had been Mary Carney, a chaotic and insufficient parent who might or might not have been involved in casual prostitution. Had this been Edgar's supplier? Certainly, he had maintained contact with her in a sporadic way.

'Oh!' said Michael softly to himself. 'Oh, I see.'

He looked out now to his precious view. In the distance was Mount Zeus, clad in handsome grey shale and surrounded by greener mountains as if by a small assembly of lesser gods. When the sun hovered golden just before sunset, he liked to let his fancy drift to the time when ancients peopled the basin just above his land. He saw them as faceless, like the Cycladic statuary suspended in glass cases in the museum, those profound and eyeless seers, which spoke in wordless tongues.

It was Michael's fantasy that one day his farmer's plough would turn some up, these smooth, marble, obsessively carved mannequins, striking identical poses, arms folded, rectangular heads uplifted . . . maybe to the gods. Now he closed his eyes and felt, as he often did, the near presence of their makers, benign spirits who oversaw the trimming of his vines, the mulching of his potatoes. It helped him when perplexed to ponder it, that there was nothing new under this sun, at any rate. What was happening now had happened before and would doubtless happen again in a long coil of unfolding cycles. The science of life was to be at peace. That was what he must do: recover his peace.

He wrenched back the chair from his oversized desk, shoving Edgar's pictures aside. What was he to do about Gerry? He had checked his first two impulses, one to tell his wife immediately, the second to ring Godfrey. Clearly, Harriet Washington thought it should be done; as, clearly, she was afraid to do it.

He sighed and shook his head. If he, like his wife, had been Venetian, there would have been an outright feud between Godfrey and himself . . . but they were English. Rather than quarrel over the shoddy and peculiar way Godfrey had dealt with their mother at the end of her life and with her affairs after her death, Michael had simply trickled away. Perhaps it was moral cowardice, perhaps resignation, but Helen's longing for Greece had coincided with his own loss of appetite for Ashdean and for a family who, he had to admit, sucked one in and drained one dry. On principle, he did not like to agree with Eleni who declared that every day away from Ashdean was a gain, but privately he had to admit there was a lot of truth in what she said.

One thing in Harriet's letter perplexed Michael: that she seemed so frightened that Gerry Carney would seek out Godfrey on his release from prison. Surely he would have sought him out before this point if that were what he wanted. In any case, there would be no need. Why did he think that, he wondered? He rumpled his hair frantically, as if to find answers under it. And then it came to him very clearly. From the moment he had first read Harriet's letter, he had known exactly what he was going to do. If Eleni didn't like it, and she wouldn't, she was going to have to put up with it.

He picked up the letter again. Although it wasn't scented, something emanated from it, the smell of soap perhaps, or hand cream, that brought Harriet Washington vividly to mind.

Suddenly, he felt acutely sorry for her. Was it the way she had expressed the letter? There was feeling in it, compassion for this poor man. Poor Harriet, what a trial for her! One had never imagined what a good person she was, visiting prisons and all that. Michael flushed, remembering how he had misjudged her. He'd thought her brittle and a little cold, a vain woman with her actress smile and stage-set house. All along she concealed a kind heart – probably quite a sensitive one too. Her mask had only protected a vulnerability. Averell had been the more amusing of the two and she'd never been a match for him with his mordant wit. Besides, he'd treated her shabbily. No, Gerry was not Harriet's responsibility, as her conscientious letter seemed to suggest. This was a family obligation.

Michael frowned when he considered the battle that lay ahead. He must gird his loins. There was only one honourable thing to do. He would invite Harriet and Gerry Carney to stay. September was a lovely month in Naxos, the tourists just ebbing away, the heat abating. What better place for them to find their feet again, the two of them . . . one after a disastrous marriage, the other after not only a frightful time in prison, but a lifetime of neglect – quite unconscious on Michael's part – by the family who might have sustained him.

The dinner party had been a huge success and Eleni was prostrate the next day on the chaise longue her great-grandmother had imported from Paris. She made an agreeable picture, her black hair with its swoops of grey flung loose over the scrolled back, her robe de chambre in broderie anglaise draping to the floor, and her little feet unconsciously arranged like Mme Recamier. Michael looked at her blinking. It still astonished him that she had married him. In triumph, as she was now, her whole being was suffused by a dark glamour that he found bewitching.

Eleni was pleased with the meal. Had Michael liked it? Of course he had – the effort showed. 'Well, I shan't do anything like that again in a long time,' she said.

Michael was making a show of reading *The Times*, necessarily a day late and one of his few luxuries. He watched for his opportunity. 'M'mm,' he said. He hated to bring her down from her cloud. It made him writhe inside to spoil her good mood. But as the dinner party had progressed last night, he had become more and more convinced that his decision about Gerry Carney was the right one. How could he sit there at table, laughing and enjoying himself, if one of his own relations went in real need? Was that Christian? Michael tried to be one. Behind the paper, he murmured a prayer for strength. His eye caught sight of the small crucifix on the wall. Both Catholics, they kept this and an icon of the Virgin in what Orthodox Greeks would have called 'the beautiful corner'.

They were seated in the colossal hall that did for a drawing room. A pair of antique Turkey carpets, each large enough to swamp an ordinary room, lay end to end leaving a gap between the two on the sagging wooden floor; it dated from the seventeenth century, so there was nothing to be done about renovating it save to keep woodworm at bay and shore it up from underneath. They had managed to rest Eleni's piano on a couple of supporting beams, else it would have fallen into the cellar. The ceiling was seven centuries old, its Romanesque carving intact. Although the beams listed a bit, they were exquisitely ancient, above them a stout thatch made of interwoven twigs and branches.

Eleni had inherited furniture to scale and she had preserved the Greek traditional overstuffing. There were tight, plump armchairs, a pair of high, rigid and formal leather sofas and all sorts of good bric-a-brac. Everything was a little too smothered in hand-made lace and tatting, Michael privately thought, but it was authentic. A superb pot-bellied stove kept them warm in the winter (backed up, it must be said, with a pair of electric fires). He particularly liked her family photographs of stiff grandfathers with walrus moustaches and stiff grandmothers, hieratic as icons in piled-up hair and lace.

Michael folded his paper and stood up. Three grand windows opened on to to a view the harbour far below, and from the balcony below he could see the Palatia, a spur of land that juts out into the sea where the Portare, the ancient gate of an unfinished temple, stands. It greets every traveller to Naxos from its mound above the sea like a threshold to the island, a gigantic marble frame. He glanced at it now, and for some reason it struck him afresh.

'The Portare,' he said to his wife, 'is a gate from nowhere leading nowhere.'

'Sorry?' she said. 'What brought that on?'

By night, he thought, the black inner space of the Portare, bounded by tactfully illuminated marble, seems to suggest a living emptiness within. Why had he not thought of it before? He put his hands behind his back and cleared his throat.

'My love,' said Michael. 'I've been waiting to tell you something.'

Eleni's head swivelled, her eyes widened. 'Cassie!'

'No, goodness me! Of course I'd have told you anything about Cassie. It's something else and came as a bit of a shock to me . . .'

'Our shares! The market's crashed.' (Eleni had once been a Communist.)

He shook his head, took Harriet's letter from his pocket and gave it to her. She looked at him, mutely questioning, then put on her half-moon spectacles. After briskly perusing the letter, she put it back in the envelope. 'Michael . . . no!'

'No, what?' He was stalling. Again, he asked for strength, and strength came.

'You were going to ask them to stay.'

'I am,' he said, choosing the present tense over the conditional.

'You're not!'

'Helen!' This was his more intimate name for her. 'I'm sorry, but I'm afraid I must. Surely you can see why.'

The last sentence was a mistake. Helen saw everything. 'I do indeed!' Her voice started that threatening upward climb. 'You believe this? It's incredible! Why did we never hear of this Gerry before? I can't imagine Edgar missing the opportunity to milk the family! If this urchin existed, your brother would have crippled him like an Indian beggar if it meant getting money from Maeve! And to do her justice, she would have bought the child like a slave if it meant saving him from Edgar and his charming "lifestyle".'

Michael agreed but didn't say so. There seemed no reason to add that the emergence of Gerry made the coils Edgar had writhed in seem deeper, more peculiar than ever. The night before, while Eleni snored gently beside him, he had lain awake, his mind worrying into the gaps, poking and prodding the whole anomaly of his brother. From that sharp sense of an inexplicable loyalty to Edgar, which he concealed from Eleni and half-concealed from himself, corollaries arose. He'd been through it all before, how he'd felt this useless guilt about Edgar. Even in childhood, he'd been curiously protective of his brother. And maybe that was it, his inability to help Edgar, that always tinged his feelings with shame and regret . . . that or Queen Maeve's favouritism, which he had accepted uncritically while his brothers had starved in comparison! All these elements had combined, rising to crisis pitch in Michael at Edgar's death. He'd never fully understood it, why he'd felt so especially responsible.

Shortly before dawn this thought came: if ever there was a second chance to help Edgar it was now, and through his son. Queen Maeve would have wanted it. Surely, even the best side of Edgar would have wanted it. Michael wanted it. Who, being part of the family, could not have felt a visceral compassion for the innocent by-blow of such a walking human disaster as his brother? And when he had seen this he had fallen into a deep slumber, finally at peace. Gerry Carney was like the unexpected light from a dead star. And Michael needed to know him.

His wanting to know was, of course, where his wife's chief objection lay. His was a family, she thought, where one should leave well enough alone.

'Oh, Michael,' she continued, 'you simply can't let it alone, can you? Wrapping up Edgar, as if it were possible! I knew he'd surface again. I just knew it!'

Michael squeezed his eyes shut and sank his head between his hands.

'And if you must be such a noble martyr, please don't implicate me! Even if he is Edgar's son, he's a convicted *criminal*. How does Harriet Washington, of all people, know what he's in prison for? He could have told her anything! He could be an axe-murderer for all we know. And why has she decided to tell us all of this? It seems an extraordinary way to behave. If she's worried about this man, surely she should seek the prison's help! Or Godfrey's!'

Michael said nothing. It was the best way, he'd discovered. She would rant and then weep and then apologise, so he battened the hatches. She also knew, and he knew that she knew, that when he actually did make his mind up, there was no shifting him.

'Oh, it's *all my fault*, I know . . . Mrs Mean! I'm the one who has to do the dirty work, point out uncomfortable truths, save you from your own dotty goodness! I'm only kicking myself that I wrote to Harriet in the first place. I only wanted her to talk up Cassie's cards to friends, put it on her social mantelpiece!' She ended her tirade in spiteful triumph.

He said quietly, 'Helen, that isn't true. You told me yourself that you felt sorry for her because Averell left her. You always felt sorry for her and you know it!'

Helen looked down a nano-second and he knew she was ashamed of herself.

When first they married he had found such scenes alarming, but as time went on their rows took on the aspect of bullfighting. There was a rewarding moment when he saw where to thrust a bandoleer. He had pierced the skin above the shoulder blade and it slowed her down.

'Come, they need not stay for very long,' he said. 'In any case, they might not come at all. I simply want this poor chap to know, well, that one never deliberately abandoned him . . . that he does have family. That we do care.'

She tossed her head, mostly for effect, he observed, but she did continue. Seeing victory in sight, he listened only to half of what she was saying.

'I wonder if you've thought this thing right through, Michael. Suppose he is actually Edgar's son. Has it crossed your mind that we might be in for your brother's carbon copy? Have you considered this? Do you really think we could go through that again? She says he's a thief, as if this were some kind of grounds to love him. Have you wondered what he needs the money *for?* Edgar ran through a fortune and you know as well as I do where it went! Don't you remember what it was like? The pleas for cash? The promise of reform? The so-called "drug-induced psychoses"? And then there was the cruelty. I'm not putting up with that. I'll never forget the look on his face . . . you know, when he decided one of us was ripe for cutting down to size. Why, when he had your mother in his sights, he almost licked his lips!' She shuddered with genuine disgust.

'What do you think it might have looked like to a little boy?' Michael was astonished at his own anger. Then quite without meaning to, he got up, threw the paper on the floor and slammed out of the house.

And that was the end of that. Although they were a little chilly with each other for a day or two, Michael wrote his letter to Harriet and posted it.

11

GOSFORTH CAME ON DUTY Monday morning only to find that Hythe had been rushed to hospital with a heart attack. Touch and go, they said. The landing staff had saved his life.

Even so, no one had thought to contact next of kin.

Gosforth shut the door to his superior's narrow office. As often, the Principal Officer wasn't there. He sighed and picked up the phone. Only a few months back the papers had been full of a case at another prison: a young offender had died of peritonitis following a burst appendix. The medics had responded too late, the lad's parents hadn't been called.

You'd think they'd learn, but no. His boss was in a meeting. No one else had bothered to inform Hythe's cousin. Either they didn't have the time or they thought it was someone else's problem. With the understaffing, it was probably no one's fault.

Gosforth liked the sound of the cousin, the things Hythe let slip about her. Inmates often felt a mystical devotion to remembered women; it was amazing how a prison sentence could change the script of a relationship that had been bad or worse on the outside. He'd known men who made icons from photos of wives they'd battered or those who transformed violent, inadequate mothers into household saints. Though Hythe was disproportionately proud of his cousin's few letters and infrequent visits, there was a sense that she hadn't abandoned him. The relatives of this sort of inmate often did. Hythe had shown Gosforth one of her notes.

It had surprised him, for he had rather made up his mind that Hythe's posh connections existed only as some inflated fantasy of himself. The cousin's hand was well formed, not only educated, but singular. Gosforth had a mental image of her, a tall, willowy blonde with chiselled features and a hesitant smile. She had taken Hythe's 'book' home with her to read after the last visit and the inmate had been asking every day if there were post for him.

Poor Hythe. These days, he looked out for Gosforth, peering down the landing, venturing something that resembled a smile, hailing him from the dinner queue with a lordly wave of the hand. Whenever they encountered one another, Hythe would make a little offering, usually of an authorial nature, always drawing attention to his illustrious connections. He seemed obsessed with class, burning with fervour that only the dispossessed could have. Whatever his pedigree, it had given him none of the traditional advantages. When Hythe spoke he seemed to be squeezing the life out of a South London accent that refused to lie down and die. Squirrelled bits and pieces, such as Cassandra's note, appeared from his pockets, things that revealed a pathetic snobbery that made Gosforth squirm.

There was, for instance, a tatty book of snapshots, photos of his fateful trip to Greece – a journey Gosforth imagined that anyone else would prefer to forget. Gosforth remained to be convinced that Hythe was entitled to boast of the coat of arms carved on the stone lintel of a doorway – the entrance, he said, to his 'family's ducal palace'. In another picture, he sat rigid on an uncomfortable-looking sofa, which occupied a small space in a large room. Gosforth hardly recognised Hythe as he had been then, a slim youthful-looking man with a sulky Elvis pout. He was dressed in clothes that seemed wildly anomalous, a blazer and Paisley tie. A tall woman with white hair, dressed elegantly in cherry red, stood above him beaming down. Gosforth, curious, asked who she was. The idea that someone had once loved Hythe to the extent of that fond smile seemed disjunctive. 'That's Judas Iscariot!' he snapped and angrily shut the book.

All this was progress, Gosforth supposed, these little scraps the prisoner shared with him seemed a prelude to larger confidences. Mindful of *Crime and Punishment,* he waited, patient as Raskolnikov's nemesis, to hear what Hythe meant by the word 'innocence' in order that he might confront his guilt.

And yet each ragged oblation unnerved Gosforth as much as if his cat had triumphantly brought him a savaged bird. His flesh crept against his will. Now, Hythe might be dying.

Did it matter? Hythe was grotesque. Gosforth breathed out, relieved to admit it to himself. The man troubled him none the less. He wondered if people died in their sins any more or if hell had gone off the boil. With a twinge of guilt about the poor monster, he picked up the phone.

An hour later, having found that part of Hythe's file was lost, he managed to extract Cassandra Hythe's number from the Admin Block. Everything in Grisholme took twice the time it took outside, and that was on a good day. By the time he finally reached the cousin, there had been two disciplinary issues to be solved; a rat had been sighted in the kitchens; and one of the officers on Hythe's bed-watch had called in to say that his wife had totalled their car and was herself in hospital – Charing Cross, five miles away. Gosforth felt driven to his knees.

'Is that Cassandra Hythe?' Gosforth didn't know if she were Miss, Ms or Mrs. Maybe he should try 'Lady' or 'Your Grace'!

'Speaking.'

'This is Senior Officer Gosforth ringing you from Grisholme Prison. I'm afraid to say that your cousin Hy . . . Gerry Hythe . . . is dangerously ill.'

'Oh dear! What? Why?'

Gosforth explained that he'd had a heart attack and faced the two-pronged danger of a second one or of another stroke.

'Is he . . .?'

'It's very serious, but they think he may pull through. You may visit him if you wish . . . he's really quite unwell. He's in intensive care.'

'Oh, dear.'

'You are his only . . . he's put you as next of kin . . . and I do know he very much looks forward to . . .'

Miss, Mrs or Ms Hythe said nothing.

'He may die,' Gosforth added bluntly.

'I'll have to see if I can get someone to pick the children up from school,' she said. 'If so, I'll come as soon as I can. Is there anything I must do or must not do? Anything I may or may not bring?' She spoke with an even sarcasm.

'You can bring flowers if you like, but it's a little beside the point. Just bring yourself.' He nearly added 'madam'. He supposed that she was, after all, one of those dislikeable women who drive Range Rovers from point to point in their useless lives. All the same, he had a sudden desire to meet her. 'Midday, I shall be relieving one of the officers at the hospital. We're short-staffed and his wife has had an accident.'

Cassie, stung by the officer's judgemental tone, put down the telephone. So Gerry was at death's door. She had just taken the boys to school and was finally settling down to work on a new idea she had for a children's birthday card . . . a treasure hunt. It was as if a crocodile had appeared in the bright blue lake she was drawing: not a jolly green one with a white, zigzag smile, but an old and hungry reptile with practised jaws. She'd been to see her cousin only last week, and now she would have to go and see him again. How selfish she was to feel that way!

In truth, it always took her time to recover from her visits to Gerry and, though she forced herself not to clutch at John and Alexander afterwards, she found herself watching for unwholesome signs of friendliness in men she would otherwise consider benign. Because their father had left them, the boys, nine and ten, tended to look for reassurance. They'd followed the local builder round all day when he had come to put up some cupboards.

She glanced at her design. Tears of frustration pricked at her eyes. But she'd brought it on herself. Was it pity or vulgar curios-

137

ity? Family feeling or a compulsion to shine light into the Hythes' dark cupboards? What mixture of motives drove her to visit Gerry? And now there he was, open-mouthed need that she could never satisfy. Suppose he did die? Was there a point in his staying alive?

She squeezed her eyes shut in an effort to erase this thought. In reparation for it, she went to the extraordinary lengths of getting the boys billeted, possibly for the night, with a friend who could fetch them from school. If Gerry died she would have to make the arrangements with this Gosforth. Could he be buried in Ashdean? Near Uncle Edgar? Near Harriet? Why not? she thought.

At first she did not recognise Gerry in his white hospital gown – an angel robe, they used to call it. She wasn't sure she had the right patient until she looked down to his wired-up arm and saw that he was cuffed and chained to the bed. She gave an involuntary cry of pity.

At the sound, two prison officers who were talking to the sister turned their heads, on alert as if Cassie had been about to wheel the bed into a lift and make away with Gerry.

'What is the meaning of this?' she cried, looking from one to the other. 'This is outrageous!' She pointed to the shackles.

One of them, a middle-aged man, had the beetroot complexion of a heavy drinker. He stared at Cassie with cold, veined eyes. The other, a younger man but apparently his superior, stepped forward.

'I'm afraid it's in the regulations, ma'am,' he replied, but he looked down, studying his highly polished shoes in embarrassment, she thought.

Gosforth was, indeed, embarrassed. And Cassandra Hythe was quite different from the way he had imagined her, small, vivid and rounded. For some reason, she reminded him of a robin, defending its nest against two stalking cats.

'You must be Hythe's cousin,' he said. She nodded. 'We spoke earlier on the telephone. I'm Senior Officer Gosforth and this is Officer Grimston.'

'So two of you are needed in addition to the shackles!' She made a gesture towards the comatose Gerry.

'I'm afraid so. That too,' he said miserably.

Mr Grimston, worthy of that name, Gosforth always thought, heaved himself down on the chair next to Gerry's bed. He folded his arms across his chest and glared at Cassandra Hythe.

She coldly ignored them both and went to her cousin. 'Gerald? Gerry? It's me, Cassie. So sorry you're unwell.' She waited for a response but as there was none, she eased gently from the bedside and thrust a bunch of oriental lilies at the officer. 'Shall you put these in water or shall I?'

The sister came up and, in answer to his cousin's enquiry after Hythe's progress, told her that there were no flowers allowed in intensive care.

Hythe's mouth was a slack O; he drew laboured breaths through an oxygen mask. The nurse scrutinised Cassie, obscurely triumphant, Gosforth thought, as if she had observed signs of moral contagion in the visitor, a disease caught through earlier association with the prisoner.

Gosforth shook his head. 'I'm sorry,' he muttered, ashamed of the sister. 'I didn't think.' For all Cassandra Hythe's anger, she was instantly likeable, an open, attainable sort of woman.

'You keep them. I can't bear to take them home.' She was on the verge of tears, he could see.

Gosforth floundered. By all rights, he should stand up to this woman. That was what Bill Grimston was thinking, he could tell. She couldn't be much more than thirty, he judged, and he was embarrassed that he found their short interchange obscurely erotic. She was not conventionally pretty, but her features were strongly moulded and gave the suggestion of character. Well, being an inmate's relation, she was off bounds for him.

He tried to deflect this unwanted surge of interest. Although there was an undoubted resemblance to Hythe, especially around the eyes, her face had the look of a developed individual. It was as if a potter had thrown the prototype of an idea in Hythe, binned it, then found the figure he wanted in his cousin. Her dress, slightly unconventional, suggested some Bohemian occupation, and Gosforth noted that she wore no wedding ring.

It was only noon, but already it had been a long day. Hythe's landing officer was in a rage at the prison doctor who had missed all the signs of the heart attack and who might even have prevented it if he'd bothered to give the inmate a couple of aspirin rather than the eternal paracetamol. The officer had just happened to be passing down the landing when he heard the tell-tale noises coming from behind the inmate's locked cell door.

As if by telepathy, Cassandra Hythe turned her head. 'He was complaining of pains in his chest,' she said, 'when I saw him, just the other day. I suppose there's no point to him in your eyes.'

Just as he thought it was high time he made some effort at self-defence, she blushed, looking down. He noticed how her long lashes brushed her cheeks. 'I'm sorry,' she said. 'He's told me that you've been kind to him.' She flashed a glance at Officer Grimston and Gosforth was glad that he had not been on the receiving end of it. 'It's the shock, that's all.'

Why did she seem so familiar to him? Gosforth wondered. It was partly the resemblance to Hythe, but the way she gestured when she spoke, a certain expressiveness in her eyes, reminded him of someone else. Ah, he had it. His father's second wife was a Cypriot. They had three children, his half-sisters, who all worked in Limasol, one of them a tour guide. Of course. Hythe had told him he had a Greek aunt, who must be Cassandra Hythe's mother. 'It is upsetting,' he said awkwardly.

Cassie pulled her thoughts around herself, pinching her mouth. The shock, the drive, the shackles, the nurse's unwonted opprobrium and, more than anything, the unwelcome, raw pity she felt for Gerry, unmoored her. She was ashamed of herself. It was nothing less than hypocrisy to blast this Gosforth when she remembered what she'd been thinking about Gerry only that morning. She did owe him an apology. Yet she was sure it must take a certain mind-set to spend a working life curbing other people's liberty, no matter what they'd done.

Gerry's chest rose and fell, his flesh waxy, nostrils pinched. He looked about as culpable as a turnip.

In Cassie's art school days, she would have thought any constraint on liberty an evil. And now Vassilis, with his big teeth and specs, grinned perpetually at her, a photo sealed in a shiny tomb of Naxian marble. Cassie's mind snapped shut, excluding memory. Her father had taken it so hard, harder almost than the child's own father who bore his cross with a Balkan stoicism. And her mother had descended into a Greek fury, the kind that perpetuated wars.

Gerry's existence seemed stretched out on the graph that bleeped above his head, each heartbeat a gain. 'All the same, he's not an animal,' she thought.

For some reason, this put her in mind of the 'Hythe Chronicle', as Gerry styled it. She had forced herself to read it, battling through the impenetrable grammar. It was as if a ghost were trying to communicate with the living, by various tappings and automatic writing, a message from the other side, indicating soul.

'He gave me a bit of this book he's writing,' Cassie said finally. 'I understand you told him he could get it published.' She turned her head and let the despair in her eyes meet Gosforth's. Did he know how irresponsible it was to have given Gerry false hope? No one would ever read, or want to read it.

Gosforth blinked. 'What?'

'Oh!' she said. She saw what had happened. Gerry had made similar mountains out of her own small encouragements. 'I see,' she said, softening. Gosforth attracted her. Was he a Scot? She believed so from his accent. She looked away, confused. A Scot with a deeply authoritarian personality, she added to herself.

She tiptoed over to the bedside once more. 'Gerald? I've been looking at your book. Jolly good bit about old Aelric and Richard!'

'I liked that too,' said Gosforth.

They smiled at one another, she involuntarily. 'Presumably under the circumstances I may touch him?' Cassie said. He nodded, so she took Gerry's hand and gave it a gentle squeeze. As she did so, he frowned and with an apparent effort, he opened his eyes a crack, then closed them again as if this basic and reflexive movement had exhausted him. He tried to say her name.

Gosforth went to tell the sister that the patient had regained consciousness.

On a Tuesday morning in early May Harriet received Michael Hythe's letter inviting Gerry and herself to Naxos. She was just on her way out the door. She'd planned to walk down to change her books at the library then stock up at Waitrose, a routine she had got into before her 'Gerry Wednesdays' as she called them. They left her shattered. She never surfaced from them properly until the weekend. It was a bit like going to the bottom of the sea in a bathysphere, she once told Boo. Coming up too quickly gave her the bends. Boo had frowned, pondering it. Was Harriet becoming a little too introspective? A little too intense? she asked.

Harriet had been wounded by this. Boo was an extrovert, not sensitive and creative. It was pointless to get her to understand. It was up to Harriet to understand herself, she decided. So she invented her own little rituals to help her cope. The day before her visits, she would lay in supplies to feed her preoccupation during the time it took her to recover. Often she found that her conversations with Gerry would repeat themselves in her head verbatim, as if she had left a tape recorder running and had to replay it several times before she could safely stow the contents in her memory.

She read Michael's letter going down the King's Road. It was a lovely morning, lambent even through the fumes of the rush hour snarl.

Harriet had not expected this result. She had expected Michael, living so far away, at best to write some anodyne message for her to give to Gerry. She'd had it in her head that Michael returned to England from time to time and it occurred to her that on his next visit he might suggest a meeting, lunch perhaps, on neutral territory. She had a pleasantly recurring fantasy of herself, Gerry and his uncle sharing chops at Simpson's or somewhere like that. Boo's visitors weren't allowed to have contact with inmates after their release, but surely a meal with Gerry and Michael didn't fall into that category. In her dream of meeting him, Gerry would have managed to get a job, a better one from her influence . . . or maybe through it. She liked to imagine the thrill of the reunion, a moving silence, an embrace. Presumably they would take it from there. Harriet had already picked out what she was going to wear, a cashmere and camel cardigan and skirt, very smart, and some big earrings. Everything would be taken forward by an encounter of this kind and nothing lost. This was the most she had hoped for.

The idea of escorting Gerry all the way to Greece, however, fell about her head like wet clay and stopped all thought. For some reason she concealed the letter – though from whom it would have been hard to say – in the zip compartment of her handbag; but she wanted to take it out again directly to re-read it.

Of course, what Michael suggested was impossible! Apart from anything else, she would be obliged to tell Boo. The rules were plain enough and Harriet had already bent one of them a little too far. More importantly, she wasn't really ready for spending whole days with Gerry. In fact, it made her feel uncomfortable, vulnerable. In Waitrose, she fumbled through her mental list and managed to swipe half a dozen eggs on to the floor where they broke, all six, and had to be cleared up by a sneering cleaner. She bought beans instead of the broccoli she'd planned and went home without sugar.

Harriet took the letter out in the privacy of her drawing room, and smoothed it on the table as if this would iron out the problems it created. Michael had clearly considered his reply; his draughtsman's hand made every word seem carefully composed. There was a need, he said, to bring family problems concerning Edgar to a resolution. He was glad for the opportunity to do this both for Gerry's sake and his own.

She didn't know why she had expected a lighter response from Michael. She had even imagined him shrugging the whole thing off as an improbable story. How was it she had thought that he wouldn't take her seriously? And why did it unnerve her so that, much more than serious, the tone of Michael's letter seemed almost grave?

Could Harriet reassure Gerry that there had been no conscious decision he knew of to exclude him from the family, Michael asked. He was delighted to learn, no matter how late, that Edgar had a son, his nephew. He would prefer to meet him before he raised the subject with Godfrey.

She spun about, studying the letter like a psychic with a crystal. She was appalled at herself. What had she been thinking of, dragging memories of Edgar back to people she hadn't seen for years? Michael's careful writing said more about the pain Edgar still caused him than if he had boldly described it. Harriet was an only child. How would she have felt about a brother who had died in a dustbin like someone in a Beckett play? Suppose she had been confronted with a long-lost nephew who was in prison? It didn't bear thinking about. Her cheeks flamed.

And now she had unsettled Michael so badly, what on earth was she to do? Having raised the matter, she could hardly bury it again. As for Gerry, either she had to show him the letter or conceal it.

Suppose she gave it to him to read. There was no way of controlling his reaction. Once he knew she had written to Michael, he might be furious at her. She flinched. Whenever she displeased or vexed Gerry, always quite unintentionally, there was a moment like a dead spot in time when his eyes grew blank, his muscles clenched in stillness. She'd end up fumbling for an apology.

The letter was sure to disturb the crazy patch where Edgar lay in Gerry's mind. Even if it had the opposite effect, what then? She would have to commit herself to this journey, wouldn't she?

Suppose she kept it from him. Had she any right to do this? Here she had found a family for a lonely prisoner who needed all the support he could get. There might even be a legacy in it for Gerry, much less the healing that might come from the Hythes' kindness. And now Michael knew about him there was nothing to stop him from writing to Gerry in Grisholme. Anything could happen then. Harriet really did not know what to do.

Boo would know. Harriet picked up the phone then put it down. Boo would be livid! She might even prevent her from visiting Gerry again. And if she did that, what might he do? The old question came up, the one that had prevented her from talking to Boo about the Hythes in the first place: the sudden withdrawal of her nurture and support might unhinge him. Harriet was no psychiatrist, but one didn't need to be Sigmund Freud to know that now he'd started the process of letting out the deep buried anger against Edgar, and the Hythes by association, he might go haywire if he were wholly cut off from her. What was to stop him going down to Ashdean to finish the job he'd intended on his first visit there? A vivid picture came to her of Gerry in the church-yard, bludgeoning Edgar's tombstone with a sledgehammer. Why, he might even attack Godfrey!

Harriet stood at her window and looked down at Cadogan Street below. Passers-by carted bags of purchases from Peter Jones or popped in at the little school across the road. Taxis thundered by. Suddenly, the idea that Gerry would seek out where she lived loomed as a real possibility. What would she do if she saw him there in the street, gazing up? If she gave him up suddenly now, who was to say he wouldn't take it in his head to stalk her? She had read stories like this in the newspaper. He might even take revenge on her for allowing him to express the terrible feelings he'd hitherto barely acknowledged to himself.

The more Harriet argued down her growing panic, the worse it became. She had planned a bit of smoked mackerel for lunch, but it lay in the fridge uneaten; her stomach seemed ringed with nerves.

She paced about. She could always ring Michael, discuss it with him, get him to back off a bit, then decide. Yes, she could tell him she didn't think Gerry was ready to meet the family yet. Maybe she could propose her original idea, that in time they could all meet up in England, thus saving her the penalty for having made such a stupid mess of everything.

It was a mess, wasn't it? A horrible, horrible mess.

Harriet began to cry. First, the tears started in her throat, then at her eyes and, in a moment, without her knowing where it came from, huge sobs welled up within her, forcing her down in a spindly chair where she rocked back and forth. It wasn't just Gerry, was it? She had been an inadequate wife, an inadequate mother, a failure as an actress. What was she to do with the rest of her life? Suppose she lived to be eighty. She had twenty years of emptiness ahead of her. She couldn't even do a little charity work without making a complete hash of it. And now the one flame, the flame of Gerry, that warmed her existence, wavered before her inner eye, ready to be snuffed whatever she did. The base of her diaphragm heaved reflexively, aching as if clenching itself around an infinite loneliness. Finally, exhausted by weeping, she staggered off to bed and collapsed.

She woke an hour later, curiously refreshed. She rose and made herself coffee. How extraordinary to have such an outburst! She looked about the drawing room, half expecting to see the contents of it strewn about as if a great natural force had heaved the earth up. Everything, of course, was still in place. She caught sight of her face in the mirror, then went to the fridge and sliced two rounds of cucumber to soothe her puffy eyes. She felt sore but better. Tomorrow she would tell Gerry about the letter and see what he said. She needn't add in the invitation unless it seemed right to do so. And if things got out of hand, then she could always confess to Boo. After all, she *was* just a novice. She had always expected too much from herself and maybe she *had* made a mistake. Well, if she had, Boo might even forgive her.

Averell had always called her a perfectionist. In fact, painful as it was to acknowledge now, he'd cited this as a reason for his defection, not being able to measure up to the inhuman standards she set for herself. It was true, wasn't it? Much as she hated to admit it.

The next day she set out for the prison firm in her resolve. If Gerry was angry with her, so be it. She had acted with the best of intentions. The train from Victoria rattled across the bridge and she looked down on the river, full for early May, the swollen tide almost at the edge of the Embankment, but the day was balmy and the little gardens below the trestle bloomed in a maze of waxy magnolias and fruit trees. Harriet felt light and airy. There was a production of *The Cherry Orchard* at the National, she had noticed in the paper. Maybe she would see if she could wedge herself in that evening. One couldn't go wrong with Dame Judi at the helm as the self-deluding Lyuba. Harriet was almost merry. Her little cry had been cathartic after all and she couldn't think what she had been making such a fuss about.

It struck her at the bus stop that Boo might even be happy to be able to turn a blind eye in this case. Obviously, it was a good idea to get Gerry in touch with his kind uncle! The soft focus of the spring light gilded Vauxhall.

Yes, Michael had always been a treasure, the more so for a gentleness that Averell had mocked. 'Typical mama's boy,' he'd called him, laughing at the way he peered through his specs 'like a short-sighted giraffe'. Yes, it was gentleness and family that Gerry needed. Sensitivity. To ask Boo's permission for bringing about a meeting or to consult her might be to tie her hands, forcing her to the letter of the law when all along the spirit of the voluntary job was to connect prisoners to themselves and fit them for the outside world in the hope that they would never re-offend.

The Visitors' Room was full that day, it being the half-term and mild. As luck would have it, Gerry was in a receptive mood.

He'd had a good fortnight. The prison English teacher had praised an essay he had written on window boxes and had told him that she was going to try to take cuttings from her mother's geraniums using his special tips. Gerry was 'well pleased', he told Harriet.

Harriet said she had something to confess, but Gerry wasn't paying attention. She noticed how he watched the children straining at their mothers, romping against their fathers. So he liked children. One day he might even marry, she thought bravely.

'I took the liberty,' she said, 'of writing to your uncle Michael.' Her heart knocked at her ribs and she felt obscurely panicked. What she had said she couldn't now unsay.

His eyes left their drifting round the room. He blinked. It was as if someone had turned a switch on full. He said nothing.

'I'm sorry,' she said humbly. 'I should have asked you, but I didn't want any disappointments. I got an interesting reply yesterday.'

He put his head to one side, still saying nothing. She couldn't read him at all. She half expected him to stand up and knock her down, despite the attending prison officers.

Her breath trembled. She looked at her hands that twisted in her rosy linen lap, the threads of her skirt with its nubbly weave. 'He wants me to assure you that he never knew of your existence until I told him,' she murmured. 'He says he is delighted to know he has a nephew.'

'My uncle,' was all that Gerry could manage to say. He was stunned. It was like one of those telly programmes she was ashamed of watching, *This Is Your Life*.

'He told me to send you his greetings.' She shrugged. It seemed so pompous a thing to say within the walls of Grisholme, even though the actual message had been nicely put.

'Does he know I'm here? He does know, doesn't he?' Gerry seemed as breathless as she.

Harriet nodded. 'Yes. Yes, he does.' And then because she sensed his need as if it were her own, so that her whole chest burst with pity, she added, 'He knows where you are and he wants to meet you anyway.'

Gerry gave a timid smile, his softened face and eyes were like those of a child, nose pressed against the glass at Hamley's. 'He does?' He was quite altered, she thought.

'Yes!' she flowed towards him. It was all she could do not to embrace him. 'Yes, Gerry, he does!'

And she went home, giddy with her success.

12

MICHAEL HYTHE GREW POTATOES for export. Though the farm didn't make a lot of money, most years he more than broke even. He loved his spuds, firm and waxy, good for salad. They came out almost clean from the rich, crumbly soil; he stored them in the crypt of a ruined monastery that stood in one of his fields: it had once housed Benedictines, but it was a home for bats now. The problem was always getting the potatoes shunted to his wholesaler who sent lorry loads of vegetables to Athens and beyond. A few years ago he had purchased a second-hand lorry but it continually broke down. This frustration, in addition to the need for hiring hands to shift the heavy crates, had lost him a lot of revenue. The Christmas before he received Harriet's letter, however, he had done a good deed which promised to repay him a Biblical fourfold. Yiorgos was a godsend.

Eleni had been against his taking on the man and his son. Yiorgos, formerly Mehmet, was an Albanian who arrived in Naxos on a bad November day when the boats just about made it into port through the gales that blew through the Aegean. He emerged from the ferry with two plastic sacks for luggage and his ten-year-old son Ali, a malnourished tow-headed boy who simply shivered and stared blindly into the harbour. The pair sat on the sea front in the wind and the rain. They had nowhere to go and they spoke only a bare amount of Greek. Free-floating Albanians were objects of fear and sometimes loathing. Mehmet and Ali ended up in the police station charged with vagrancy.

Mehmet came originally from Tirana but in the 1970s had escaped to Yugoslavia and married a Kosovan woman. They had four children and were well respected in the community. When in 1989 the state passed laws to limit the autonomy of Kosovo, some Serbs invaded his town bent on annexing property. They went in to confiscate the house Mehmet and his wife had built with their own hands. He had not been at home; she had resisted. When he returned, he found Ali clutching her hacked corpse. The battered bodies of his three younger sons had been stuffed down the well. The barbaric details of this story were very distressing. No one really knew how Ali had escaped the massacre, if he had witnessed it or who had perpetrated it. Either he could not or would not speak of it.

Mehmet snatched up a few possessions and his one remaining child. Together they made their way across the Greek border and, finally, to Athens. It was unclear how they had sustained life, but everyone knew Albanians thieved and begged. How they had ended up in Naxos was anybody's guess, but the consensus was that they had probably stowed away on a ship to avoid the police.

No crime could be traced to them, however, and the general plan was simply to send them back. Mehmet begged to stay. In order for him to do this, he had to have a job. What was more, he and Ali would have to convert to Orthodoxy – rather a tall order, Michael thought, when one considered at whose hands the child's mother had died.

Mehmet agreed. He wanted to be Greek, he said. He had never practised Islam; it was simply part of his national identity, not an active faith. His family had been secular Muslims who, before the troubles, had got on well with neighbours of every religion.

It remained for someone to stand as guarantor. Michael was neither Greek nor Orthodox; Eleni was Greek but not Orthodox. It was perhaps for this reason that she had been so much against Michael's offer of rescue. With her English connections and dissenting faith, she often struck patriotic poses.

The Hythes had an empty house on the farm, a laïko with one room hardly distinguishable from its chicken coop. Michael's wholesaler somewhat grudgingly stood as godfather to Mehmet and Ali and, being immersed under the auspices of the Orthodox cathedral with its miraculous, deep-eyed Virgin hung with trophies, they emerged new born as Yiorgos and Vassilis.

Under the faintly scornful eye of the Catholic Manolis, Michael's farmer, Mehmet/Yiorgos worked like an ox. No one could slight him. He cleaned the long disused hut, whitewashed the walls (putting an icon up for good measure), re-thatched the roof and got the chimney going. It appeared he had been a mechanic. Before long he transformed the shaky lorry, having correctly identified a fault on the camshaft. He dug and he hoed and he lifted crates, not minding how hard he worked nor how cold it was that winter; he stopped only when evening fell. Michael quietly paid him over the odds and was rewarded by a fierce gratitude that slightly unnerved him.

It wasn't just the money. The boy united Michael and his farmhand. Vassilis, so recently Ali, was sent to the local school. With little Greek, he was put in a class with much younger children, but he learned quickly not only to speak but also to read and write. He had, surprisingly after his experiences, a gentle nature; far from being humiliated by standing so tall amongst his classmates, he endeared himself with the teacher by helping her out with the 'babies'. He was almost too good to be true.

The teacher, Kiria Irini, was the childless wife of the local Orthodox priest. No one knew how she had managed to get a teaching qualification, but she'd picked one up in a youth it was impossible to imagine. She was not of modern Greece. The other teachers, cool girls with plans, did not like the image she gave the school. She would have been a saint except for the hairline crack in her psyche that reduced her to an eccentric. She became vehemently attached to Vassilis, encouraging a sort of desperate piety in him, which did him no good with the other boys. She was sure he'd be a monk the way he talked, even a bishop! He was her 'kalo paidi', her blue-eyed boy. He liked to tell her how happy he was to be a Christian now, because he knew his mother and his brothers were alive in heaven where they had become angels adoring God for ever. And he would meet them there if he was good. Irini hadn't the heart to tell him of their probable fate in the after-life when they had died Muslims.

Vassilis was a strange child. During Easter week, Michael had seen him in the procession of the icon from the church, wedged between the priest and Kiria Irini. Clean and dressed in his best, his blond hair slicked down, his blue eyes flashing with enthusiasm, he lunged at passing tourist cars crying, 'Christos anasti!' Christ is risen! It would have been an edifying sight but for the look about his eyes that, like a photographic negative, seemed to reflect a shadow of horror. What did he remember of the massacre? Flies? Blood? Terror fixed on his mother's dead face? 'He is risen indeed!' Michael had replied, according to custom and his own belief, but still it was unsettling.

By Pentecost the teasing had started and the bullying was about to begin. The child seemed to expect nothing from life and bore his cross with stoicism, never complaining of the catcalls.

Vassilis loved Michael. Whenever he came to the farm, the boy would hear of it. He dogged Michael's footsteps, trotting behind him at a little distance in hope of a word or two. His smile would crack his face showing big, tombstone teeth. He wanted to learn English, reconnecting the lessons he'd started in Kosovo. He already knew phrases such as 'Please, mister, I am hungry . . .', survival English, one might call it. Michael and the child communicated in their own brand of Esperanto. It emerged that some American tourists had been particularly kind to Vassilis and his father during their flight. Michael had been their salvation. So Vassilis associated the English language with beneficence.

As months went by, Michael began in earnest to help Vassilis with his studies. He kept the lessons short and light. Vassilis would sit at the kitchen table in the pyrgos drawing pictures and assigning them neat labels in English, 'boat', 'cow', 'potato'.

Michael would make sure that Anna, the farmer's wife, gave him something nourishing for tea. He would lick a milky grin from his lips, his forehead pinched in concentration. As time went by, his face filled out and took on colour. No amount of fresh air and wholesome food, however, could make him look like a child. It was almost as if his increasing good health had been applied like cosmetics, rouge and blusher, to a midget with elderly eyes. At other times, Michael observed him walking about the farm in deafened isolation. Predictably, he became fond of the dogs and when the bitch whelped Michael gave him one of her puppies.

As to the boy's character, it seemed early days to determine what he might turn out to be. Michael ventured that his other-worldliness did not especially predict a religious vocation.

Even after Vassilis's death, Michael kept the secrets of his drawings – all save one. Now and then, his pictures would show evidence of the holocaust in which he'd lost his family, blood spurting in red crayon; a neat, white house he scribbled over in black. At these times, he would go pale and sit very still at the table. Michael never elicited more from him than he was prepared to give. He would fold his hands and remain quiet until the child was ready to go on with the lesson. Most of the time, Vassilis would give a little shake of his head as if to dislodge unwanted visions. Once, however, he brought Michael a picture he had drawn at home. It was a well, laboriously constructed, brick by brick. The cheap paper lay on the table between them. After some deliberation, Michael picked up his pen and carefully wrote the word 'well' underneath it. When Michael glanced up, Vassilis was crying . . . not like a child, though. Tears made their way down his immobile face like rain on a window.

'My brothers,' he said.

'I know,' said Michael, simply.

Although the drawing was listed as evidence in Gerry's trial, it never came up.

Vassilis seemed grateful for Michael's response. Michael made no move to touch or comfort the child. To have done so would

154

have shown a lack of respect for him, he thought. Vassilis would talk about it, but in his own good time.

And so, by the time Michael heard from Gerry, father and son had matriculated into their new identity as Yiorgos and Vassilis. With the coming of spring they seemed settled happily in Naxos. Despite initial prejudice against them, they were building a reputation as solid citizens.

Gosforth wasn't sure how it happened, but he found himself in the Dog and Fox with Cassie Hythe and counting himself a lucky man. It was probably, he thought later, because she was upset about Gerry that she hailed him across the pub; and when he asked if he could join her, it had seemed the most natural thing in the world. It was not until he was buying her a drink that the impropriety of the situation struck him. Sharing even a ploughman's lunch with an inmate's next of kin might be considered a sackable offence, but by this time it was too late. And it was just a pub; they had entered it separately, and it was lunchtime. It was right across from the hospital and, when his second officer on bedwatch had unexpectedly turned up early, Gosforth had innocently gone in for a pint.

He had one of two choices. Either he could abort the lunch, or write a memo to the governor logging the impromptu meal. He hesitated for a moment at the bar. Cassandra Hythe sat across the room kneading her temples as though they ached. She had made a loose braid of her heavy hair to keep it off her neck in the heat. Her olive skin and delicate profile gave him a little stab of delight, which he quickly suppressed. He would inform the governor. She hardly came from a criminal family; he doubted she was part of a paedophile ring! Besides, it was certainly not going to lead to anything. She didn't like him very much and, after the bollocking she had given him earlier, he wasn't too sure about her.

Maybe it was the faint aura of privilege, so disjunctive with Hythe, which made him curious about her. She was hardly conventional and too spirited to be the sort of middle-class cabbage his mother wanted him to marry, but whatever else Hythe was lying about he'd been accurate in one respect. His cousin lived in a sphere where ease of manner was bred in the bone.

He was suspicious, however, of the facility with which she had managed to draw him to her. The idea that Hythe was in his power might have given this Cassandra a motive to nobble him. Well, he was up to it. If she wanted to elicit classified information about Hythe or ensure the inmate received some perk as a result of this meeting, he'd soon ferret it out.

This did not stop him smiling as he wove his way between the packed tables with the drinks. She was gazing in a quizzical manner at the baguette and cold, pressed cheese on its bed of shredded lettuce she had ordered, gastronomically challenged by it. She prodded a pallid slice of tomato.

'It's real, after all,' she said. 'I had my doubts.'

Gosforth's laugh sounded goofy and self-conscious to his own critical ear and he managed to slosh part of his pint into the steak and kidney pie that stood congealing at his own place.

They smiled at each other. He placed her glass of white wine next to her plate with the utmost delicacy. In her flowing green dress, she looked a little like a pre-Raphaelite heroine. Even with the muzak rendering of 'I'll Do It My Way' that pumped through the pub like recycled air, she made it leafy for him, something to do with William Morris. He tried to drown this consideration with a gulp from his pint.

She leaned forward. He braced himself against what looked like touching sincerity in her eyes. 'I feel really dreadful, you know,' she said. 'I was very rude to you back there in the hospital. And now you've gone and bought me a drink!' She spread strong fingers wide and shrugged, a fluid movement. 'You're very forbearing.'

'It's nothing,' he said awkwardly. 'It *is* very upsetting to see those shackles, especially when someone's so ill. But it's Home Office regulations and there's nothing we can do.'

'Poor Gerry.'

He wasn't sure he'd go that far. He tasted the steak pie and made a face. 'I think we could get the Dog and Fox under the Trades Description Act,' he said.

She giggled behind her hand, like a girl.

Gosforth tried not to be chuffed that she liked his little joke. 'I shouldn't be talking about him, you know,' he told her. 'Not with you. In fact, I shouldn't be "consorting" with you.'

She looked up in mild surprise.

'It does make sense. Suppose you were his moll.'

She clapped her hands, delighted. 'Or, of course, I could offer you a bribe,' she said. 'Only I forgot my chequebook.'

Gosforth did not know when he had felt so at ease with a woman. Suddenly the rule book, which he had taken such pains to memorise, seemed a travesty of law. Cumbersome, ponderous, legalistic, it was slowly turning him into the sort of man he'd never been. 'Seriously, though, it's so incongruous, your being his cousin . . .'

'It is to me as well,' she said, shaking her head. 'I can't tell you how incongruous. He's long-lost, my wicked uncle's son.'

This enlightened and relieved Gosforth. 'So it's goodness of heart? The way you visit him.'

'I wouldn't put it as strongly as that . . . I don't know why he's latched on to me. I never even knew he existed until a few years ago. He just emerged.' She talked with her hands and it put him again in mind of Cyprus. 'But everyone else has abandoned him, even his own mother . . . and you can't wonder why.'

For some reason, she abruptly withdrew into herself, looking small.

Losing the flow of her spontaneity bothered Gosforth. 'I often think how devastating it must be for relatives,' he muttered. 'Especially when the crime is . . . well . . .'

'Heinous? Gerry's broken the mould for black sheep, I suppose. I can't say it's easy to come and see him.' She shuddered. 'It

157

churns me up terribly. I have two boys of my own, you see. And the victim . . . my family knew him. Apart from everything else, what Gerry did devastated my parents, especially my father.'

'Why do you visit him, then?' Gosforth wanted to light a cigarette but thought she would be sure to disapprove of smoking, so thought the better of it.

'I wrestle with that.'

He was quietly amused by her look of moral earnestness. It was a long time since he'd seen that expression on anyone's face.

'The truth is,' she continued, 'I don't really know why. There's something irrational about it.' She looked up from her cheese salad with candid eyes. 'I suppose I was curious at first. But I don't think I would have become involved if it hadn't been for an old neighbour of ours who got sucked into his orbit. When she was dying she became obsessed that Gerry would commit suicide in prison.'

'Inmates do,' said Gosforth, shaking his head. 'But I wouldn't associate that with our Gerry, as you call him.'

'Harriet was possessed by him!'

They looked at each other, mutually bemused, he thought, that the pallid man whose bedside they had just left could have provoked such an extreme state of mind.

'Oh, poor woman, she wrote and wrote to him. He wouldn't answer her letters . . . so she begged me to go and see if he was all right. I could hardly refuse . . . You don't smoke, do you?'

With mock sighs of relief, they both lit up, angling their cigarettes defensively at one another. Gosforth had a delicious sense of getting in deeper than he had planned, but it also alarmed him. Her vulnerability was almost as exotic to him as her idiosyncratic clothes.

'The first time I met him I could have killed him myself, for all that he'd done. And added to that, he had the temerity to despise the dying woman! He still blames *her* . . .'

'For everything!' Gosforth cried, despite himself.

'So you've heard it, too!'

'He's innocent. Of course. Nothing short of a national scandal that he's in gaol.' His wry face made her laugh aloud. He felt dashing, a man with a hidden genius for comedy. There was no point adding the lengths to which sex offenders were prepared to go to justify themselves.

Cassandra Hythe shook her head. 'I sometimes do wonder, you know. I mean it was awfully convenient to lay the boy's death at Gerry's door. After all, he must have known that an involvement with any boy would make him chief suspect in a case like that. And he is so categorical about his innocence . . .'

'Guilt belongs to other people in his eyes, always and perpetually the victim himself.' Gosforth was inwardly enraged. 'Your Harriet, for instance.'

'Oh, she bore the blame, all right. She never forgave herself. What made me so angry was that everyone let her, as if she'd plotted the whole thing from the beginning. Even my mother thinks she was subtly at the bottom of it, but then my parents blame *themselves*, and so the whole sick cycle of guilt is never-ending.'

Gosforth ate a morsel of pastry. It was probably better to reverse out of this topic, but he couldn't think of a way to do it. 'I imagine that something like the death of a child touches everyone with remorse.'

'It touches me!' she said, somewhat wildly. 'I can't get over this feeling that I am in some way to blame, that I have something to redeem or recover because of it. And this, when I was a thousand miles away from the scene of the crime and knew nothing about Gerry until it had all happened. I sometimes think it's because I was brought up a Catholic. Guilt had to be met and dealt with; it wasn't an imaginary number on a sliding scale. Once you've stopped practising, it colours everything you do in a vague way. There's a sense of unease . . . that you're responsible.'

'It has nothing to do with that. It's because he won't take responsibility for what happened. He makes other people do that work for him.' Gosforth was unwontedly crisp. Cassandra Hythe looked at him with new interest. 'He projects it out and you're mug enough to pick it up for him.'

'He can't. He doesn't know how to face it.'

'Or won't.'

'I don't know why I'm telling you all this.'

'Because I'm a stranger on a train?' Gosforth said, feeling suddenly very sad. 'Because I have unique experience with sex offenders?'

'It, whatever it is, gets in everywhere . . . like sand, a feeling of discomfort,' she said wringing her hands. 'Now he's ill, there'll be no stopping it. For years I had a partner. Now he's gone, I say good riddance, but just seeing Gerry tempts me to ring him up, talk to someone . . .'

Gosforth's heart skipped a beat, but he forced himself not to grin openly. 'You're talking to me.'

'You said I shouldn't.'

'Well . . .'

'Sometimes I think I should go back to the church. St Thomas Aquinas or somebody like that surely had some perspective on this kind of thing. Why God permits evil, whether Gerry is mad or bad, why I pity him when I see him then loathe him afterwards, why I can't just write him a stiff letter telling him I can't cope with him . . . or whether I should do so . . .' She shivered, lighting another cigarette. Gosforth noticed her hands were trembling.

'It's to do with my family. He's something to do with my family, something oppressive. I dream about him. He's always guiding a sealed container lorry into a loading bay . . . with a look of triumph in his eyes.'

Gosforth reached out to her but put his hand on the table instead and started shredding a napkin. Someone in the smoky middle distance near the bar had been playing the one-armed bandit and a shower of coins clattered down to his whoops. Gosforth wondered if he was going too far in hoping that he had found a kindred spirit. 'Aren't you missing something?' he said.

'What?'

'Look, I don't care what sort of DNA he had. Maybe he had a dreadful childhood, who knows? Bad luck. Most of us have something. My parents were divorced but that doesn't make me a child abuser, does it?' He stopped himself, having revealed too much. 'You know something about his form, I expect?'

She shrugged. 'He makes no secret of his past . . . not now. Poor Harriet hadn't a clue, though, not until it was too late . . .'

'That's typical. The old shell game! Ms Hythe . . .'

'Cassie,' she said.

Gosforth beamed uncontrollably.

'Cassie, then. Every day of my life I have to deal with people like this and if you can reach a deeper conclusion than I have, then put it on a postcard and send it to me. Everyone has temptations, some worse than others and usually nothing so frightful as wanting to molest a child. So what do we do with them? We talk ourselves down or go for a walk. We tell ourselves it's wrong . . . at the worst, not expedient. But when Hythe . . . sorry, Gerry . . . had these temptations he acted upon them, again and again.'

Cassie caught her lip in her teeth and laughed. 'So you're a Catholic too, then!'

He shook his head. 'It was in my family but nobody ever bothered about it . . . Look, the point is, they're a special breed, these sex offenders. Often they don't recognise their own motives until it's too late. So how could your friend Harriet or your parents or whoever recognise the signs? They'd probably never met anyone like Gerry.'

'I'm not sure that gets us much further,' Cassie said, a little primly, he thought.

'But they're so manipulative!' He exploded with the exasperation of trying to explain what was unquantifiable to him. 'Can't you see how manipulative they are? Life is all about power to them; sex is meaningless unless it is a matter of control.'

Cassie put her head to one side. 'Do you think they are actually . . . well, evil?'

He frowned in concentration. 'I'm not sure what that means.'

'Nor I,' she said, 'but the Sacred Heart would have failed me if I dismissed it as a category.'

By the time they left the pub, Gosforth, who had promised himself to confine this conversation to an absolute zero of trivia, had given Cassie Hythe a rundown of his deepest aspirations. It appalled him, the kind of male display he was putting on, yet, watching himself as if he were bound and gagged, he was goaded to higher and higher struts. By now, she knew: that he had a degree from UCL; that his subject had been archaeology; that he had his own flat; how it was furnished; what car he drove (a Mazda); that he was aiming to be a governor one day; that he hoped to run an open prison; that his priorities would be education and psychology; that inmates needed to be given responsibility; that they needed to be treated with respect if they were to respect the lives and property of others; and more besides. He liked real ale; he knew the name of the wine she was drinking and why it probably wasn't very nice. Also, he liked baroque music. His name was James.

And as he was not a dishonest man, he sat down that afternoon and wrote a memo to the governor, this time requesting an interview. Whatever else he did, Gosforth was going to see Cassie Hythe again.

By mid-May the Hythes had given up on Harriet and Gerry. Much to Eleni's relief, they began to put Harriet's letter down to her credulity, a sudden enthusiasm that had backfired. She might have made a mistake too embarrassing to correct. Perhaps this Carney fellow had proved to be a con man, a mere predator who had long ago encountered Edgar in some disreputable haunt and hoped to take advantage of the acquaintance. So, six weeks on, they were not expecting a reply to Michael's invitation. When the letter came it was written on lined paper by Gerry Carney and was misspelled.

Dear Uncle Michael,

I got your address off Harriet because she told me you wanted to meet me and asked her and me to stay. I've been thinking about it. She says Im very bitter against my dad and it would be a good idea as long as you know. I called him Edgar. I hope you dont mind. He wanted me to. He told me that nobody in your family would have any use for me exept in the end when he was going to tell his mum because he was skint and a junkie. I dont think you really want to know me because Im a con. Harriet just wants it to be that way.

I dont know if I want to stay. It would take me back but Im curious to. Also its nice of you. I have been a thief but I want to stop so dont be afraid Ill steal your things. I would like to talk about Edgar to someone who knew him. Thanks. Are you sure you want me? Harriet says you didnt know about me and I acept that but dont do it just because you feel guilty about me, okay?

Love Gerry

Michael and Eleni were both keen swimmers. The day the letter arrived they had been on their way to Agios Procropius beach for the first bathing of the season, and so they took it with them, tucking it into the bag with their picnic lunch.

'Well, there it is,' said Michael as he stripped the gears of their antique Fiat that served as a runabout.

'That's for sure,' said his wife, her eyes fixed on the road. The letter had a presence, as if it sizzled in the back seat, melting the cheese in the sandwiches she had made.

'Is there anything to say?' he asked partly as a challenge to her unexpressed disapproval. He might as well have received a communication from the planet Venus.

'Only that Harriet should have written herself, I think,' said Eleni. This clear, hot day was to have been so pleasant.

They chugged past the salt marsh, the pale sea grass undulating in a mild breeze. 'Yes, she should have.' What possible reply could he make to Gerry?

'Does it sound mad to say that she shouldn't have given him our address?' Eleni asked.

He knew the rhetorical note in her voice and that it would ascend. 'I agree I don't like the feeling,' he said to head it off.

'Of course, *he* might be all right, but think of the sort of people he lives with . . . professional burglars, armed robbers . . .'

She had a point.

Abstracted, they parked and trudged across the sand to their favourite spot only to find it occupied by half-naked Germans. In the lee of the mountain, the sea was calm. They walked down the beach, plunged in their umbrella and unfolded the sunbeds. Eleni had a trim figure but in a costume her once-smooth olive skin, always so soft to the touch, now sagged. Ruefully she put on oil, pounding it in as if to eradicate the stigmata of age. She did her husband's thin back with practised skill, rubbing in the oil like a nurse preventing bedsores. The sea was every colour of blue, with inflections of dark cerulean and light azure. The tassels on the umbrella fluttered in the clean breeze.

'It's surreal,' she said at length. 'How can he be Edgar's son? And write like that?'

Michael needed her.

What had he expected from Gerry anyway? Certainly not this. Why did it trouble him? How he wished he was at the farm so that he could take it into his study there, just letting it lie for a while, absorbing it. And yet he took his wife's capable hand, pressing it for want of anything to say.

Why indeed had Harriet passed their address on to Gerry? Of course it was irrational to object, because he had already issued an invitation to Gerry. Still, it made him feel uncomfortable.

No, that wasn't what bothered him. His imagination wandered back into the drawing room of the Kastro house. The large, airy space with its ancient beams, its ordering, its tranquillity never failed to comfort him. On the east wall hung a portrait of his great-grandmother, the daughter of an earl. It was a good picture; the artist had also painted Tennyson. The sleek loops of his ancestress's hair framed a delicate oval face, her wasp waist with the rich puff of silk skirt made her look a bit like an inverted flower. This was the great-great-grandmother of the author of the smudged, untutored letter.

Was this snobbery? He hoped not, for he had always detested it. Edgar, of course, had been a howling snob; if nothing else, a gentleman. And there really had been nothing else.

A memory of Edgar came to him now. Why it provided a link with the sad little letter from Gerry he could not tell except that it was as disjunctive. Edgar had possessed a formidable charm. No matter how low he sank, he seemed to wave from the depths with an immaculately gloved hand. In his way, he'd had atrocious manners, an upper-class vanity, that way of making others feel small beside him, small and less interesting. He suggested a Nietzschean superiority where he broke rules by a sort of divine right, rules that others were expected to keep. Perhaps this was why the knowledge that Edgar's son was semi-educated came as a particular shock.

As if reading his thoughts, Eleni said, 'Edgar had enough money all right! Do you think it ever occurred to him? Surely his child meant something to him? Couldn't he have . . .?'

But she did not need to finish the sentence. Edgar's money had been something of a sore point, particularly with Godfrey, because his chaos had funnelled so much of it from the common purse. Their mother poured cheque after cheque into the Edgar project until she was finally persuaded that it did more harm than good and the trust was set up. Even then, Edgar could have provided a good school for Gerry. So it was hardly Gerry's fault that he didn't know where an apostrophe went.

Michael shook his head. There was no point in laying blame anywhere, not till he knew more. Maybe this Carney woman had got hold of money Edgar had given her to educate Gerry. Still . . .

Eleni opened a small bottle of retsina and offered some to Michael in a plastic cup. His stomach churned and he shook his head.

There was something disturbing, too, about the paper the note was written on, clearly standard prison issue, grey with a blue bar across the top. Even though it had travelled all the way to Greece, the note had a distinctive odour. Was it boiled cabbage? And then there was the writing with its sharp wedges crossing the 't's as if a heavy humour hit the writer from time to time during what seemed to be a laboured composition. What surprised him – upset him – was the gracelessness of the reply.

'I'll swim first,' he said and he waded into the water, still not fully warmed from winter. Inch by inch he bathed ankles then knees.

Was this really Edgar's son? He supposed it must be. His brother came to mind full blown as if he had been there biding his time all along for this hidden key to turn the lock.

It must have been during the winter when Michael was working on a small, smart block of flats in Battersea that a sudden fog had come down so thick one evening that he couldn't get back to Ashdean. He was not sure why he decided to call on Edgar. By this time, they had minimal contact. But it hit him as an impulse and he crossed the river, virtually feeling his way on foot all the way to Pimlico to beg shelter for the night from his brother.

Edgar lived in crummy splendour near the old Casa Pupo, which had sold those hideous rugs, once so smart, and thick peasant china at an inflated price. Michael made up a script, even though he didn't have to, about how he had little money on him and could not afford to sit out the weather in an hotel. He supposed it was curiosity rather than anything else that induced him to find out how Edgar lived. In some part of himself, Michael was impatient with the shibboleth his family had made out of Edgar.

He rang the bell for so long that he nearly turned away, but eventually Edgar answered the door. Michael was surprised at how pleased his brother was to see him, secretly touched, he thought, that he had been appealed to in a crisis. He walked in expecting an opium den, walls blackened with smoke, the floor strewn with needles and ordure, but the appurtenances of Edgar's habit that he'd imagined – rubber tourniquets, carved boxes holding glass straws and white stuff – were clearly tucked away. To gauge by other times, he was only slightly stoned. He had been writing a poem, he said; but added that Michael was not to confuse himself with the man from Porlock, it was hardly *Kubla Khan*. He said this in a self-deprecating way that in no way reflected his true opinion of his talents, Michael was sure. Edgar considered himself another Baudelaire and often boasted that he was on the verge of publication.

From their mother's description of the place, an active squalor should have overflowed the sink, tumbled from cupboard doors, scrunched up filthy sheets and smeared the bathroom with sticky hairs. It was a bit more chaotic than mere bachelor's mess, but it could have been a lot worse. Edgar even found some clean sheets. The walls were painted scarlet, the mantel black and there was a small, perhaps valuable collection of theatrical tinsel pictures. Edgar offered him a joint and only shrugged when he refused; he didn't bother lighting up himself. They had a supper of scrambled eggs on toast and Edgar cooked it. The evening was remarkable for being so ordinary. He began to think, as he slipped into a pair of his brother's pyjamas, that Edgar's addiction had been greatly exaggerated or that Ashdean set him off, pushed buttons in his skull that made him explode into those sarcastic rages they all dreaded.

While they were eating breakfast the next day he noticed a box of toys shoved next to a pottery bread bin. Whose were they? he asked. Perhaps Edgar was quietly screaming for a fix, for he snapped at Michael to mind his own business . . . then apologised. He had a girlfriend ('Don't tell Mummy. She wouldn't approve. Not Quite Our Class, Dear') and she had a kid who had to be entertained.

Out of this longer memory, it was only this moment of Edgar's face and voice that he retrieved so sharply. A rare pleasant time between two brothers dissipated like the fog that had cleared overnight.

The idea of a girlfriend had puzzled Michael then, as it did now. Up to the waist in cold water he struck out, and in the shock of freezing purity his mind cleared. Even poor wretched Queen Maeve, whose Catholic piety had been distinctly conservative, even ultramontanist, had put forward Edgar's struggle with his sexuality as a reason for his habit, but she only used it as a stick with which to beat herself. All of it had to do with her failure as a mother, and so she lost sight of who Edgar really was.

He pushed the salt water vigorously from his chest, in and out, flailing his legs in an effort to keep warm. Beneath him little fish darted casually in the clear shallows. Maybe Gerry had been the owner of that stash of toys. Not Edgar's son at all; his mother might have been merely a supplier. A child could learn an awful lot from overhearing adult conversations. And yet Harriet had mentioned a birth certificate. And would Edgar really have kept Action Man and Dinky toys for someone else's child?

He decided that his dip had been long enough, and floundering to the shore towelled himself off.

'You're not going to brood too much, are you?' Eleni said sharply. He shook his head. Ever since his depression, she had monitored his moods like an ECG. He had been hospitalised and it was fair to say that Edgar's death, no matter how tangentially, had set it off.

And it was true to say, too, that this isolated memory now did seem a harbinger of that disturbing melancholy that sometimes opened up beneath his conscious mind. The icy water that had just buoyed him up in the sea seemed to have lingered in his veins, penetrating his chest. He lay full in the sun and closed his eyes. There was nothing for it but to telephone Harriet and find out more before he made a very cautious reply to Gerry's letter.

13

HARRIET WAS FINDING IT DIFFICULT to sleep and this was something new. She had started nodding off during the news; a soporific heaviness deadened her mind so that she could hardly drag herself to bed. The moment she lay down she would crash into a deep slumber for a couple of hours, then wake with a start as if someone were in the room. The first few times it happened, she was convinced that someone had broken in. The illusion was very real that an intruder had cut the telephone wires and was moving inexorably towards her bedroom. Harriet would lie there petrified, unable to move or cry out.

Maybe it was a consequence of her visits to the prison, but she began to think nervously that, these days, even very elderly women got raped or beaten up. A report on *Crimewatch*, which she could no longer bear to switch on, had recently shown a reconstruction of the murder of a woman about her age. A devout Christian, she had been bludgeoned to death by a down-and-out she'd befriended.

The bout of insomnia, coinciding as it did with Michael Hythe's telephone call from Greece, seemed to have an obvious cause. Once she had convinced herself that the 'burglar' only embodied her fears about taking Gerry to Naxos, she decided to weather it and not bother the doctor for tablets.

Harriet wondered if instead she should talk to a priest, but now that the old canon had retired she no longer liked going to confession. She needed someone who could really understand her and it was difficult to talk to Father Luke, who was so young. Last time he had been dismissive, she thought, giving her one Hail Mary.

Soon after she had started to visit Gerry, she had been spurred to seek his advice because she'd had an embarrassing dream, but when it came to the point, on her knees and in the dark, she found she couldn't mention it. One could hardly take responsibility for a dream, after all! So she had floundered, unable to get to the nub of her unease.

It was difficult to say what it was. Generally, Harriet was not prey to sexual desire. More specifically, there was something off-putting about Gerry in that respect, though she could not define it. No, there was something else that wormed away at her; it was like an undertow deep within herself, almost beyond her conscious thought, that sucked her into Gerry, as if he were the cold, impersonal moon and she the tide.

She had ended up telling the priest she was helping a poor prisoner and she was getting a bit too involved. Was it right? Father Luke clearly wasn't able to grasp what she was on about. All he could do was counsel detachment. One mustn't take oneself too seriously, he told her, and this had hurt her feelings.

But it was Michael Hythe who preoccupied her now as she coiled around in sweaty sheets. Was she imagining that he sounded agitated on the phone? Especially after he had initially given her so much encouragement about Gerry, it was a bit much that he seemed to be having second thoughts! Not that he put it that way. In fact, he had such wonderful manners that only later she realised the extent to which she had been driven to justifying herself. At the end of the call, she'd been dry at the mouth and exhausted. Well, everything she'd told him was true, wasn't it? Why then did she feel so furtive?

An odd effect of hearing Michael's disembodied voice was how it recalled Ashdean, as if neither of them had ever really left it. When she moved to London, Harriet found it disturbing that blank spaces occurred in her mind's eye when she tried to recall certain specific things that had been recently commonplace to her. Now, she couldn't get the village out of her head.

These recollections flooded back but fitfully, in an oddly disjointed way. Her sensation was that she was seeing Ashdean accurately for the very first time. The prison had done that. So had Gerry. How could she have been so blinkered, and for so many years, to the sort of harsh reality that he had been forced to suffer? It filled her with shame now that she had accepted the ethos of privilege enshrined in every aspect of village life without ever once questioning it.

On her night voyages, Harriet seemed to fly weightless over Ashdean, looking in at windows, hovering invisibly in drawing rooms where snobbery and parochial stupidity were like escutcheons flaunted with pride. A bit like Wendy escorted by Peter Pan, Gerry managed her return as animus and guide. In his company, the contours of the village were shockingly changed for her now.

What a wonderful place it was to bring up children! Everyone said that. In fact, she and Averell had decided to live in Ashdean for this very reason. Whatever she said about it now, Emma had had an idyllic childhood, winning rosettes at gymkhanas, gambolling about the orchards.

It wouldn't have been quite so idyllic for Gerry. Not with his accent, not with his slatternly mum. Suppose Edgar had honoured his obligations, taken his son on, introduced him to the village. 'Ghastly little oik!' she could hear her neighbours thinking, smug in their dozy Eden. Not that they would have said it. They would have acted on the thought instead, excluding him.

She supposed that was harsh, but it felt good to be angry. Why hadn't she admitted before how angry she was? With her new vision of things, the very hops on the vines and the apples on the trees seemed plumped up with hypocrisy. She hoped she was not becoming a socialist.

Harriet had never been good at answering the questions she asked herself. She would ponder over them doggedly, as if chewing a pencil at a difficult exam. She wondered now if this new indignation she felt against Ashdean had some connection with Michael Hythe. Maybe she was really angry with him. As this would be most unfair, she decided that she could not be. He had every right to question her about Gerry. And his worst enemy could never call Michael smug or a hypocrite.

His call had come just as Harriet had been on her way out to Marks and Spencer, but it had been an hour before she put down the phone and by that time she'd forgotten what she wanted there.

Thinking about it now and rationally, Harriet rummaged around the conversation trying to put it in some sort of order. One would have imagined that finding a long-lost nephew in prison would preoccupy Michael more than anything, but it seemed to be Edgar's concealment of Gerry that really upset him. Why he took it as a slight on his mother she could not fathom. 'She adored children!' Michael's voice across the wire had been tense with emotion. 'Edgar knew that. She would have dropped everything to help the little boy, look after him. She would have sold the family silver rather than think he wanted for anything!' And though Harriet agreed with him, saying that this was her reading of Maeve Hythe's character, it hardly seemed the point.

Most nights Harriet had to get out of bed, make a cup of tea and stare at the milky fluid until it went cold while chunks of memory went by like overloaded carriages on a slow-moving freight train. There she was, back in Ashdean, making tarte tatin for the cake sale and nobody bought it. Her campaign for a mobile library fell flat. Harriet knew she tried too hard, but she couldn't stop driving herself. She had never really fitted in, and that was the truth.

She had been a great one for dinner parties. Although Averell provided her with a cook, she had taught herself a lot and liked to dabble. At one time, she toyed with the idea of doing the Cordon Bleu course and setting up a business. If only she had! At least she would have something now. But Averell didn't like his wife to work. That didn't stop him from asking her what she did with herself all day, but never mind. It was what she didn't do at night that really bothered him. The more time she lavished on perfecting the house and the food, the less likely it was that she would have to offend him by refusing what he too often so urgently wanted. She could simply conk out, knowing that the success of these social occasions made him proud of her, an idea he could cling to instead of her. Why he put her off so, she never could understand. It was shameful to her that she was so indifferent to what everyone else seemed so mad about, but the act itself was more humiliating still, not the sort of love she had imagined and longed for as a girl. Never mind, she thought. There was no point in raking over that now.

Harriet realised how much she had changed since the divorce, and for the better. She looked back with a shudder at garden parties on the trimmed lawn and at the meals she served on a table polished to a mirror shine. She had always tried to make these occasions special, a bit above the common run. Although she wouldn't have admitted it, she would have loved it if one of the Sunday papers, having heard about her parties, had come down to Ashdean to photograph her house, print her recipes, ask for her secrets, hints and tips. She masterminded menus, instructing the dowdy cook in the use of novel ingredients long before they became fashionable. Harriet discovered sun-dried tomatoes before anyone else, and once she decided to serve smoked eel on a bed of samphire as the first course to an Elizabethan dinner party.

Samphire was hardly staple fare in Ashdean's greengrocery and it had been Helen Hythe's bright idea that Harriet might find some on the Marsh, where long ago it had been collected as a delicacy. They decided to make a day of it, driving out in the direction of Dungeness where Helen had heard that someone sold the stuff. Thinking about it, Harriet could not see why the memory of this jaunt kept bobbing through into conscious focus now. It was a bit like a tune that insists itself and becomes maddening.

Perhaps it was the prospect of seeing Helen again, but there were many other memories to sort and shuffle. It was probably something to do with the strange and dream-like quality of the place.

That day Harriet and Helen had started out early. They'd have a pub lunch, enjoy the air that blew so fresh in from the Channel over the dykes that shored the land from the sea. There had been another motive for Helen to make the trip, and Harriet could not quite remember what it was. Ah yes, it had to do with *King Lear*, in which samphire played a part. Could Helen have wanted the Am Dram group to put on *Lear*?

Harriet had no sense of direction. Once they had left the familiar lanes near Ashdean behind them, she found herself confused. Descending into the Marsh, they drove along flat, wind-blasted roads bordered by ditches, where fields of pale reeds undulated in the wind. The scene was wild, almost romantic, with grey towering clouds and gusts of fine rain.

What an odd day it had been. Helen, usually garrulous and cheerful, seemed edgy, obscurely upset when Harriet lost her way. Harriet forbore to point out that Helen had no idea of the exact location, or the name of the place they were looking for. She just kept on saying she would know it when she saw it. The more they trundled across the chessboard of fields and reeds, the more they strayed from their objective, a farm shop stuck in the middle of nowhere. Apparently the farmer engaged in what Shakespeare described as 'the dreadful trade' of gathering and selling samphire. Harriet reminded Helen about how they had laughed that a mere vegetable could have appeared in so dire a light in great tragedy, and this somewhat restored her good humour.

In the warm car they began to relax, chatting about this and that, then, for some reason, Harriet mentioned Maeve Hythe. At this, Helen became abrupt, finally admitting that she'd used Harriet's exotic shopping spree as an excuse to get out of Ashdean for the day. Her mother-in-law was driving her wild. Edgar had just been to visit and this always meant an intense post-mortem with his every word dissected, his every motive scrutinised. If

Maeve would only let him alone, Helen cried, maybe he would sort himself out.

They jaunted on and Harriet, distracted by Helen's voluble critique of Maeve, took a wrong turning. She found herself driving down a spit of land fringed with dune grass, heading towards the sea. They had overshot their mark and somehow reached Dungeness. The nuclear power station was dead ahead.

Harriet stopped the car. A tall chain fence with razor wire postulated some heavy investment in security, but the gate was open so that she could have driven in if she had wanted to. There wasn't a mortal soul in sight. For a moment, she and Helen stared, dwarfed and helpless, at the plant with its lethal Martian look. Weird white spheres like gigantic, bulbous fungi ballooned above them, oddly graceful against the March sky, and the mighty honeycombed towers of the power station hummed before them, self-generating and bizarre as if its efficient working had no need of human intervention.

Harriet put the car in reverse and turned to Helen to apologise for her mistake but, much to her surprise and embarrassment, she realised that her friend was crying. She braked. 'What is it?' she asked, thinking that she must have underestimated Helen's concern for ecological sanity.

'Have you ever wished anyone dead?' Helen said, oblivious to her own tears, it seemed. She seemed more like an Eleni now, intense and Greek. Her eyes were trained on the power plant.

The passions were foreign to Harriet. 'No,' she said. 'Not really,' she added, so as not to sound judgmental.

'If I thought I could limit the damage to my in-laws, I'd set a torch to this place and blow it up. With particular attention to the blessed Maeve's bloody knot garden! "Nuke the lot," as your Averell would say. That's what should be done.'

Even at the time, this outburst seemed extraordinary to Harriet. Now, thinking about it, it seemed odder still. The words were flamboyant enough, but Eleni's tone, the set of her jaw, shocked Harriet in a way that melodrama never could. Helen turned and glanced at Harriet, smiled slightly as if to her incomprehension, then deftly opened her handbag from which she withdrew a tissue to wipe her eyes. 'Samphire?' she said. 'Let's get some.'

Harriet retraced the route; they drove on away from the sea in their quest for the maritime vegetable which, ultimately, they found. But the image of the monolithic nuclear plant that ticked and droned, dividing atoms on the salt flats, stayed with her as minatory, a factory for deranging and displacing the tiniest components of life.

During her nightly vigils Harriet first struggled to make some sense of this and other disconnected memories, then tried to avoid them altogether. It was a bit like sorting out drawers after someone had died. The temptation was to shove it all into a suitcase and stick it in a loft. In the end, she decided that she would look at it all at some later stage. It didn't do to become too introspective.

In any case, she told herself, her main task was to help Gerry make contact with his family. What was the point of picking over the past when she was presented with so worthy a goal? As for Michael's remaining reservations, there seemed little point in distressing Gerry with them now. He needed confidence to face the Hythes, not the sense that they doubted or mistrusted him in any way.

During her talk with Michael she had managed to clear a few things up. She really ought to be pleased with herself, she thought, the way she had established Gerry as a Hythe beyond Michael's second-thought doubts. Armed with Gerry's memories about Edgar's random visits to him as a child, she was able to build a credible picture. There were facts here that only an intimate of Edgar could have known. She didn't mention the violence. There seemed no need, especially when her delicate allusions to how troubling Edgar had been to Gerry seemed to make Michael wince. He recognised his brother's hand in this, all right. She could tell by the long silence that ensued. Nor did it seem too difficult in the end to convince him that the combined chaos of Edgar and Mary Carney was too great for them to form any plan as concrete as the introduction of Gerry to his grand-parents. The sober and awful truth was that Edgar had not been able to focus long enough on the boy's care to do this. What was more, it was hard to see how the mother was lying about Gerry's paternity when the family resemblance was so striking.

Poor Michael had floundered on over the wire. He hated to say it, but he did have a responsibility to Eleni. She was not as com-fortable as he was about . . . well . . . Were Gerry's crimes such that they had to be at all worried? After all they had been through with Edgar, Eleni was particularly concerned about drugs. And Gerry's letter to them had not made him sound really keen to visit Naxos, had it? Frankly, if it were optional to Gerry and if Gerry were dangerous in any way . . . He let his words trail feebly off from ending nearly any sentence that he spoke.

'Drugs! Good Lord, no!' she had cried. Gerry had a horror of them! And as for being dangerous, well, they only had to meet him. She felt perfectly safe with him – perfectly! In fact, it was a stretch of imagination to believe that he was in gaol at all. He liked to talk about gardens. He was a gardener – with green fingers like his grandmother. He told her he'd got into bad company but he was finished with all of that.

Gerry's spirit seemed to whirl through her as she spoke, almost as if she had allowed it to collect in the depths of her own soul, like ectoplasm waiting to be released by a medium. Other-wise how had she been so eloquent about him? Hectic spots formed on her cheeks as she justified him. *Of course*, he wanted to meet them! Maybe he had expressed himself awkwardly, but what could they expect? He had been so hurt, so let down. Wasn't it better that he was honest with them? He had to learn to trust – a slow process after the prison, the children's homes, the bad schools and the foster parents. He wanted to be accepted all right, but for the man he was, not the man he could have been if things had worked out differently. All of this tumbled out of Harriet as if she were a dedicated social worker called as a witness for the defence in the trial of a delinquent child. It ended in a passionate plea for Gerry.

In the end, Michael agreed to answer Gerry's letter generously. They ended up by setting a provisional date for the visit. Of course, Harriet would undertake to come too? This was understood?

Before Harriet realised what she had done, she had set herself up as Gerry's guarantor. It would have to work out, she thought when she had put down the phone. She would make it work, wouldn't she?

Somehow she had not expected Michael's reply to be so swift. On her next visit to the prison, Gerry was in a state of high excitement. His eyes glittered over Harriet as if he were about to cry. Without saying a word, he took out his uncle's promised letter and, unfolding it with an exquisite care upon the lino table, gave it to her to read.

My dear Gerry,

Thank you so much for your letter. It affected me deeply to hear from you. I think it only natural that you should be anxious meeting your father's relations. Edgar must have been a difficult parent, and there is no sense in pretending otherwise. I do assure you that we had no knowledge of your existence and this in itself must be painful for you to contemplate, for my brother should have told us about you. He must have known we would have been willing to help in every way.

Our invitation to you has nothing to do with assuaging guilt. It is my genuine hope that we can talk, perhaps in a way that will help both of us. Naxos is a beautiful island and a good place to recover from the pain of your present situation.

Best wishes,
Yours ever,
Michael Hythe

It was the first time Harriet had seen Gerry look fully alive. His shoulders were thrust back so as to give him nearly an inch of height. His voice seemed lower, more resonant and, though he always smiled to see her, there was a depth of expression in his eyes. It surprised her to realise that he had never before looked fully at her. Their visit was spent in her listening to his busy plans.

In the prison library he had found a book on Greece, and he had pored over it. The pictures of bright blue sky and water, of bleached, white, ancient marbles, of crumbling castles and leaping dolphins, of old churches with pictures of saints that looked wise . . . all of this he thought of, dreaming of it.

It was a lovely June day. Even the grimy windows of the Visitors' Room could not conceal the perfect weather. Harriet's eyes kept drifting for some reason to the pools of sunlight that fell through a high transom. Gerry kept touching the letter, convulsively talking. Why did she feel empty? Usually she clung on to the last moments of the visit and now she kept wanting to get up and go, out into the early summer sunshine. She felt drained, but stayed as she always stayed until the officers started to make the move to collect the men and return them to their cells.

As she turned to go, an odd look stole over Gerry's face. Harriet stopped, suddenly alert. 'Are you all right?' she asked him.

'D'you think he knows anything about Greek vases . . . my uncle? What do you reckon? Edgar was keen enough. You could say they were his hobby and I learnt a lot from him.' There was enough turmoil in his eyes to give her the effect of a mild electric shock.

'I don't understand what you mean.'

'Well, you know, bowls and that with pictures of men . . . drinking . . . myths and stories.' Gerry's eyes shifted away.

'Michael's an architect, not an archaeologist. Why don't you ask him? He probably knows something about vases, living there.' She didn't mean her voice to sound cold, but it came out distorted in this way.

179

Gerry shook his head sharply as if trying to dislodge something in his ear. 'It don't matter. It's nothing,' he said. *'Doesn't* matter. Edgar was pretty strong on that too. English. Grammar.'

And perhaps it was this last troubling moment that further disturbed her sleep, making her restless and afraid.

Now that Gerry was out of danger, they had put him in a side room off the ward in order to accommodate the officers who came on a rota to sit by his bed and ensure he did not bolt. He even had a private bathroom. In order to use it he had to be unshackled and then shackled again when he was finished. There was telly and whichever officers were in charge stared at it all day, except for Mr Grimston, who was a crossword fanatic. They saw *Casablanca*, snooker, Gary Rhodes and Oprah Winfrey, who featured victims of child abuse.

Gerry asked if he could have a Bible. He did not know what sense to make of the heart attack, but it had felt like being an insect thrown against a giant windscreen. The pain had been intolerable. He felt something inside him had changed, not the heart – something else. But then how could it have changed anything? His stroke, years ago in Greece, had changed nothing but his body, racking his limbs, slowing him down, greying his hair. Then, he had been conscious, though paralysed, and able to hear the British consul wishing him dead. This time, they wouldn't operate on him for fear of strokes . . . or was that their excuse? The terror ate him up, but it made him feel very alert.

He had read the Bible once before – not all of it, of course. After his second offence, when he was very young, he had thought turning to God might help. Religion helped you get parole, but that was not the only reason. He realised that he was becoming like Edgar.

The first time he wanted a boy had taken him completely by surprise and so what happened then could have been an accident. He was only sixteen. He'd had a couple of illicit pints at lunch for the head gardener's leaving party and he wasn't used to drink.

He'd stumbled into the park toilet to take a leak. The boy was too old to cry, and maybe this was why he had taken shelter in the toilet. He had a tough-looking crew cut and a sallow bullet face, but he had grazed his knee in the paddling pool and he was crying and peeing at the same time, his bathing shorts round his ankles. One thing led to another and Gerry was ashamed, even though he had been let off with a caution later because there was no evidence other than the boy's witness. Besides, he was only a kid himself. In those days, the word 'paedophile' belonged in textbooks, not to the tabloids.

But the second time was by design . . . and it didn't seem so wrong when he was doing it. After all, it wasn't buggery because he, of all people, knew how painful that could be and he would never hurt a child. What was more, he started being honest with himself. Even though Edgar had terrified him, hurt him and sometimes revolted him, there had been times he'd craved the touch, the attention. Once in a while, he'd wondered if it was love, his body in an uproar like that.

He was hurt . . . hurting. For a long time he contained the fantasies, but bit by bit they built to an insupportable level. He tried to but could not forget the exquisite first time which grew in his memory, with which he solaced himself through lonely nights in Elephant and Castle where the council had managed to get him a flat. Edgar was dead, his mother didn't want to know, he was thought to be useless at school and he was too old for children's homes at eighteen. He became a Socrates with ancient wisdom in his engorged senses. It was only modern prudery that decreed he should desire the voluptuous girls with pert breasts, girls who sneered at him from posters on the Underground. The spare delicacy, the pure athleticism of a boy's body challenged the vulgarity of women, their engulfing, distressing fleshiness. Gerry began to hoard pictures, even tearing some out of library books; he took up swimming in the local baths at weekends and school holidays. He kept telling himself he was only looking and would never touch again, but the thought of another opportunity spiked his mind like gin, adding a buzz and a fizz to every aspect of life. When the delicious moment of surrender came, he got caught. The trial was oddly wonderful, the judge in his ponderous wig, his brief defending him, the appalled jury. It was like having a drama put on, one that he had scripted but in which he seemed to have no real role except that it was all about him.

Prison was different. From the moment the cell door closed on him, he had been in a state of shock. He would have topped himself but for the Anglican chaplain, Church Army, a nice old geezer who took the trouble to seek him out; he didn't moralise at Gerry. All of us were sinners, he told him. If Gerry came to the foot of the Cross he would be saved. So even though he'd never been baptised, which the vicar wanted him to be, Gerry did Bible studies and attended services, but what the Cross was and where its foot stood in relation to himself, he never learned. All he derived from his reading was the knowledge that a millstone should be tied around his neck and he should be cast in the sea . . . albeit that the chaplain talked about grace and they all sang how amazing it was. God knew how long ago that was, almost thirty years he reckoned.

Mr Grimston laughed when Gerry asked for the Bible. He was an atheist and said we'd all end up in the dustbin sooner or later. He did get the Good Book, though, from the sister who kept a copy presumably for extreme situations, for it was brand new and never cracked.

Gerry turned to the Book of Revelation. He flipped through. There was a sea of glass, a beast with horns, angels with vials, a whore, a woman clothed with sun, a dragon . . . and then a pure river, the water of life.

Though he could not make head or tail of it, it struck him that there could be neither head nor tail to something as final as a time when history stopped. The end of the world must be, he reasoned, the end of history. Time stopped . . . and a chaos of images ensued.

Gerry wondered if he had died during his heart attack and been brought back. He'd read about out-of-body experiences but he didn't think he'd had one of those, which were all to do with lights and tunnels and happy relatives in gardens. He felt, rather, that he had returned from a long journey. Everything looked different to him, even the officers who, all of a sudden, seemed human. He was in a heightened state of awareness. Living things, the tree outside his window for instance, seemed precious, precarious, to be treasured as ephemeral. He was grateful for the taste of water.

The Bible was a good weight in his hands. He riffled through its pages quizzically, hoping that his eyes would lock on to some verse or phrase. The words seemed like fractured light, prismatic, not solid. He could not concentrate on them, but if he closed his eyes, there was a jumble of images. He was surprised at how much of it had to do with healing. That's what he took out of it anyway.

Gerry took to theological argumentations with Mr Grimston, who seemed willing to put down his puzzle for the sake of a good debate. The other officer simply gazed at the TV. Gerry wasn't saying there was anything to religion, but supposing there was?

Mr Grimston emphasised the here and now. Why didn't Gerry go to work on his offending behaviour pattern when he got back to Grisholme? See the psychologists. Try to get his head sorted. That was a proof of remorse, wasn't it?

Gerry said he had not been thinking about remorse, but about Heaven. If there was one he wanted to go there.

'With your form?' said the officer and returned to his brain-teaser from the *Telegraph*.

Gerry wondered if he should be baptised and asked to see the hospital chaplain. Before the priest could arrive, however, Gerry had the stroke they had feared and was back in intensive care.

14

HARRIET HAD BEEN PUTTING OFF her obligation to invite Boo to dinner. Boo was very busy of course. Now they had screened the first of her three documentaries about prisons, she was much in demand, so much so that she had farmed out Jolly Labrador to her son in Fulham rather than burden Harriet further.

Boo's vivid character travelled well across the airwaves. BBC2 was thrilled that the controversy she provoked bumped up viewing figures. Harriet had to admit that she was impressed, awed at times, by Boo's instinctive touch with the medium. She stuck to a simple message and refused to let it get hijacked by the slender girl presenter who looked as if she had a string of degrees. No one, no matter what atrocity he or she had committed, was beyond redemption, Boo said. This was bottom-line Christianity. Not according to some viewers, whose angry letters said she was a dangerous fool, or worse. An equal number hailed her as a gin-slinging saint.

Boo was no diplomat. Women's groups seethed at her careless remarks about rape. The NSPCC did not think it helpful to hear child abusers described as modern-day lepers who shouldn't have to wear bells round their necks. One hated the sin but loved the sinner, Boo said. Even murderers could be quite ordinary people who had been driven beyond endurance.

Harriet privately drew a firm line at some of Boo's more out-rageous statements. Someone who hurt a child could never be forgiven, surely. Still, Harriet remained loyal to Boo whose qualifying remarks had been ignored by hostile reviewers of the first programme. If anyone had asked Harriet, she would have told them that Boo was pretty tough on crime but didn't believe that criminals should be written off. The raves balanced it, and Harriet cut a good one from *The Times* and slipped it through Boo's letterbox.

When she had finished filming, Boo went off to Tuscany for a few weeks with an old schoolchum. By the time she returned, Harriet had decided to have all the curtains and upholstery cleaned (partly because she was at last rid of the dog). She wasn't feeling very well . . . nothing serious, just not a hundred per cent. Maybe she was just ageing . . . she'd always been vain, she told herself; she found herself peering in the mirror a lot. Crows' feet were definitely collecting around her eyes and the poor sleep was making dark circles under them. She decided to take herself in hand and sought advice from the creamy ladies at Peter Jones whose cosmetic counters she haunted. She invested in a really heavy-duty moisturiser and a booster for fine lines around the eyes. Her guilt at the expense was part of a covert thrill she always took in the rich scents, the gold packaging. At the hairdresser's she flipped through *Vogue* to study an article on the miraculous effect of safflower oil. Her eye lit on an advertisement for Haven Hall. Harriet had never considered a health farm before, but she toyed with the idea until she picked up the telephone and found herself booking a week's break.

It was only six weeks before she and Gerry took off for Naxos and that would be no holiday. Best to get herself in shape.

It was bliss! They kneaded her, steamed her and pampered her. Her nails had never looked so good. A dietician made her see sense about her weight: she had become too thin. They piled on the calories and gave her a programme of exercise. She walked the muted corridors in her white silk kimono to mud baths and re-read P. D. James. She had knots in her neck like fists when she arrived, but as the week went by they loosened. She had the vague sensation that she was recovering from a major operation. The divorce, the move, the new interest in prison visiting had all taken their toll, she reckoned.

A sleek paramedic in a white coat recommended a herbal remedy for insomnia: it worked! They also coaxed her into aromatherapy. Harriet clutched her lamp and essential oils, rushing with them back to her room like a child on Christmas morning. The tranquil aura of medicinal frankincense and myrrh permeated her room while she napped. It was only the resident osteopath she didn't like. He dropped a hint that maybe some counselling was in order, for stress. Harriet decided that she'd had her bones cracked quite enough, thank you. Then she met a charming threesome in need of a fourth for bridge.

She fizzed back to Chelsea, ready for anything. If only she could afford Haven Hall more often! In its tranquil, scented cloisters she had felt completely safe. It seemed extraordinary to think it, but her life had been like one long siege. She had been the lonely child of critical parents who regarded her as an inconvenience. Her marriage to an insensitive man had isolated her even more. What had she always been so afraid of? A failure to measure up, perhaps. At Haven Hall, cool professional hands had soothed her; she could lose herself in the lovely big grounds where no one could reach her to judge or criticise. For once, since she had met him, Gerry and his prison seemed far away. The intensity of her involvement with him began to look a bit absurd and a lot of it seemed to vaporise in the Turkish bath.

Her batteries thus recharged, Harriet decided it was time to tackle Boo. Apart from anything else, Boo had dropped a hint after Sunday Mass. 'I *never* seem to see you any more. I *do* miss our little times together!'

She had promised herself that she would sound Boo out, and at Haven Hall it really had seemed a good idea that she should. When the major developments occurred between Gerry and the Hythes, Boo had first been out of town and then out of the country. Now the prospect of the trip was doing Gerry so much good that Boo might very well be pleased. She might even praise Harriet for using initiative.

After all, the Hythes now seemed very keen to meet Gerry. And Harriet was a very old friend of theirs. She supposed that if Boo reacted badly she could always cancel. But not if she behaved stupidly! Harriet was set to purchase the tickets in a few days' time, having tracked down a special deal from Olympic Airways.

Apart from anything else, Harriet was beginning to feel a little socially awkward about just hailing her friend at church then beetling off. Boo had brought her a silk stole a few months ago as a thank you for minding the dog. Harriet had of course written her a note for the expensive gift, but good manners dictated something a little more than that, and she had noticed that Boo looked just a little bit hurt when she mentioned how long it was since they had properly met. She flushed when she thought of it. She did not want Boo to get the idea that she was in any way jealous of the fame the telly had brought her. So she issued an invitation, and with a flourish – they were to celebrate the success of the series! This way, she wouldn't have to talk about Gerry if she didn't feel entirely comfortable about it.

As the day approached, however, the idea of spending a whole evening with Boo made her increasingly anxious. An old dread, which she hadn't thought about for years, came to her in fitful dreams. She was a young actress again, and playing a scene that was crucial to an important play. A first-night audience, spiked with critics, lurked in the dark behind footlights. She opened her mouth, but nothing came from it but a thin wail, and she woke in a sweat.

A celebration was to be a celebration, though, and Harriet outdid herself, marinating a rack of lamb, fiddling the shells off quails' eggs for a piquant first course involving rocket and all sorts of other things. She slaved over a crème brûlée. She went all the way to Berry's for the wine; she starched and ironed the damask napkins so that they puffed up like soufflés. The silver was in a shocking state. How had she let it get so tarnished? She supposed before Haven Hall she had been mildly depressed, but now her energy was on overdrive. Boo survived entirely on microwave meals, used paper napkins if she used napkins at all. She would have been thrilled with poached eggs on toast, provided there was enough drink. Still, Harriet felt goaded on to greater excesses of grandeur.

The morning of the tête-à-tête dinner party, Harriet received a letter from Emma. She was coming to London in September. Would her mother put her up for a few days? Unfortunately, Tom had to be at school so he was staying with his father, but Emma was doing an interview with Salman Rushdie for the *New York Times* . . . 'a big deal' for her. She thought she'd broken into the magic circle.

For some reason this agitated Harriet terribly, especially as Emma's letter was an affectionate one, a surprise in itself. She said she been thinking a lot lately, and wanted to spend some time with her mum. It was the sort of reconciling letter Harriet had prayed for, a sign that maybe Emma was finally growing up.

But Harriet would be in Naxos with Gerry.

She could hardly change her plans now, with only a month to go. She walked round the drawing room waving the airmail paper in her tarnish-covered gloves. Harriet caught sight of Emma's face in the one framed photographic portrait she had. Her pugnacious jaw, unsmiling mouth and bold eyes seemed to follow Harriet around the room. Harriet had longed for a baby girl to dress up, not a tough tomboy.

Well, there would be time enough to make up for the letter she'd have to write telling Emma she was going to be away. She smiled to herself. There was no reason that Emma shouldn't use the flat in her absence – she could water the plants.

That evening Boo arrived with a wonderful pot of lilies, blooming now in August, their delicate trumpets curled to perfection, stamens exposed. 'You *shouldn't* have!' Harriet cried and set them in front of an ornate mirror so that they twice adorned the room. She wore her grey silk, simplicity itself, a pearl locket at her throat and, of course, Boo's precious stole. Suddenly, Harriet felt a surge of confidence. It was a bit like the theatre, after all. She almost laughed at herself. She had set the stage, and had been her own wardrobe mistress. This time, though, there were no lines to remember, not as in her awful dream. This was an ad-lib job, and Harriet was in control.

Boo sighed, gazing down at her stomach and patting its fatness. 'You always remind me of a painting!' she said to Harriet, 'A different one each time, depending on what you are wearing. Tonight it's one of those powdery French women with tall hair.'

Harriet eyed her reflection with pleasure. 'In my heyday . . .' she said ruefully, then went on effusively about how well Boo had looked on the telly programme. 'You should wear make-up more often,' she said. 'It suits you . . . just a little foundation and mascara . . . it does wonders.' She poured drinks and toasted Boo's programme.

The gin took the edge off the day. Boo had a way of kicking off her shoes in Harriet's flat without actually doing so. She threw herself back in a silken chair, lit a fag and closed her eyes with pleasure. Notwithstanding her residual nerves, it amused Harriet to note that, even with the more expensive clothes afforded by her windfall from the television, Boo was clueless. She had bought some white duck flares and a voluminous tunic, riotous with pastel flowers. It was endearing, but she did look a bit like a child's birthday cake. 'Heaven!' Boo said, sipping gin and ton. 'I've been barging round Grisleyhole all day moving and shaking. There was a suicide on F Wing.'

Gerry lived on F Wing.

'Oh?' Harriet wrinkled her nose at the bubbling tonic. She scooped at the lemon slice and sucked it. 'Who?'

'Not Carney.' Boo glanced at Harriet. Harriet smoothly offered her some olives. 'He was only a kid,' she added.

Harriet shook her head. 'Awful!' She could not afford to let her relief show, but maybe this was the time to start putting out feelers. She could lead with some remark about how Gerry had received some good news.

'Why?' she asked instead.

'Why did he do it? They're trying to get to the bottom of it. He had one of our visitors coming to see him . . . that's where I came in. It reminded me of how careful we must all be,' she said, struggling with the olive pit. 'She's devastated, poor lass. But I'm convinced it had nothing to do with her. She told me all along that he was being threatened and I did approach the Board of Visitors.'

Harriet thought of how Gerry's face was so often drawn, tired with fear. He had told her about the drug barons, the poofters and just plain bullies who shared his life, his meals, his exercise, his English class. He told her of men being beaten up in the showers or in what he called 'the recess', and how officers turned a blind eye.

'He was a nonce,' said Boo, crushing out her cigarette. 'A sex offender,' she added, seeing Harriet's incomprehension, 'or so the rumour goes.'

'I thought they were all on the Rule!' Harriet cried. 'Aren't they on an annexe in the prison? Remember Tony? The one I saw for a while? He was only too glad of the protection.' Harriet privately thanked God that he had been sent elsewhere. He was a pallid little man, anxious, unctuous and balding, so eager to please. She hadn't been able to think of anything to say to him. He was so different from Gerry, such a crushed, sad man.

'Oh, the location isn't much to go by. They move about the prison. Sometimes they've been sentenced for something else, another kind of crime which doesn't bear any relation to their previous convictions. Sometimes there's no room on the unit. Some even brave it out because they hate to go on the Rule. It marks them, you see.'

'I don't know about you, but I'm starving!' said Harriet, rising abruptly. 'I must do one little thing in the kitchen and then we can eat. More gin, do, though,' she indicated the silver drinks tray which she had polished that morning to a rich shine. They'd settle down to dinner first, then maybe she would present Boo with the fait accompli.

'The rumour about this chap who died,' Boo yelled through into the kitchen, 'is that an officer who had a grudge against him might have put it about that he was a sex offender. But we think it was another prisoner.'

Harriet fussed with the vinaigrette and turned the lamb off to let it rest. She'd nuke the beans in the microwave. Her stomach felt cold, her appetite annihilated. Well, she'd been putting off this evil day for quite a while, hadn't she? And it really wasn't easy to know where to start. 'You will not believe the most amazing coincidence,' would have been a good opener a few months ago. She supposed she could always add, 'Things developed so fast . . .'

'On the other hand, maybe he was a paedophile. Maybe he couldn't live with himself.' Boo waltzed into the kitchen with her freshened drink. 'Harriet, that looks lovely! They're a special crew,' she continued, 'and nobody knows what to do with them.'

Harriet placed the carefully constructed salad of quails' eggs on the table and lit the candles. 'In acknowledgement of your brilliant series!' she said with a mock bow.

'A rococo feast!' cried Boo. Indeed, there was something of Fragonard about the delicate room with its pinks and blues, a drift of lace here, a glint of gilt there, caught in the soft light of the candelabra. Boo said grace. She always did, even for a scotch egg.

Harriet did not want to know about paedophiles, especially as she thought Boo had been far too charitable to them in her broadcast. She lightly changed the subject to Haven Hall until Boo glazed over. She herself was going on an Ignatian retreat at the beginning of September. Would Harriet like to give it a whirl?'

The lamb cut like butter. This was the moment, the main course, when Harriet had planned to bring it up, what she had done about Gerry, and now she had an opening. Indeed, Boo fell silent.

Harriet poured the claret and inhaled the nose of the aromatic wine. It looked as if she had other plans, she told Boo. In fact, she'd only heard that morning from Emma, whose alienation from Harriet Boo was wont to deplore. As she opened her mouth to add that she had something else to discuss, Boo, fuelled by the good drink, launched in on the bolshieness of daughters these days. Harriet forced herself to smile at the anecdotal evidence and selective memories that built up a case against girls. The moment, having retreated, seemed to have slipped beyond her grasp. She pumped Boo about Scotland and the film crew; she lauded every detail of the production.

After the rich feast, they snuggled down to coffee drunk from Harriet's Royal Doulton demi-tasses, which they balanced on her spindly inlaid table. Boo's hands around the little cups looked like paws. Why not have a cognac? they decided.

Boo had a hollow leg and a cast-iron head; not so Harriet. She stretched out her feet in front of her, resting her head on the chair, the fumes of the brandy palliative and exalting. Suddenly, she was pleased with her dinner. It really had been awfully good. When she got back from Greece, she'd make more of an effort to entertain, relax with friends. A surge of generosity welled up in her. She was truly happy for Boo's deserved success! And she'd write to Emma congratulating her on the Salman Rushdie coup! Put a little extra effort into the letter. Maybe she and Emma had both been mean-spirited in the past. She should welcome what looked to be a first move on the part of her daughter.

So she was unprepared for the shock that Boo delivered, and perhaps this was why things went as wrong as they did.

'Look, Harriet,' Boo said, her eyes screwed up against the smoke from her umpteenth cigarette, 'how much do you actually know about Carney?'

Harriet struggled up to a more dignified position. 'What do you mean?' she asked cautiously.

Boo stubbed out the fag. 'I was talking with the S.O. on F Wing today . . . you know, about this poor chap who hanged himself. Only a few cells down from Carney, as a matter of fact. You might take this into account when you next see him. It will have upset him.'

'Oh, poor Gerry! Of course. Of course I will.' Harriet's blood turned to ice.

Boo leaned her elbows on her knees. Her face was both ugly and wise. There was a kind of beauty about her, though hard to translate into terms that the unguent sellers at Peter Jones would understand. She gazed full at Harriet. 'I don't want you to break any confidences, obviously, but Gerry himself may be at risk. If you know what I'm talking about, we'll say no more.'

'He's always frightened of bullies . . .'

'Do you know why?' Boo asked her abruptly.

Only much later did Harriet realise that just beneath her consciousness she had suspected all along what Boo was about to reveal but never finally did. She shook her head and smiled. Boo looked very far away, almost surreal.

'I'm sorry. I didn't know till today, but poor old Gerry has pretty heavy form. You should pat yourself on the back because the S.O. was telling me that if it hadn't been for your visits, he would have thought Carney the most likely candidate for suicide. Except for this offence Gerry has been in and out . . .'

Harriet had no idea she was going to snap. Suddenly, she was irrationally enraged. It was the drink, she told herself, but even that did not account for the heady feeling of moral indignation. 'Gerry tells me everything,' she said stiffly.

Boo sat back, startled at her vehemence.

'I'm sorry,' Harriet said automatically.

'It's all too easy to get homed in on these men.' Boo spoke with an even gentleness that Harriet found patronising. 'When I started I had one of these intractable cases like Carney. You see, they have no sense of proportion themselves . . . and no boundaries, as the shrinks like to say. One tends to lose one's own.'

Harriet had never had a violent impulse before. She wanted to jump up and slap Boo hard across the face. What was she implying? How dare she! Instead, with a rustle of silk, she moved her hand towards the coffee pot. 'Shall I make some more?' she enquired.

There was an uneasy silence between them. 'No, don't bother. Heavens! *Is* that the time? I must be getting home,' Boo said.

They burbled politely enough at the door, but Harriet couldn't close it fast enough behind Boo. She leaned her back against it and she started to sob. The stupid, self-righteous bitch! Fuelled with her own sense of self-importance! What did she know about Gerry? Thank God she had not divulged their plans. It must have been sheer instinct that had protected her.

Harriet's head spun, but she finished the claret as she shoved even the good china into the dishwasher. All right, so Gerry did have a record. She'd worked that one out already, hadn't she? It wasn't until she had fallen into bed, the dishes half-done, her make-up only half removed, that the dead spot appeared in her, sinking her stomach. A record for what?

But then she passed out and by the next morning she had forgotten it.

15

THE FOLLOWING DAY, Harriet cut off all relations with Boo. She rose early, briskly finished the dishes, vacuumed up the crumbs and then, with no trace of the hangover she should have had, she composed a note with cold finesse. Usually, she made several drafts of letters for she had little confidence in her powers of expression, but it came out pat in one version. She thanked Boo kindly for trying her out as a prison visitor, but she had discovered it was not for her. She had decided to resign from the scheme.

Yes, she told Boo, she really had become too involved. Her pen hovered over the paper for one moment while she considered including a sentence about not feeling trusted, but that was implicit, wasn't it? Besides, Boo might come back at her with her precious guidelines and, as humiliating as Harriet found this, she had to hang on to the truth. She knew she had interpreted them very widely indeed, to say the least.

As soon as she had pushed it firmly through Boo's letterbox, Harriet realised that there was little reason for the note. Only a few days ago, she had seen Gerry for the last time in the Visitors' Room: their next meeting would be when he was out of prison. How could she have blocked out this pressing reality? Throughout the whole course of her conversation with Boo the previous evening, she had actually believed that nothing had altered and that she would be continuing her visits to Gerry in Grisholme. Like a drunk who strives to retrieve mislaid hours, Harriet tried to conquer panic. 'No matter,' she muttered to herself as she strode away to the receding barks of Jolly Labrador who'd been clawing at the door to greet her. There was a principle involved here, and she felt liberated at last from Boo's narrow-minded approach. Whatever happened when she returned from Greece, she would never have to take on another prisoner . . . at least, not with Boo controlling her activities!

Poor Boo, she was very upset. She came round in response to the letter, banged on the door urgently, but Harriet hid in the folds of the drawing room curtains until she went away. The next day, Boo prodded through a note. She knew she could be tactless, she said. Maybe she had said something inadvertently. Please would Harriet reconsider? She'd been such a boon all round, to the prison and to Boo personally.

Since childhood, Harriet had been the same. There was no court of appeal once she had made up her mind. Averell had called her inflexible, even ruthless; true or not, there it was. Given the scope of her enterprise, Harriet had no choice but to leave Boo hanging. Nothing and no one was going to threaten this trip.

As for the things she was intimating about Gerry – well! If anything had made up Harriet's mind to quit, it had been the inference that she was too naive to grasp his true nature. A trust more absolute than Boo could imagine existed between Harriet and Gerry. Maybe he did have 'form', as Boo called it. Maybe he'd found it awkward to discuss, but Harriet was sure it was nothing vile. Their relationship was one of delicate nuance, shifts of mood and feeling. The subtlety of inflection that went for currency in their friendship could almost be set to music. In fact, it had all been like a modern ballet, a complex pas de deux danced against the stark background of Grisholme, something Boo could never understand.

The more Harriet thought about Boo, the more she realised that a slow disillusionment had been creeping up on her for a period of some months. Boo had changed since she'd become a telly star. The OBE had gone to her head. She had little idea any more about the real problems inmates faced. As far as she was concerned, 'befriending' prisoners meant a calculated do-goodery that had nothing to do with the simple love they needed. Well, Boo could think what she liked.

Harriet picked up the telephone and, tweezing her credit card from her wallet, she bought the aeroplane tickets she had reserved, using the back of Boo's abject note to jot down details. She'd be a great deal sorrier when she heard of Gerry's metamorphosis!

It was only when she had made this final leap that it struck Harriet: it wasn't as if she'd given in her resignation with any selfish or calculating motive in mind, but now she considered it she had inadvertently put herself in a better position. If at one time she had worried about the constraints imposed on her by Boo's guidelines, such as not 'consorting' with convicts after they left prison, her formal withdrawal from the scheme must bear some legal weight. As an ordinary citizen, Harriet surely had every right to see whomever she chose. Now she had quit, she could no longer be touched. As for Gerry, he would soon be out, free from all constraints. Even probation would have no power over him, he had told her. He could travel where he liked and do what he would. They were both free now, free to become more sure friends, free to make of their severally damaged lives a new start.

Though Harriet barely admitted it to herself, the truth was that the idea of seeing Gerry outside the prison walls still made her uncomfortable. What would it be like, being with him in the normal way? For some reason she could not picture him doing anything mundane, like travelling on the Tube, say, or buying toothpaste. Well, one thing was for sure – she could hardly invite him to her flat, because Boo might spot him. This was yet another hidden benefit of her severing relations with Boo. Now, if she needed it, she had a cast-iron excuse to warn Gerry away from Chelsea, and it relieved her mind considerably. Besides, she and Gerry had already arranged how to meet.

With a chill of fear, the last time she'd seen him she had written down her telephone number on a piece of paper and slid it into his hand as they had said goodbye. He was to ring her when he got out, and they would take it from there. To her surprise, Gerry had not seemed perturbed in the least when, even then, she had started making hints about his not coming to see her. She'd thought he would sulk.

Quite the contrary, he explained to her that as he had managed to cling on to his council flat in Elephant and Castle, his first wish was to go home and sort things out. A friend had been popping in to look after the place, he told her. Harriet found it hard to imagine such a person, and something like jealousy pricked her when she thought of his having an independent life. Gerry was quite decided about the business of reconnecting with 'the out', as he called it. It crossed Harriet's mind that he had some wish to avoid her, but she dismissed it. With only a week between his getting out of Grisholme and their departure for Greece, there was a lot to be accomplished. She had assured him she'd help him get together an appropriate wardrobe. As he was nervous of meeting the 'toffs', she'd joked about a lightning course in etiquette.

In the days running up to his release, Harriet was in a delirium of anticipation. She found she could not settle to anything, even some simple knitting she'd bought to keep her hands occupied. She concentrated her energies on avoiding Boo, altering her daily schedule. She even took a roundabout route to Westminster Cathedral, attending Sunday Mass there in order to avoid an embarrassing meeting at St Mary's. There, she eyed the bank of confessionals apprehensively. But what had she done wrong? She hadn't exactly lied to Boo. It was more like a disagreement with a boss. Looked at in one way, a further and spiritual benefit of her resignation was the element in it of sacrifice. Being a part of the scheme was something she had really valued; staying on might, now she thought about it, have put her in a dishonourable situation.

Harriet sang the responses to the Mass, *Christe eleison*. And as she engaged on the procedure of the liturgy, her eyes drifted upwards with the soaring of the music, until her gaze stopped on the gigantic Byzantine crucifix that hung, like a Damocles sword, she thought, over the nave. It always unnerved her, this heavy, hieratic cross, whenever she visited the Cathedral. Suppose a bolt slipped in the vaulty ceiling; she could see it swinging and crashing down. Perhaps for this reason, a weight of seriousness descended on her, displacing the hectic anxieties of the last few days.

She had made these decisions about Gerry out of love, hadn't she? It seemed important to establish that. There could be nothing sordid or wrong when love was the motive, could there?

It was not what she considered a prayer, nor did she take what responded in her as revelation. All the same, Harriet was grasped by a thought as spare as plainsong.

Love meant what it said. She had taken a path; if she chose to call it love then love it must be. There could be no going back, no shirking of consequences, and no expectation of reward.

There was a moment of stillness that only took the space of a few alleluias uttered by the congregation rising for the Gospel, but it seemed a great deal longer than that. Slowly, Harriet bowed her head, as if in assent. It was like a vow, she thought. How arduous this might be to keep she saw between one blink and the next, and something in the vision made her tremble.

When the great day came, Harriet woke at 5 a.m. She had definitely decided not to meet him at the prison gates. Gerry would be released around 9 a.m.; he had told her this was the normal time. But he wasn't expecting her. The night before, she had downed as many herbal sleeping pills as she could safely take, but she had lain with eyes wide open until two, sinking at last into a fitful doze. Suppose he had lost her telephone number. Suppose someone had stolen it or confiscated it. Besides, how dreary could it be to leave prison on one's own, with no one there to give a welcome. Harriet found herself on her feet at dawn, telephone in her hand. She'd take a chance, surprise him with a minicab to take him home. It was a spur of the moment decision, but a generous one, she thought. Why had he mentioned the time he'd be let out if he hadn't hoped she'd be there?

Harriet made a desperate attempt at camouflage in case her arrival at the prison should coincide with Boo rolling up. She rummaged through her cupboards until she found an old khaki dress and flat shoes. She hadn't the patience to do her hair properly so she slapped on a headscarf. She might have been anyone, a taxpayer, personnel, a dog owner. The cab driver was curious as to her business at Grisholme. Harriet wished she had the composure to say that her husband was in the Mob, but instead she turned her head coldly to one side, gazing at the river as they crossed Vauxhall Bridge. Why hadn't she thought of it before? Without her there to meet him what would he do? Walk to Elephant and Castle? Or stand in his humiliation at the bus queue, 'jailbird' written over his pale face? She only hoped he had been right about the hour. How stupid it was to make this a surprise! It was only eight, but suppose he had already been let out? Maybe he was wandering south London, clutching at his few small possessions, dazed and confused. What kind of a friend was she who would let him down on this of all days?

As it happened, by the time the taxi drew up before the gates of Grisholme, there were about ten minutes to spare. As Gerry had told her, shortly after the clock struck nine, an officer emerged from a small door in the main gate, and started to usher out the prisoners who were being released that day. Harriet was breathless and trembling as first one man and then another passed through, blinking at freedom. Where was Gerry? A group of people she hadn't noticed as the cab drew up swarmed to meet a tough, muscled convict with a shaved head. It looked like a big East End family, the sallow women in leather mini-skirts, the barrel chests of the men dangling with gold jewellery. Their features were sharp – moulded, perhaps, by a perpetual watchfulness that made their broad smiles look out of place.

Harriet searched the street with her eyes. It suddenly struck her that the friend Gerry told her about might be there too. Could it be this girl he was supposed to be engaged to? The one he'd broken the window for? She peered from the back of the minicab, headscarf pulled forward like a helmet. The pavement was empty save for two other men newly released, whom no one greeted or met. They strolled out with a superficial nonchalance, bearing their bits and pieces in tell-tale plastic sacks. They seemed to flap out into the south London drizzle like disoriented birds, cut off from a flock, wounded and dazzled. Maybe she had made a mistake about the release date. Maybe they had found an excuse to keep Gerry inside. But then, after a little wait, there he was, last in the queue. It took a moment or two before she recognised him.

Gerry stood on the pavement dressed in street clothes, black jeans and a checked shirt. Some of the other men had shaken hands with the officer in charge of the release, or at least waved an ironic goodbye, but Gerry had passed through the gate without giving the smallest acknowledgement.

Harriet was surprised to see how ordinary he looked, like a workman, perhaps on legitimate business. He swiped the lock of hair from his brow as if it maddened him. He was holding a duffel bag and his eyes scanned the terrible road as if all his senses were assaulted by the fumes and grinding lorries. Harriet opened the minicab window, put out a hand and waggled her fingers. 'Coo-ee! Gerry!' she called softly, at once abashed at this ridiculous greeting. When he saw her he hardly looked surprised. Either he had guessed that she might come or he was too stunned by his newfound liberty to take in her gesture of solidarity. But she was overwhelmed to see him.

'Friend of yours?' the cabbie asked.

'Actually, yes,' Harriet said in her most mandarin tone.

They said little in the car with its swinging air freshener and squawking radio. Maybe it was the result of her sleepless night, but almost at once Harriet felt sapped of energy. As for Gerry, he sat cautiously in the corner, almost prim with his hands straight on his squeezed-together knees.

Harriet was not without savoir-faire even in this situation, she discovered, exhausted as she was. Somehow she had blundered into a private area. She had no doubt that he was pleased with the lift and with her attentive concern, but she had the delicacy to see that he did need 'to get his head sorted', as he was wont to say, before they could engage with each other in this confusing new development. So Harriet instructed the driver to take Gerry home and, scribbling down her number for him again just to be sure, she told him to call her when he was ready. His tired eyes thanked her dumbly and he managed an uncertain smile. She left him at the foot of an enormous tower block, as monolithic as the prison itself, she thought, and she spent the journey back to Chelsea trying not to cry.

Maybe her sense of time was distorted by the toll it took on her to wait so passively until he got in touch, but it seemed an aeon before Gerry rang. His voice was friendly, if a little distant, and Harriet found herself adding up the sum of his words, scrutinising the gist of remembered phrases when he had rung off. He was ready now. The gas was back on, he said, and the electricity; obviously the phone. He consented to meet her in Piccadilly the next morning. They were to do a big shop for Greece. Of course he would be pleased to see her. Why not?

Harriet arrived early, slightly embarrassed to be meeting someone at the foot of Eros. For a panicked moment, she thought he was going to stand her up, until she suddenly realised he had been there all along. He had been sitting at the base of the statue idly feeding pigeons with a scrap of a burger roll he told her he'd had for breakfast. How could she have missed him? He seemed to blend into his surroundings; he could have been a tourist, a shopper, homeless, a stage-hand from one of the theatres on Shaftesbury Avenue. Perhaps he had been quietly assessing her from his perch, for he waved, identifying himself only after she had circled the statue several times. With a small shock, Harriet realised that they were both in equal measure happy and unhappy to see each other. The change of their circumstances was more radical than either of them had imagined it would be, she thought, but Harriet took him in hand. She had booked him in at a men's hairdressers in Jermyn Street, an establishment appointed to the royal family. Although the gentlemen's barber blinked at his new client, he fell to. Harriet waited in St James's Piccadilly where the Anglican religion of her childhood and married years seemed to have been re-scripted to include forces and powers of the earth and the New Age. Stands and placards stood about proclaiming the holiness of trees, the active interaction of angels with those adept at summoning them. She circumambulated the church, too agitated to sit down.

In later years, Harriet was to treasure the moment of Gerry's transformation. When she returned to the hairdresser, his neck was being dusted. He gave her a broad grin in the mirror; his dark hair was princely. Helped by its waviness, it swept back and tufted up behind the ears. No longer Carney, he was a Hythe, as polished and pomaded as if he were on his way to a hunt ball. Harriet gave the barber a handsome tip along with the credit card that was going to take heavy damage that day. The man smiled discreetly, making her peer at him in a double take. But she decided that he was pleased with his handiwork, her pleasure in it . . . and the gratuity.

What a time they had, those few days! It was so giddy that sometimes she had to sit down, close her eyes tightly and breathe slowly to stop the eddies of nameless panic. At night, she curled into a foetal ball, her ears stopped with wax plugs. Fancies hopped through her mind like imps allowed to stay up late in hell. Between Gerry and herself there was only a bus ride now: the bolts, bars, keys, chains . . . even the dogs were gone. There were no prison officers to regulate their friendship. In place of Boo stood only her discretion.

And yet it was anarchic and wonderful to be a fairy godmother to Gerry. She had chosen his clothes carefully, steering him away from Gap. She wanted him to appear in a way that would reassure Michael and Helen Hythe. Harriet was determined he should possess at least one good jacket, so she stumped up for a solid blazer at Hackett. She made him over into a gentleman, buying him good shirts, silk ties, some decent casual things for hot weather. His foot fitted the improbable glass slipper better than she could have imagined. The clothes sat well on his wiry shoulders, and at times she could see Edgar in him just as if he were being brought out of the humble chaos in which he had been reared, like a brass rubbing. Mice transformed themselves into shop assistants, as helpful as could be at the sight of her Platinum Visa, and pumpkins turned to black cabs in which Gerry lounged with surprising ease and confidence. If there were sniggers at the unlikely pair, Harriet chose not to hear them. Still, if it was thrilling, it was also disturbing to be with him, walking freely together through Green Park. Audaciously, she gave him tea in Fortnum's where she tried and failed to raise the subject of his appalling table manners. Gerry buttered a whole slice of bread and stuffed it into his mouth. He left his spoon in his cup. Harriet decided to lead by example, clinking her spoon in the saucer, dissecting her tea-cake with exaggerated finesse. As for his accent, maybe it was her imagination, but since his release it had broadened, almost as if he were guying her efforts to launch him into the Hythes' exalted orbit.

She drove her bank account into the red with all she heaped on Gerry and she didn't stint herself either, buying an elegant swimsuit and some cruise clothes. To do him justice, he worried at the expense. She told him he could pay some of it back when he got a job. Of course he could. But some things were outright gifts, the blazer and the shoes she bought him at Bally.

At the end of two days of shopping mania, Gerry asked Harriet back to his flat. Their feet were throbbing on Oxford Street. Could she sew? he asked her. The trousers they had bought needed taking up a fraction and he was hopeless with a needle. He was afraid he hadn't anything to offer her except tea or coffee, but maybe she'd like to see where he lived. There was something in the manner of his asking that put Harriet off.

Perhaps if she hadn't been so tired, Harriet would have followed her instinct, as strong as if one of the empowering angels of St James's Piccadilly had erected a plate glass window between her and her intention. But as there seemed no earthly reason why she should refuse Gerry, it seemed a bit offensive to say no. It was hardly as if she wanted to get off with him, did she? Or he with her. In fact, Harriet was beginning to suspect that Gerry wasn't interested in women . . . nothing she could put her finger on. Her intuition was based on the most threadbare evidence, the interchange, perhaps, between himself and men's clothiers, a lack of response in his eyes to the beautiful young women who paraded the West End, brazen with chic and money. It was nothing she could fully put into words to herself and, if she had been able to admit it, she would have had to allow that it added a piquant edge to her feelings about him. Even out of prison, he retained an air of mystery, of being just out of her reach, an exotic man, maybe with singular needs. So she consented. The truth was, she was curious.

Harriet had no idea what to expect from the nineteenth floor of a council block where the lift was broken, except breathlessness. She had never visited a council flat before. They trudged the urine-smelling staircase. She tried not to hold her breath or to avert her eyes from the graffiti sprayed on the walls. The few neighbours they met on their upward climb thought she was a social worker.

She was surprised, therefore, to find that Gerry had created an inner sanctum high in the jerry-built tower block. The furniture was cheap but tasteful, modern, along Conran lines, and he had kept to simple lines and neutral colours. Gerry told her he'd had to muck out when he returned. His 'friend' had let all the plants die and left the place a tip. It dawned on Harriet that Gerry had managed to sublet the flat during his imprisonment; she began to suspect that there was no friend at all. He banged on the kettle in his midget kitchen and asked her to sit in the 'lounge'.

Harriet wondered if she should try to persuade him to call it a 'sitting room' if he meant to refer to it on Naxos, but she decided against it.

While he was clattering away with mugs she looked around, slowly absorbing more. By the window there were some hooks for plants, presumably all taken down because they'd died, but she remembered how he had described his geraniums and she thought how effective they would have looked against the beige decor. There was a television with a large screen, expensive-looking, built into a large bookcase where there were rows and rows of untitled videos. But there were a few nice books, too, about gardens and gardening . . . Gertrude Jekyll and Capability Brown. What really took her eye, though, was a whole wall of prints Gerry had hung above the sofa. Each one depicted a scene from childhood. Most of them were old engravings: there were Victorian boys by a swimming hole and a scene with a tiny lad cuddling close to Father Christmas. The best were modern, particularly some stunning etchings of children at play. The chief piece of the collection was a slender youth bearing a cup aloft. Harriet got up and squinted at the picture. It was entitled 'Ganymede' and was signed with a scrawl . . . an original! The boy was naked, wonderfully and terribly realised, as if the gift of immortality had only just been conferred upon him. It was lovingly framed in black and gold.

Just then Gerry came in with the cups on a tray. He froze for a moment, his face a curious mixture of feelings.

'Gerry, this is superb!' Harriet cried. 'Wherever did you get this lovely drawing?'

His expression relaxed. 'Do you like it?'

'It's amazing. You didn't do it yourself?'

He shook his head. 'It's by an artist friend of mine. I met him at a club I used to belong to.' He shrugged, passing it off. 'The rest I got on the Portobello Road.'

The anxieties Harriet had about Gerry's finding a niche in

the Hythe family were somewhat allayed. She looked at him solemnly. 'You have real taste,' she said.

'I'll do, then? With me new gear an' all?' he said with an unpleasant vehemence.

Harriet flushed. 'I meant to give you a compliment,' she said.

'I'll get the trousers,' he said shortly, putting the tray down on the coffee table with something short of a bang.

And she was forced to kneel at his feet, her mouth full of the pins he provided while he stood oddly triumphant, legs astride. Harriet made an effort not to touch him. She felt deeply uncomfortable and left as soon as she could with the pinned trousers, her coffee untouched.

A day went by in which they did not communicate. He was obviously nervous about the trip, she thought to herself as she unpicked the expensive cloth. And she must allow for the trauma of getting out of prison. Still, Harriet felt a little bruised by their last, odd encounter and she decided that if he could sulk so could she. She pressed the turned-up light summer gabardine to a knife-edge. If he wanted the trousers he could jolly well ask for them.

It was a great relief to Harriet when her plot to keep a distance worked. Although Gerry didn't apologise for his bizarre behaviour, his voice bounced on the phone in that vivid tone people use when they are trying to paste over an unacknowledged quarrel. What was more, he was asking her out to dinner. She had given him so much, been so generous, he'd like to repay her in some small way. Could she name a place to eat? He'd got a windfall from Social Security, back payments for the time when he'd been 'out of commission'. He insisted.

Harriet thought and thought about it. At last she lit upon what seemed to her the perfect choice. In the library she found the name of a Greek restaurant in Bayswater, highly recommended and inexpensive. The food and ambience were authentic, said the *Good Food Guide*. What better way to celebrate his release! It would give the trip to Naxos a kick-start.

When she rang him back, Gerry seemed delighted with the idea. It was amazing how his moods fluctuated. And so they booked a table for the night before they were to board the midday flight to Athens. Harriet made an extensive toilette, chose a floating dress, the best of her collection from the middle range of grandeur and, as a last thought, put on the garnet pendant Averell had so long ago given her for a wedding present.

She and Gerry were finally on their way.

16

HARRIET AND GERRY WERE AT SEA before she realised that there was no going back. Even if she took the return boat, nothing could be altered now. He had made sure of that.

This realisation came to her at first from a distance, then, like an oncoming ship, it grew larger. Gerry stood at the railings, gazing into the Aegean as if nothing had happened. The big ferry slipped past barren islands baked to a dusty ochre by an eternal, unblinking sun. The sky was the spectrum of blue with every modulation expressed in tints and half-tints of azure and cerulean, hyacinth and aquamarine. But he, not ten feet from her, was her only horizon.

Now she knew, there was no unknowing.

She had it from Gerry himself.

How long had this taken to sink in? Days measured in slow hours. It was like the knocking at a door in the dead of night, only a dream until, portentous and terrifying, it finally wakes the sleeper to bad news. Gerry was dangerous.

And she was responsible for him.

Harriet did not know what to do. She was surrounded by water and she didn't speak Greek. How had she allowed herself to board the ship with Gerry, knowing what she knew now?

Harriet shivered into her cotton cardigan, the warmest garment she'd packed. Whether it was actually cold, she could not tell. The September breeze made crisp wavelets which spanked the hull; gulls above bucked the wind. It should be hot, she thought irritably. They should be gliding. But Gerry was in his element.

Harriet looked at the sky and tried to speak to God, but glanced away. She had never before made a mistake on this scale. The immensity of blue seemed to answer her with yet more light and she craved nothing so much as darkness. What was she to do now that she had failed in every respect to take appropriate steps?

Averell had once told Harriet that her conscience was like an adding machine. Why had he said that? In what context? She could not imagine now to what circumstance of their mundane lives that remark had applied, but she remembered his contempt. Whatever, the calculator now hummed into life. She strained, frowning, wrestling with it. As a child she had made a list of her imperfections every New Year's Day with resolutions to improve. There were no measurable quantities of goodness here that could reduce the awful sum of truth.

To begin with, she could have aborted the journey at any stage. That this should occur to her now, when they were but a few hours from Naxos, amazed Harriet, deepening a painful horror at herself. Gerry had given her that opportunity. They didn't need to be on the ship. In fact, she could have ripped up the aeroplane tickets, grounding them in London.

And yet it never crossed her mind. For the last two days she'd been robotic, a mechanism wound up by Gerry and travelling with him. If only she could be rid of this suffocating nemesis! It went mercilessly on, computing her errors.

Given that she had embarked on the journey, she'd still had a chance at least to challenge him and make conditions. On a three-hour flight from London to Athens she had ample time, but she failed to voice her misgivings.

Gerry, why? she could have said. When they'd supped on moussaka and Greek salad on arrival, the tourist taverna had been as good a place as any to say, 'Gerry, why do you want to do these dreadful things?' But a part of her had been excited to be in Greece and with him, sitting out under the leafy acacia trees.

Afterwards, they strolled in the Plaka where saucy T-shirts, hanging outside the shops, blew in the warm breeze and Priapus, mass-produced, lined the pavements like an odious guard of honour. His member, almost infinitely repeated, saluted her nauseated mind, a line of high-kicking chorus girls. She'd hustled the sniggering Gerry by. Rather like a nanny, she'd propelled him up to the dark base of the Acropolis, herding him away from the issue of sexuality, rather than raising it, dealing with it. Instead, she regurgitated bits of information she had gleaned from her guidebook. They returned to the Hotel Grande Bretagne where she'd extravagantly booked two rooms, all her fears unspoken.

It had seemed rather awful to spoil his fun. He was more interested in his princely bathroom than in the Parthenon.

Harriet's long and agonising night ended in a resolution to confront him at breakfast: why did you wait so long to tell me? But he was so nervous about the imminent meeting with his relations that she once again forbore to dredge up any unpleasantness; she had been silent, too, during the long bus ride to Raffina where they had boarded the ferry to Naxos. She blundered on, powerless against the momentum of travel, checking in, checking out and changing travellers' cheques from pounds into drachmas.

Harriet sank into the slatted bench where she huddled, heedless that the stiff sea breeze unmoored strands of white hair from firm pins. She supposed she was getting old. She was only in Greece, but it felt as if she'd journeyed to Pluto.

All morning she'd fussed about catching the boat, swamped in the terror of missing it, a little old lady who takes an age to put her change back into her purse while a queue is fuming.

Whenever she looked beside her there was Gerry, standing like a monolith, almost waiting, she thought, for her to do something, to say something, to make a move. She was fidgeting over tickets, flapping about luggage, worrying over exchange rates. She was straining to remember the inscrutable alphabet, the smattering of Classical Greek she'd learned at school, when really they should not be going to Naxos at all. He was unbalanced. And now she was herself. She reeled and wobbled like someone crawling out of crashed car.

Harriet had never been good at choices or able to see alternatives. She could have said no to Averell, to Ashdean, to a loveless marriage and years of mindless boredom. She could have stuck to her acting, but basically she liked being told what to do. Easier than making a mistake. Befriending Gerry, and on her terms, was the first independent thing she had ever done, and now look what had come of it! His crimes. What crimes! He was like a bomb ticking. It was staring her in the face that without her intervention it would go off. And yet she felt paralysed. Had she deliberately blinded herself to the possibilities that lay within her grasp?

Her mind drifted miserably back to the restaurant in Bayswater. To his stunning revelation, she could have said, 'Gerry, you have badly misled me and you've made a fool of me with your uncle. The trip to Greece is off.' She could have got up and gone home. It would not have been easy, but she could have put an end to the whole thing.

Or could she?

Although Harriet had not taken her eyes off Gerry for the last fifteen minutes, she narrowed them now to take him more fully in. The deafening wind buffeted his princely hair. He seemed blissfully unconscious that anything out of the ordinary had happened except that he was abroad for the first time, for the first time on board a ship. This had exercised him not a little. He'd been manic, commenting on every new sight and sensation from the rocking deck to the belching funnels. At long last, he'd settled down and was leaning over the railings watching the sea for dolphins. That had been her idea . . . telling him there might be dolphins.

She was desperate for some peace to think things through.

He'd been driving her mad all morning, pacing from stem to stern, fetching drinks from the bar, poking his nose into forbidden areas on the ship.

Were there dolphins in this part of the Aegean? She had no idea, but she told him he was bound to spot one if he were patient. They were good luck . . . she'd read that somewhere.

Who was he anyway? What was she *doing* with him?

Suddenly Gerry's new clothes looked crazy. As he hunched over the railings, the shoulder pads in the jacket hiked up, making him look like a space man. Against the vastness of the sea and the unreal sky, he seemed to shrink to the size of an overdressed child on his way to a grown-up party. Why had he told her? And then? Twelve hours before they were to embark? It was a game to him, wasn't it? A theatrical game involving disguises. Unmasking one illusion, he made a deeper magic. She had not, after all, been powerless to act, not even at the eleventh hour. Had he hypnotised her?

The night before they flew, Harriet crawled into bed sickened and shattered, descending into an awful narcolepsy. A decent human being would have rung Michael Hythe instead. Even if it meant getting him out of bed that night, she should have told him the truth. At the very least, she should have given him a chance to decide whether or not he wanted to meet Gerry on the basis of the reality he had demanded of her. Although Harriet flinched from this thought, it pursued her as if it had a vengeful life of its own.

Alternatively, she could have pretended to Gerry that one of the Hythes had fallen gravely ill. The journey was off. Even at the airport, she could have said this.

But she had not. She was shipping him, her wooden horse with its hidden freight, into the Hythes' Troy. If she told them now, they'd be devastated, even if half of what he'd revealed to her was true.

She closed her eyes now to the after-image of green. Was God without pity? It was wrong to think that, the canon once told her, but the knife at Isaac's throat flashed in her mind. She was going to have to steel herself and plunge it in: Gerry must be sacrificed.

The brutality of this thought startled Harriet into an uneasy, inner silence.

Must he be? Surely, that was a bit extreme.

To be fair, with a part of herself she still did not believe all he'd told her. When she'd met Gerry at Heathrow to catch the flight to Athens, she began to wonder if she'd imagined the whole thing. He'd been in high spirits, cracking jokes. No one would have thought he had secrets, dark or otherwise. He was the picture of the plain man off on holiday. A cold trickle of fear had leaked through her veins, however, as he snapped up the duty-frees, a kid in a toy shop. He got a free gift, a tinny radio, with his Marlboros. He selected a rock station and jived in the departure lounge.

For a few edgy moments, she'd tried to convince herself that their talk had been cathartic. Maybe that was why he was so cheerful. Bit by bit, though, she found herself blinking at her own memory, as if she had suffered a temporary lapse of sanity. But then he was so bobbish, snacking on nuts in the aeroplane, deliriously ordering gin then wine with lunch, chatting away, that she thought she must have misheard him. Gerry's admission of guilt had been like the flash of an explosion of which there was no visible sign. Well, maybe it *wasn't* true.

Harriet did not know why she wasn't angry with Gerry. She had a feeling she should be. Instead, a sickening pity swept through her. Earlier, she'd watched him stride across the ferry's sun deck where a group of young, well-heeled backpackers lay sprawled across their knapsacks soaking up the sun. Their long limbs were loosely entwined, their easy smiles flashed white teeth. Oh, the ease with which they laughed and talked! She observed them glancing up at Gerry as he skirted round the happy pile they made. His stiff and stunted movements proclaimed his otherness. With his new polo shirt buttoned too high, he looked like a theology student at an American college where some small sect grimly monitored the end of the world.

No! He had betrayed her trust and she must excise all easy pity from her heart. Only a demon could have committed the crimes Gerry confessed to. A monster. Here she chafed away at her own sins, making petty flaws grow huge in her eyes, while all along there was real grandeur about Gerry's wickedness. It sent a weird thrill through her to think of the vast evil he'd gone in for, as if she had come across a tarantula in a bunch of supermarket bananas. There could be no sympathy with this, no concessions to it, no collusion in it. When she arrived, she must tell the Hythes . . . perhaps in front of Gerry, making an example of him, making him pay.

Harriet opened her eyes. The wind ruffled Gerry's hair, her Gerry. The nape of his neck was poignant, his enthusiasm for dolphins touching. She ached with the memory of how she had been looking forward to this voyage. She was curious to know – just curious – why it was he had chosen the moment when they had been in such a high mood of anticipation, when the evening had promised to be so wonderful.

There's something you ought to know, Harriet. It's not easy to talk about, but you've always been straight with me.

The ship hit a swell and the sea foamed up glinting in the sun. It had seemed a good idea to drink to the spirit of Greece their last night in London, get themselves in the mood, so she had suggested ouzo, not knowing how strong it was. If they'd had less to drink would he have told her?

I wasn't about to tell you in Grisholme. Somebody might have overheard and I could've been done . . . murdered with no one the wiser! Besides, I didn't think you'd come back to see me. I wonder if you ever knew how much those visits meant to me. I lived for them! But I'm sure of you now. I know I can trust you. Can I trust you, Harriet? You must never breathe a word of what I'm going to tell you . . .

Harriet had given her solemn promise, gladly and with misty eyes across the table. They had reached an apogee. It was the crowning success of her patient love that he planned to give away what seemed to be so deep a confidence. And yet as he spoke, his eyes had shifted about cannily like a spy. Maybe he was frightened of being overheard.

Ever since I was aware, you know, of sex and all, I've had a bit of a problem. I don't want you to think I'm gay, Harriet, because I'm not! One day I'd like to get married and have kids, you know.

She supposed she'd seen it coming because suddenly she thought of Boo. Harriet's hand went to her garnet pendant and she felt the weight of it in her palm. The nurturing presence of Boo was gone. With a twinge she felt its lack. She gathered up the chain and let the garnet swing, inspecting its red depths in the candlelight. 'What are you trying to say, Gerry?' she asked him, coaxing him. She had injected a note of understanding into her voice, she was sure of that, but she was frightened and did not dare look at him.

It's when I get stressed out! I'm not gay! I get these fantasies and they play on my mind, and there's lots of reasons for it. It's young men. I think about young men. And then it sort of turns into my doing something about it . . .

Harriet had asked him how young.

Not that young! Ten or twelve. Maybe sometimes not as old as that. I never hurt anyone!

The ship rocked and her head spun, just as it had in the pretty restaurant with its starched tablecloths and its napkins perked into mitres. At the time, she had remained smiling. She even put her hand across the table, frantic in her disbelief, and touched his fingers lightly. 'Young men' of ten or twelve? It was grotesque!

But Gerry wasn't finished. He went on to give her some details of the 'affairs' that had put him into prison. Most of them had been schoolboys, but he admitted to a rent boy or two. The pupils of his eyes were dilated, making them almost black. He'd known all along she would understand.

And Harriet assured him that she did understand.

When she did not the least bit understand.

She'd still care for him, wouldn't she?

Of course she would! she told him.

The whole point was . . . and this he had assured her . . . she had changed his life. Yes, she . . . Harriet. Now he knew her, he could put all this behind him. He'd never had a reason before, but with her help, he was sure he could break the habit. He made it sound a bit like giving up smoking.

Now she knew Gerry's secret, Harriet felt so ashamed. It was as if she herself had perpetrated these crimes, as if she, like Myra Hindley, had been a handmaiden to Gerry's Brady, providing him with innocents.

You still care, Harriet? You won't dump me, will you? And you'll never tell? You'll never tell anyone? You promised.

Harriet listened to the mesmerising churn of water that slapped against the sides of the ship. She shivered again, her thin white cardigan insufficient against the wind that blew her own words back to her. 'Yes, Gerry, I promise. Your secret is safe with me.' Had she really said that? *Your secret is safe with me?* She'd grabbed the nearest cliché in her shock and pain. Were hackneyed phrases binding? And yet, even against the breeze, she felt an odd warmth spread through her, a relief. Suppose she had rung Michael. You didn't have to be St Augustine to see it. She would have broken faith with Gerry . . . and her word.

Come to think of it, what was it she had actually promised Michael Hythe? Insofar as she knew it at the time, she had told him the truth about Gerry. If it meant breaking a confidence, was she really obliged to tell him now?

My God, they were going to see Michael in about four hours! How could she now look him in the eyes? For a fleeting moment, Harriet wished the ship would sink. She would rather drown than be in this predicament.

The boat ploughed on, though, making good time, the brisk wind behind it. Harriet glanced again at Gerry and prayed that a dolphin would appear to amuse him. He was intent upon this child's quest. In the few weeks since he'd left prison, she had noticed how little things frustrated him and made him fractious. He'd been gazing at the water for some time now and he was sure to feel let down if the sensational animals failed to appear. It was too cold to sit out on deck, but she was instinctively afraid to let Gerry out of her sight. The alternative was to join the widows inside.

When they boarded the ship she had spotted them, the group of black-clad women who now occupied the second-class bar like a band of demonstrators bent on wrecking whatever was left of her holiday mood. Harriet had never been to Greece before. Who were they? Why were there so many of them? They buzzed around the ladies' loo like flies and lurked along the aisles of seats inside the boat, opening parcels and closing them, clacking away in their harsh language. She had shrunk from them as they waddled on at Raffina with their picnics and knitting. Perhaps if she knew Greece, she could put them into some context. Maybe they were nuns, not widows at all.

Yet this was all too modern, the idea of nuns. The black-shrouded crones, perhaps thirty or forty of them, seemed a visitation from archaic times, hardly women at all, more embodiments of vengeance or fate. How old were they? They looked immortally ancient, as if they had never been young. It was impossible to tell, for the bloom on their olive skin was prematurely deadened by their funereal dress. They filled Harriet with a peculiar horror.

And yet the women looked happy enough, even excited. The group was led by an Orthodox priest, also in black; he had a long white beard, his hair caught up in a snood under his geometric hat. They had been praying on and off since Raffina. Harriet wondered if they were escorting a body to be buried on one of the islands on the ship's itinerary – Tinos, Syros, or Naxos itself. She hadn't seen a hearse drive on to the ferry, but any chaotic arrangement seemed possible. Maybe the coffin lay stacked in the car deck, lost somewhere between the smart luggage of tourists and cardboard boxes done up with string. Perhaps there wasn't a dead body; perhaps the women were on some kind of pilgrimage. Whatever they were doing, Harriet found them ominous and wished to avoid their company.

Quite without expecting it to happen, Harriet found herself incensed, boiling with rebellion. What an idiot she was! It was a great relief to think this. She was worrying now to the point of obsession! Of course the women weren't ominous! And why was she mixing up Gerry with someone like Ian Brady? The two of them were understandably anxious about this meeting with Michael, she was tired and she was getting things out of proportion. Just because Gerry was not the man he seemed didn't mean that he was going to do something dreadful. He had, after all, told her what a difference she had made to him. There was no need to panic. Just because he had odd sexual proclivities didn't mean he was dangerous. And was there any reason to humiliate him in front of his new relations?

The knife at Isaac's throat fell from her grasp. She'd like to pick it up and hurl it into the bushes. Her conscience was no conscience at all but an inhuman, remorseless, driving force, goading her to frenzy. She'd go mad if she carried on like this!

Now she thought of it, would Michael and Eleni actually want to know the details of Gerry's crimes? They had been afraid of drugs because of Edgar. That was natural enough. What would it serve to expose Gerry? Some scruple of her own? Wasn't it better to give him a chance first? Whatever he'd done it was surely wrong to brand him. And, much as she was repelled by all he'd told her, her deeper loyalty was to him. What sort of a friend was she anyway?

Reason flooded into the vacuum her scruples had vacated.

Was it likely that he'd get up to much in Naxos, especially when she knew his tendencies, his weakness? No, the best thing was to coax Gerry, once he'd settled in, to confide in Michael himself. In any case, who knew? The plan to get the Hythes to care for him might fizzle out, a squib made damp by social inequality . . . or just plain indifference . . . or mutual dislike. She'd feel a right fool then for jumping the gun. If it was true that Gerry needed her help to overcome this thing, it wouldn't do much good if she alienated him by breaking her word. She was being stupid, dramatising herself, playing out Sophoclean tragedy in her mind, all because of a Greek chorus of old dears who were probably chatting about the cost of living or their grandchildren. The last time she'd looked through the porthole, they'd been eating hard-boiled eggs out of waxed paper and great hunks of bread.

The ship's tannoy crackled, making Harriet start. *Sas parakalo*, it said. She had it from the phrasebook that this meant 'if you please,' she remembered now. A torrent of Greek followed. It was a modern country, not some mythic place where Furies lurked or goddesses were born upon the foam.

Gerry, who had been motionless all this time, turned. Had he been brooding? Was there was a veiled antagonism in his eyes? She mustn't look for trouble! The disembodied voice announced in English that lunch was being served.

'I'm starving,' he called over to her.

For all of her justifications of him, Harriet could not endure another meal with Gerry. 'The sea air has given you an appetite,' she cried. An inspiration came to her and she turned her head to hide her pinched face. 'Why don't you go and get a bite to eat? I'm afraid I'm not at all good on boats. Just the smell of food . . .' and she turned to give a weak smile.

He laughed, coming closer. 'You do look a bit green. And here I was thinking it was me that was making you sick.' He added this with the faintest twist of the mouth. His eyes searched her face.

She shook her head . . . too vigorously? 'I think I'll stay out here,' she said indicating the sea, 'just in case.'

He moved abruptly from her side, but gave her a nice wave.

'I'll come in and get you if there are dolphins,' she called after him.

'Great!' he cried and, seemingly reassured, went in to discover the canteen.

Harriet was not sure the sea was 'wine-dark', but there were great purple stains like spilt wine fanning out in the clear turquoise water. It was probably seaweed, she thought. She shivered harder. Maybe she was sick after all.

Intensive care wasn't intensive enough as far as Gerry was concerned. He was in torment. Maybe they'd given him some medication that affected his memory. It throbbed erratically with pictures returning like strobe lights at a disco. Why couldn't he talk? He wanted to talk. Maybe he'd had another stroke, but he couldn't ask because he couldn't open his mouth. No one seemed to speak around him. Did they think he was dead? The nurses tended him though he couldn't see them. Maybe they would declare him dead while he was alive. Maybe they would bury him alive or, worse, harvest his organs, cutting his chest and taking out his heart without an anaesthetic.

It was like being down on the Block in solitary, this drift of time, where day and night were meaningless proportions. Yesterday, childhood, a few years ago . . . maybe even the future itself came and went.

Or it was a broken mirror in which he saw his face in the least fragment of exploding glass. He was being infinitely repeated down a long corridor. Now and then they gave him something to relax his muscles, at least that is what he thought it was. At these times, memory came in state, fully dressed and in sharp detail, a formal visitation.

He was with his mum. Why was everything strewn across the carpet with its whorls of green and grey? He tried to help her but he couldn't move. She was too ashamed to accept his help anyway. She had a black eye. It never before crossed his mind that she had been ashamed in front of him. She was crawling on her hands and knees, picking up the mess. She had big breasts that strained against her tight jumper and she made that abject noise. You'd put her out of her misery if she was an animal. One of her teeth was broken. She just kept telling him, 'Go away, piss off!' And he would be pissed off too, pissed off into care until she could 'cope', until she got rid of one in the series of 'uncles' who acted out this

221

and similar scenes with his mother, scenes in which she was punished for crimes of sex he never understood. You didn't have to be a shrink to work out that was why he'd become such a wanker.

His memory lurched towards Uncle Michael. It confused him to have an uncle who was a real uncle. He thought he saw the lanky old man's face, a flash like insight in a crowd going down the Strand. What was he doing in the Strand? But then Gerry was back in the flats. She must have been guilty, mustn't she? With the beatings she took. There she was again, crawling on the floor, looking for her contact lenses, she told him. If he ever woke up, maybe he would ask to see her. Why had he never felt sorry for her before?

And there he was again, as if in a video, planting municipal zinnias on a roundabout. Cars were whizzing around him, big lorries too and one of them was going to crash into him before he could complete the design. It spelt something but he couldn't read it. All he knew was that he had to dig and plant, dig and plant the repulsive orange flowers.

There were some humming dead spots that wiped each distinct picture. Suddenly, Harriet was sitting opposite him at a table in a restaurant. He shrank, trying to battle the image off, but she wouldn't go away. There was a starched blue cloth and starched blue napkins, a candle between them. The colours were like the Greek sky. Harriet beckoned him over the table with her index finger. She looked like royalty with that crown of hair and he had the impression of jewels. What was she asking him to do? Kiss her? It made him sick. But you could never tell what it was she wanted. She offered him a bit of food but he refused it. The scent of aniseed filled his head.

If she fancied him he couldn't handle it. She was in control. You could tell from her dainty figure, her oval nails.

Gerry wondered what had happened to time and place. He was in two places simultaneously, splitting from himself now so that he could see as if he had four eyes. He observed himself talking to Harriet and he was also inside himself. It surprised him to see how young he looked. He was very good-looking – how about that! A sharp dresser. No one could have thought he'd been in prison. And he wasn't in prison, but free. It always felt like being on ice without skates for the first few weeks, exhilarating, with moments of black terror.

She was needy, that was it. He actually felt her clutching at his ankles as if she had extra hands, but he saw her too, with her eyes so full, her elbows not touching the table, but propped against it. The ring she was wearing nestled in the soft flesh of one finger. There was a richness of colour and smells, more intense than life. All around the table was dark and, except for the candle, he couldn't see any light at all. She was bewitching, a witch. The little flame shot and guttered. She was toying with a pendant and he couldn't look away.

Quite suddenly, Gerry didn't want to have anything more to do with her. He had no idea why this had come on: it just had. He liked her. It wasn't that he didn't. Now and then he thought he loved her. She had a pretty little mouth and took bites of food with her white teeth, so polite, so lady-like. All of a sudden, he saw himself do it. It was like being his own ghost, a moment not remembered but re-lived. Himself who was watching tried to stop himself who was speaking.

Himself who was speaking thought that Harriet had a right to know the truth: at this precise moment, he also felt a visceral thrill at telling her, at talking about it to a woman. He felt and thought these four things at once: revulsion, gratitude, love and a subtle form of erotic cruelty he had never before experienced. It was a terrible risk.

In vain, himself observing tried to stop it.

'There's something you ought to know, Harriet. It's not easy to talk about, but you've always been straight with me . . .' and then it came out, how he'd done things with boys and that. Then it was she who became a ghost. It shocked him to see her fade. He'd tried to rescue her from the dead and now she was turning to shadow, her arms outstretched. 'Gerry,' she was saying, 'you know

I accept you, whatever you have done.' But he could not see her face because it was too late.

Sas parakalo, sas parakalo, the tannoy said again. From her vantage point, Harriet was startled to see the widows assembling in the stern of the ship. *Tha ftanoume stin Tino stis deka lefta*, the voice continued. The boat was arriving in Tinos. There was a surge of prayer from the black-clad women and their priest. Ahead of her, the island loomed and Harriet noticed a huge marble building crowning its acropolis. Clearly modern, it gleamed in the sunlight, something between a temple and a five-star hotel. The ship thrashed and churned as it slowed, turning to back into the port. As they neared it, Harriet picked out yet another group of black figures. At first she thought they were large animals, what kind she could not tell. They were inching slowly up the broad thoroughfare that led to the white building. With a sharp intake of breath, she realised that they were human beings, moving heaps of black rags. They were crawling slowly and painfully on their hands and knees up the hill. For some reason, Harriet found the sight deeply repugnant.

'Ah, Tinos,' said a male voice behind her. Harriet whirled around. A well-dressed man about her age had been observing her. If he'd had a hat, he might have tipped it. 'I see you have been watching the penitents,' he added, in a German accent, Harriet thought.

'What are they repenting?' she asked, awkward at having her thoughts read.

The man eyed her appreciatively, but no more than a gentleman should. 'Surely that is between themselves and God,' he laughed. 'Do you know Greece?'

She shook her head. 'This is my first visit.'

'Tinos is a place of pilgrimage,' he said. 'There is a miraculous icon of the Virgin in that building you see at the summit of the island . . . it's a shrine. It's frightful on the Feast of the Assumption, do keep away from it in August. All Greece descends on it.

It's their Lourdes . . . piles of discarded crutches in the church
. . . that sort of thing.'

'It looks crowded enough to me now,' Harriet said, for the port
was clustered with soberly dressed Greeks, some looking to catch
the ferry on the outward journey, some milling about clutching
souvenirs. The boat thundered in, the powerful noise of the
screws making it seem impossible that it should touch the lip of
the quay so lightly. There was a great noise of chains being
undone and the huge stern of the ship descended to form a gang-
plank for cars and lorries that fumed out into the crowd.

The German looked at his watch. 'Today is the eighth of
September. That would be the birthday of the Virgin if I remember my Jesuits well.'

'Does she require them to be so abject?' Harriet whispered.

'I suppose it depends,' said the German. 'But mostly people
come for healing.' He gave Harriet a charming smile, taking in
her graceful figure in the shirtwaist dress she had chosen for the
voyage, her respectable cardigan.

Before she knew it, Gerry was behind her, grasping her elbow.
'The food's shit,' he said, 'just like in the nick.' He released his
hard grip just before she gasped out in pain. The German, with
the discreet and knowing smile of a seasoned observer, backed
away. Perhaps he was a doctor. Who knew? Harriet, mortified,
was left with Gerry as the boat slowly thundered out of Tinos
harbour.

'If there are miracles,' she prayed silently, 'Please save Gerry . . .'

But in a few moments, the island was out of sight. Gerry went
inside the ship and slouched in a seat where he glowered in
silence, finally sleeping until Naxos.

The German, who disembarked on Syros, caught Harriet's eye
as she stood on deck. He gave her a wave and a smile oddly full of
understanding.

17

CASSIE HAD INVITED James Gosforth down for the day on Saturday, but as it turned out he ended up staying for dinner. After that, it seemed silly to oust him, especially as the boys eagerly hoped that he would still be there on Sunday morning. A strong wind had got up from the Channel and swept across the Marsh, needling the cottage with rain. So with one thing and another, Cassie made up the bed for him in the spare room, and found a clean towel. Whether he hoped for more than that or not, she could not say. Unsure of her own feelings, she was not prepared to make life more complicated than it was already. Some awkward laughter and nervous smiling, then, went into saying goodnight . . . who should use the bathroom first, that sort of thing. She had a spare toothbrush, but Donald Duck was on the handle. Well, there it was. Quack! She had two children.

Once in her bedroom, with its old exposed beams, she glimpsed herself in the dressing table mirror, then drew nearer, curious at the reflection. Her face was flushed, probably from sitting by the unseasonable fire she'd made; when she realised she looked happy, though, Cassie proceeded to be matter of fact. She knew what it was to risk everything; now she was frugal with her love. Oddly enough, her boys' father had been in touch just the other day. She always called him that to herself, 'the boys' father'. 'His name is Keith,' she muttered to herself. 'Keith,' she repeated. Keith had written to her.

Peering at her face more closely now, she decided she looked positively haggard. Cassie sighed. She really should have sent James packing at tea-time. He had feelings too. Wasn't it compromising them to put him up for the night, even as a friend? The vestiges of Keith clung to her, making her feel small and failed, unworthy of love, and maybe incapable of it.

She brushed her long dark hair, trying to tame the curls, then gave it up as a lost cause because of the wet weather. Luckily, the rain had held off until late afternoon. She could not deny it: they'd had a marvellous day.

The moment she had invited James, she was sure it was going to be awful. It put her in such a panic that she had considered ringing him and begging off, but that had seemed a shabby thing to do when it meant she would have to lie. It was her own stupid fault, and she would have to take the consequences, even if it meant long silences and bruised feelings. Rushing up to Gerry's bedside for the second time in a fortnight, she told herself, had left her in a weakened state, and she had been feeling pretty fragile anyway. Only a few hours before the hospital phoned her with this bad news, Keith's bizarre letter had arrived on the mat.

Cassie gave a sharp laugh and turned from the mirror. A creak from the spare room told her that James was getting into bed, and she blushed crimson, like the teenager she had been when Keith had first taken notice of her, his star pupil. From the constraints of Ashdean, her art school days had seemed sprinkled in fairy dust. Everything about it was wonderful, her tutor above all. She remembered how breathless she had been when he had asked her to go out with him. Slowly, he had opened her naive eyes, initiating her into the belief, among other things, that he was the British answer to Rothko. That he was not emerged only slowly over the years. Cassie even felt guilty when she produced babies rather than inspiration.

When first he'd left them Cassie had tried to arrange for him to see the boys, but he visited them in a sporadic way, and when he did he upset them. John, more closely attached to his father than Alexander, had worried her dreadfully. In the end, everyone seemed happier when he stayed away, including himself, Cassie always thought. This was why hearing from him on the very day of Gerry's stroke had rattled her so badly. She had to read the letter several times to believe he was making a demand for joint custody.

The chances of his achieving this, given his track record, were slim and Cassie knew it. All the same, she spoke with her solicitor for an hour before she finally calmed down and realised that he didn't have much of a case, and would probably forget to pursue it even if he had.

It must have been at the back of her mind, then, that her visits to Gerry Hythe could be used against her if questions of custody arose, because when the hospital rang informing her of his pitiable condition she felt unaccountably threatened. But Gerry had no one else; she had to go. Arming herself with a pack of cigarettes, she puffed her way through half of them as she plied her way once again up the motorway to London. She maintained contact with a sex offender, a relation whose predilection was for boys! *And* she was a smoker, she thought, crushing out an offending, half-finished weed. If Keith made good his threat, how would that look to a judge? By the time she arrived at the hospital, Cassie was grimly battling off hysterics. So she was in equal measure annoyed and relieved to see Gosforth.

Gerry was thirsty. As on her first visit, she became possessed by an unreasonable rage, this time at the nursing staff. He was conscious – this she knew because, in response to her voice, he started patting his mouth with his hand, the only part of him that could move. Why wasn't he on a drip, she wanted to know? She had read about elderly patients being deprived of food and water so that, dehydrated and starved, they died, relieving the body politic of nuisance and expense. Cassie became agitated, thinking that the hospital was conspiring to kill Gerry because he was a criminal. She lost her temper and started throwing accusations about.

When Gosforth intervened, calming her and the antagonistic sister as well, she was surprised at the gratitude she felt. Stony-faced though the staff were, they hooked Gerry up to a drip, but even after they had done this and swabbed his mouth he kept on moving his hand convulsively to his lips. He wanted to talk, that's what it was. He probably wasn't thirsty after all. Cassie felt a fool. Gosforth must think her an unbalanced termagant from the way she had behaved both times they'd met. She did have a quick temper, but it appalled her that she'd thrown her weight around. She sat there miserably squeezing Gerry's hand and talking to him about anything that popped into her head, mostly their grandparents. He always wanted to hear about their grandparents and the manor house she had eschewed, not knowing then that he even existed, not knowing that he might have had his own rights in the matter.

Cassie racked her brains for pleasant memories and was surprised at how few she had. She'd loved her parents' house, a shambolic old Georgian rectory, not exactly a jewel in Ashdean's crown, but homely and pleasant. She saw her grandmother fairly often, but visited her in the manor mostly on family occasions. She'd already given Gerry an edited version of Christmas lunch, and the Easter egg hunt on the lawn that all the villagers were invited to join. The garden – she settled on that. How Gerry would have loved Grandma Maeve's knot garden! One of the village ladies had copied the pattern for a needlework cushion. Most people assumed the maze was Elizabethan, but Grandma had invented it herself. Now and then she would look after Cassie for the day, and they would play secret games in the walled enclosure. Cassie sometimes believed that the maze was a map of a distant land. Grandma Maeve used to say that fairies had parties there in the moonlight, and she told old stories of Celtic sprites and spirits, of strange raptures in which handsome men were transported to beautiful kingdoms where they would be pledged to imperious fairy queens. Thereafter, even if they wanted to, they were never able again to live in the real world. Cassie had always been frightened by these stories, as she was a little by her grandmother. She worried that she might be 'taken', as Grandma put it. But Grandma would say, 'Not you, not ever.'

Cassie babbled on at Gerry until her own mouth was dry.

She found it hard to explain to herself why she was so frightened that Gerry might die. Maybe it was because whenever she stopped talking, he would pat his mouth again until she continued. Gosforth had put his hand on her shoulder. 'Enough!' he whispered. 'You've done enough for one day.' It wasn't as if she loved Gerry. In many ways, she abhorred him. And what would she lose if he died but a burden?

Cassie was unaccountably afraid for him. Maybe the old, often terrible, certainties of childhood lay dormant in the mind until crisis set them off, but she had to fight off an impulse to call the hospital chaplain lest Gerry die an unrepentant death. For whatever reason, a dread arose, primeval, irreducible and nameless. When she thought about Vassilis drowned, hell for Gerry seemed a part of God's justice, not the purlieu of a medieval bogeyman. Cassie shrugged off this theory. Maybe it was simply the idea that Gerry would die chained to a bed in a vacuum of lovelessness. His face was paralysed, his eyelids sealed, his legs so rigid that he looked like a mannequin.

That was how James Gosforth's first trip to the house on the Marsh came about. As they left the hospital, he murmured something about taking in a concert. He had talked to the prison governor about seeing Cassie. Rather than put him through the agony of explaining the reasons behind, and the conditions for, his boss's benevolent ruling, Cassie cut him short. She put him out of his misery and invited him down for the day. She liked him despite herself. Apart from anything else, she was curious about him. He did not seem to fit into any category.

The house creaked in the wind, the rain lashed the windows, and Cassie sought the depths of her bed in the dark. The moment James had stepped into the kitchen that morning, she knew it was going to work. Out of uniform, he was transformed. In his faded chinos and linen shirt, he no longer seemed alien. She imagined a lot of women would think him rather a catch. He loved the country, he told her. What a wonderful house – was he right in thinking that part of it was Saxon? Of course, he was.

As for John and Alexander, he glanced once at their wide, mistrustful eyes, greeted them with a nod and let them be. While he chatted to Cassie, he included them lightly in the conversation without the sugary guile that children detest. How it happened she did not know, but within an hour they were piling into his car with the boys' kites. Before anyone knew it they all seemed fast friends, charging round the beach, untangling strings, making jokes. The boys were deeply impressed that James got the kites to fly; the wind whooshed them airborne where they sailed like gulls above the sea. The power plant at Dungeness hummed and ticked in the middle distance, almost cordially, it seemed to Cassie. Afterwards, James insisted on buying them all lunch at an ancient pub. The boys had crisps and ended up larking about on the swings in the garden while she and James sipped the dark brew he liked and they talked about Gerry. He seemed a little improved. The doctor thought he might pull through. He had regained the use of his vocal cords but no one could yet interpret what he was saying.

The day comfortably bled into evening. The boys were fast asleep even before she went up to turn out their light. Because of the sudden change of weather, Cassie lit the fire. They split a bottle of wine and went on talking . . . a lot about him this time. This seemed something he rarely did. He spoke at first slowly, glancing at her with quick, reflexive eyes.

Gosforth listened for movement from Cassie's room, simply to catch the whisper of her bedclothes. The scent of her and the cottage with the wood fire, mingled with the sea wind, filled him with all that was fresh and clean. There was no point in pretending he was going to sleep, sleeping without her, but it was enough for now to be there in the house. For one thing, he had an intuition that she really did need time. He didn't like the sound at all of the man she referred to so crisply as 'the boys' father'. For another, it went against the grain with him to scandalise her children. He had tried to make sure they were included in everything all day. They'd be only too swift to spot in him the ulterior motive of Cassie. Gosforth remembered hating a man who used to call on his mother. Not that they ever got up to much, he was sure, but the smell of Old Spice had disgusted him ever since and he'd thrown away the sweeteners of toys that were meant to keep him out of the way.

He lay still in the dark, gulping. He had not talked about himself to anyone for so long that it must have come out gormless. He had addressed her like a public meeting, declaiming his opinions. He sensed that it was his job, as much as her ex-partner, that got between them. Did she want to know why he worked for the prison service, he had asked her? He hadn't really told her that he hoped he'd make a difference, had he? Gosforth squeezed his eyes tight shut and muttered an obscenity.

Cassie had been impressed by the way he'd talked. He'd wanted to make a difference, he said, then, with a wry humour she liked, he added, 'That's what people say now, don't they? It's as if we all kept some kind of balance sheet for intractable social problems and I'm talking about a sum on one side that says "before Gosforth" and a sum on the other saying "after Gosforth". The truth is, the difference hasn't been that much.'

She was glad he'd been able to talk to her, quite flattered really. 'Just because reform happens to be an imaginary number it doesn't wreck the equation,' Cassie said, pleased to have turned this sentence out. Maybe it wasn't clever after all. He had smiled. She hoped he thought she was clever.

She was a bit out of his league, Gosforth supposed. Everything in the cottage had the imprint of her quirky individuality, and her confidence to express it. Even the smelly old spaniel that waddled round vacuuming up crumbs seemed the right spaniel, the only dog that would have gone with the room or the pictures on the wall, paintings of her own. There were a lot of Greece, especially a rectangular monument he thought he remembered from his studies, which she had treated over and over again in shades and attitudes of light and darkness. But it was only when he'd said he felt he was being dragged down into a simple containment of evil that she drew her feet up under her in the big basket chair, sat with her head to one side and really listened. The chair had a hood. She rested her chin on one pointed finger. It was easier to talk into the shadow created by her dark, unruly hair.

Sometimes, in his mind's eye, he had a brief, tormenting glimpse of the backs of houses flashing by, as on a train building speed out of a station – houses in which small victims, like trapped birds, flung themselves terrified against the walls and windows while all along a father or an uncle or a family friend crouched, awaiting the fall, the mortal exhaustion. For every one who was caught, how many others got away with it?

How did he switch off? she wanted to know. She told him again what happened whenever she went to see Gerry. But the wind outside and the crackle of fire drowned her soft voice. She muttered anyway, as if she were talking to herself. But he had looked up; she was watching him cannily. As his mind now started to drift and he began to settle, he saw himself reflected in that glance and smiled. He wasn't all that bad, was he? He kept fit. His job wasn't exactly boring.

He had found himself holding forth a bit on things he knew he really shouldn't discuss. He didn't mention names, but the faces of prisoners came to him as if he were communicating who they were. Strolling around the exercise yard of a morning were inmates who had tortured children; watching telly of an evening, those who believed that their victims loved them and enjoyed the gross indecencies that had been perpetrated upon them. Talk about guilt! There was guilt so deep that it seemed to emanate from the primordial abyss. And yet . . .

Once he had started, James talked compulsively, as if the words were air and he had to breathe them. Cassie had known instinctively to withdraw into her chair and sit quite still. Mentally, she sketched his profile, moulding it finer perhaps than it was, but his face, now animated, informed his angular jaw and wide brow with genuine feeling. He was sitting under her pictures of the Portare. After Vassilis died and she went out to Naxos to comfort her parents, she had comforted herself, she supposed, by drawing it obsessively until she calmed down. Since childhood she had loved the great, archaic gate, and was always the first to spot it from the sea when the boat approached the harbour. Her mother liked to call the Portare an anthill for tourists, but her father, who'd gone native with a vengeance, instilled in her all its lore. Cassie realised with a start that, from the way she had arranged the room, visitors always had to sit beneath this wall full of gates she had created, repeated, magnified, diminished in nearly every shade of light and darkness. There was one still more to do. This was the Portare at night, when the monument was lit from below, so that it became almost a beacon for the ships that came and went at all hours. But she wasn't good enough to attempt it yet. The vision came to her in various ways. The illuminated stone became either a frame for darkness, or a gate into it. Sometimes it seemed an imaginary focus on somewhere deep in the universe. Whatever Cassie heard, she had always translated into images. And so she listened intently to James, mostly, as it were, with this inner eye.

There was a force to his words, a quality of mind behind them as if what he detailed to her were atrocities witnessed by a man returned from a secret war. There was a moment when she saw what she must do with the night-time gate; and then it was gone.

If Gosforth had known what she was thinking as he spoke, he could not have asked for a more hopeful indication of their future. Instead, he apologised, abashed at talking about himself so much. 'No, I really *am* interested,' she said. 'Please go on.' He must have been an idiot to take her at her word. Now he thought about it, she had probably even asked him to stay the night out of good manners. He had almost certainly missed a hint that he should go. Yet he had plunged on regardless, taking up her entire evening by telling her how he felt.

There were officers he knew who hated these men they worked with and called them vermin. That was *their* way of switching off, and he almost envied them sometimes. When day after day one discovered fresh evidence of human depravity, contempt became an analgesic for the pain of thought.

'But you do think,' Cassie had said gently.

Then he had become clumsy and he knew it, but as he talked it ceased to matter. How could he explain the quirk in himself that often made him find them moving, these men who were supposed to be monsters, even someone like Gerry? He was sorry he had to say that, but Gerry was one of the most intractable cases. He struggled to articulate their complexity. Maybe it was because they had nothing else to lose; maybe it was because they were a bit like children themselves, but he had seen more goodness in them than he sometimes saw outside. Twisted into the dreadful knot of their desires were weird, shining strands of kindness or generosity or humour. There wasn't any 'they' to it, and once you plunged into this morally confusing area of shared humanity, you were either saved or lost yourself, but at least it was an education. Oddly enough, the one thing he'd miss about the job was the jokes.

A curious peal of mirth came from Cassie. Gosforth glanced at her, suddenly aware that he was becoming a little humourless. And then they had laughed together.

But it wasn't funny, of course, and he'd gone on. It astonished him how many could endure the insidious brutality of prison. Often with great pain some admitted their guilt and longed to make reparation. The worst of it was, the obsessional syndrome that made them offend often rendered their attempts to reform useless. They'd totter out, braced up with good intentions, only to return. A lot of officers dismissed their efforts as manipulative, but James wasn't so sure. Their tendencies were so deep-seated that they often lied to themselves, rather than to others, about the intractable and irreducible canker within.

Did Cassie know how difficult it was, dealing with this day in and day out? Maybe he had expected the prisoners to be tabloid devils, complete with horns and tails and fangs. When you worked with them it made it worse, not better, to realise their teeth were like anyone else's and just as painful when drilled. They had hobbies, harmless foibles and legitimate interests. One man was mad on vintage cars; another had discovered a taste for George Eliot. A group of them undertook to sit up all night with suicidal companions, a lot wrote poetry, they liked Mars bars and tinned peaches, they corresponded with their grannies. There were men inside whose bones had been broken by their own parents in childhood, men so inadequate or mad that they could hardly be judged to have volition. Sometimes behind their cell doors late at night you'd hear them sobbing.

And then they were back to Gerry.

Cassie wished she could sleep. Was James asleep after all he had told her? The loo flushed in answer to this question, but maybe it was one of the boys.

It welled up in her how touched she was at the attention he had paid to John and Alexander. Perhaps it was an antidote to the unwholesomeness that saturated him every day to be so good with young children. The boys had conked out smiling, their steam let off, their energy well spent on the race along the beach. Yet she balked at something about the job James Gosforth did. One read enough about it in the papers, the prison 'canteen culture' with its toxic mix of cruelty, racism, sloth and ignorance. As much as he had railed against it that evening, there was an obscure sense of its dankness clinging to him. Although he read the *Guardian*, Cassie felt certain that the *Sun* was the ruling planet of the penal system.

She sat up in the dark and hugged her knees. How could she be so hypocritical! If Gerry were to live to finish his sentence, would she let him near one of her boys? She wasn't that much of a libertarian. James Gosforth, in all of his incontrovertible decency, stood foursquare between Grisholme and her children. And what about Vassilis? If she were honest with herself, the prison walls could not be too high, nor the keys James wielded too formidable.

But the conversation had been disturbing, there was no doubt about it. When she'd started babbling about Gerry, she'd taken the wrong turning down a dark road. She hadn't really admitted it to him, had she – that she continued her visits to Gerry partly out of fear? The truth was that he threatened her – not because, if he survived to get out, he might do something to her family, but because he was of it. Gerry . . . Hythe.

Maybe it had not been as impulsive as she thought, asking James down to the Marsh, a man whose business it was always to *know*, in whose knowledge there was protection, whose presence could provide a barrier between herself and . . . *what*?

She supposed she'd been silly, rattling on about how she wanted to get the truth from Gerry, and not only about the dead boy. If Keith had not written her his threatening letter, she would have consigned the issue of 'bad blood' to where she had stowed it long ago, in a locked drawer of her memory she rarely opened now. Because it had been Keith who'd got her going when the papers had smeared her family after Vassilis's death. Even though she'd told herself he would say anything, especially to get at her parents who had tolerated his duration with patient martyrdom, his remembered cruelty still struck at her like knives. Had she really told James what he had said – that he was glad the Hythes were out in the open now, her bloody family? That they ought to work 'the fucking pervert' into their escutcheon? He had even implicated his own children's chromosomal heritage in this slur.

Gosforth sensed she was awake for he heard rustling, so when he went to take a leak the opportunist in him checked to see if there was a light under her door. He went back to bed a little ashamed of himself. And one shame led to another. Grisholme's governor had not exactly given him carte blanche to woo Cassie. Liberal and kind he'd certainly been, but trusting too in Gosforth's common sense. There had been various recommendations, but none of them assuming the circumstance that he would fall head over heels into the situation in which he now found himself. He bunched himself now, crossly, under the duvet. Of Cassie, he was sure. And yet he should have foreseen the potential for harm in her, well, mad family.

The rain had stopped, the moon was out and Gosforth watched it sail across the sky. He wondered where it was taking him and what it illumined. It was not that he suspected that Gerry would or could commit any further crime. If that were the case, he would have been blunt with her about going to the police. It was more his sense of being pulled into a web that did not yet, but might still, lead first to little compromises, then larger ones.

Gosforth had a sudden, vehement wish to seek out this ex-partner of hers and punch his lights out. Why was he so aggressive? He folded his arms across his chest in the dark and scowled. The insult about the Hythe family escutcheon that 'the boys' father' had lodged at Cassie might have been puerile, but taken with inklings he had gleaned from Gerry, inklings indeed he had gleaned from her, there was a misgiving he could not shake off. What could he base on the snatched narratives he had to hand?

He'd uncovered only little pieces – if he had remained an archae-ologist, they wouldn't add up to a vase.

All the same, he was stuck with the impression that Cassie had a dragon. It pleased Gosforth, this image, as it stalked out of the mist of his confusion. The crux of the matter seemed to be that she recognised, but only dimly, what manner of beast it was.

The series of choices he might have to make became clearer to him. He could leave Cassie tied to her family tree, of which her cousin was a significant leaf. Her cousin was his prisoner, poor sod, and that might make a difference to what Gosforth as an officer did or did not do in future. The most obvious course of action was to throw himself on the governor's mercy, and put a moratorium on seeing her at least until Hythe died.

Or he, an odd St George, could lie in wait for the dragon to emerge from its cave, then strike with the force of the knowledge he had to hand before it devoured her. It irritated Gosforth to see himself in this romantic light, but it shone all the same, almost counter to the moonlight, on his restless imaginings.

He liked reason, and tried it again. There was nothing to suppose that Cassie Hythe was tied to any tree at all. She was as balanced an individual as he had ever met, with that Greek inde-pendence of mind he liked in his half-sisters. And she was tough. She'd raised her children well, and against some odds.

All the same, as she had spoken her fears, almost whispering them into the fire, he'd clicked into a kind of watchfulness which, he supposed, was a core value in his job. Something was amiss about the Hythes, on the loose, that padded about in the wake of the boy's death. Or murder. Was it the story of her father's shattering breakdown after Hythe's visit to the island? Maybe it was some of the things she'd said about this Ashdean place, where Hythe's junkie father had been buried. And the snobby uncle she'd spoken about. Why had he sold the family seat after the scandal? Why had first her parents, then she, refused to live in it? One did not give away lightly a heritage of eight hundred years.

He hoped she'd thought he'd listened, because he had listened and very carefully, but none of this complicated family story seemed to make much sense. Then, there it suddenly was, sharp as an alarm bell. For all that Gerry Hythe was gravely ill, in prison and cut off from any society that included children, he still had power to do harm. Gosforth sifted this in his mind now. It was when she had spoken of her urge to discover what her cousin knew that it struck him, and struck him on behalf of her children too. If Hythe really did have some missing piece in his possession, and if Cassie crossed him . . . Well, the poor bastard was on his way out anyway, and he adored her. It did seem an overreaction to take this line. But Gosforth had the distinct impression that Cassie had been shielded all her life, but insufficiently. It was the way she spoke of Naxos.

She probably wouldn't have provided her own small piece of the puzzle if he hadn't been resisting the temptation to sweep her into his arms. Standing up to go to bed, they had shifted from foot to foot, circling the question without raising it, and so he asked her about her paintings, the ones of the marble gate. He did really like them. He was honest about that yet, to his pained frustration, she had taken refuge in them, spiralling off about the island and her Greek grandfather, the house her mother had inherited – the house that Gerry's crime now defiled and haunted.

He was in love with her, wasn't he? As he articulated this in his mind he realised the truth of it, rather in the way he would know he had flu at the first or second heavy sneeze. He swore and, pulling the covers hard around his ears, he finally went to sleep.

Not so Cassie. She did not know the time, but she expected she would be pretty wrecked in the morning. So she tried to play the game she had explained to James, one that she'd invented for herself as long ago as childhood as a way of getting to sleep. Then it had worked in almost all situations – the night before exams, after awkward colloquies with Grandma Maeve who, almost like a ghost herself, would grieve and keen for Uncle Edgar to Cassie's private ear, times like that. It had developed over the years, and after what Gerry had done it was difficult to engage upon. But oddly enough, what was central to it survived even that.

It was simple. She would imagine arriving in Naxos for the holidays, the porters at the quayside greeting her, her Greek coming back to life after the slumber of winter. Everyone knew her and she knew everyone, and she would try to call each face to mind, a bit like counting sheep. Sometimes this alone would send her off. But if this charm failed, she would carry on in her imagination, running up through the town, finding her way through the labyrinth of streets like Ariadne herself with the ball of wool, not stopping till she reached the tall gates of the Kastro where she would draw breath. Then she would sneak, hiding behind a wall or crouching behind the perfect little cathedral as she stalked her grandfather's house. It was a game they always played in real life. She always knew he knew she was coming, but they both pretended he did not, and when she arrived she would pounce, jumping out of the shadow of his little front atrium with its pots of bougainvillaea, its geraniums and lilies. He would cry in mock alarm, and then he would take her up and swing her round in his big hug, and she would pull on his whiskers, and he would pretend it hurt him, and then he would take her in and give her portakalada. Then she would sit on his tall, overstuffed chair, sip the orange juice and look at the blue sky and the bright flowers and swing her legs: safe. Yes, she told him, at last able to articulate it, Naxos made her feel both safe and clean.

In the morning, she was wakened by the rude racket of James Gosforth and the boys trying their hand at a makeshift breakfast, and imitating warlike noises that sounded like low-flying aircraft.

18

WHEN THE BIG FERRY churned into port, Michael recognised his nephew at once, picking him out of a horde of arriving tourists. He spotted Gerry before he realised that the woman trundling luggage after him was Harriet. Eleni had declined to meet the boat, pleading the necessity of putting a final touch to the guest rooms, but Michael turned his head to the side as if she were there, saying softly to his startled Greek neighbour who was touting for hotels, 'He looks like my father.'

Gerry, who had wheeled a large case down the gangway, stood squinting at the sun. He might have been anywhere, the middle of a field. He made no recognition of the crowds around him as they pushed and shoved. Grown children greeted elderly parents, wives their husbands, sweethearts each other. A party of French tourists, well dressed, well heeled, flocked prettily around a young Greek who looked like a graduate student with a summer job he was surprised to find agreeable. Michael thought Gerry must be very nervous, which would explain his stiffness. He held his shoulders rigid and clenched his fists, a man about to be shot.

Michael hadn't seen Harriet in a long time. He supposed it was no surprise that she had aged considerably, given what they'd heard of Averell Washington's behaviour. As ever, she was smart, though. In her blue dress with the pure white hair crowning her head, she suggested the sea and breezes. She craned her neck for a sight of him and he slipped out of the waiting crowd, taking a deep breath as he did so and expelling it through his nose.

'Oh!' she cried as if she'd been hit instead of greeted. 'Oh, Michael, there you are! How lovely!' She made a pass at the air twice, kissing him on both cheeks. Gerry turned his head slowly. He and Michael observed each other slowly. And he looks like Edgar too, Michael thought, down to the bony forehead and green eyes.

'How do you do? You must be Gerry,' he said proffering a hand at last. 'I am your uncle Michael. Welcome to Naxos.'

Gerry took his fingers in a weak grip, hardly a handshake at all; it felt more like the brush of anemones in the sea. 'Cheers!' he said, 'Hiya. Nice to meet you.' It was as if he were wearing sunglasses but he wasn't, his eyes were so opaque.

'Did you have a good journey?'

'Oh, lovely!' Harriet dived in to save face for the motionless Gerry.

'There can be squalls this time of year,' Michael said, making for the luggage. He hoped she wasn't going to leap into every pause, but then she must be nervous too. 'This is quite a day for us all,' he added. 'You must be very tired. I should think you long to get settled. It's rather a way up I'm afraid, and there's no getting there by car.'

Without further ado, he mastered Harriet's case and the three of them made their way through the thinning crowd across the sea front and into the labyrinth of winding alleys and passageways that constitute Naxos Town. It is all of a piece, a conical city that rises in vertical ascent from the port to the acropolis. The town was drowsy now in the early afternoon, when children were home from school and families had a meal and a siesta. The seller of foreign newspapers greeted Michael as he trekked by with Harriet and Gerry. The women in the zacharoplasteia likewise looked up; they were twisting squares of tulle around parcels of sugared almonds for a christening. Quickly scrutinising Harriet's smart clothes, they waved at Michael. Eleni patronised the shop and would be able to answer questions later.

Michael had been worried enough about having Gerry in his

own home, but it hadn't struck him before that his neighbours might have reasonably objected to the visitor if they'd known his last address. Gerry didn't look like a burglar, though, Michael thought nervously. Surely, if he and Eleni gained his trust . . .

Up the flagged incline they went, past the old white houses mostly now turned to tourist shops where scarves fluttered in the breeze and picture postcards stood on racks not yet brought in from the heat of the day because of the newly arrived boat.

'Look at that, will you!' Gerry cried suddenly, as they turned a winding corner.

Michael and Harriet glanced at each other in veiled relief that he had finally spoken and in enthusiastic tones. A deep pink bougainvillaea poured generously down an old wall that buttressed the ascent. Gerry's eyes flashed. 'I've never seen anything like that before!'

'Magnificent, isn't it? Harriet tells me that you know a great deal about plants and flowers.'

Gerry nodded stiffly, shy once more. 'I did once.'

'You've come to the right place, then. There isn't a Greek on earth who doesn't have some kind of a garden. They cultivate even the most difficult plants in olive oil tins. You should see it when the lilies bloom in every doorway. And the wild flowers are beyond description!'

They wound up, trudging now up a great stone flight of steps. In the background a tape was playing flute music. A wind chime tinkled in someone's balcony and the breeze blew the high leaves of the shade tree under which they passed.

'This is something else!' Gerry said and he smiled, for the first time looking straight at his uncle. An Orthodox church, newly whitewashed and gleaming in the sun, rose above them on a corresponding mound, its scrolled façade sharp against the pure blue sky. The air was soporific with the afternoon heat and the scent of late summer roses emanated subtly from walled gardens hidden from the eye.

'I think you'll like our house then,' Michael said, pleased. 'I hope so . . . but we have a farm too, out in the country. You might be interested in that.'

'Do you grow produce or keep animals?' Gerry asked. They had all but forgotten Harriet. Michael turned round and courteously stopped when they saw that she was lagging behind. She has indeed aged, he thought. She looked frail, almost elderly. 'Oh dear, I should have warned you about the climb,' he called down. 'Everyone here has thighs like goats from rushing up and down this hill!'

Gerry laughed uproariously. It was out of place. Sticky for the poor chap. Michael softened. Since they started the ascent, little eddies of mind had whirled up then away – a recognition, an awfulness of knowing this was his brother's son. He had an impulse to reach out and touch Gerry as if to brace himself and his nephew, making a balance between them, the fulcrum of it Edgar.

'Shall we sit while you catch your breath?'

Harriet shook her head. 'The sooner we get there the better. I had no idea I'd become so unfit.' She looked at him with a worried air. She was understandably apprehensive about this, her project. Michael wondered if she had kitted out her protégé for the visit. His clothes looked new and seemed to sit poorly on him. He remembered Edgar's seamy urbanity. He'd been a bit of a dandy in his own way with his old, good tweeds. Poor woman, she'd gone to such trouble and expense. He felt a twinge of pity.

Another bend in the road and they were on the final leg that led up a flagged street to a medieval gate. The walls girding the acropolis were old and mellow with crenellations sweeping round in a graceful curve. 'I've taken you in the back way because it's easier,' said Michael.

'There's a harder way?' Gerry joked and Harriet gave a mannered laugh. Some neighbours, a trader and a restaurateur, were playing backgammon in the shade of the wall; they looked up and greeted Michael as the little party passed under the arch with its thatched eaves, and into the Kastro.

Michael dreaded the next step, his wife. Harriet's case weighed a ton and his fingers slipped sweatily on the handle where 'AW' was engraved in gold. The impedimenta of Averell, he supposed. Perhaps Harriet and Eleni would form a new bond based on indignation at her husband's shabby conduct. On a level passageway now, he watched Harriet as she went ahead, shoulder to shoulder with Gerry, one would say, except that she was a head taller. His legs, Michael noticed, were slightly bandied; there was something not altogether gelled about his body, as if God had been absent from the full creation of Gerry. Harriet's gait, now graceful, drew attention to it, the way he rolled as he walked. Perhaps he'd had some childhood disease, or maybe . . . Michael didn't want to think of the effects of heroin on an unborn child. Could a father transfer this? The mother could, but then he'd been through this before in his mind, thinking of the mother, wondering about her. How had Edgar met her?

'This is utterly lovely!' said Harriet, waving her hand at the charming scene. They had reached a fork in the road. Pointed arches and doorways topped with marble lintels gave complex vistas of the citadel which swept upwards in a unified whole . . . stone interlocking with stone, a burrow of passageways tunnelling and white flights of steps going nowhere, scaling the ancient walls. Ancient escutcheons, lozenges and stars and hearts, marked ducal thresholds, and towering palm trees thrust into the sky, their leaves clashing gently in the breeze, audible in the silence.

And they were there. Carved over the front door was the Bellini crest, a dove descending. Michael took his key and opened to a pretty courtyard filled with vines and tubs of red geraniums. The inner door was open and standing in a spacious hall was Eleni, her hand extended; she smiled, but her eyes were cold. Michael's heart sank.

Harriet had never been so nervous in her life. A memory of the stage came back to her, waiting in the wings on first nights. Her mouth was dry from the climb and from the terror. She bit the tip of her tongue, an old trick to get the saliva going. She talked herself down. Everything had gone pretty well so far, hadn't it? She had to give credit to Michael. His own emotions were clearly moved by the meeting, but putting Gerry at ease seemed his main concern and Harriet realised that she missed the skill of gentlemen. Her agonising worries on the boat began to recede. With someone as well-bred as Michael (and she had to face the fact that this did matter), they were sure to work things out. The beauty of the island, too, surprised her, its tranquillity. She must concentrate now on Gerry's debut.

On arriving at the house Harriet caught her breath. She hadn't really taken it in, the scale on which the Hythes now lived. It was as if she had rehearsed Gerry for *The Mousetrap* only to find he must play Hamlet against a lavish set of Elsinore. How was he going to cope with this? Even with Godfrey and Sophie, it might have been easier for him to manage Ashdean Manor, the sort of property, after all, one saw advertised in *Country Life*. This place . . . well, it was a miniature palazzo. Behind the unassuming stucco façade there was an easy and unostentatious grandeur to the well-proportioned hall that she and Gerry entered. He looked around, awed. Harriet flushed with embarrassment at the way he gawked.

'Helen!' she found herself crying in her confusion. She clutched at her old friend as if they had been the dearest confidantes divided only by time and distance. Helen braced her by both shoulders and, keeping her slightly at a distance as if she had a cold, kissed Harriet on both cheeks.

Suddenly, it made tears prick at Harriet's eyes to be reunited with Helen/Eleni; for the first time really since the divorce, a genuine gratitude for someone who had once been familiar to her leapt in her heart. 'How well you look! What a lovely house! How kind of you to have us!' Harriet found herself burbling.

Eleni thawed into giving Harriet a squeeze, this time more affectionatet, then, holding her at arm's length, gazed into her

247

eyes. 'It's been such a long time.' For a moment she held her in this way, looking at her quizzically; then, releasing her, she turned to Gerry, offering her hand. She spoke now with a perfect courtesy that Harriet knew to be mistrustful. 'I am happy to meet you,' she said. 'Good of you to come all this way. Would you like some coffee? Or would you prefer to rest from your journey and have coffee later? Perhaps some water? A Sprite?'

Harriet noticed that she had acquired a faint Greek accent.

Gerry looked wildly to Harriet for social direction. 'I think we're fine, thank you so much,' she said.

'Then perhaps just to get your bearings we'll have a guided tour,' Eleni said, as if to lodgers. She was wearing jeans, probably couture, Harriet thought, and an expensive-looking white cotton jumper with a cowl neck. Eleni looked almost as magnificent as her ancestral house and yet made Harriet feel overdressed. She threw open the double doors from the hall with conscious flair and they followed her into the vast space of the drawing room, united by the amazement she had wanted to elicit from them.

The room, with its high rafters, looked out upon the sea. Indeed, the view from the tall windows first gave the impression that the world outside had been transmuted, liquefied into an iridescent blue. This agreeable impression was delightfully offset by a decor that might have seemed fussy elsewhere, but was exact in its effect there. Stuffed sofas draped with lace stood braced to attention round spindly tables; sepia photographs of moustachioed Greeks and their rigid wives, embroideries and tapestries hung about the walls. There were grand chests, elegant tallboys, dried flowers, but it all hung together.

'It's beautiful,' Gerry murmured. 'Do you really live here?'

'Of course,' Eleni was brusque but she laughed, and Harriet could tell she was pleased.

'Over there,' Michael spoke so abruptly that everyone looked around. 'Over there is your great-great-grandmother . . . Gerry. That portrait. Do you see?'

An odd silence followed this. Harriet looked in the direction he indicated but she bit her lip. Guilt pinched her like bad shoes. Michael was being truly good to Gerry, not just considerate. Imagine initiating this stranger, a man – she now knew – who had been in prisons half his life, into the family hierarchy like this! It was a generous thing to do and her worst instinct was that Gerry was unworthy of the gesture.

The ancestress in question smiled down on them. Gerry stood stock still, his lips parted.

'She was Lady Montescue, her husband was in Gladstone's government: Clarissa Hythe.'

Lady Montescue held a sliver of a hand towards her cheek, accentuating the dimple therein. Her glossy hair with its rich ringlets shone to a high polish. No earthly passion but kindness could have touched her heart. Her adorable mouth could not have uttered a disagreeable word.

'Thank you,' Gerry said softly, glancing at his uncle. 'Thank you very much indeed.'

Not knowing exactly what to do or where to put her hands, Harriet drifted to the window, where Helen stood. Only she wasn't Helen any more, was she? Harriet couldn't imagine how she had shared a school run with this exotic, European creature. 'You can see the Portare from here, our famous monument.' Eleni waved a hand towards the harbour far below. 'Did you notice it coming in? Sometimes I think I can catch sight of Ariadne down there, her ghost wailing at the desertion of Theseus.'

Harriet smirked nervously.

'You're right about the resemblance,' Eleni murmured sotto voce. 'He is Edgar to the life.'

Harriet gave a perfunctory look at the distant marble relic. The mound on which it stood was now alive with tourists, dwarfed by the Portare.

'It looks like a gigantic window . . .' Harriet said.

'Yes, people say that,' Eleni replied. 'But it's a door.'

Harriet thought she heard a catch in her friend's voice; swiftly she glanced at Eleni whose head was fixed towards the sea. 'So lovely to be here,' she repeated. 'So kind of you.' But Eleni made no reply.

'But your rooms!' she said at last. She bit on the words decisively. 'You must be exhausted!' And she went into a discursive tale of bad boats or missed boats or uncomfortable journeys in boats. Michael stood with Gerry at the other end of the room. Although he was a full two heads taller than his nephew, he looked oddly inconsequential beside him. Perhaps this was because he stood in the shadow and Harriet's eyes had been affected by the bright sunlight. Since she had met Gerry she had never seen him in such high definition. He held himself erect. Maybe the beautiful room provided a flattering backdrop; maybe it was a result of his introduction to Lady Montescue, but all at once Gerry seemed, finally, to fit. His face relaxed into an engaging smile as she and Eleni approached. He was holding a large photograph album.

'Uncle Michael said I could look at these . . . at my leisure,' he said. 'It seems I have grandparents too! Harriet! I have . . .' he could not finish. 'I have . . .' And he shook his head from side to side, tears in his eyes. 'Thank you, all of you.'

19

ONLY AFTER DINNER did Harriet and Eleni find themselves alone together. A walled stone terrace extended from a parlour below the drawing room, overlooking the harbour. The two women, wrapped in shawls against the night air, took their coffee out and sat huddled in the lee of a hefty turret. The meal had gone far better than Harriet expected. Was she imagining that Eleni had been avoiding her all evening? Harriet felt wounded.

Michael and Gerry lingered with cognac in the drawing room above. Their voices, Michael's deep and Gerry's nasal, rose and fell in the background like a radio chat show, tense and spuriously friendly. Now it fell to the two women to make conversation, there seemed little leeway for a beginning. Ashdean had groomed them both to excel in uncontroversial chat and so they 'caught up', weaving at details of their lives like two lacemakers at work on doilies.

Far below them the town spread out, lively and spangled with light: from a way off, a large ship was making for the harbour, its white bulk ghostly on the distant water. The deep tone of its horn ruptured the air and immediately the quay was alive with cars and lorries that seemed to appear from nowhere. Porters with their barrows, tourists with their backpacks, surged forward into the general mêlée. Inside, the men continued talking. Though Harriet strained to catch the words, only isolated phrases emerged. 'My father . . .' she heard Gerry say. 'Your grandmother . . .' Michael said, but it was impossible to piece together the fragments of sound into an intelligible whole.

Eleni had certainly killed the fatted calf. Walking into the well-appointed dining room earlier, Harriet groaned inwardly at the social assault course this was going to be for Gerry on his very first night. The table seemed needlessly arrayed with silver cutlery, laid neatly in ascending order of courses. Was she right in thinking the grandeur excessive? It proclaimed a social rigour, a policy of no concessions. Not that it was pretentious. The Hythes had no need to pretend. The feast was either a compliment to Gerry or a warning, Harriet thought; perhaps both. A protective desperation clutched her heart.

They sat down to a confusing array of meze: tiny fish that needed expertise to eat, a variety of vegetable pâtés, meats. Gerry hadn't bothered to wear his new tie for the occasion; he hadn't even changed, so he wouldn't have showered. 'Watch the others then copy them,' Harriet whispered helplessly.

He startled her with a contemptuous look. 'I'm up for it, Harriet,' he said, unfurling his napkin on his lap. At least he didn't tuck it under his chin.

But he was a bit of a chameleon; there seemed no doubt of that. Maybe there was more of Edgar in him than met the eye.

Not that anyone mentioned Edgar. Even though the thrust of every word implied a deep enquiry into the connection, the Hythes clearly felt that family matters were not for general consumption. Perhaps what evoked Edgar most was the way in which Gerry slowly took command of the table. The few times Harriet had met Edgar he'd always made himself the focus of attention, his Byronic hair scraping his collar. He seemed to swagger, even sitting down. Gerry had none of his father's assurance, but as the dishes came and went and the drink flowed he began to gain a curious control: he was not constrained, he seemed to say, by the awkward protocols of gentility.

Prison was, of course, a subject everyone was at pains to avoid but Gerry brought it up, dragging it into the conversation with surprising finesse. Michael was carving the chicken Eleni had roasted . . . oh, with such herbs! Gerry received his plate. He spoke with cheery frankness. 'I wish they could see me now on F Wing!' His eyes bulged in mock surprise, a caricature of Oliver Twist.

'It must be a terrible place,' Michael said solemnly. Harriet smiled to herself at his reverential tone. She had come a long way since Grisholme had seemed alien, formidable in its horror. Even the evil smell of the prison seemed familiar, as if she had actually been locked up herself.

'The food was garbage,' Gerry said, 'but you get used to it . . . food, prison. It's a routine you get into. There are plenty who prefer it to the outside, if they're honest with themselves. It's warm, it's dry; things happen on time; you don't have to find the rent or pay the gas bill or deal with relationships.' He tucked into the chicken. 'This is great!' he told Eleni. 'You're an ace cook.' Gerry menaced the tender breast with his knife, and conveyed a large chunk to his mouth, dripping the buttery juices on the cloth.

Eleni drew back like a cat retracting itself to a new position of watchfulness. 'Thank you.' All four swilled a little wine in unison.

'Mind you, I was lucky. I learned my lesson,' Gerry continued. Harriet noticed small but significant shifts in his diction. It was as if he spoke in the vernacular for effect now, putting it in inverted commas. In other, subtle ways his behaviour was re-adjusted. She could not pinpoint how, but it irritated her. He looked different, almost confident, the wavy hair on his brow boyish, his eyes filled with that kind of keenness she associated with a certain kind of public school, not Grisholme. Harriet felt a surge of anger at the fraud, then pain. Why should he have to pretend at all, put on airs?

She peered at Gerry across the table. Was it the drink or simply being with old friends? Slowly a sense of unreality grew on her. Had he really molested children? Maybe it was a test. Maybe he was testing her to see if she would accept him unconditionally.

For the second time that day, she began to wonder whether what he'd said was true.

'That's good to know,' Eleni said dryly, but whether Gerry heard her or not was unclear. Michael shot a look at his wife and stepped into the breach.

'It must be a difficult lesson to learn,' he said gently. 'Impossible in some cases, I understand.'

Again, Harriet could not escape this new impression of Gerry as a clean-cut boy who'd got mixed up in bad company, smoked behind the gym or got drunk on some under-age spree. He looked at his uncle with a candid gaze. 'It's true, what you say, but I had help . . .' he swept the gaze towards Harriet and raised his glass in her direction.

The Hythes looked uncomfortable and Harriet squirmed.

'I did nothing,' she said lamely.

'Why am I here now?' he asked then, lowering his eyes, continued to eat. 'Most people don't bother,' he said to the plate. 'Not like Harriet.'

Michael could barely take his eyes off Gerry. The quality of his regard was hard to fathom. 'It's nice to hear,' he said at last. 'Nice to hear genuine gratitude.'

Gerry beamed a smile at his uncle. Their eyes met, gazes locked. They were mesmerised by each other, she thought.

'What do you intend to do now you have left . . . Grisholme?' Michael continued. 'Have you had any thoughts?'

'I don't know . . .' he flicked little glances at Eleni. This drew attention to her in a way that made Harriet uneasy. Her face had become hard in the sense of being opaque, but she was not to be drawn. 'I suppose I thought I might try out some charity work,' Gerry continued. 'I'd hate to see kids get mixed up in the sort of thing . . .' He stammered and Harriet froze. 'Perhaps not that. Actually, I've heard of ex-cons who have gone into the Probation Service. I wondered if I'd give that a crack. Harriet has given me so much confidence. I could finish my education, you know.'

'That's very constructive,' said his uncle, 'a good idea.'

'I have another one,' Gerry said, looking modestly down, 'but it's probably unrealistic.'

'What's that, Gerry?' Harriet asked. She had not spoken for so long that her throat needed clearing and the words came out hoarsely.

'Well, I do know something about gardens, I suppose you could say. I wondered about starting a garden centre.'

'That's not unrealistic. Is it?' Michael asked. 'It sounds better to me than probation . . . it gets away from the whole . . .'

' . . ."sordid business", as my father used to say?'

There was a moment of disquiet, far deeper than could have been reasonably expected at this slightly contentious remark.

Gerry had become rather tipsy, Harriet realised. He gave, however, a quick smile. 'It *is* sordid. Prison is and so is crime. I'm finished with it!'

No one knew what to say. He speared a potato and ate it, mouth open.

'No, my ambition is a bigger one. I thought I might specialise in roses. I've got an idea for a new rose, a pink one. You know, I once helped set up a display at the Chelsea Flower Show and I met a lot of people in rose growing.'

'I didn't know that, Gerry! You never told me that.' She spoke in an overly bright way, covering for him. Why, after what she knew, was she doing this?

Gerry turned to his uncle and studied him intently for a moment. 'You said that it was nice to hear gratitude. But words don't mean much, do they? After all Harriet has done for me, I want to show it. Do you know the rose Mme Antoine Marie? It's a hybrid tea, scented with big flowers. I'd like to breed something like that, but a deeper pink. And I've decided what to call it too. I thought about it night after night in prison when I couldn't sleep. I've decided to call the new rose "Harriet Washington"!'

There was a frozen pause in which tears came to Harriet's eyes. She didn't cry, though. 'Good Lord! What nonsense!' she said gruffly to Gerry's insouciant gaze, but she flushed. 'It's a sweet thought, Gerry,' she added, in case she had hurt his feelings.

Harriet and Gerry scrutinised each other over the table. He turned first to Michael then to Eleni with an enigmatic smile. 'You won't ever know what it's like to be in prison,' he said, 'until they bang you up and you hear that cell door close behind you for the first time.'

An odd but respectful silence ensued.

But now Harriet and Eleni had been sitting on the balcony for a good half-hour. The evening star hung in crisp definition over the Portare far below in the harbour. Harriet kept glancing at it. An activated blackness seemed to well up from inside the illuminated lintels, as if the gate were a frame for dark thought, thought that had not yet articulated itself to the conscious mind. She was trying to listen to what Eleni was saying, something about her brother-in-law Godfrey and the manor. He'd been trying to open it to the public on certain days but no one was interested in seeing it. All this she had from Cassie, little snippets.

Harriet glanced at her old chum and idiotically remembered her buying chops at the butcher. How could this woman be Helen, a core guest at Harriet's annual garden party, full of verve and flashing black eyes, that slightly unconventional vertebra in the backbone of Ashdean society? What had shifted in her to make her so inscrutable? She was now as illegible to Harriet as if even her thoughts were written in Greek letters. It seemed she had thrown her Ashdean years in the Aegean, like so much unwanted baggage. Eleni, not Helen, was treating Harriet with the remote courtesy of a new acquaintance. And why was it she said nothing about Gerry – surely some remark was called for?

'I was so sorry to hear about you and Averell,' Eleni ventured at last. She pulled her fine-spun Black Watch wrap up to her chin against the night air.

Harriet's breath came out slowly. At least Averell was not an impersonal topic. It startled her a bit to realise that she barely thought about him these days, but an answer was required and she gave the sort of sigh that she thought Eleni expected.

'Oh dear, I hope you don't mind my bringing it up,' said Eleni.

'Not at all! No, I'd like to talk about it. It was a dreadful shock, of course. We'd been together for so long. But now I look back on it, we were never what I'd call "compatible".'

'If it's any use to you, I could never bear that Sally person,' Eleni said. 'Ghastly, pushy woman!'

Harriet smoothed her silken purple skirt, like moth wings in the dark. She shrugged. 'I never really knew her. Just by sight. In fact, I discovered that I was the very last to know about her and Averell. I remember bumping into her in the Co-op just a few days before I learned. She was affability itself. You know, in a padded jacket and Barbour.'

'The quintessence of Ashdean, I would have said! Oh, it was a horrid place. I'm so glad we're out of it. So must you be.'

'Averell needed her, or so he told me.'

'For *what?*'

'You know!'

For some reason Eleni started to giggle. Despite herself, Harriet laughed too and kicked off her painful shoes under the wrought iron table.

'The mind boggles!' said Eleni with neat acidity. 'A bit hard on Emma, though. It is at any age, I understand. How's she taken it?'

'You know Emma.' Harriet wriggled her toes and slid the shoes back on. As they were speaking, another ship had arrived with sudden speed and was backing down on the quay. Voices from a tannoy reached all the way up to the balcony. 'Emma takes everything hard.' Harriet pursed her lips. Her daughter. Emma was staging yet another crisis: she was mortally wounded that Harriet wouldn't be in London for her visit. 'She's doing well for herself professionally though. As we speak, she's interviewing Salman Rushdie for the *New York Times*,' Harriet added.

'I'm impressed!'

Harriet had a sharp urge to say, 'She's a selfish little cow!' It was an expression Gerry had used when she told him about her daughter. How could it occur to her to say such a dreadful thing? Instead she said, 'And Cassie?'

'Also a professional success,' said Eleni, 'but the boyfriend . . . sorry . . . *partner* . . . Ah me!'

'It's a different generation,' Harriet said, though they might easily have said it in unison.

'They were so sweet together, Emma and Cassie, when they were little! Do you remember?'

'I always loved Cassie!' Harriet cried. 'She was so original. And kind. Cassie was a kind child. Do you remember how she tried to set up that animal rescue station? I remember her weeping wretchedly when they died, baby hedgehogs, things like that.' It was dark and Harriet wanted to say it in the dark. 'Emma is like a man. She has the mind of a man.'

Eleni said nothing. 'Daddy's girl, I suppose,' she said softly, after a moment.

Harriet felt the awkward pressure of censure but could not see Eleni's face well enough to determine how severe it was. 'Yes, I have to confess that hurts me. She has entirely taken her father's side.'

'What does she think about your prison visiting? Gerry? You know, she must admire that!'

Again, it was hard to read Eleni for what direction this might take. 'She's not interested.' The truth was that Harriet had not told Emma about Gerry. She waited, making an act of will not to twist the fringe of the woollen shawl Eleni had lent her.

'It must be terribly difficult, a very exacting job. I'm sure I couldn't do it!'

In the lull between them, Harriet noticed that the ship, swiftly arrived, was as swiftly gone, its stern like the tail of a glow-worm now upon the open waters of the Aegean. She could hear Gerry's voice from the room above stumbling out a long description or explanation. Perhaps he was telling Michael his secret. The very thought gave her a cold blow to her stomach. Why, she could not tell. It was what she wanted, that he should come clean and confess, get everything out in the open to the Hythes and thus spare her a hideous moral burden.

'It's very rewarding,' she said carefully. 'If one can do it, one can; if not, well . . .' She paused. 'It is difficult – what was the word you used? – "exacting" for you to have Gerry to stay like this. You needn't have, but . . .'

'Michael needed to,' Eleni said abruptly. 'He never completely recovered from Edgar's death.'

'I'm sorry.'

'Why should you be? You only wrote a letter. Suppose you hadn't? Michael had a right to know, I think, don't you?'

It was an ameliorating thing to say, but the angle was wrong, the angle of sound, the edge on Eleni's voice.

'What do you think of him?' Harriet could bear it no longer.

Eleni said nothing for a moment. 'It's you I'm thinking of.' She spoke carefully.

'You dislike him then!' Harriet could hear her voice rising and trembling but there was nothing she could do about it.

'I didn't say that. I hardly know him.' As fleet as a bat in her dark shawl, she leaned forward. 'Harriet, you've been through a ghastly divorce after over thirty years of marriage! Dear Harriet!' She grasped Harriet's hand.

Harriet was outraged and pulled her hand away. 'There is nothing, really nothing like that between us, I can assure you!'

'Does he know that?' Eleni asked.

'Gerry isn't interested . . .' she nearly said 'in women' but stopped herself.

'Harriet, I'm sorry. I imagine it is a sore point. Do forgive me. Let's be friends.'

Normally, Michael was not a heavy drinker, though in Ashdean he once had been. Since moving to Naxos, he had gradually fallen into step with the more abstemious Greeks; besides, his peaceful life made drink less necessary. That night, however, they'd put a lot away. It wasn't as if they were drunk, Michael told himself, but Gerry was garrulous now. He sat hunched with elbows on wide-spread knees, fiddling with the empty balloon glass between his legs, a signal for more brandy. Alcohol had stripped away his thin veneer, making his voice rasp, a file sawing through the hard substance of his life story. It wouldn't do to seem bored.

In any case, it wasn't boredom that made Michael stifle a yawn. Gerry had been talking in an obsessional monotone for what seemed hours, about his awful childhood. To listen to the catalogue of harshness and neglect was oddly tiring, especially when all of it was due to Edgar's obsidian pride. Why hadn't he asked the family for help? Maybe Gerry's mother had been frightened of losing him if the Hythes stepped in. And she would have had a point. The woman sounded barmy, and Queen Maeve would have spared no effort to get him away.

'. . . so you see,' Gerry was saying, 'Edgar did have plans to bring me to Ashdean.' He put the glass down on the table, pushing it slightly forward, then opened once more the album of photographs Michael had earlier given him. He flipped through.

'I never knew what my grandfather even looked like until now,' he continued, 'but Edgar always told me that he was waiting for him to die. And then he did. He did die.'

Michael woke up. 'What did you say?' It was like sifting through papers where the relevant document lay hidden near the bottom of a pile. 'He was waiting for our father to die?'

Gerry nodded, evidently pleased at this reaction. 'After that, Edgar said he was "putting the matter in train". That's how he used to talk. Of course, I was a little old to be appealing by that time, but Edgar said your mum would probably want to meet me, and he mentioned his brothers, but not by name. He never told me your names, like he thought I might call you or something. He was going to bring me down, introduce me as his son. I got excited about it, see, that's how I remember. Then I heard nothing more about it. Not long after that, they told me Edgar was dead, that he'd died abroad. And we all know what a load of cobblers that was.'

'How old were you then? When Edgar . . .' Michael had been thirty-four. It was Godfrey who broke the news to the family; Godfrey who'd had it from the police. Godfrey had gathered everyone in the hall of the manor. He had stood with his back to the fireplace and Michael absurdly kept thinking of Hercule Poirot. Maybe this was because Godfrey looked around the room at the assembled family, scrutinising each face as if one of them had murdered Edgar. Their mother had screamed, but he and Godfrey and Sophie remained transfixed. He remembered that he had known then how everything would change. Why Edgar's death rather than their father's would make such a radical difference he did not understand then nor now, but a deep, intuitive sense of oncoming wreckage whistled up his nostrils. It had been Helen who had gone to comfort Queen Maeve and even then he had seen how odd this was, given how much they disliked each other.

'I was fifteen,' said Gerry. 'I was with foster parents. Edgar had kind of lost interest by then,' he added bitterly, a curious afterthought.

It was hard to believe Gerry was forty. He looked at the very least ten years younger.

Suddenly there was Edgar before him in his mind. Edgar hiding from Daddy. Well, he was so often naughty. He was hiding behind the bookcase in the nursery. 'Don't tell him. Don't tell him I'm here. I'll give you a sixpence.'

Against his better judgement, Michael gave them both more cognac. 'So I expect you don't really know whom to believe anymore,' he said gently. Not after you've been told so many . . .'

'. . . lies.' Suddenly, Gerry looked up at him from the sofa. Their eyes met and, for a fleeting moment, Michael experienced a burning sensation. It was as if the anger in Gerry were so intense that it had distilled itself into a caustic poison. They both looked away. 'Yes, you've got it,' Gerry went on. 'It's true. I never do know just who to believe.'

Michael sat down a little heavily from the drink. 'Do you think it is possible to believe me?'

His odd nephew withdrew into a silence for a while. Across the room, the painted smile of their ancestress smirked from the shadows. Michael was filled with an overwhelming sadness. He struggled to grasp it. What was it? Throughout dinner, while everyone was trying to be nice, he had felt strange sensations of sudden, nameless anger . . . not at Gerry, nor at Edgar. It was almost as if his mind had an extra limb he had long ago given up as useless, a limb that started now to tingle and smart. It was impossible to trace these little eddies of rage or track them down as being aimed at any one person or event. And now the sadness was the same.

There could now be no question of Gerry's authenticity as Edgar's son, but the reason for such identification lay neither in his resemblance to Edgar nor in his familiarity with him.

'Yes,' Gerry said, after long and careful thought. 'I really do think I can believe you.' He looked up with the flash of a smile so enchanting that it quite took Michael aback.

'Well, as I told you in my letter, I can promise you that if Edgar spoke to anyone in the family about you, no one told me. You see, his addiction made him so unreliable.'

'And Godfrey?' The eyes were shrewd and mistrustful again.

'I shall write to Godfrey. Then we shall see what he has to say.'

No, the certitude came from another source. It was a broken spirit that Edgar and Gerry shared. A fracture to the soul had been passed down, a deep interior wound. Gerry was a Hythe, all right.

It was perhaps the drink, Michael thought, which fuelled his resolution. There was no going back on Gerry. He had to take him up . . . and take him on.

20

GERRY WAS RETURNED to Grisholme only two weeks after he had been admitted to hospital. He had regained a certain amount of mobility and, though he slurred his words like a drunk, he could speak. There was nothing anyone could do but keep an eye on him and supply him with medication. And yet he was happy to be home where every day was the same.

The good news was that he had a roomier cell near the Centre where he could be observed; the bad news (or so he thought at first) was that he had a cellmate now who could observe him, Lennie, a Scouser. Lennie was twenty-five, a suicide risk who was always crying, and Gerry was supposed to keep an eye on him, too. Lennie was being victimised by bulls who were fighting over him because he was pretty. In the old days Gerry would have thought himself a jammy bugger indeed for sharing a cell with this approximation of a child, but his health precluded any such interest now. That he was alive at all, much less ambulatory, was a miracle, and just getting through the day was a struggle. Maybe it was nearly dying, maybe it was the medication, but Gerry wasn't interested. Besides, Lennie was straight. He had broken the arm of his girlfriend's baby because it, too, had been crying . . . endlessly, endlessly crying one hot summer night. This was his first offence. Lennie wore a rosary round his neck; the Catholic chaplain visited him often.

Gerry liked the look of Father Joe, a lanky Irishman with a good sense of humour. Whenever Lennie had a chat with the priest he came back to the cell looking better. Lennie wrote a lot of religious poetry, which he showed to Gerry who had a reputation on the unit as an intellectual. Gerry told Lennie his father had been a poet. He surprised even himself by saying this one thing that didn't make Edgar seem like a monster. What was more, Gerry flinched with involuntary pity as he suddenly remembered how gutted Edgar was that no one believed he was a serious artist.

Lennie's poetry was dreadful by comparison, Gerry knew that much, but he didn't say so. And it oddly touched him when he heard that Father Joe had read one of Lennie's poems out at Mass. 'Sentimental,' Edgar would have called it. Lennie had a holy picture of the Virgin, which he tacked to the wall along with a raunchy pin-up that Gerry found most distasteful. The Virgin, shrouded in powder blue, smiled sweetly as if she understood the need for the hairy, bulbous tart with her wetted lips. But such pictures were an ineffectual insurance policy against rape.

Gerry asked Lennie in his new Dalek voice if he could talk to Father Joe himself. It was on impulse. Lennie took him along to the Mass and Gerry liked it. It wasn't like the one he'd been to on Naxos where he couldn't understand anything. One of the lads played the harmonium and there was an old nun who was mobbed at the end of the service by men wanting to have a word with her. A lot of men in the prison were brought up by their nans (not Gerry! not he!), and Sister Louis had the twinkly look that signalled unconditional love.

That day Father Joe preached a sermon about forgiveness because the Gospel reading was the story of the Prodigal Son. 'Father, I have sinned against Heaven and against you and I'm no longer worthy to be called your child.' Gerry found tears pouring down his numbed, stricken face and didn't even know what they were until they splashed on his folded hands. Lennie got Father Joe to talk to Gerry afterwards and Gerry asked him if he could be baptised. He'd thought about it in hospital, he told the priest. He wanted all of his sins to be forgiven before he died.

At first, he was offended when Father Joe told him, 'Let's wait. You come to our confirmation class, why not? And see what it all involves.' But on thinking it over later, Gerry was glad. The other lot, the evangelicals in his youth, had snatched at him like piranhas at a lump of bleeding meat. So he went in for it. And Lennie was that proud of himself for making a convert!

What impressed Gerry chiefly about Father Joe was that he wasn't allowed to have sex with anybody at all, which took him right out of the conflict. Some of the other inmates sneered, saying that priests could be the worst of all, but Gerry's instinct was that this did not apply to Father Joe. The signals were missing. Gerry thought it must be hard for him to stay pure like that, and that at least he wasn't smug. Father Joe knew it might be difficult to . . . well, he saw the problem. Gerry began to look forward to the classes. Inmates said whatever was on their mind. There were comfortable chairs and Father Joe had good taste in pictures. Gerry was drawn to the Pietà where the mother mourned her dead son on her lap; he had seen the crucifix off and on his whole life, but now it began to make some sense to him and he found his eyes travelling to it all the time. Here was someone dying in real agony, killed as a criminal, mocked, laughed at, treated like shit, treated like a sex offender, really. But He loved you no matter what. It seemed profound to Gerry. He had never thought about it before. He began to be anxious that he would die before he could be absolved. He began to yearn for the Eucharist, which the other men were allowed to receive. 'Not yet,' said Father Joe. 'Wait.' And it brought tears of anxiety to his eyes.

How long would it be? Well, the bishop was coming in the third week of September. He would be baptised, make his First Communion and be confirmed all on the same day. Gerry began to pray in earnest. He and Lennie would start and end the day with prayer. He also began to think about his sins and wonder if they really would be forgiven. Father Joe emphasised how the inmates should be willing to make reparation for the things they had done and he never minimised how dreadful these things were. Oddly enough, this came as a relief to Gerry, though not to everybody. It helped him to think that making a number of small efforts could reduce the tariff. Father Joe told them the past was the past but there were little ways in which they could make amends, maybe write that letter they hadn't written, apologise. Maybe say prayers for their victims and their victims' families, begin to reconcile themselves to their own families, tell them how sorry they were about the grief and shame they had caused. In addition, he asked them to think about people who had wronged them, people who made them angry. Maybe it was time to stop putting blame on others. This wasn't an easy option, but although Father Joe talked about the right and wrong aspect of things, Gerry never felt he made moral judgements. He was the inmates' friend.

So Gerry began to think a great deal about Harriet Washington. It was a terrible struggle because wave upon wave of anger assailed him until he thought he would go under, drown in the rage he felt. As he went through the list of people he hated, it became so formidable that he panicked. Edgar, his mother, Eleni Hythe and, to some extent, Uncle Michael drew from him incoherent feelings so violent that he found himself trembling, his health in danger. Father Joe told him to start on a modest scale, just to say a written prayer every day, taking each hated person in turn, quietly, methodically, not expecting his feelings to change. It wasn't his feelings but his intentions that mattered, the priest told him. If he prayed for that person, he intended good for that person whether he liked them or not. 'Give your anger to God,' Father Joe said. 'He knows all about it anyway. Just leave it with him, to his justice and his mercy.' And Gerry did all that he said.

One of the inmates on the course had been abused by his father from an early age; Gerry listened carefully, saying nothing, to Fred's story. Father Joe was careful to point out that people who had been abused didn't always become abusers; there was no hiding behind that. 'Don't pass the buck!' he told the group. 'Tell yourself, "It stops here."' Nevertheless, he got Fred to write a letter putting everything in it he wanted to say. The next Sunday, he put the letter under the chalice at Mass and offered it up to God. The group talked about the pros and cons of sending it. Gerry thought it would be a big mistake. He could just see Edgar's face if he got such a letter saying how much pain he had caused, how he had set up a pattern of sexual obsession in Gerry's life, how Gerry would forgive him if only he asked. Writing to his mum, now, that would be different. He'd thought about her in hospital, after all.

Fred posted the letter but his father sent it back with no reply. Father Joe said now it was *his* problem. Gerry didn't notice Fred feeling much better, though.

The result of all this activity did jog Gerry's memory. He began to worry that maybe the boys . . . well, maybe they hadn't liked his games after all. He'd been a precocious lad himself, advanced for his age in every way. Wasn't he? He began to feel insecure about it. It was common knowledge on the unit that kids were ready for sex much younger than people liked to think. Talk about 'denial', they would say – it was society that was in denial!

Gerry remembered the intensity of physical feeling Edgar had produced in him, an involuntary pleasure that his father took as consent, and then the servile craving that crawled up into his loins. Fear, pain and pleasure formed into a knot which he could never untie. Just hearing Fred's story brought it back. Like Gerry, Fred's mum had slapped him hard when he tried to tell, and there was a feeling of being worthless after that. Dirty, too. Edgar used to tease him, telling him he was asking for it. 'You dirty little bastard!' he used to say after the act, cuffing Gerry's head in a matey way. When he was about nine, he'd come on to a younger kid at school and there'd been a ruck, lots of questions asked about home. But he'd never grassed on Edgar and still he wondered why.

Gerry had his favourite mental snapshots from past exploits with which he often relieved himself. The more you told the story to yourself, the better it became. Maybe it was something one of the men in the group said, maybe Fred who'd been through some of the experiences he had shared, but the well-worn memories started to look a little different and they didn't help him to relax when he called them up. One night he was trying out the memory he kept for best. Suddenly, it started to bore through his skull – as if someone with an outside television channel were broadcasting the hateful and unwelcome news – that the face he had thought contorted in pleasure had been contorted in emotional agony. This spooked Gerry so badly that he considered giving up the group, and he skipped a meeting saying he felt ill.

Maybe to get the devil off his back, he started to remember Naxos. He grasped at scenes that welled up in his mind like waking dreams from a past he'd put the lid on. He couldn't quite make sense of what he saw in his mind's eye. Things didn't add up the way he remembered them. He supposed he was experiencing what they called 'flashbacks', only they appeared randomly and had little to do with the actual trauma he had suffered at being wrongly accused. Apart from anything else, it had all happened so fast, his meeting of the boy and then the boy's death.

So she'd left him money, had she, Harriet! Thirty pieces of silver, that's what it was. Money she'd ensured he could never spend. Even if he lived to see his release date, he'd probably have to spend the rest of his days in a flat-cum-cell in some police station. 'For his own protection,' of course. They'd never let him go and live with Cassie because of her boys. Maybe they'd even section him and make him live in a special hospital. It would take two shrinks all of ten minutes to decide he had an 'untreatable personality disorder', which meant he'd never be allowed take a walk in the park again. If only Harriet had left him alone, he would be a free man now, not even having to register with the police because his last offence against children had been before the changes in the law. Harriet was probably writhing in hell at the moment. Gerry wondered what sort of tortures the demons had invented for jealousy. As for 'bearing false witness against your neighbour', that was in the Ten Commandments!

Gerry couldn't remember how long he and Harriet had been in Naxos, maybe a couple of days, before his aunt started having her 'headaches'. He smiled thinly at the memory of her vaunted migraine problem. She had burnt herbs like a witch, and had taken to her bed. Later, when he met Cassie, she innocently told him that her mother had never had a day's illness in her life. He'd known all along that Eleni hated him and suffered every moment she had to spend with him. So it fell to Uncle Michael to show him round the island. And as he felt he'd known the boy all his life, he wasn't sure which day it was when he had first met Vassilis. He wished he had the date now, he would have kept it precious, like a birthday. The love of his life had appeared like a god just after that disastrous trip to Melanes.

Gerry didn't like sightseeing much, but he would have jumped off a cliff to please Uncle Michael. Naxos was stuffed with ruins. It was like being in a graveyard or a rubbish tip strewn with old bits of marble where everyone said oooh and ahhh. He supposed he would have more time now for the churches, scores of them, but they weren't exactly friendly, like the chaplaincy, and he was supposed to appreciate the faded pictures on the walls of saints and angels looking stiff and Jesus whose eyes bored straight through him. Harriet gushed away, of course, crossing herself and kneeling. And she chattered away about the older bits they visited, the archaic rubble, as if she and the ancient gods had been mates which, given what happened, they weren't! Gerry didn't know why they couldn't spend more time at the beach. He thought maliciously of Harriet's varicose veins. She couldn't even swim!

He also wondered why Uncle Michael didn't have a better motor with all that money they had, just a tin-can Fiat, and he had to sit in the back because Harriet was a *lady*. He'd give her lady! She was winding him up so tight he thought he'd lose it, which is what he did. But that was part of her plan, wasn't it? Why couldn't Harriet have had the diplomatic headaches? She insisted on tagging along everywhere so that he and his uncle could not talk properly. She made him feel like a kid. Anything he said over the backs of the seats made him feel like he was butting in.

They spoke in Edgar's language and Gerry found himself falling in. Edgar used to mock the way that Mary Carney spoke. He was a good mimic and Gerry would flush with shame when his father aped his mother's speech, her mannerisms. 'Good diction', as he called it, was one of the many things Edgar forced on Gerry, who abandoned it whenever he escaped. Now it all came back to him, the clipping of consonants, the broadening of vowels, and it made his mind buzz as it had done in the past, the effort to reproduce his father's accent. He wasn't a yob; he was a Hythe now, with ancestors. He didn't want Michael to get the wrong impression. It was slavery he felt for that man, something like the adoration Father Joe said was due to God alone.

The very first night in Naxos, Gerry noticed that his room, an old study, stood apart from the others in the house. The walls were at least three feet thick – you could tell by the way the window was set. It seemed only too familiar, like prison, though it was a great deal more comfortable, every surface covered with embroidered cloths. Right away he spotted the advantage to his uncle of this isolation, and so prepared himself for the nocturnal visits he imagined would be inevitable. Gerry's heart pounded, his hands sweated. He would lie awake clenched in a foetal ball. When nothing happened, he was oddly disappointed at this sign of Michael's indifference to him.

He hunted for his father in Michael's eyes, the splay of hands on his knees, his voice and his brow. There were signs with which he had an absolute familiarity, quirks of speech that brought back flashes vivid with pain, a sense of irretrievable loss. At the same time, Michael seemed to have taken up where Edgar ended. There was more of him; he was a full person. It startled Gerry to realise how stunted his father had been.

By day, Gerry felt compelled to please his uncle in every particular. He tried to make the sort of clever remarks Edgar had enjoyed; he tried to be suave and cool; he swore allegiance to every attitude his uncle had; and he took a fervid interest in the historical bits his uncle loved, begging for every detail like a spaniel for snacks. He supposed it was an ill wind, because it all stood him in good stead now. He liked the Middle Ages. He went up towers and down alleys learning heraldry, and spouted it all back at the dinner table like a schoolboy, his palms sweaty on the damask napkin. When his uncle, with that mild smile of acceptance, praised his efforts, Gerry basked in the approval. He had never craved the love of any single individual more in his life. That was why it was so wrong, so terribly wrong, the thing about Vassilis.

After the boy's death, Gerry had written Michael a letter from prison telling him all this. Michael had never replied. So Father Joe could take his letters and stuff them! Gerry went back to the group, but he became wary of Father Joe for several sessions. It wasn't Michael's problem that he never answered the letter, it was Gerry's problem. For several nights in his cell, Gerry re-lived the agonising crush he'd had on Michael Hythe, the searing knowledge of rejection.

The morning they set out for Melanes was an archaeology day. Gerry couldn't imagine what was so special there, some statue or other they had to see. Sometimes he wondered if he had disturbed something in that place, a ghost or something. Later they were going to the farm, which was what he was looking forward to. They jounced about in the Fiat. It was very hot that day, really boiling. Harriet looked absurd, that much he remembered, in a girlish flowered dress and a cartwheel hat she'd bought on a shopping trip to the quay with Eleni. Harriet was wearing so much make-up that it looked as if her face would fall off. She was preening herself in the front seat, making flirtatious comments to him and to his uncle as they set out from the base of Naxos Town and made their way eastwards into the interior. A lot of men would say what Harriet needed was a good seeing-to. He imagined with relish her fallen breasts, her withered skin, what she would look like naked and unmasked. She was working in her cryptic way to undermine him, to make him look small and stupid, talking about archaeology with a knowing smirk. He could see she was trying to show off to Michael. Why had he never noticed before what a phoney she was? Edgar would have called her 'middle class', his worst insult. 'Arriviste' was another word he liked.

Michael, on the other hand, was the genuine article in his battered Panama. He chatted away, giving bits of information to Gerry in a completely unpatronising way. They were going to see a kouros, he said. He explained that this was the statue of a boy on the verge of manhood, but that was nothing new to Gerry. He'd thought of the Ganymede he had in his flat. He'd kept up with another ex-con some years back who worked in the film industry and made porn on the side. The drawing was a present for some introductions Gerry had made; he had to admit it was beautiful, not just a turn-on. And so he perked up at seeing something like that. He knew all about the Greeks and boys from Edgar.

Uncle Michael acted as if he didn't know anything about this, but that was just for Harriet because he dwelt on it, going on to say that the ancient Greeks of this period had made many of these statues. There were a lot in Athens and in museums all over the world. They stood tall and rigid, their faces carved in a mysterious smile called 'the archaic smile'. The kouros they were about to see had never been finished and lay in its quarry, a quarry of great antiquity, to this day. It might be, Michael told him, a statue of the god Apollo.

Long ago, Edgar had told Gerry about Apollo and Endymion in support of his claims upon Gerry's person; in the car he suppressed a snigger at the name Apollo but said nothing. Maybe it was a signal. Maybe Michael would visit him that night. It made him feel awkwardly randy to think of this. They drove on. In the distance, beautiful mountains glowed in the morning light, one as if it were made of gold, the others mottled by a passing banks of snowy cloud in the deep azure sky. For a moment, Gerry had a glimpse of the god in his mind's eye, gold and with golden hair, a body fit and hard. The Fiat descended into a valley and bounced into a shady car park. Gerry felt alive to the probability of mystery. There was the sound of running water as they got out of the car and traipsed up a woodland path to the ruin. He imagined forest spirits murmuring and teasing. Butterflies with wings like the flags of pageants sailed above wild stalks of flowers in a clearing and crickets made a sleepy hum as they tracked their way towards a walled enclosure where the kouros lay. He had it in his head that Michael was leading him, gently grooming him, like putting a beautiful bridle on a horse, taking him to see the secret boy. And they would both know. They wouldn't have to say anything. He could give a sign. He felt a delicious sense of erotic ease.

Why it affected him the way it did when he saw it, Gerry still did not know, but it upset him when he saw that the huge fallen statue was dark and its right leg was broken. It wasn't a statue at all, more a lump of stone. Instead of the light-filled child he'd been expecting, it lay there as if someone had toppled it; lichen blossomed on its ravaged body. Its features were erased. Maybe it was Harriet's endless emoting or the heat or the tension, but Gerry's first reaction was rage. The kouros was broken! You could tell it was meant to be a boy because of its swelling little package, a worn bump! But it was grown old. A superstitious fear made Gerry clammy. Cicadas sawed away in the glade, a menace. Some old earth force was singing to him a tune he understood but in a language he didn't know. The lump of darkened stone was repellent.

Of course, he hadn't said anything. He just stood numbly glaring at it. Michael didn't even seem to notice, though maybe he had. It cut Gerry that he didn't feel the impact of the broken boy. He was even cheery and sauntered off to get them tickets to the site and some cans of drink from a stall further down the path. 'Gerry, dear, are you all right?' Harriet asked him.

Suddenly, this was all Gerry could take.

The rage swelled, burst and oozed. 'Bitch!' he said. If Michael hadn't come back, Gerry would have struck her.

That was why she grassed later on . . . one of the reasons, anyway. He might as well have struck her. She sat on a stone near the fallen head of the obscene statue and put her own head in her hands.

'Harriet!' Michael cried, looking from one to the other of them.

'It's all right. I think it's the heat!' she said, bravely smiling. 'I'm simply not used to it.' She wondered if they might go directly to the farm where she could rest a bit. Harriet, her meek smile, her fainting spell, her disappointed love! It made Gerry tremble with fury still to think of it.

They drove in silence to the farm, the mood of the day altered. He could see that Harriet was trying not to cry, but it gave him pleasure that he had hurt her. Either she was a really good actress or had been a terrible one. She took little sips of Fanta and put the cold can to her forehead. Michael wasn't fooled . . . or was he? Yet again she was trying to undermine Gerry, making it look like his fault.

Gerry felt like an angry bee trapped in the car. When they arrived, he all but sailed out the window into the free, warm air.

It came back to him now as he lay on his bunk: the farm with its rich smell of earth, the crumbling medieval tower, its walls baked in the sun. It seemed planted there like the potatoes, organic, a part of everything that surrounded it from the mountains to the distant, sparkling sea. There was a joyous bark of dogs and, before he knew it, they were surrounded by a pack of collies waving their feathery tails. Standing to the side, grinning, were two men, one gnarled like a tough old nut, the other middle-aged. And, suddenly, there was Vassilis. He seemed to come from nowhere and then he was everywhere, plunging up and down around Michael in the mêlée of dogs. He was fair and slender with deep-set eyes and he wore spectacles in wire frames. If it hadn't been for those spectacles!

Here, Gerry's mind slammed shut.

He'd hardly noticed that Mr Gosforth had been on his annual leave, but he was glad to see him when he returned. He was becoming afraid of religion. Mr Gosforth asked him how his book was getting on and he explained he was unable to write now. The officer looked chuffed about something, but only said he'd had a good holiday.

That night, Gerry woke sobbing from a dream he could not recall.

'Are you all right?' Lennie asked.

He couldn't speak.

Lennie reached a hand down and, after a moment's hesitation, Gerry gripped the fingers and held them until he drifted back to sleep around dawn.

21

HARRIET COULD NOT BEAR to look at Gerry so she stood apart, pretending to admire 'the farm'. Not since adolescence had she felt such humiliation. She kept thinking that everyone knew it. Even the dogs seemed to sniff it out, shunning her. She hoped her flaming cheeks would be put down to a touch of sun.

It was stifling, very hot, but beads of cold sweat collected on her brow. A squat tower, that appeared to serve as a farmhouse, stood in an enclosed courtyard. Its walls were baked to a biscuit colour by successive aeons of sunny days, and tufts of weeds grew from the cracks in the ageing stucco. A green lizard darted over a buttress, giving Harriet a start. Its jewelled presence made the fortress look all the more forlorn; against the pure azure sky, its stark bulk dwarfed her, making her head reel.

'Are you all right?' Michael asked her.

Harriet jumped out of her skin at the sound of his voice. She gestured helplessly at the tower. 'Medieval?' The façade had only two windows, high up, like a dungeon for Rapunzel or Philomel.

'Merely seventeenth century,' he laughed; then, more seriously, said, 'Harriet, you really don't look at all well.'

Gerry's nasal voice abraded her ears. He was joking with the farm lad who answered in high-pitched broken English.

'I feel a little sick,' she told him. 'Sorry to be such a bore.'

'Oh dear. It's probably heat stroke,' Michael said. 'You really had best lie down. Salt. You'll need rest, salt and plenty of water.' He fussed about her.

'Gerry . . .' she started to say.

'Don't worry. I'll take care of him. He'll like seeing the farm.'

But she wanted to fall sobbing into Michael's arms. His virtues were so English in this foreign place, qualities she'd taken for granted all her life. How had she lost track of them? Who had taken them away? Kindness, fairness, self-control. He blinked at her through his specs, his forehead creased in attentive concern.

Gerry's eyes! The way he had looked at her, calling her 'bitch'!

Before she knew it, Michael had rustled up Kiria Anna, the farmer's wife, who emerged from the kitchen with a great air of knowing what to do with an invalid. This was the way her concern translated itself into English, for she led Harriet into the old tower house in the universal language of genuine solicitude. It was blessedly cool inside and furnished with a monastic simplicity. There were stairs to trudge. Out of a back window, Harriet could make out the sparkling of the sea in the distance. Kiria Anna unlocked a door high in the tower and showed Harriet into a musty bedroom. She threw open a narrow window and rolled up dust-sheets. An iron bedstead stood against a whitewashed wall, above it a crucifix. Harriet felt a bit like Lady Jane Grey. The walls were so thick. There must have been three feet from the window-sill to the outside wall.

There was a basin and ewer on a marble stand and a hard chair. Even the floors were stained white. Harriet sat, trying not to slump, while the solicitous Greek woman plumped up the straw mattress and put on sheets.

As her eyes lit idly on the crucifix, it suddenly looked alien, not salvific. Perhaps the immense, hot sky of Naxos, the fathomlessly old hills put the modern age into this harsh perspective. The carved ivory Christ seemed to fling His pierced hands upward, diminutive and helpless against an implacable eternity.

Harriet barely noticed the comings and goings of Kiria Anna who, giving a final touch, trundled in with a carafe of water. This, she indicated with sign language that involved pulling up buckets, came from the well. The water, with its tang of iron, was refreshingly cool. The woman gave Harriet a few salt tablets to swallow, shooed her towards the bed, then crept away.

Gerry had moods, mood swings. They'd always been abrupt, even in Grisholme, so there was no sense in breaking her heart over this one, her porcelain heart. Oh, she'd looked after it all right, never putting it at risk as others did. So she had no practice in assessing the scale of pain she felt that Gerry had turned on her.

Lying on the bed, Harriet retraced her steps through the forest glade towards the sleeping kouros. That had been her impression of it, as though its toppled grey marble length lay in primordial slumber, its gigantic feet up on a mossy stone. Her brain rattled with the fantastic notion that the broken statue had spoken to Gerry. He'd stood stock-still. At first she thought he'd heard something. It had occurred to her that he was in his element now. Shade and stone, leaf and bush evoked the Pan he sometimes was, not a spirit to be confined, but one at home with fauns and satyrs, free to roam.

Then she'd caught the working of his jaw. Michael had vanished down the path so it gave her the opportunity to check on Gerry. They hadn't been alone together for days and she was beginning to wonder if he was avoiding her. All she'd done was ask how he was! It was as if she had unwittingly stepped on some totem animal or failed to give some long forgotten honour to the pagan energies that seemed to seep through the base rock of Naxos like radon. 'Bitch!' It wasn't the word, but the way he'd said it. His cold green eyes in the wood had looked her up and down, not as if she were an animal, but as if he were the genius of one whose disdain for her was part of a larger abhorrence for anything human.

Her head began to steady now. Maybe it really was the heat. Besides, they had all been drinking so much, putting it away every night in increasing quantities. Why was that? She hadn't remembered the Hythes as heavy drinkers. Never mind. Alcohol dehydrated the system. She felt her pulse. It didn't seem to race so now.

Out of the susurration of voices below, she identified Gerry's. It was all she could do to restrain herself from jumping up and peering out of the window. What was he doing? But she fell back on the bed, afraid that he would spot her.

Surely she'd mistaken his look of contempt – what had she done to deserve it?

Averell had a terrier bitch, Patsy. An image of Patsy came to her, in season, hindquarters splayed, presented. She'd disliked the creature and wanted it spayed.

It was just a vulgar epithet, she told herself firmly, and there were worse. He could have said something worse.

Harriet tried to give in to Kiria Anna's mimed instructions and closed her eyes. She was overwrought. The bed was made up with linen sheets, handwoven. The straw palette, surprisingly comfortable, rustled. As she listened, the voices of the men below receded towards the field beyond. One of the dogs barked excitedly in long, bell-like yaps just short of a howl. The noise maddened her. She held her hands over her ears. Tears sprang to her eyes but she did not cry.

Sex. Nowadays everyone reduced everything to sex. It sickened her. Her thoughts jumped to Eleni, how she'd subtly implied that Harriet was making a fool of herself with Gerry, a man young enough to be her son. Oh, surely Gerry knew her better than that! 'Blessed are the pure in heart,' she thought, the beatitude slipping into her mind from thin air. 'For they shall see God.' As if to taunt her, a raunchy image came to her of herself and Gerry naked, him pinning her against a wall. A confused sort of anger burst in on her thoughts, a sudden impulse to smash the carafe, wreck things. It appalled her. She lay very still as if hiding from it until it went away.

If only she could talk to someone! She longed to pour out her soul to an open ear. But tell what and to whom? Why, oh why, had she not spoken to Boo when she had the chance? Well, Boo wouldn't have understood, she thought irritably, not the special feelings that she had.

On Sunday, Gerry had accompanied them to Mass. Eleni had thrust her missal into his hands at breakfast, making it impossible for him to wriggle out of church. Maybe she had plans to save his soul. Harriet was trying, really trying, not to resent Eleni. All that self-vaunting candour was a bit hard to take, especially when she left poor Gerry in little doubt that he'd have to do a lot to gain her trust.

At any other time, Harriet would have admired the little Catholic cathedral on the summit of the Kastro. Its baroque façade masked a much older foundation, domed, Greek romanesque. It stood in a flagged square surrounded by mellow Venetian mansions, a rare tourist attraction in the Aegean. Once inside, the four of them uneasily shared the front pew. Harriet tried to appreciate the icons the Hythes courteously pointed out. The altarpiece, a full length Byzantine Virgin, was like a column of thought come alive with deep, glowing colours. The Infant Jesus perched on Her arm like a finial, as if He were the ultimate statement about Herself, not a child at all. Harriet tried to pray to the Virgin but words would not come. Instead, her eye wandered to a side altar where the Archangel Michael wielded a sword in a titanic battle against a cringing Satan whose vile, scaly figure left no room for uncertainty about the nature of evil. Gerry made little attempt to conceal his boredom, and his restlessness embarrassed Harriet. She stumbled after the Greek liturgy with English thoughts, but the words she remembered slipped from her like beads of glass, polished by over-use and without the value of meaning to her now.

Afterwards, when the congregation trickled out into the light, the Hythes' Greek neighbours gathered round to meet Harriet and Gerry, who had recently started to smirk as if he expected a round of applause for everything he did. Harriet slipped away. The priest stood on the steps. She liked his face and the way he'd said the Mass, with faith and dignity. Maybe she could trust him with her secrets. Her knees wobbled with fear at this sudden impulse but when he signed to her that he did not speak English she was obscurely relieved. She wouldn't have known quite what to tell him. Her moral dilemma was receding in any case. Increasingly, it seemed officious to inform on Gerry. He'd paid his debt to society and, after all, he had the right to some privacy, she told herself.

But maybe it was the Hythes themselves who seemed proof against any discussion of Gerry's true nature. The Kastro house had the faint air of an embassy in a wild outpost where, like diplomats, Michael and Eleni received the oddest guests with practised manners that fortified them against anything sordid. Harriet shuddered, remembering Gerry's criminal needs. Could she really tell them?

Nothing in Naxos was as she had imagined it – not the house, nor the island, nor her old friends, nor Gerry himself. The night before, she'd dreamed she was tied up in the back seat of a moving car, only there was no driver. She awoke with a cry, overwhelmed by a sense of impotence.

She gazed now at the wall where the sun flooded in, making a patch of white light. Outside the dog had stopped barking, and an almost active absence of sound hung heavy on the air. It was as if the whole world had deserted her at the top of this silent tower. Harriet was not far off panic. A cold sense of being trapped invaded her.

'There is absolutely nothing wrong,' she whispered to herself, almost relieved she could hear her own voice. 'You're acting as if something has gone wrong and it hasn't! It *hasn't!*'

And yet a sense of nothing being right needled her. She picked at the coverlet with obsessive hands. Not even Boo could have objected to the way the visit had gone so far. If Edgar Hythe had wronged Gerry, Michael seemed intent on making it up to him.

Wasn't this the result she'd intended? That Gerry and Michael should strike a bond? Again, a wave of nameless alarm swept over her. It was like finding a lump, or imagining one, during a routine self-examination, but she scolded herself. Why not concentrate on the good things? Michael's decency fulfilled her dearest hope. Suppose he'd rejected Gerry. What would she feel then?

It was true that Eleni was awkward, but then Averell had always said she was a bit of a diva. In contrast, Michael hadn't put a foot wrong since their arrival, she reassured herself. For one thing, he was utterly sweet to her, never missing an opportunity to include her. He understood all she meant to do for Gerry, didn't he? He didn't misconstrue her motives.

And she hardly resented his kindness to someone she so longed to help! Now she thought about it, Michael Hythe had behaved admirably. He wasn't giving Gerry vain promises about the future. Instead, he offered a kind of grave sweetness. It was like watching someone feed a maimed fox with eyedroppers of milk. The effort cost him, though; that she could tell. His face weighed heavy in repose and now and then he closed his eyes, exhausted.

Harriet took sides with her reason against her instinct. The truth was she had imagined a greater freedom in the visit, more of a range in which she could act. Ever since the trip was mooted, she had indulged herself, building up the trip in her mind's eye, making a paradise of Naxos. She'd even invented a complete Greek temple, rather like the gazebo in the park of a stately home, where she would sit and gaze out to sea. Above all, she would have space and time to talk. In this rosy fantasy, Michael and Eleni were transformed into dearest, deepest friends. She'd confide in them all her schemes for Gerry as if he were her wayward son, someone who needed managing. She'd forge an alliance with the Hythes, other grown-ups she'd bring in to help her save him. They'd need some coaching, of course, if they were to help Gerry gain confidence. Harriet had seen herself giving them guidance, winning their support.

As for Gerry and herself, she'd imagined a beach on which they would wander, wading barefoot through frothy wavelets, curling their toes in the white sand, forging an intimacy that needed no words. Well, they were there for two weeks; maybe things would relax. If one had these silly ideas, reality was bound to disappoint!

But Harriet hadn't banked on Gerry's response to Michael.

Yes, it was this that troubled her. It had shaken her, taken her by surprise. If Michael scratched his head, so did Gerry. He followed his uncle everywhere with hungry eyes and had taken to showing off at the smallest opportunity. He was spinning about like a child drunk on the sort of over-stimulation nannies deplored. It obscurely revolted Harriet. Why?

After Edgar's beatings, she supposed Gerry would become devoted to a kindly uncle, but his frenzied attachment was so sudden! She wasn't feeling cheated and excluded, was she? That would be unfair, possessive. Still, she kept wanting to say to him, 'Calm down, Gerry. Don't rush things. There's time enough.' What was more, he was alienating Eleni, fawning over Michael like that. Eleni watched Gerry, a sphinx, her eyes barely moving. Whether she despised him for his new clumsy pretensions or whether she was jealous, Harriet could not tell. Perhaps Eleni was afraid. Yes, that was the impression Harriet got.

Harriet had to face it: Gerry was nobody's ideal long-lost nephew, but this didn't quite account for the psychic osmosis that seemed to be passing between the three Hythes. Maybe this was what troubled her. Maybe this was why a surreptitious dread grew on her, bordering on a premonition of disaster.

There was a nerve-wracking undercurrent, she had to admit. Since arriving in Naxos, each successive evening became more difficult and complex. Like a fog that starts with a few puffs of mist and then descends thickly, a heavy atmosphere had started to choke back words and stifle questions.

During the day, when Michael kept them on the move seeing sights, they jollied along well enough. The jaunting was, more than anything else, like a treat given by a kindly relation to a schoolboy whose parents work abroad. Gerry might have been taken for a fifth former on an exeat, awkward, ashamed of his

Adam's apple and in need of a hero to worship. But if, on trips to the beach or to Byzantine churches splendid with old frescoes, Michael conveyed the mood of half-term, he seemed unable to sustain it under his own roof. Nor could Gerry.

At the beginning, Harriet had judged it all Eleni's fault. And she was not bearing a grudge – if Eleni was cynical about Harriet's motives, then let her be! Harriet flushed angrily. In any case, they'd made it up when they'd gone down to the harbour to buy the cartwheel hat. Eleni had been full of compliments. Harriet's skin was so fair, so young-looking. What did she use? The hat itself drooped on the chair back now, looking faintly absurd. They'd bought it as a joke in an effort to revive old friendship girlishly.

It was important to be fair: if aloof, Eleni was hospitable. One could not fault that. She knocked herself out on good dinners. Harriet must soon take them all out for a meal as a thank you.

For some reason, she found herself laughing aloud in the silence, a sharp, barking sound, cold to her own ears. Eleni! Though she provided food, she gave no blessing to the meals; she was merely present. Someone as sensitive as Gerry was bound to pick this up. No wonder things were sticky. In her desperation for things to go well for Gerry, Harriet served up a patter of trivia at each meal for Eleni's delectation. It was miserably hard going, distracting her hostess, and often as not she lapsed into silence while Gerry recycled the lesson of the day in fervid appreciation. Where could he find out more about the Crusades? What was an escutcheon?

The previous evening an ominous leak of family secrets began to show, spreading like a damp patch on the company. They had spent a quiet Sunday visiting the museum not two hundred yards from the house. Eleni excused herself from even this unambitious venture, saying that a friend of hers was ill. She needed shopping done and cheering up.

Harriet didn't believe in this sick-visiting business. Nor did Gerry. She could see by the look on his face. Eleni had managed to duck all the expeditions round the island, each and every one. Either it was friends needing attention, shopping or the migraines she was martyr to. She knew the signs when one was brewing; it was best to keep out of the sun. This was such an obvious lie that Harriet couldn't see why Eleni didn't gag on it. She stiffened whenever Gerry spoke. If it was true she were seeing some sick chum, she was sure to be moaning about her unwanted guests not offering calves' foot jelly. No matter. Harriet refused to mar this precious time for Gerry by getting her feelings hurt.

So, on Sunday after Mass, it was again up to Michael to show them round what turned out to be a distinguished collection of Cycladic artefacts. Gerry hadn't wanted to go and had hinted for the beach instead, but he wasn't about to pass up an opportunity to be with his uncle. Once inside the museum, though, he was all rapt attention.

It was a fascinating exhibition and Harriet tiptoed round the glass cases, breath held in wonder at the planed marble figurines that stood propped in rows before her. They were of the deepest antiquity, their abstract white heads upturned as if in prayer to a long-forgotten god. Harriet had shivered a little, wanting to reach out and stroke the smooth white statues with their totemic eyeless gaze. And there were rooms of vases, impossibly old. Michael was on grand form: this was something he clearly enjoyed and he took a touching amount of time and trouble explaining to Gerry the meaning of the best exhibits. There were terracotta pots painted with octopi and dancing men and snakes. Uncharacteristically, Gerry had nothing to say in response. He stood aside from his uncle's explications, his arms folded like the Neolithic statuettes, his eyes oddly hot with feeling.

That evening, something came up about French poetry. Eleni was talking about her sick friend, an expatriate Frenchwoman, who was intending to spend her time recuperating by translating Baudelaire into Greek! At this point, Michael mentioned Edgar – he did come up from time to time – and how his brother might have been a linguist if he'd taken the trouble.

Edgar had loved Baudelaire and could have made his mark as a translator. Suddenly, Gerry's face darkened and the conversation stopped.

Harriet was suddenly very much afraid. With an agility born of the dread of an outburst, she jumped in – neatly, she thought – with an Ashdean memory of Cassie bound to please the Hythes. Cassie had a gift for languages, didn't they think? She'd helped Emma with her French.

Eleni kept her eyes on Gerry the whole time, but she did not miss the chance to preen. She had taught Cassie herself. No wonder brilliant Emma had been floundering. That school in Tunbridge Wells hadn't been all it was cracked up to be . . . and so expensive.

Perhaps he had been simmering, the memory of his father too painful to be kept silent, but apropos of nothing Gerry spoke, and in a way that made the Hythes shoot each other looks in the ensuing stillness. Nobody moved.

'Edgar had a thing about books,' he said. 'You'll know his shop on the King's Road, won't you?'

After a frozen moment, Michael inclined his head, stiffly in assent.

'He used to take me. The owner was never there, though, when I went. He liked to show me rare books an' all.' His face was set in an implacable sneer. 'I went back when I got out of prison, stood outside for a minute on the pavement. I just wanted to have a good look, bring him back to mind, but all I could see was my face in the glass. I look just like him, don't I? Except shorter.' Maybe it was the impacted bitterness in this remark that made everyone feel so uncomfortable.

Gerry leaned forward a little, a faintly conceited look on his face. In a complete non sequitur, he said, 'I wonder if anyone can tell me why those vases we saw today are so clean.'

'Of course they're clean!' Michael said with surprising sharpness. 'They're very ancient and valuable.'

'They'll keep the dirty ones in the basement then,' he said, with triumphant menace. He gave a knowing smile, but said nothing more.

The seemingly unconnected remarks about the rare bookshop and the vases seemed to set Michael off, making him sober and reflective.

Was it Harriet's imagination, the tension at breakfast that morning? Eleni sent her apologies: despite her precautions, another migraine had arrived. A smell of aromatic herbs drifted on the air. Maybe she'd be all right by that evening; on the other hand, maybe not. Michael had driven them out to Melanes, eyes maybe too closely on the road. His features, usually expressive, seemed locked as if interior thoughts formed within him to which no one else should have access.

Harriet propped herself on her elbow and took another sip of the cool well water. She was being a great baby! How could she possibly plumb the depths of what passed between the three Hythes? It had nothing to do with her. Couldn't she see how Edgar haunted them? His shade reached out and clutched at their memories, dragging them back into a nightmare none of them could shake off. They couldn't even bear to talk about him. He must have been even worse than Harriet had thought. Before they were to exorcise the man, they had to be sure of one another. How glib it was of her to have thought that this could happen overnight!

She took another sip gingerly from the cup. The sharp edge of the crucifix caught the corner of her eye and she craned round to look at it again more fully. Love, she thought. They preached love at her and all along she . . . no. A thought surfaced, too vague to be recognised, then sank beyond retrieval.

Jesus: they were always bashing on about how low He could go in order to redeem . . . As low as Gerry – as low as that? It stood to reason, but the logic of it failed her. How far was He prepared to sink – to what depths?

Harriet fell back on the pillow, oddly cynical, but she was too weary to feel guilt at her rebellion. Besides, she hurt so much. She was enmeshed in pain, as if it were a net.

And yet, tired as she was, a wordless sense came to her, jumbled and confused, that to love Gerry *was* to suffer. She stumbled after it for a moment, trying to formulate a thought around it. 'He descended into hell . . . the third day . . .' Down into the deep sea of Gerry's crimes, weighted with the millstone his perversity deserved, she fell oddly weightless herself.

It came to her obscurely, then, that whatever mistake she had made in getting this far with Gerry, not to go the whole length with him was the worst thing she could do. It must terrify him that she knew his secret. Could she now abandon him? Wasn't this what she was really doing if she herself took fright? Suppose she did tell Michael, whom he adored? How small that seemed, now she thought of it – how mean and graceless!

A sense of Gerry flickered along her nervous system as if he actually inhabited her mind. He touched her still, achingly. A moment came and then, seeming too terrible, she let it go.

No, she was not in love with Gerry Carney. She had not let herself go to such an extent. Somebody who went after boys? It was meant to be a redemptive thing all along. Like Jesus. She remembered being in Westminster Cathedral the Sunday before she had left London. Was that only ten days ago? Something like that; it seemed an aeon. There she had felt such certainty that she would stay the course with Gerry, no matter what pain it might bring: that she must offer nothing but a perfectly selfless love. How had she thought she could do that? Especially as now the words, both 'love' and 'selfless', seemed fraught with so many contradictions that they were rendered meaningless.

Brainstorm that it was, a new thought swept through, lighting Harriet's mind with flashes of insight. All along the truth had been under her nose – Gerry was mentally ill.

Why deny it? This was nothing to do with good or evil, the recondite lore of the Fall. Her own slippery emotions were irrelevant in this case. She grasped at the idea, clutching it to her. A litany of his oddities came to mind. His insulting behaviour to her that day was no sign of rejection, but sickness. Wasn't it?

Harriet opened her eyes and stared at the ceiling. It merely looked as if she had lost ground with Gerry. In fact, she had gained it. He knew his family now. All because of her, he had a history.

Let him come to terms with it! This was only the first painful step in his rehabilitation. As soon as they returned to England, she'd tackle his illness at source. Harriet was sure there were good clinics that dealt with the sort of . . . problems . . . he had. It flooded through her, a great relief at having something to do for Gerry. She could afford it! Really first-class psychotherapy. She'd give something up if need be. Suddenly, Harriet saw the scope of the enterprise. He'd need tactful and constant sustaining if he were to grapple with the real issues that troubled him. It wasn't as if she were losing him – why, they'd only just begun.

How shabby it seemed to her now, her disgust at his honest admission of those terrible desires that haunted him. Possibly he sensed it; maybe she had deserved today's ugly moment. He needed acceptance, not prudery. Gerry was deeply disturbed, and this visit was providing ample evidence for the reasons behind the disturbance. If Edgar still made the Hythes so squeamish, what havoc must he have wreaked on a child's delicate mind? Harriet tried to imagine what sort of psychiatric care Grisholme had offered Gerry – not a lot, she imagined. Together, once they were home, they would gently unpack their memories of the trip and she could coax him, she knew she could. He had something to live for now, an incentive to get well, be whole. He had Michael to please . . . and he had her, yes, love. Her unconditional love, free from anything mean or low.

Harriet felt a little better; much calmer, she persuaded herself. Gerry did love her. He'd told her so many times in a roundabout way. And here she'd been concentrating on the bad things, not the good.

On Saturday evening just as the sun was setting, Michael had taken them both on a walk out across the breakwater to the spur of harbour where the Portare stood. Gerry had really enjoyed that and so had she. She tried to focus on it. 'Think happy thoughts,' her mother had often said, 'and you will always be beautiful.'

She had never seen anything like the deepening passionate pink of the sky, the waves crashing on the rocks below. They seemed combed with gold and the froth leapt up like a shower of crystals in the dying sun. Hadn't that been a good moment with Gerry – standing together in the marble frame? She'd asked Michael to take their picture and he'd obliged. What was more, Gerry had wanted one of Michael and herself together, capturing 'the two people I love most': she thought that's what he said. No, it was a direct quotation – why had she forgotten these, his very words? She hoped the picture would come out. She'd frame it, she decided, and keep it on her desk, always to remind her. So it wasn't all doom and gloom, she said brightly, aloud in the silent room.

After the photo session, Michael had told Gerry the story of Ariadne. Before they knew it, a small audience of tourists gathered round beside the mammoth stone gate where he sat on a fallen plinth. The wind buffeted Harriet's ears and snatches of the myth came to her. She gazed up at the great Ionic lintel with its ancient bosses and beyond it found the first glimmer of the evening star. Bit by bit, she drew closer. She'd never heard anyone tell a story like that, not without reading it from a book.

Gerry sat next to him mesmerised.

'I want you to imagine,' Michael said, 'that your mother was a great queen, but with one terrible flaw. She was obsessed with desire for an animal, a huge, terrifying bull. Now, imagine for a moment that she managed to gratify this frightful lust . . . which she did! And nine months later, she gave birth to a freak they called the Minotaur. Your parents could not bear the sight of him but they didn't dare destroy him either, and so they imprisoned him in a labyrinth. He may have been half-man and half-bull, but

290

he was also your half-brother. There he sat in the centre of this maze, in grief and rage propping up his huge horny head with his human hands. From time to time he'd bay for blood. Maybe you got used to the idea that your parents even sacrificed human beings to him. Was it out of shame, or did they just want to keep him quiet?

'Then one day, a ship came in, loaded with beautiful young men and girls, every one of them doomed to die. And there he was! Among the crowd of terrified victims, you spotted the most handsome man you ever saw. It was love at first sight and you couldn't bear to see him slaughtered, and so you went to him in secret and gave him the key to the maze. You knew that in doing this you would lose your whole family for ever and that, no matter how vile, it was your brother whom your lover would kill . . .'

Harriet could almost see the skein of wool unravelling from the hands of Theseus, hear his footpads as he sought the centre of the narrow, winding maze built by Daedalus to contain the monster. The squeals and bellows of the tragic Minotaur rang in her ears; the flight of the royal lovers, with Cretan ships pursuing, pleasantly agitated her as if she didn't know the outcome.

Even Germans were listening as he wove the tale. Even people who probably knew the story stood around.

'And so Ariadne sacrificed her family, her home and her kingdom for Theseus. But what I can't manage to understand is why anyone ever thought of him as a hero.' Michael was warming to his audience, hotly taking sides. 'He was simply using Ariadne. Her brilliance, her beauty, her courage . . . he even used her love to gain his own ends. To think, with all of his promises to marry her, that he abandoned her in this very spot!'

The sound of the sea orchestrated the story; the high portal glowed in the fading light. When Michael reached the climax where Dionysos arrived in his leopard-drawn chariot, it was as if the god jumped straight through the empty centre of the illustrious stone doorway, swooping up the princess, ascending with her to the heavens and setting her among the stars.

'And so, for all that Ariadne suffered in losing a mere man,' Michael concluded, 'she obtained the love of a god!' The tourists applauded spontaneously, but he shook his head with modest disclaimers. They should have heard his wife's father, he said. Now there was a storyteller!

The three of them had strolled back along the harbour, at ease, suddenly unified in pleasure at Michael's little triumph. It was hard to think that this was only the day before yesterday. Surely she mustn't get too discouraged! Harriet felt drowsy. Maybe there was some medication that could help Gerry. She wasn't going to leave a stone unturned.

She closed her eyes. And then, quite suddenly, the tissue of assurances fell away and without any warning, Harriet started to cry.

22

IT HAD BEEN THE WORST ROW of their married life and Michael had made up his mind. If his wife found it so difficult to tolerate their guests, then he wouldn't encumber her any longer: they would stay at the farm, at least for the next few days, and he had already arranged it with Kiria Anna, giving her a substantial bonus and orders that night for a special meal in the rustic old hall.

He rarely lost his temper, though, slow-heating mechanism that it was, when it achieved a high temperature, it took a while to cool down. Right now his mind was hopping around on an emotional griddle. To the startled Harriet, he announced that he was going back into town to fetch some overnight things; adding a long circumstantial list of reasons for this impromptu change of plan, he only managed to convince her that he was lying. Poor woman, he thought, it hardly mattered. She was showing all the early signs of a breakdown, a furtive morbidity he knew for himself too well. How had she ever thought herself capable of managing Gerry? It was Gerry, he suspected, who was managing her.

Eleni, however, was no such delicate creature. Her histrionics were pointed, guided missiles programmed to gain her ends. Her terrible tactics were based on the premise that she always fought a just war. Well, he wasn't going to let her get away with it this time.

In truth, they rarely fought, only squabbled. She vented her feelings; he was inclined to brood. They disliked quarrelling, and tended to make up quickly. On Sunday night, however, she'd gone past the unspoken boundaries that need to be observed in long marriages. He stood now at the foot of their bed where she lay, oddly small, in the darkened room.

Migraine! A convenient excuse. She looked almost fearfully at him as he packed his overnight case, swiping a clean shirt from a hanger, jerking the drawer for maximum effect on the 'headache'.

'Michael . . .' she pleaded. She was always the first to be sorry.

He tightened his lips and nodded courteously to her. 'I shall be away for a few days at the farm. You will be glad to hear that I shall be relieving you of your unwanted guests.'

'I shouldn't have said . . .'

'No, no! You're entitled . . . as you never stop reminding me, it *is* your house.' He shut the door hard and stalked into the room where Harriet was staying. Normally, it would never have occurred to him to go into a woman's room unasked, nor rummage through her drawers, but he did so now with a firmness and definition that surprised him.

Poor, weak Harriet with her vain struggle against age! The dressing table was littered with pots of unguents. He decided he couldn't get into that. She'd have to do without her war paint for a few days and, quite honestly, she'd look better without it.

The room was Cassie's when she came to stay and, for a moment, his eyes rested on little mementoes of his daughter's childhood, a Royal Doulton ballerina on the mantle, a picture she had drawn and he had framed of her Bellini grandfather.

It was a sadness to him that Aidan Hythe had shown no interest in Cassie when she was born. Michael had hoped that a grandchild would succeed where he and his brothers had failed; but maybe his father disliked babies. What would he have made of Gerry? Before Michael could dismiss the thought, it flashed across his mind what Gerry had said about Edgar's waiting until his father was dead to bring him to Ashdean. He saw it: Gerry, a skinny little boy with bird bones, tucked up in the nursery with eyes wide over the coverlet; pale Gerry playing wanly on the lawn, solitary under the big old trees . . . a picture came to him of someone too vulnerable entirely to be subjected to his father's gaze.

Michael didn't know why he had always taken it for granted that he was considered a separate entity from his brothers when his wife had always thought it odd. Perhaps it was the difference in religion. Maeve had explained to him that she had lost her faith, but on his birth had regained it.

There was no need for her to add that her marriage had broken down: he had never seen it function. His first discovery of old photographs, however, had stunned him: black-and-white snaps of them laughing together on a Spanish holiday. How and why they had become alien to each other he never understood. They shared the same large house, but only came together when it was necessary to put on a show for the village. In a curious way, however, Maeve was loyal to her husband. She never ran him down. In fact, she heightened his reputation with her sons, making them mute anywhere near his study door lest they disturb the scholarly recluse she made him out to be. They were off at prep school, each one of them, before the age of seven, but from time to time Michael's path intersected with his father's. There was a kindly smile he did not like for the hard eyes above it: it made him feel uneasy and afraid.

On Michael's marriage, the large-hearted George Bellini had taken him up and made him into the son he never had but wanted, sometimes to Eleni's chagrin. The two men became real friends and enjoyed popping about the island together on the Hythes' annual holidays there. They talked about potatoes and architecture, but it was the affirmation of himself that slowly and effectively thawed Michael, giving him back the warmth that was naturally his, adding a self-confidence he'd never had. When his father-in-law died, he found himself unable to control his weeping at the funeral. The Hythes were not given to public displays of emotion, or to confessions from the heart. At the time, he had blurted out to Eleni that her father had meant much more to him than his own, and a surprising bitterness emerged that left him feeling raw and guilty.

This was one of the many reasons her words to him last night cut so deeply. She'd pointed out what needn't have been said. When would she learn that some things were better merely understood not stated? Aidan Hythe had never cared what happened to any of his sons, least of all Michael. He had rejected each and every one, she had said with a blood-curdling Greek directness that saw no compromise.

He didn't want to think of it now; his wife's insinuations about both his parents were the crux of the row. He tried to keep his anger at bay, but it smouldered as when they cleared the crops in Naxos, burning stubble in the fields. You'd think the fire was out and then it would erupt again.

Resolutely, he tackled the drawers that Eleni had, with much grumbling, cleared last week for Harriet. He knew women were for ever changing their underwear, and so he fished out a bra and some pants; his eyes averted from the froth of lace. Of course, it only scored a point for Eleni to be thinking, as he was, that Harriet was getting on a bit for such frippery. A nightdress seemed in order. Maybe she kept it under her pillow, as his wife did. And it was so. More froth emerged . . . it must have cost a fortune.

Of course, Harriet was in love with Gerry. Why spell it out? Especially in words of one syllable. In a cold voice he knew to be his angriest, he had demolished Eleni, taking her to task for her evil mind. Couldn't she see the pathos in Harriet? The poor woman, sixty if she was a day, yearned after a much younger man who obviously had no interest in her. Last night before dinner, as they stood together on the balcony, Gerry had muttered something Michael didn't quite catch, something about 'alternative sexuality'. An odd way to put it, but Michael had assumed he meant he was gay and quickly changed the subject.

That Harriet was oblivious to Gerry's indifference made it all the more poignant. She became arch and kittenish around him, not sensing his distaste. She had got Michael to take her picture with Gerry . . . oh, everywhere. Yesterday she'd asked for one in the drawing room, even changing for the occasion into a bright red dress that accentuated her figure and her creamy skin. Gerry slumped into the sofa, sulky as an adolescent. It was hard to place him in any other age group, even though chronologically he was a mature adult. Harriet beamed down, her hands placed just above his shoulders like an infatuated doll-maker dangling her own, badly executed puppet for the world to admire. She adored the odd little man. Wherever he went, her eyes followed him with doggy devotion. It was almost unbearable to watch her humiliate herself in front of someone as, well, as mad as Gerry. On that point at least, Michael and Eleni were agreed. The argument, if one could call it that, was what to do about it.

Michael glanced at Cassie's china ballerina. Harriet was more brittle. It was no wonder that she doted on such a cold fish when reciprocated love would almost certainly involve too much rugged handling. Averell Washington had treated Harriet like a princess. It was common currency in Ashdean that he had a wife who constantly demanded sacrifices of him. When Cassie wrote telling them he had bolted with the gamey Sally, Michael had felt a guilty twinge of male solidarity.

Eleni could be so harsh! So unyielding! So rigid! For a moment he wondered what it would be like to sleep with Harriet – sort of a revenge fantasy, he thought – but there was something really offputting about her and he couldn't put his finger on it.

So Eleni found the visitors disturbing, did she? So Gerry gave her the creeps? 'How do you think it makes me feel?' he had shouted, knowing that her riposte would be that he had brought it on himself.

He had shouldered the burden, all right, and with no help from her. To keep them on the move was the only tolerable way to deal with them. That had been his strategy, to cart them around the island seeing sights, distracting them like children. Given that he was running out of stamina, he wondered what alternative he had for the duration of their stay . . . More beach? Gerry had liked that. Maybe the farm was the answer after all. They had traipsed the fields all afternoon while Harriet was sleeping and Gerry had burbled with enthusiasm, the artificial edge to his voice quite gone. Maybe it was the presence of the boy. At least someone seemed to like Gerry. Vassilis had tagged along, practising his English and feinting basketball shots as they trudged happily past the furrows. In the end, Michael had come up with a plan that seemed inspired at the time. There was no proper flower garden at the farm. Would Gerry like to stay there and design one? He jumped at the chance.

Harriet and Gerry made nothing seem neutral. Although he had no right to complain, Michael was drained in just under a week. Wherever they went, a subtext of powerful feeling projected itself on to mountains, oozed into the sea, inhabited rocks. One would think the Melanes kouros was uncontroversial enough, and yet as a result of seeing it that morning Harriet had collapsed with the vapours and as for Gerry . . . Michael didn't like to think about it. He'd walked into the clearing where the fallen statue lay, having gone just long enough to buy a few cold drinks, and there was his nephew, Edgar redux, quivering with that arctic fury he so well remembered. Anything could set it off. Even as a child, Edgar's quixotic moods governed the household. They had not been the ordinary tantrums of a child with inadequate control. It was quite the other way. Even their father seemed curiously dominated by Edgar and, though he punished him heavily, there was a sense in which Edgar had the upper hand.

Suddenly, Michael had an urge to run to Eleni, repair the damage, bury his face in her breasts and tell her this latest and weirdly monstrous development, this sense of Edgar exhumed at Melanes beside the fallen boy. But he thought better of it.

All Eleni had to do was to supply meals. They'd even got Maria in to help. Suppose one of her sisters had died, he asked her, leaving a troubled child to set straight – wouldn't she expect his full cooperation? She'd demand it! How could he turn away Edgar's son?

As a gambit, that remark had been a mistake. Eleni told him exactly why. And now she wished she hadn't said it. Well, she could suffer in silence, his most powerful weapon and one she could never withstand.

He swiped a frock from a hanger and folded Harriet's few things carefully, as he'd seen Eleni do, then went in search of a toothbrush. His eye caught some rosary beads on the night table. Did it never occur to Eleni that Harriet might be struggling against temptation? Such a charitable thought would never enter her head.

When it came to searching out Gerry's room for bits and pieces, Michael became afraid of what he might find. He opened the door to the old study gingerly. He could hear Eleni's voice: *Do you want to know why I called my daughter Cassandra? I'll tell you why! Because none of you has ever listened to me and I am cursed by always being right!* What rubbish! Cassie's name had come from her maternal grandmother and had nothing to do with sibylline predictions.

There was a thumbed science fiction thriller on Gerry's bedside table. The cover sported lavender creatures with cyclops eyes. It looked good fun to Michael. He popped it in the bag, then went back to fetch Harriet's rosary for inclusion, as a compliment to her piety. Back and forth he went, pacing the distance between the two rooms as if in doing so he could survey the strange emotional territory his two guests occupied.

Gerry's room, his father-in-law's old study, was immaculate, as if he hadn't slept there at all. The roll-top desk was locked where George liked to sit and where they'd share shots of raki, smoking and telling stories. It was no good wishing he hadn't put Gerry in that room. Michael wrenched a shirt from the wardrobe and stuffed some boxer shorts in the bag. Why did he feel like a thief? He wanted to put Gerry's things back, creep out of the room and close the door, an odd thought considering his nephew's conviction for burglary. Edgar had been light-fingered, Michael suddenly remembered with a grim laugh. Even before the drugs, he would take money from their mother's handbag and steal sweets from the village shop. It gave him a buzz, he said, but Michael always wondered if that was really it.

No, he was not going to dignify his wife's undignified screechings. *Can't you see what he is trying to do? One wrong move from you and he'll dig things up and you'll never know . . . you'll never know if they are true or false! Michael, can't you just let the past be the past?*

Whatever Gerry was, there was no sense in which he was using the situation. There had been no pleas for cash, no mention of future involvement with the family. His demands seemed modest enough: he wanted answers. After all, the poor soul, he was no less a victim of Edgar's drastic enigma than the rest of the family, and with more right than most to get at the truth.

Michael shook his head at the conundrum of his brother that seemed to deepen every day with the little shards of new evidence Gerry's most casual remarks turfed up. Eleni had always been completely unable to see how brutal she was and how intemperate in her keenness for making connections. He had thought her lust for revenge on his mother had abated, but no, not so.

Thank God she never knew about his father and the book of vases! All along he'd known what dangerous ammunition that would be for a loose cannon like Eleni, and time had proved him right. Imagine what she would have made of Gerry's words at dinner last night if he'd been stupid enough to confide in her. It meant absolutely nothing, of course – it was mere coincidence that Gerry had been so odd about the pots and crocks in the museum.

Michael shoved the business about the vases away from him. Memory was never a reliable tool. In any case, the bookshop that Gerry mentioned, the rare bookshop on the King's Road, had been quite enough to set her paranoid imagination racing into high gear.

Keeping Edgar out of trouble had always involved a high degree of maintenance. Their mother was for ever taking the train up to London in order to fund some new scheme or to lend her respectability to it. In this way, their parents had lost what few friends they had. Godparents, cousins, even Maeve's own brother who ran a West End gallery had all been dragooned into rescuing Edgar, then stung by his unreliability. At the very least, he'd turn up for work for a few days and then bunk off; his worst antics included mild embezzlement. Their mother had kept him out of prison by repaying what Edgar had stolen and squandered.

The rare bookshop, though, was different, mostly because it had very nearly worked. The proprietor, Colin Phipps, was Maeve's distant relation, a frail old man who suffered from crippling arthritis. He must have been pretty desperate to take Edgar on as an assistant, but he did it in order to manage bad days. At first, all seemed well. Edgar liked books and even enjoyed going to auctions. He became, everyone agreed, touchingly proud of his increasing knowledge of vellums and bindings. It was a quiet trade, just his speed, nothing in it to over-excite the mind. With a huge sigh of relief, the Hythes believed that Edgar had, at long last, found his métier.

Phipps was a kindly old Catholic gentleman whom everyone dismissed as having little to do in life other than be pious. He was a type, the mainstay of daily Masses, who occupy the back pews of churches in a grey haze of unassuming devotion. Yet he turned out to be more formidable than anyone supposed.

He took the scapegrace under his wing, encouraging him quietly. Michael remembered what it was like, the tranquil years when Edgar seemed to be making genuine headway. Maeve blessed Colin Phipps every day. In turn, he managed, with considerable tact and skill, to convince Maeve that Edgar's addiction was not so engulfing as perhaps she had assumed. Of course, this bore out Eleni's theory that Edgar's taste for heroin grew in proportion to his mother's hysteria about it. He was unquestionably hooked, but he was hardly sleeping rough and he did function. Where everyone else had failed, Phipps got Edgar to a discreet doctor he could tolerate. Maeve's grip on Edgar relaxed as the Phipps effect kicked in. He gave private progress reports to the grieving mother, punctually, once a month. All of them were good.

Michael needed no reminding from Eleni about how bitter the blow had been when it came. One weekend, Edgar turned up on an unexpected visit. For the first time since anyone could remember, everyone was cautiously pleased to see him. He'd gained weight, his colour was good; he was even civil. Sunday lunch was prepared for the prodigal, and his brothers arrived at the manor with their wives.

It was characteristic of Edgar that he waited to drop the bombshell until they were off their guard. He'd always had a cruel streak and he preferred to exercise it before an audience. Maeve had made his favourite pudding, personally; she'd gone to lots of trouble. A trifle. He liked a trifle. He waited until she smilingly unveiled it. He'd decided, he told them, to quit his job. Nothing could induce him to work any longer with Colin Phipps. His mother's face predictably fell and that was all he needed. Edgar leaned back in his chair, relishing his power over the silent group. Perhaps they'd like to know why. A few days before, Edgar, rummaging around at the back of the shop, had discovered a locked case. Curious about it, he had searched for the key. It hadn't taken him long – and voilà, within lay a nice little collection of erotica that Phipps must have been hoarding over the years . . . men with children mostly, he told them, but also women with animals.

'So you see,' Michael muttered aloud now into the empty hallway, 'there was no mention of Greek drinking cups back then, was there!' Still, he felt confused.

Whatever the type of smut Edgar had described that day, Michael and Eleni had been dumbfounded, and more by the strength of Maeve's reaction to this news than by Edgar, who was predictably triumphant with the desired effect. The table palled in a squeamish silence while the slow recognition of a peculiar kind of horror spread over Maeve's face.

At this, Godfrey shoved back his chair and left the room. Everyone else was locked into place, pinned and squirming, while Edgar and his mother stared each other down.

Michael and Eleni had walked home, badly shaken. 'It's almost as if he's blackmailing Maeve,' Eleni had said. It had made sense at the time, but she had remembered the incident during their quarrel last night and repeated it, twisting it out of context.

Poor Phipps. He'd been axed from the family tree even though, for once, Godfrey had had the presence of mind to check out the story. There was no doubt that Edgar was lying. He had been using the money entrusted to him to buy up this pornographic material. It was Phipps who had uncovered it, and Phipps who had threatened exposure to the police . . . unless Edgar fell on his sword and resigned. Maeve never believed this, and Michael put it out of his mind.

So Gerry had been to the shop. What of it? Did that give Eleni justification for all sorts of morbid suspicions? She was appalling, truly appalling – how dare she? Michael's heart thudded with rekindled indignation. Edgar probably just sat the child in a corner with a soft drink and a bag of tooth-rotting sweets. And what gave her the right to assume that Phipps had known of Gerry's existence, and reported it to Maeve? How could she possibly leap to the conclusion that his mother had known about Gerry all along? Or that there was some other dreadful family secret Maeve was hiding or with which she had been colluding? Just thinking about it made his blood pressure rise – to think that just a moment ago he had started to weaken! No, he was not going to apologise for what he, in turn, had said to her: that she had made his mother's last, miserable years intolerable! Let her tears of contrition for her hasty words flow! Maybe they would clean her up, give her the nasty purge she deserved!

Michael zipped up the bag, marched to the door and slammed out of the Kastro house. In the years to come, he never regretted anything so much as that childish decision to show Eleni up, make her sweat it out. He strode down the sunlit alleyways, descending through the medieval gate down to the port where his car was parked. He saw neither friend nor neighbour, nor the big ferry arriving from Athens on the deep blue sea, nor the late afternoon sun pouring gold on Naxos like Zeus on Danaë.

The still, cold dread hadn't gone away; his rage had not dissipated the small, sick feeling in the pit of his stomach. Michael sat in the baking car, his hand idle on the ignition key. It was nothing; it meant nothing; there was no tangible connection between vases and shops, only the suggestion, only mindless panic that linked the two. He started up, shifting the gears and steering automatically. Like one of his own donkeys, he instinctively knew the route that led to the farm. His mind was vividly present in Ashdean Manor where, he presumed, Godfrey would soon be opening the letter he had just sent about Gerry Carney, Gerry Hythe.

It was the day after his father's funeral over twenty-five years ago, when his brother Godfrey had called him in to help sort out papers, books and effects from the study where Aidan Hythe had lived and even slept in self-exile from the human race. For some reason, it had rankled with them both that Edgar wasn't there. They complained of him, condemning his hardness of heart when for the first time he seemed oddly necessary. Why Michael had the impression that he and Godfrey were wearing protective masks and suits, he did not know, but the memory came to him in white as if they had been dressed to handle radioactive material. Even the musty smell of the room came back to him, the dreary light from a mullioned window that was never washed. The desk was old, but not a good piece of furniture, simply massive. Tall Godfrey looked small beside it. He cracked a dry joke about having to stand on the carpet in front of the desk while their father considered the number of strokes he would get from the cane that lived, almost like a panting animal, in the corner. A look of resentment came over Godfrey's bleak face. 'Mummy saved you,' he said. 'By the time you came along . . .' he had hesitated, not finishing the sentence and Michael hadn't wanted him to finish it. He brusquely cut in with some question about where to pile the books.

Curiously, Godfrey stopped in his task of sorting the bills and correspondence taken from their father's drawer and, going to the window, he gazed out on to the lawn. 'You do understand how important the manor is to me now, don't you, Michael? Sophie and I will never have any children. *He* made sure of that.' Godfrey paused. 'I think I am going to seal this room off,' he added, a strange afterthought.

At the time Michael had not known what to make of this, but was delighted to have the manor and the matter of his mother's old age taken off his mind. Only later did he became angry with Godfrey, when Maeve was relieved of her money, shoved off in a wing of the house and never driven anywhere unless he or Eleni came to fetch her. Reasonable enough for them to help, he sup-posed – but her tears and suffering, her complaints that she'd been 'thrown in the dustbin'! Poor, wintry Godfrey, he had thought that day as they stood in the study, for Michael had always conceded that his two elder brothers had come off the worst . . .

He'd been embarrassed, none the less, by this vulnerability in Godfrey, especially as he was feeling vulnerable himself, and he turned to the books, piling them up so that they could be por-tioned out between the brothers. The room, their father's refuge for so long, smelt like a disused mausoleum. It was then that his hand rested on a volume bound in black oilskin that he assumed must be a journal of some kind; he dreaded having to read it. It fell open, almost as if it had a will of its own but probably because it was obviously well used, stained with thumbing.

The pictures had never left him, even though he had shelved them in the depths of his mind. The book was a collection of plates taken from drinking cups used by Greeks in the fifth century BC. Men with huge phalluses capered around, in and about first one kylix and then another, while slim-hipped boys with simpering glances received their advances in every position. It was like a *Kama Sutra* for pederasts. Michael gave an involuntary gasp and turned to show Godfrey, but he realised that Godfrey already knew what was in the book and was watching him. He gave a withering laugh that conveyed an instruction. 'I don't think anyone need know about this, do you?' Godfrey had said at last. 'Especially not Mummy.' And he threw it on the pile of papers to be burned.

After a near miss with a lorry thundering towards the port, Michael drew over and parked the car in Sangri. He went into the local bar, asked for a stiff ouzo and sat staring at the dusty road until he realised that if he arrived too late at the farm there would be lapses and lacunae he would have to explain.

Cassie studied the menu in the Greek restaurant off the Bayswater Road, her favourite. She was waiting for James Gosforth to make his way up from Peckham once he had finished his shift. She checked her watch and decided the traffic must still be diabolical. September in the rain, it always choked London.

James had her mobile number. She checked her bag to see if it was switched on. To her annoyance, the battery had almost gone. A faint signal showed one message. She prodded the stupid thing, but it died on her. She hoped it wasn't the boys. No, she'd rung the sitter earlier. Something had probably come up with James; he was reliable. She glanced at the door again; she hoped he hadn't cancelled. Almost certainly, he was caught in the bowels of the Underground, but he was half an hour late. Another fifteen minutes and she'd find a phone and ring the prison. Cassie debated on whether or not to order a drink and decided she needed one. She'd been to see Gerry that morning, and even though she'd spent the afternoon shopping in a desperate and deliberate frivolity to offset the visit, she felt whacked. Lots of things had come up and she needed to digest them, James or no James. Besides, her feet were killing her.

The circling waiter caught her eye. Cassie exercised her Greek and asked for a white wine spritzer. They were off in a clatter of language – he came from Paros, imagine that! Whatever rivalry existed between the two adjacent islands vanished as if blown out to sea by the northern autumn. Before she knew it, the proprietor looked in. A lively discussion ensued, inevitably of politics. Cassie's Greek wasn't up to this, so she was doubly relieved when the door opened and James arrived, his mac dripping and his hair plastered down with rain.

It wasn't the weather – she could tell from his face that something else was wrong. When she looked up, the Greeks had whisked away his soggy coat and melted into the restaurant, blending into its cosy light as if they were props on a stage set.

He sat raking his fingers through his hair, padding his face down with his palms. He took her hand. 'Cassie, I'm sorry. Gerry died two hours ago. I tried to get you . . .'

She put her head to one side, quizzically, like a bird. 'But how can that be? I only saw him . . .'

'I know. I'm so sorry.'

'Oh my God. My mobile went flat . . . was that you? There seemed to be a message.'

'I did leave something, but it was a bit garbled. I couldn't tell you, not just like that. Besides, I had to sort out the body . . . you know. Well, perhaps you don't.' He looked as if he expected her to bear a grudge. 'I knew I'd be seeing you. It was all so sudden.'

She waved it away, swatting it like a fly. 'He didn't commit suicide?'

He shook his head. 'Why? Did you think he would?'

'I don't know why I said that. We had a good talk, better than ever before. He died in the prison then. You didn't get him to hospital.'

Gosforth said, 'I need a drink.'

They were silent for a moment while the waiter re-emerged. Cassie felt that something was missing between them: Gerry. The gulf his death created surprised her, even though she felt only sad. James stared at her as if trying to dig up what was behind her eyes. She sensed an emotional panic in them both.

He poured a little water into the ouzo, clouding it, and drank, his eyes closed, as if it contained no alcohol. 'There was an appalling choice,' he said. 'I don't know what you'll say, but I think Gerry made it for himself.'

She leaned into it, into the light of the candle with its chimney that stood between them. 'Poor James,' she said softly. 'Oh, James, what was it?'

'Well, we've talked about his getting religion, haven't we?'

'He was on about it this morning . . .'

'About five o'clock, when I was going off duty . . . you know, to see you . . . shower, change . . . change out of the prison . . .' He squeezed his eyes shut. 'I don't know how much more of that place I can bloody take.

'The panic button went. They were banged up before Association and I had some odds and ends of paperwork. Everyone scrambled. I stepped out of my office to find it was Gerry, crushing pains in his chest. His cellmate raised the alarm. Of course, we called the medics. That was done, I promise you.

'His cellmate was jumping up and down, gibbering, going mad. "Father Joe," he kept saying, "Get Father Joe!" It was heartrending. He kept hanging on to Gerry, crying. "C'mon Gerry, you can make it."

'Anyway, to make a long story short, there'll probably be an inquiry. By the time the chaplain got there, the medics were waiting to get Gerry off to hospital. He was in real agony. I'm so sorry. It was a straight choice, but Gerry nodded . . . I'm sure I saw him nod. Father Joe must have seen it too because he called for water and he baptised Gerry and said the Last Rites.

'And then he died.'

A relief so profound she could not credit it gusted up from Cassie's Catholic past. 'Thank God,' she said.

'They couldn't have got him to hospital in time. I'm quite sure of it, but they're saying if they'd got into the cell before Father Joe they could have saved him.'

'Saved him,' she said. 'For what?'

'I'm sorry. It was . . . a nightmare, actually. And I was responsible, in charge. It was pure instinct. It just took over. I had no idea I'd act like that.'

Cassie shook her head. After a moment, she said, 'It sounds insane, I know, but Gerry has died and gone to heaven. Don't you see?'

Gosforth stared at her. 'You don't blame me?'

'I am starving,' she said. 'I recommend the mezedes, a whole plate of them. It should be quite sufficient.' As she put the order to the waiter, by now avid with curiosity, she added. 'Why should I blame you? In the eyes of the Church, you've sent him to paradise and shall probably go there yourself as a result.'

'But you don't believe that.'

'Don't I? Well, I'm only telling you what was hammered into me. It must be on the hard drive. As you told me the story, it seemed absolutely the right thing to do.'

James looked down at his hands. 'He never admitted that he killed the child. He should have been sorry!' His voice came out awkwardly as if he were a child himself, complaining of unfairness.

Cassie felt a little giddy, detached from the whole proceedings and grimly amused. 'You *did* miss out!' she told him. 'Baptism is trumps. The Byzantine emperors used to wait until the last gasp to be baptised . . . No matter how great the sin, baptism cancels it. Theoretically, Gerry is pure as an angel now. He could have killed ten children, cooked and eaten them and it would make not the slightest difference in the eyes of God. Simple, isn't it? And as for the Last Rites . . . well, if extra were needed . . .'

'It's medieval!'

'Is it?' She helped herself to some kalamares and pushed them his way. 'You think I'm hard, don't you?'

'I think you're as shocked as I am. It'll hit you later.' He ate, but little. 'I've seen them die before. I had to cut down a man who'd hanged himself once. You can't imagine that, can you? The trouble is, neither can I even though I know I did it. I was able just to blot it out. But I never *knew* him.' He gave a contemptuous snort. 'It makes it easier if they're numbers to us, surnames.'

'You knew this one, though, didn't you?' Cassie's appetite for the kalamares deserted her as quickly as it had come on.

'This one was Gerry to me . . . through you. Gerry, Gerald . . . His cellmate told us the name he'd chosen for the ceremony next week – he was going to be the godfather, he told us. Gerald Basil. He was adding the name Basil.'

Cassie worried an olive pit from her mouth. She rested her chin on her hands and thought for a long moment. 'Did you learn any Greek in Cyprus?' He shook his head. 'That's the name of the victim, Basil . . . Vassilis. He chose the name of his victim.'

'Holy God!' said Gosforth.

'Quite.'

They were sharing a demi-carafe and found they had consumed it in a short space of time. 'Shall we go for it? Another one?' he asked.

She nodded. 'Why not?'

'I drink too much,' he told her.

She shrugged. 'I'll tell you something else. Today is the anniversary of the child's death.'

'You're kidding!'

'It is, isn't it, the 15th? That's the day Vassilis died. And I don't know . . . and I will now never know . . . whether Gerry did the deed or not. Today, he told me his version of the story, perhaps because of the date, maybe because of the impending baptism. And I'll leave it to you to decide what you think. For myself, I honestly can't say.'

23

THE SUN WAS SETTING by the time Michael returned to the farm. Harriet stood at the gate, watching anxiously as his car bounced towards her: it disappeared into the rosy shadows of bends and hollows, then reappeared, a small moving bubble on the long dirt track that never seemed to get closer. In the late light, the dusty road was like a satin cord shot through a bolt of rich cloth shaken out below the darkening mountains beyond. The smell of lamb roasting with wild herbs met the scent of evening in the courtyard. In the distance, at an arc to the car and bisecting the circumference of her horizon, Gerry and the farm hand's boy were apparently deep in conversation. They moved slowly across a broad field near a small copse of trees. They had been standing there for quite some time.

Her new resolve was beginning to crumble. The scene before her, far from bearing omens of the catastrophe she dreaded, exuded sylvan peace. What could be more natural and wholesome than the picture they made, a man, a boy and a dog taking a stroll in the twilight? Evidently concluding what they had to say, they were now making their way back to the tower house, going slowly over the hummocks, gesticulating as they went. The dog trotted behind them, its tail waving like a flag. Sheep bleated in the distance; grasshoppers, crickets, cicadas hummed and chirped. As Michael's car travelled nearer, so did Gerry and his young friend; they would reach the courtyard where she stood within moments of each other.

Well, maybe it wasn't meant to be, her talk with Michael. She had calculated on nobbling him while Gerry was out with the boy, but hours passed without a sign of him, leaving her in fearful solitude, powerless against the magnitude of her imaginings. Just when she thought that she and Gerry were about to settle for the afternoon, the child had manifested himself.

At the back of the tower, there was a terrace built into the hill with a hazy view of the distant sea. After Michael's departure for Naxos Town, Kiria Anna had led her out there with much smiling, Gerry in her wake. Before Harriet knew it, she was ensconced under a fig tree in a deckchair plump with cushions, a jug of lemonade by her side. What a view! The Aegean sparkled beyond the velvet headlands. She felt rested, better. What was more, Gerry was sorry for his behaviour that morning, she could tell. He was positively friendly, even flattering her a little. She felt completely restored. She realised she had not been so comfortable with him since he had left the prison. He needed time, of course he did, time to readjust to the normal world.

And he was full of plans. Maybe Michael could be persuaded to build a swimming pool with a gazebo for changing. Gerry had looked at the space. There was room. Certainly, a garden designed around a pool would have great possibilities. Didn't Harriet think so? They chatted on, carefully avoiding what was personal to them both. Gerry paced the terrace, excited and creative.

At first, she didn't notice the boy. He must have scrambled up to the top of the dry stone wall that separated the farm from the outcropping of the terrace, but when she looked up he was sitting there; legs dangling, he banged his heels, scuffing his dirt-caked sandals. He was peering at them, curious. Whether Gerry sensed him or saw him, all conversation dried. His eyes swivelled towards the child and his lips parted in a smile. He stood aside, making a sign to the boy in a wordless invitation. The boy grinned and hopped down, his feet pounding on the hard stone. Harriet hadn't taken him fully in before. His rough-cut hair was bleached by the sun, his wiry body deeply tanned. He wore a worn T-shirt with 'Hard Rock Café' inscribed on it over a faded orange circle, and a pair of hand-me-down jeans. He must have been about eleven years old. His teeth were big for his head, his feet large: soon he would be growing into them. He had deep-set eyes that blinked slowly behind thick spectacles; and, though he was all smiles, there was something flat in his expression, as if he were in some respects older than Harriet, an important resource in him exhausted and dried up. He looked from side to side, worried perhaps that Kiria Anna would find him there and shoo him off. He trotted up to Gerry, again grinning his toothy smile.

'Hiya,' Gerry said, his voice throaty. He made a move to ruffle the boy's hair perhaps but then, thinking better of it, retracted his hand. Harriet felt trapped in the sagging deckchair, supine and helpless as she observed them.

'Mister Gerry?' the boy enquired. He nodded to Harriet, acknowledging her politely.

'Mister!' Gerry guffawed, throwing back his head in a laugh at once self-conscious and delighted. 'Just Gerry, mate. Plain old Gerry. Call me Gerry.'

'You want to see something? I show you something important.' The boy's eyes lit briefly, making him look younger. It was the look of childish conspiracy. 'It's a secret, a secret for Kirie Michali! Something he likes, something he wants. You want to help me?' He looked down at the cobblestones, at once shy as if he had presumed too much.

Gerry's face reddened, flushed with the sun or pleasure. The space between him and the boy seemed charged with a subtle energy as if it were magnetic. She made to heave herself from the cushioned chair. 'Gerry . . .' she said, not knowing how to end the sentence she had begun.

Later, she could never remember whether he had thrown her one glance or whether he had ignored her entirely. It was all so quick. 'Sure!' he said to the child. 'Sure, I'd love to help.'

The boy put his finger to his lips and beckoned Gerry towards the wall. They wheeled together, a single unit, up and over it like birds taking to the air.

'Ela!' she heard the boy call out. 'Ela, Hera!' and at once a dog barked excitedly. There was the sound of feet on bracken, and then they were gone.

The whole weight of Harriet's back was pressed into the chair as if she were being hurled into space. She closed her eyes. 'Gerry,' she said, 'Oh, Gerry.'

Even then, the irretrievable loss of him . . . for ever afterwards that was when she marked the point of it. It wasn't simply that she really accepted from that moment what he was, but the force of it, the strength of it, the hold it had over him. If he had encountered a god or an angel, Gerry's face could not have been more transfigured by the child. 'Oh, Gerry. Oh no!' she said.

But surely he wouldn't, not here. She struggled to her feet and quickly made her way through the house and out into the courtyard. The whooping boy, Gerry and the dancing dog were making their way up the shallow bowl of hills into the field beyond.

She opened her mouth to call out, to call them back, but her voice died in her throat. Her exhaustion became palpable, like a wall of water, thrusting her down, crushing the air from her lungs. Harriet braced herself against the dry stone wall. When she had recovered her equilibrium, Gerry and the boy had disappeared from sight.

She must tell Michael. She had to do it. There was no reasonable moral alternative. No matter what she had promised Gerry, the stakes were much too high. Slowly and very shaky now, she made her way back to the terrace at the back of the house and began to rehearse what she would say.

'Michael, I have something important to tell you . . .' she whispered sotto voce to the arena of noble landscape that stretched below her. She dried. How was she to put it? Cards on the table?

'Your nephew is a paedophile. I believe this puts your farm-hand's boy at risk.'

Maybe more subtly. 'It would appear, after all, that Gerry's problems are deeper than I at first supposed.'

She imagined Michael's face, first incredulous, then stunned.

'I knew, but I didn't tell you,' she found herself murmuring to his imagined anger, his need for explanations.

'I didn't tell you because . . .' She struggled for a reason.

'Well, I didn't know there would be any children here, you see.'

Tears pricked her eyes as she pictured his stinging rebuke. Hadn't he specified that she tell him what they were in for with Gerry? What about Cassie's tiny boys, whose photographs were on display all over the Kastro house? Had she considered how likely it was that they might be introduced at some later stage to Gerry?

Harriet bowed her head in shame. However Michael despised her, she must and would do her duty. And yet she still found herself torn on the point of self-justification:

'I didn't tell you because . . .'

'Because I didn't tell you.'

'I didn't tell you because . . .'

A space opened out below Harriet's conscious thought as if the floor of her mind had turned to glass. She seemed held over it, giddy with it and appalled. She flinched and tried to close the gap once more, but it was too late. Not to herself, surely not to anyone could she explain it – why it had happened and how she had fallen so hopelessly . . . in . . . well, was it in love? What did that expression mean anyway? Simply in.

The boy had jumped over the wall, Gerry after him. Harriet's fantasy jumped after them both, dragging them back, furious, outraged. 'How could you? How could you, after all . . .'

Gerry's face was illumined, eyes shining for the boy. 'After all I've done! After all I've been for you!' For one transcendent moment, Gerry had looked wholly alive. It was as if the boy had a secret key that unlocked his full humanity, making him complete.

That was the face that should have shone on her; it was she who was meant to transform him. This epiphany belonged to her. It was what she had wanted of him in way of consummation, and now the platonic construct lay shattered. She was eclipsed by a boy. She had not loved anyone in her whole long life, not her mother, nor her father, nor Averell and certainly not Emma. Instead, she had exacted love from them, hoarding it, lying in wait, afraid to return it. And now she had seen what this urchin could do to Gerry she understood what she had invested and why the crash had come about. A hot fury came over her. She could have taken the boy by the shoulders and shaken and shaken him, slapping him on one cheek then another, over and over again. She could have beaten him and kicked him. She could have killed him.

Even when Emma was born, Harriet had never cried out in pain. She did so now, a long reedy wail that might have set the farm dogs howling if she had not stuffed her knuckles in her mouth. To love him so hugely and in this way was depraved enough, but to be in torments of jealousy over an eleven-year-old boy, to have such evil imaginings about a child reduced her to nothing. And, having seen that, she broke down and wept.

She supposed there must be something to good breeding: after a while she had pulled herself together and gone back through the house to the courtyard in the front. She would watch, yes, keep an eye out. To her relieved surprise, the boy and Gerry were again visible. Whether or not they had only just emerged from the copse above the field she did not know, but their distant figures seemed relaxed.

And now here was Michael at long last pulling into the courtyard. He glanced at her and she at him. A strange exchange, an expressive sadness, seemed to travel between them. She made to speak but stood there dumbly as he got out of the car.

'Are you all right, Harriet? Are you better now?' he asked, the pattern if not the soul of courtesy. He seemed distracted, nervy.

'I'm . . .' She couldn't tell him. As much as she had steeled herself to do it, she had no strength left to draw on. 'Gerry's with . . .' She gestured lamely towards the darkening field. There was no evidence of wrongdoing. The dusk was rapidly taking hold, but she could clearly see that the boy was chatting, happy and serene. Gerry too was calm. If some traumatic event had occurred, this was hardly likely to be their mood.

Michael looked up and watched their final descent towards the tower house. 'Oh, I see,' he said curiously, as if he really did see, as if he saw straight through her.

Surely she was imagining it. She looked down, however, suddenly mortified. Were her shameful feelings so transparent? He and Eleni must have been talking about her, a mixture of pity and contempt for an old woman's folly.

As if to verify it, he added very gently, 'It's kind of Gerry, you know. Vassilis hasn't made many friends at school since he came here. He's an awfully lonely little boy.' He swung the small suitcase out from the front seat. 'I hope Eleni's packed the right things.'

Harriet felt a blush rising that made her eyes smart. Her passion unmasked now, she stood without any defence against Michael's gentle reproach. She looked quickly away towards Gerry and the boy. She was humbled into the dust. Her need to confess, to betray him had been no more than the hell that had no fury like a woman scorned. 'Poor Eleni. Is she feeling better?' Harriet mumbled.

He shook his head. 'We were saying maybe it's one of these viruses, now that you've been stricken too.'

'Could be!' she replied, so falsely cheery that she cringed to hear herself.

A little beyond them, Gerry was parting company with the boy, who ran off in the direction of his father plodding home from work at the end of the day.

He strolled up to them, all smiles. 'Brilliant afternoon,' he told his uncle. Really, sometimes it was hard to believe Gerry wasn't about twelve years old himself.

He rubbed his hands in a child's glee. 'There's a secret!' he said, 'A surprise. And, Uncle Michael, you'll love it when you find out!'

'I love this place!' Gerry told Michael. 'I could stay here for ever.'

They were as drunk as owls, the two of them having left it until Harriet went to bed to get stuck in. Somehow, they'd managed to get upstairs to Michael's study and were lounging like sultans in two stuffed, battered armchairs that had been filed in the room for future renovation. A couple of oil lanterns stood alight on the mantel, but the moon outside was so bright that it looked like a map on a schoolroom wall; its neon glow came through the tower window, casting sharp shadows on the floor.

'I'm glad you like it,' said Michael. 'You can get away from the women up here.'

Gerry spluttered a knowing laugh. 'Why do they make everything so heavy? Can you explain that? I don't fucking understand 'em. Sorry. Don't bloody understand 'em.'

'Fucking's all right.'

'Phoa! You're telling me!' But at his own stock quip, Gerry dried and sat staring boss-eyed at the brandy bottle in front of him. The smoke from his cigarette drifted towards Michael making his eyes smart, but he asked Gerry for one. He lit it and coughed.

'It's their nerves,' Michael said. He thought wryly about his own but forbore to mention them. 'And they're always looking for trouble.'

'True!' said Gerry pointing his index finger in the air. 'That's very true. Mind you, I never got the hang of them, so to speak. They're all dykes in prison. Makes you wonder about Harriet, don't it?'

Michael disliked the turn this conversation was taking. He held up his hands for a halt.

'Yeah, I know, but she pisses me off!'

'Harriet really cares for you. She loves you, Gerry.' During dinner he'd felt so sorry for her. And he got the distinct impression that Gerry was winding her up, waxing lyrical about his day in the hills with Vassilis. Gerry couldn't keep a secret, at least not with a skinful of wine in him. The boy, he told them, had it in his head that he knew where a cache of Cycladic figurines was buried – clearly a fantastic notion, it sounded, but Michael had been touched when Gerry told him the gist of their conspiracy. Vassilis had cooked up a scheme to find the treasure, and Gerry, being seen as equally indebted to Michael, had been pulled in to the plot. 'He hopes to dig it up in time for your birthday,' Gerry had said. 'He idolises you.'

It was hard to see why Harriet looked so disapproving at the plan they had in mind. They were taking a picnic the next day to a secret place in order to start the search. But then she did look very odd, on the verge of tears throughout the meal. In the end, she rose abruptly from the table, declaring she needed an early night, which couldn't have relieved Michael more, he had to admit. What would he do if she started to make a spectacle out of herself?

It was partly for that reason that he'd decided to kill a bottle with his nephew. With his wife emoting in the Kastro and Harriet going barmy at the farm, Gerry seemed the lesser evil. With any luck they'd get to a state of total amnesia.

Gerry frowned, pinching his lips together. 'I know. I know she loves me. And . . . don't say it! She's a good person. I'll just never be good enough for her, that's all.'

Michael thought to let the subject drop, but Gerry continued after a thoughtful pause. 'It's just like being fostered, all over again. Every time you'd go to a new house, you'd meet a new lady. Every time, she'd kiss and cuddle you or get you to draw pictures or read you stories . . . then boom! You're out and you don't know why, except that the social workers tell you you're too hot to handle and try to explain but you still don't understand. A few of 'em were po-faced bitches, but mostly they were *nice* ladies, *good* ladies. Sometimes I think Harriet wants to foster me. And sometimes I think it's something else she wants.'

Michael considered Gerry for a moment through the unaccustomed smoke. Maybe the drink had impaired his judgement, but his nephew seemed to have altered. It was as though suddenly Gerry had found it in himself to speak directly from the heart. What he was saying about Harriet was unpleasant enough, but it could hardly be dismissed as coarse or dishonourable. 'You'll try not to hurt her, though, won't you?' he said aloud.

'Why did you say that?' Gerry was at once on his guard again. 'I don't *hurt* people.'

'I didn't mean . . .'

'Nobody hurts like I do!'

'Up to now I suppose your life hasn't been much fun.'

'Whatever!' Gerry said in a black sulk now.

Before he meant to, Michael said it. 'My brother.'

Gerry shot him a look full of pain then looked away. He folded his arms on his chest.

'I must say this to you. I wish he hadn't . . . hurt you. I'm sorry he did, Gerry.'

A kind of cockiness native to Gerry collapsed. 'What did you know about it? I mean, I accept you didn't know about it.'

'Still.'

'I mean, if you'd known and looked away . . .'

Michael's limbs became heavy and his stomach seemed to drop as if he were in a lift that he could get out of if he changed the subject. Why be afraid of it? They had to have it out at some point. 'Look, Gerry, you've got to understand about Edgar. It's not that there was something wrong with him, it's that nothing was ever right.' Was it because Gerry's eyes were summoning him over thin ice that he put a foot on it? 'My earliest memories of Edgar all have to do with something wrong.'

'Tell me about it!' Gerry said, oddly in command. He swilled a mouthful of brandy and put the glass back on the table like a poker player with good cards.

'What is there to tell? Only impressions. He had a sensitive nature, of that I'm sure.' Why was he rambling on like this? 'I outgrew stuffed animals before he did, for instance. Sometimes he could be very babyish and he cried a lot . . . not the little man our father wanted him to be. And Edgar was very afraid of him, I do remember that. I used to try to protect him, I tried to save him from having to go down to the study, but it was useless. My pa had it in for him.'

'*You* tried to protect *him*?' Gerry's pupils were the size of black coins. 'He used to tell me *he* was trying to protect *you*. It must have been you. He said "my younger brother".'

'Did he?' A flash of memory came back to Michael, but it was gone before he could seize it. 'My mother did that,' he said hastily, gulping because it was out before he could stop it.

'His whole story.' Gerry gave a sigh so bitter it was shocking. 'His whole story was that she *knew*. He was a trade-off for *you*. Though of course he bloody fucking wouldn't tell me your name. It all makes sense, don't you see? He said there were deals and bargains . . . that she made sure you were spared.'

Michael felt his hands go very still. He must have blenched because Gerry added, 'Listen, man, it wasn't your fucking fault, was it? No more than it was mine! You've got to believe. It wasn't your fault.'

Michael thought he said, 'What do you mean?' but it didn't matter because he could see that Gerry was going to tell him any-way and there was nothing now he could do to stop it, even if he wanted to.

For a moment, Gerry looked down at his hands, spreading and stretching them on his knees as if to inspect their cleanliness. 'He tried to make me think that it wasn't his fault either, but it was, you know.' He glanced at Michael, who realised with a shock that there were tears in his eyes. He looked no older than Vassilis.

'You won't tell anybody? I mean Harriet. She doesn't know. Can it be "our little secret", as my dad used to call it? I've lived with it my whole life. Most of the time I could put myself on a different planet . . . when it was happening. I'd pretend I was a space alien looking down on what was going on. I guess it happened to you too . . .'

Michael put out his hands, useless as in warding off a car crash. It was too late. He shook his head, both knowing and not knowing what Gerry was going to say.

'The first time, he raped me. I was eight, but he'd been working up to it for years, getting me slowly used to the idea, see? After that, it just became the thing we did and I always got a present. He liked it rough, but he never hit me like I told Harriet. She thinks he beat me but he didn't. That's how he got away with it to himself. Because whenever it happened to him, he got beaten with a stick. So he thought he was doing me a favour, being "kind". He didn't take it into account that the things he said were just as bad. He liked to humiliate me. He used to make fun of my accent, things like that. And you know why he was such a junkie, don't you? He needed a lot of stuff to help him forget what he done . . . to me.'

Nausea swirled upwards from Michael's stomach to his head. His nose fumed with brandy and when he closed his eyes his head spun.

Gerry's voice was even. It remained even throughout, sober, thoughtful, confiding, even a little dull. 'It was what happened to him that he couldn't get over. He could never connect it with what he did to me, you see, and I understand that. He used to tell me about his father all the time, how he'd come in to what he called the nursery, how he'd order him into his study for a session . . . you know. The worst was when he got sacked from school. I can say that for my dad, he was never jealous, but then it didn't matter because I never had any friends anyway. He said your mum walked in on them once. I don't know, maybe she didn't know the full extent. But for Edgar's money, she should've packed her bags and left with the lot of you there and then. You can say that for my mum, she never let herself get that close to knowing. I tried to tell her once, but all I got out of that was a thick ear.'

There was a sudden stillness between them. Michael never knew later why he hadn't hit Gerry. He supposed he wasn't really angry. What use would anger be when every wire was connected to its terminal in this engine of destruction, which hummed and ticked and glowed, neat and complete? His mother's special love for him had been no more than emotional greed, and to service it she'd sacrificed his brothers. There were no phrases he could apply to this, no stances to be adopted against it.

'I had no idea,' was all he could say.

A curious expression spread over Gerry's face . . . compassion perhaps. 'I'm sorry, I thought . . . I don't know why I thought . . . you must've been a victim too.'

'It's all right,' Michael found himself saying. 'You did the right thing to tell.' He tried to hang on to his rising gorge.

The feral look was back in Gerry's eyes, not vicious but hunted. 'They say tell a grown-up, don't they? Only you're the first grown-up I ever met.'

24

CASSIE KNEW SHE SHOULD have telephoned the vicar before driving all the way to Ashdean and so it was a waste of energy to be annoyed that he was not at home. Nevertheless, she irritably jammed a note through his letterbox asking him to ring her. It would take some negotiation to get Gerry buried in the churchyard; the undertaker was waiting for her instructions. And then there was the question of Mary Carney. Although Gosforth had assured Cassie that the prison would get the Social Services to seek her whereabouts, it was almost too bleak to contemplate. Suppose they found her . . . and alive. What would the poor woman feel, hearing about Gerry?

Cassie turned to go. It was only a matter of ten miles between her house on the Marsh and Ashdean. Maybe it was because of the rain, which was still pelting down, but the journey that morning had seemed long, almost arduous. She realised with a small surprise that, except for Harriet's funeral, she hadn't seen the village since her uncle Godfrey had sold the manor and moved to Portugal. She could see the roof from the vicarage gate. It was shiny with rain, sleek now because mended, she supposed. Well, she wished the new owners joy of the house. She only hoped they were looking after Grandma Maeve's garden.

She cast her eye over the main road, deserted in the bad weather. Maybe Ashdean was trying for 'prettiest village': flower baskets hung from the lampposts, lobelias and geraniums bedraggled by the autumn rain. Across the road, warm light shone from the bakery where her mother and Harriet Washington had bought fresh loaves, cobs and bloomers. Tourists sometimes stopped to photograph the row of Kentish shops, all tidy, russet clapboard snugly tucked together. All the scene needed was an icing of snow to make it look like an upmarket advent calendar. Cassie made a note of the thought for her next year's Christmas collection then, glancing at the churchyard as she turned to go, gave a little laugh at such an irony. She was glad it was too wet for her to make the obligatory trudge round family tombs. Not much cosiness and cheer where Edgar and her grandparents were buried. Relieved in many ways that she had to abort the wasted journey, she started towards her little Renault she had parked at the end of the path by the vicarage. Maybe it was the delayed shock from the night before, but all at once she felt drained. On impulse she made for the church, the squat Norman tower she'd known all her life. The door was unlocked; she entered, and though the church was empty she tiptoed up the aisle, found a pew at random and sat down heavily.

Only twenty-four hours ago she had been talking to Gerry, but now he was dead it seemed an immeasurable stretch of time. Her muscles felt sore, bruised as if she had been in an accident. It astonished her when she remembered that only last evening she had been looking forward to having dinner with James Gosforth, even half deciding that if things went well she might stay the night with him. She shook her head and looked at the austere Protestant cross that stood on the plain altar. The stained glass was old but not very good. It depicted the Crucifixion with the Virgin, St John and the Magdalene in stiff attendance. It puzzled Cassie why she felt so numb to James now. Even though they hadn't had an affair it felt as if they had, something long and intense which had spent itself. Maybe it was the way he had reacted to Gerry's story of the boy's death; maybe it was because all along it had been only Gerry who united them. Well, there was no point in over-reacting. If it would have been silly to throw herself into his arms, it was equally silly to reject him out of hand.

A powerful gust of wind smacked the church and from above came stair-rods of rain that pummelled the roof. Cassie looked around her at the sudden noise. If she'd wanted to escape her ancestors, this had hardly been the place to take shelter from them. She'd forgotten the plaques and statues she'd always taken for granted. In the feeble light, she made them out: from the Great War back to the Crusades, the monuments ranged round the walls, Hythe after Hythe in marmoreal commemoration. She shuddered a little at the pale gleam of carved armour, stony folds made to look like rich cloth. It was a bit like sitting in her own mausoleum.

Cassie smiled nervously as if to frowning great grandsires, a few of minor nobility, but most of them squires. She supposed there had been a point to them once, but surely not now. She could see why they had meant such a lot to Gerry. In fact, there was too much pathos in the way he had doted on the family tree she had given him. As she was determined he should be laid to rest in Ashdean, they'd jolly well have to put up with him, the ancestors. Likely as not they had lived as wickedly as he had.

Cassie shivered a little from the cold. Her hair was wet, her coat damp. If there were such things as ghosts, Gerry's would be likely to seek her here. At this thought, he was suddenly present with her as if, poor feeble spirit, he'd been waiting around in the ether for the hint he needed to make himself known. Cassie had an urge to cross herself but repressed it, partly because the Hythes wouldn't have approved, and partly because it seemed frivolous without the earnest prayer for her cousin that she was not yet prepared to make.

'Were you really innocent, Gerry?' she fancifully asked the air. Only the rain on the roof thundered in reply, but still she felt him, intensified by death into an essence. 'Poor Gerry,' she said softly.

James wasn't likely to listen to his story with an open mind. His whole life's work was to lock in, suppress and conceal society's dark shadow from itself – its own unenacted evil desires. All the same, it rankled with her that he could make up his mind about Gerry's guilt when he knew nothing but what was written on a charge sheet. To be sure, he was probably right in saying that Gerry might well have believed in his innocence without its being material. He'd been full of buzzwords – 'denial', 'distorted thinking' – all good sense as applied to Gerry, she supposed, but none of them evoking him, not as Cassie's memory of him possessed her now.

As usual, she'd steeled herself the day before to visit Gerry. This time there was no way out of it. He had written to her asking her to be his 'godmother' at his baptism, scheduled for the following week. The request had put Cassie in a quandary: she felt sure he would see this as obliging her to take an interest in him on his eventual release, and John and Alexander made that impossible. Yet it seemed dreadful to refuse. So she had demurred and thus found herself pulled in deeper because this meant she had to see him in order to explain. She tried not to be resentful. She tried not to think him manipulative for upping the stakes in this way. After all, he genuinely had no one but her.

She had arrived at the prison tense and out of sorts, expecting to be mauled into submission by his sheer wretchedness, something she always found irresistible. The humid Visitors' Room with its huddled families and fuming samovar, its tea biscuits in cellophane, forced her tension into a vice-like headache. She had almost decided to tell him that business worries meant that she could take nothing further on, a lame excuse, but no matter.

She was therefore surprised when she spotted Gerry from the door. He rose, slowly and with evident pain, to greet her, but gave her a cheerful wave.

'Cassie, thank you for coming,' he said, smiling with the bit of his face that functioned. 'How are you?'

She was a bit taken aback. Gerry usually saved this question until last, his opening conversational gambit more often than not being a threnody of grudges. On better days, his self-obsession took a more positive direction, but even though he often told her how much he cared about her and how necessary her visits to him

327

were, he was oddly uninterested in her actual life. She could see why, with his being banged up in the awful place; and in some ways, the one-way street was easier for her to negotiate. All the same, the enquiry about her health made a pleasant change.

It seemed he'd found a friend since they'd last met, his cell-mate, and he was full of excitement about the bishop coming in to baptise and confirm him. Cassie had to admit she was impressed by the rigour with which he had been catechised by the chaplain. Gerry felt he was being taken seriously, or that's what he seemed to derive from it all.

She muttered something about not having been to Mass for a long time. Gerry, with the tiresome zeal of a convert, frowned with concern. Cassie was used to blocking out this kind of thing, so she only half-listened as he took her through the saga of his 'faith journey', as he called it . . . how gruelling he'd found the course, how close he'd been to jacking the whole thing in. She found her eyes shifting round the room. A powerfully built black man sitting near them was being harangued by his tiny mother: his limbs were stiff, his head bowed in shame. A sallow kid with hair tufted like a baby's was gazing with mad eyes on a girlfriend. There was a middle-aged couple, husband and wife, silent but united in pain. All the while the guards cruised amongst them, checking for felonies like invigilators at an exam.

It had taken her a moment to realise that Gerry had started to tell her about the day Vassilis had died. His tongue, thickened by recent paralysis, made him hard to understand. 'Why would I lie to you?' she heard him asking. 'It really was Harriet's fault. And this is what I've got to do before the bishop comes. I've got to forgive her . . . for my own peace of mind . . . don't you see?'

Cassie gazed down the flagged aisle of Ashdean Church. A modern font with wheels and a stainless steel basin was tucked in next to the lectern where a brass eagle spread its wings above. If Edgar had done the decent thing by Gerry, none of this would have happened. He would have been dressed in the family chris-tening robes, and duly doused. Edgar could have ensured that he was taken up, taken in, educated – perhaps not loved but at least given . . . what? Class? Had it come to this – that she believed class really would have helped him? This sort of futile conjecture was the way Gerry had lost himself, trapped as he was in what might have been. There was no retrieving time.

His words of yesterday morning pattered on her inner, instinctual ear. Perhaps it had been his very difficulty in speaking that made him more persuasive and more articulate than she had ever remembered him. He had to choose his words, think about them.

'What really happened, Gerry?' she had asked him. Then sharply, 'Just exactly how is it that Harriet, who was nowhere near the scene of the crime, killed little Vassilis?'

She had half-expected Gerry to terminate the visit, get up in a huff and walk away. Instead, he held his ground, squared himself on the chair and painfully lifted his hands in front of him on the table parallel to each other as if to frame the story.

'Right,' he told her. 'I'll take it step by step. First things first: you'll know how the land lies at your dad's farm?'

Cassie nodded.

'And you'll know how I met the kid too. It was the day your dad showed me round the place, and Vassilis sort of tagged along.' Gerry swallowed hard. 'Look, I know you're going to find this disgusting, but I won't lie and say I wasn't attracted to him. He'd been learning English. He wanted to practise. He had this dog. I know it came up in the trial about the dog, but there was a reason and no one believed me. The day the three of us went out, there was the boy, the dog, Uncle Michael and me . . . and it was the best day – the best day I ever remember in my life.' He paused, frowning in concentration.

'I don't know why he took to me, Vassilis, but he did. He really seemed to like me and your dad was very pleased. It gave me this warm feeling being together with them, as if I belonged. We walked for a bit and then he suddenly started telling me about his life, how his mum and his brothers had died, how he and his dad had walked all the way from Kosovo. And your dad told me later it was a big compliment because he never talked about it. You see, he trusted me. That was the main thing. And I couldn't get over it, how much he'd been through, how cheerful he was. It was like his whole country had been a massive prison and now he was free.

'That was it, what got to me, not just the fact that he trusted me enough to tell me. It was this feeling I had about his freedom. He could roam anywhere he liked, the whole farm to himself . . . but it was more an inner thing. You see, he was living with his dad in the cottage they had, feeling safe at last, you know, even with his whole family dead. It's hard to put it into words but there's no way I could have hurt Vassilis. I couldn't have even touched him. He was like I wanted things to be for me . . . you know, if Edgar hadn't been Edgar. He was a dream of myself, someone who had been through a terrible atrocity, but he'd survived because the adults in his life loved him and protected him.' Gerry gestured with his good hand, frustrated.

'It was like looking in a backwards mirror, just as if I was beginning all over again a new person . . . sort of like writing a book and giving the hero a chance that you never had yourself. There was your dad, family at last, and there was the boy. I wanted to start all over again and be just like the boy, like his brother. The thing nobody understands is that from the moment I saw him I loved him. They think I meant something dirty when I told them that, but I didn't. I felt true love for the first time in my life.'

Maybe that's why Cassie now felt so cold and indifferent to James Gosforth. Last night when she had told him this he'd simply said, 'He never "hurt"? He never "touched"? He meant that he didn't bugger the child. There's a whole range of inappropriate behaviour they go in for, shocking things, and it doesn't involve their definition of "touching". They invent rules for themselves, these paedophiles, like their own private age of consent. They'll get quite censorious about someone who's molested a kid of, say, five, when their "morals" tell them six is the time of full sexual maturity! As for "love" . . . well.'

'Are you going to hear the whole story or are you going to make up your mind in advance?' she had said. He had listened but he hadn't heard it.

'The thing was,' Gerry had continued, 'that the kid loved your dad. He looked up to him. I know you won't believe me the way I've talked about him, but back then your dad meant the world to me too. I trusted him and I wanted more than anything for him to trust me. To cut a long story short, after our walk, your dad had to go back to the town and I was stuck with Harriet on the terrace there, you know, that overlooks the sea.'

Cassie nodded. 'Go on.'

'Well, everybody said that I lured Vassilis, got him into my clutches, so to speak, but the fact of the matter was that he came looking for me.'

Gosforth had snorted at this bit of information. 'Cassie, that is classic,' he'd said. 'The child always initiates the contact for these men, not the reverse! They'll say a three-year-old was "asking for it".'

She looked around the church, her reverie broken. Maybe he was right. She got up and strolled down the aisle, rubbing her arms to warm herself up. Gerry's story harried her though and wouldn't let her alone.

'He came to get me. And that's when I saw it, about Harriet. You should have seen her face! I'm sorry, Cassie, but she was eaten up . . . jealous. It hit me in my stomach and made me sick . . . a woman that age? I mean, I thought of her as a mother.' He shuddered in revulsion, a bit rich considering all things, Cassie thought.

'Anyway, partly to get away from her, I followed the boy.' Gerry looked down at his hands. 'No, I would have followed him anyway, but I promise you I wouldn't have . . . well . . . for several reasons and I'll come to them. The thing Vassilis had to tell me was

331

that he wanted to do something special for Michael. It's simple. The whole thing was so simple and I couldn't have invented it myself.

'You know how your land borders on where they're doing up that temple to the goddess . . . whatever?'

'Demeter.'

'Demeter. Yes, well, the kid was keen on the site and snooped around it a lot and had met some of the archaeologists who worked on restoring the temple. He told me they had a suspicion that there were some of those statues your father liked so much . . .'

'Cycladic.'

'Yes, those . . . buried in a field . . . that your dad actually owned. So Vassilis asked me to help him find them. He'd not wanted to ask his father because he worked so hard, but he needed a man to help him shift some of the rocks where he thought the statues were buried. I was chuffed to be asked, I can tell you. And I knew there was a kind of danger in saying yes. But the point was, I knew I'd be safe and I knew I'd be straight. You see, before we left for Greece, I'd told Harriet about my, you know, tendency. And you know why I told her? I told her so that someone would know, just in case, so that if I was tempted, I'd only have to look at her. Besides, I didn't like the idea of messing with her then, lying to her and all that. I really did want to go straight. I really did want to get better.'

'I know she knew,' Cassie had said. 'And I'm sorry to tell you that this was why she felt so awful about the boy's death. If she'd told someone, she could have prevented it.'

Gerry's face contorted in rage. 'She told all right, but not how you think! Don't get me wound up. I'll come to it. I've got to tell the story in order otherwise I'll miss out important bits.'

Cassie had folded her arms across her chest, grim and disapproving, but he hadn't seemed to notice and when he had recovered himself somewhat, he carried on:

'Where was I? Yes. When we had our meal that night, there was a lot to drink and this is important. Remember it, Cassie. We drank a hell of a lot. And I suppose if you want to be "kind" you'll say that they forgot this detail because of the drink, but I told them both, your dad and Harriet, that I was planning to go out with Vassilis all day the next day to look for the hidden treasure. They all say I made it up, but I didn't. I couldn't have imagined it if I'd tried. So why in the name of God would I try something on with Vassilis when everyone knew where I was going and what I was doing? If I'm honest with you, I've done this sort of thing before and it's not nice and there's no reason for you to look so sick because I'm sorry now, but stealth has been my best friend in the past, stealth and lying and scheming. It's so fucking terrible when I think about it. I wanted to make sure, to prove to myself that I wouldn't, that this time was different . . . that this boy was special. I wanted everybody to know where I was going so that I *wouldn't*!'

If one detail had impressed Gosforth, Cassie supposed it had been this one. Still, he had been adamant. 'I'm sure that's how he remembered it, Cassie. Memory is a funny old thing.'

Poor Gerry. Why did she feel this ache of pity? Her own memory could be playing tricks in retrospect, but as he spoke he had looked grey, his face and nostrils pinched, flesh retracted over his nose so that it stood out like a beak. Why hadn't she told one of the officers she thought Gerry was ill? But she'd let it slide.

His eyes had glittered though, telling the tale. His slurred voice gathered speed, momentum; he was the Ancient Mariner reduced to nothing but a story – reduced, she supposed, to the slaughtered albatross.

'What happened?' she asked him.

'Well, Harriet said nothing. She sat there pushing her food around her plate, giving me the eye like she was ashamed of me. If she'd had something to say, she could have said it there and then, about (and he aped her voice) "it's not being a good plan" spending the day with Vassilis. But she said nothing and then she went to bed.

'Your dad had just about had it with Harriet. I could tell he was well and truly fed up with her just like I was. He cracked a bottle of brandy and we went up to his study and got totally pissed. The point about it was, though, we had a really good talk which was why, I don't know . . . I told him lots of things about Edgar . . . It was why I expected him to be on my side when everything went pear-shaped later.'

For some reason, this had struck Cassie hard, odd because it was only a minor detail. 'I never knew you'd had a proper talk. What was it you told him exactly?' she asked, her breath drawn, her lip caught in her teeth.

Gerry shook his head. He scrutinised Cassie over the table for a long moment. 'Nothing really,' he said finally, his expression oddly gentle. 'I guess it was nothing really. It's just I thought we made a bond, which was why . . . it was why . . . well, it was another reason for me not to *do* anything.'

Now she looked back on it, he had changed tack very quickly. It bothered her. She stood knocking her hand on the pew, tapping her fingers on it as if she could type out blind some key word that would fit into the wards of her father's locked mind. Why hadn't she pressed Gerry for more detail yesterday morning? She shrugged into her damp coat and wandered towards what would have been the Lady Chapel before Cromwell. His men had hacked out the stone Virgin that once graced the small altar. The Sunday School met there now, she supposed. There were children's pictures of Jesus pasted on the wall above a mat. In one, a bearded Christ with startling, big eyes was patting a little girl's head. She was all smile with a sunny yellow triangle for a dress. Across from this tucked-away corner was what the family always called the 'Crusader Wall'. Sir Aelric Hythe lay in armour, legs crossed, on top of an undistinguished tomb. With a sudden spurt of cynicism, she wondered about the stone sword that lay down his body. How many Byzantines or Saracens had he murdered? Above him, the

Tudor Hythes, man and wife, smiled woodenly above their ruffs from a bas-relief. Could they have they betrayed Catholics to Elizabeth? Who knew and where did it end? They looked pacific enough, smug and self-assured.

No, it didn't do to go into it. But she paced all the same.

'The next morning, I slept in a bit late because of the booze,' Gerry had continued. 'And I'm coming to how important that is because I was late for the kid who said he'd fetch me from the farm at nine so we could get a good start. The thing was, I was sure there was something funny going on. Harriet and Uncle Michael . . . there was an atmosphere between them. But my head was so wrecked, I paid no attention to it at the time.'

'But Harriet didn't tell my father about your past. That's the whole point.' Cassie's stomach seized up at the thought of this. The possibility had never entered her head that her father could have known the truth and failed to respond.

Gerry shook his head. 'No, I don't think he knew. ' He looked at her curiously. 'He'd have come with us if he did. And for that matter, I wonder why *she* didn't. No, she was too much of a coward. She was too sneaky. It's something else she did, and I've never, ever forgiven it, but I'll come to it. Wait for it. It's rich!' Gerry shook his head from side to side, slowly, the picture of moral horror, but he cleared his throat and continued.

'We set off, me and Vassilis, about ten. He'd been waiting for me at the stone wall, the one that separated the house from the fields, and he'd nearly gone home because he thought I was going to stand him up. That's what I thought was the matter with him at first.'

'The matter?'

'Yeah. He seemed in a bit of a mood. Then I thought maybe it was the dog. When they talked about the dog being tied up, they said it was my idea, so that she couldn't protect him. And it *was* my idea. I never said it wasn't! But no one would listen when I told them the truth of it. I swear to you it was all about this archaeology thing. You see, I thought Hera might do her own digging if we hit paydirt. She could've broken the statues if we found them. So he agreed to leave her. But he missed her. He told me so. He didn't feel right without her.

'Anyway, we started to walk. It was a long way and the sun was up, burning hot. He'd brought a bit of a picnic and, though it was early for it, we sat down on a stone about halfway to the site and ate it. He'd managed to get some cold drinks but they were only cans and I was parched from the night before from the brandy.

'He seemed to perk up after the food. We had a game, a hiding game. It was a bit young for him, but I reckon he'd gone through so much that he'd taken a bit of time to grow up. But the point was, he enjoyed it. He said it was fun! He laughed when I caught him. He wasn't frightened or worried. Look, Cassie, if I was going to do anything, I would have done it then. Believe me, I wasn't even tempted. His face that day, his laugh. They are with me every night before I go to sleep. It was pure. I promise!'

Cassie rubbed her hands together and meandered down the side aisle where an eighteenth-century Josiah Hythe, imposing in uniform, stood struggling out of a marble military scene. It was at this juncture in the tale she had retold to Gosforth that they had locked into different positions. 'Games!' he had said. 'Innocent games? That's how they remember what they've done. The child's response, having fun, laughing. It's just part of a script. They have a selective amnesia for the truth. Cassie, it's well known! He admitted to you that he grabbed the child. Suppose he held him close and suppose . . .' Out of delicacy he let the sentence dangle, but Cassie knew well enough.

'You think I'm completely naive, don't you?' she had snapped. 'So you think he had an erection and the boy felt it, *knew*! You're saying he got the wind up and Gerry had to silence him.'

She chose a pew now and sat down again, puzzling her hands together into a basket. Of course, it made sense. She really ought to apologise to James.

'It was just a lark, nothing else, I promise,' Gerry had said. 'And afterwards, we went on in a better mood. He was telling me some stories about school and that. He was a bit miserable about it. He was getting teased because he was Albanian and also because the schoolmistress made a fuss of him. I listened to all of it. I wanted to be his friend, you see, not like the other ones. With the others I wanted just one thing.' He lowered his eyes at this little bit of Victorian euphemism, but at the time Cassie had somehow believed him. In a deranged way, he was like a man who'd use a whore but marry only a virgin.

'Well, when did things start going wrong?' she had asked, prompting him. His eyes held a far-off look, as if he had caught an ugly glimpse of himself, but from what period in his history it was impossible to tell.

He shook himself. 'That. Oh yeah. It was the thirst. That's what did it. The terrible thirst. You see, we were nearly there, walking along, carrying our kit for his dig. He kept saying "not far, not far", but it was so bloody hot! So I started to moan about it a bit, the heat. I didn't want to tell him about the hangover. That didn't seem right. But he gathered that I needed something to drink and that's when he told me about the well. And when he said the water was cool and fresh, it was like a mirage in the desert. My throat felt like I'd been swallowing razors. Did you ever see the well? Did you know about it?' he asked Cassie.

She shook her head. 'There are wells all over Naxos,' she said, 'but I didn't know we had one except at the farmhouse, not, of course, until Vassilis died.'

'I wish to God I'd never seen it. I wish I'd kept my bloody mouth shut about how thirsty I was. I mean, you'll know now about the grove where it is, right near that ruined monastery you've got on your land. I'd have died of thirst rather than this!' Gerry gave a low sort of groan and put his head in his hands.

'I thought it must be his secret hideout, you see, that he was letting me into a secret, telling me where it was. The point is, though, and nobody ever would believe me, that he didn't come with me.'

Cassie frowned now as she had done then.

'Look. Why would I lie? He never came. That was what happened whether you like it or not. I told the truth then and I'm telling it now. He pointed it out. I can see him now in my mind's eye as if it was yesterday. He said, "You go and I come after." The last I ever saw of him was then, when we split. He was walking up the hill towards the monastery. I watched him go. He disappeared into a little chapel or something, built into the side. Now, why would I make that up? It's such an odd thing for a kid to do, go into a church like that, and it was only later I learned that he was incredibly religious or something.

'If I'd meant to touch him or hurt him, I would've followed him in there, wouldn't I? But I didn't. I went down into the grove. There was an old leatherette armchair and a lean-to someone had once made, I guess. It was cool and shady. The wall of the well wasn't very high, but there was a lid on it. I let down the bucket, drew water in it, drank these huge gulps, and sat in the armchair, waiting for Vassilis to come as he said. Only he didn't show. It's true. He went up. I went down. I never laid a finger on him and, as for not saving his life, I didn't have a clue, not a clue that he'd gone back there after I finally left to go and look for him. I actually thought he had come to some harm in the church, fainted from the heat or broken a leg. I searched the whole area, called out for him, but in the end I decided he'd just got bored and gone home.'

Gerry's voice became urgent, as if his own life depended on her belief; his eyes seemed to be staring into the trauma. He looked up at her. 'At the trial, they made a lot of the fact that I had his spectacles in my pocket when I got back to the farm. It was so simple, so innocent, I never even thought to hide them. The poor kid's nose was sweating in the heat, as we walked. As we walked up the hill after lunch. He hated the glasses, he said, just another reason to be teased and bullied, so he asked me to put them in my pocket because he was wearing only shorts and the pockets were shallow, you see, whereas my shirt pocket was deep.

'I swear and promise by almighty God that I had nothing whatever to do with the death of that boy!'

Cassie studied the kneeler hung on a brass hook in front of her. Someone had gone to trouble covering it in needlework. There was a bright picture of sheep and a shepherd, Christ perhaps, looking for the lost. It was as if Gerry, spirit or memory, had forced open her head. Tears had run down his face.

'And so, are you saying,' she had said after a moment, 'that it was Harriet who made her way up the fields after you? That she lured Vassilis into the grove and drowned him? That she killed a child out of jealousy over you?'

He shook his head, his nose glutted. She gave him a tissue and he wiped his face all over, for beads of sweat had collected on his forehead. 'You don't understand,' he said. 'Harriet didn't drown him. Not physically.'

'Well, how did she do it then? *Witchcraft*?'

Gerry sighed. 'You don't get it, do you? I thought you'd get it right away. Don't you see? Isn't it obvious? It's why I can't stop hating her.'

It was the oddest and most disjunctive moment in Cassie's life. 'Am I being thick? It's true she talked to the police after the child's body was found, but he was dead by then. Surely, that was why you came to hate her so, calling her "Judas", things like that.'

A deep intensity filled Gerry's eyes, whether of rage or anguish Cassie could not fathom.

'Vassilis died in the well, right?' he said, spelling out what he seemed to see as axiomatic. 'I'm telling you I didn't put him there. Not in any way. I thought I'd given enough clues. There she is, up early in the morning. She wants for me and the boy to split, but she hasn't got the nerve to confront me or to blow the whistle to your dad. She notices I'm late down for breakfast. She also sees Vassilis waiting for me, by the fence under the tree with Hera. And so that's what she does. She snatches her golden opportunity and she goes over to him and she tells him I'm going to hurt him, that I've been in gaol for hurting children and that he can't *trust* me!'

The power of this mad argument was such that Cassie could not have broken into it even if she'd tried.

'But he knows me! He *does* trust me. He thinks he does. He likes me. He isn't listening to her. He tells her to get stuffed. He's going with me whatever! And so he does. We carry on. I don't seem likely to hurt him. We're friends. We truly are. I mean it, Cassie. But then the poison starts to drip. It starts to seep. He thinks to himself, "Why would she have told me all that – nice, sweet old lady – if it wasn't true?"

'So, by the time we get to the grove where the well is, he starts to think that being alone with me down by the well where no one can see us for the trees might spell trouble, and he bottles out.

'He must've gone to the church, then come down and hid in the bushes, waiting for me to go, waiting till I was gone. And I reckon it was then that either he just got up on the well wall or tripped . . . maybe I left the lid off, maybe I didn't put the bucket back straight and it stuck . . . I don't know wells or country or nothing like that . . . and he fell in. Maybe it was one of the bullies from his school that found him there and pushed him. Maybe he thought he heard a noise and that I was coming back to "get" him. Which I wasn't. I went back to the farm, hoping to see him there, give him back his specs, give him a good ticking off, if you want to know. But if she hadn't put him against me, frightened him, he'd have stayed with me, and if he'd stayed with me, he wouldn't have died. God knows, I would have saved Vassilis from drowning. As God is my witness, I would!' Gerry leaned forward on his terrible crusade. 'I'm not so much saying it was the boy she murdered, but it was me. She murdered the trust of the one person I loved and would never harm. Never! She murdered the beauty of my whole life and that is why I don't think I can do what Father Joe asked me to and forgive her.'

'But Harriet did not tell the child,' Cassie said.

'How do you know that?' Gerry sat straight, his arms frozen by his side. 'How could you possibly know?'

'Because it makes nonsense of everything she told me.'

'She was a liar!'

'Harriet was no liar, Gerry,' Cassie said. 'You do know she turned herself in to the Greek police when the child was discovered dead, don't you? Not you. Herself. She asked them to arrest her.'

'So?'

'It was because she hadn't told my father. And she never got over it, never recovered. Nor has he, for that matter. I'm afraid I don't think it ever crossed her mind to tell Vassilis. What you don't see, because you can't see, is that it would have made her feel so much better if she had.'

Cassie banged her fists now against the pew, then ran her fingers through her hair. How had she got mixed up in all of this? For the crime of sharing a set of grandparents with Gerry she was sentenced to an unending bafflement. She'd been sitting like a fool in a damp country church for an hour, ravelling and unravelling a mystery that could never be solved. She sneezed. She'd probably caught cold.

How convinced she had been last night that Gerry's version of things put him, with the greatest possible irony, in the clear! At least, that was how she'd argued it with James Gosforth. For if Gerry had been truthful about the grudge he had harboured all these years against Harriet, it followed that he could have been nowhere near the child when he died.

He had needed, poor Minotaur, to construct a labyrinth for himself that protected him from the ultimate and unendurable knowledge that Vassilis himself, and no other, had, during that day Gerry held so precious, got the drift, bolted and hidden himself away.

Was it Gerry's intensity that alerted the boy? It might have been something else or worse, but she hoped not. She could see it, somehow, Gerry quivering towards the child in the heat of the day, his eyes shining with the same sultry love he found so abominable in Harriet. She could see his hands trembling, his mouth moist, slack with need, the need of an adult, the overbearing and top-heavy emotional desperation that no child's shoulders could ever carry nor be expected to endure. And Vassilis had panicked. Perhaps later, when he was sure Gerry had gone, he had paid his own visit to the grove. Especially if it had been his secret hideout, maybe he had the urge to cleanse it, make it his own again. Maybe, feeling soiled, he had tried to wash – the battered armchair, the lean-to, himself . . . and had fallen in the process.

Maybe it had been more terrible than that. Cassie's mind veered to the edge of this thought, flinched from looking, but considered it. Whatever chop logic Gerry brought to the mechanics of touching or hurting, another possibility leered up at her. For a child who had survived the incalculable brutality of war, the toils of persecution and flight, for a child right on the brink of puberty, his inner fragility might have been such that Gerry was the last violator he was prepared to tolerate: maybe the sense of indignity against himself was such that Vassilis had jumped in. Cassie decided that she was not going to think this.

She was not certain, not of anything. It was probably better to focus on what James had said when he gently pointed out that the truly necessary fiction for Gerry had been love – which, as everybody knows, conquers all, is blind, forgives sins, and is, in and of itself, the emancipation from evil. So that in creating the myth of love, Gerry had uncreated the circumstances that surrounded the death of the beloved, whom he had never really loved at all, only wanted to.

Cassie sneezed again and made to go, but on an impulse that was really a decision in the end, she unhooked the kneeler with the bright sheep from the pew in front of her. She crossed herself, whether the Hythes in their rigid tombs liked it or not, and prayed.

EPILOGUE

MARY CARNEY HAS BOUGHT A FLAT in Clacton now, with a windfall, she tells anyone who will listen. She has taken up ballroom dancing and feels fitter as a result of the exercise and the sea air. Her son saw her right, she says and, in a way, he did. She has re-invented herself as a widow, changed her name to Hythe, and has even bought herself a wedding ring that goes with her new identity.

It took some effort to get hold of Gerry's money, just as it had done to conceal from Social Security the annuity she had been receiving for so many years from Godfrey Hythe. 'Blackmail', he liked to call it, but he paid it all the same, siphoning off money from Edgar's trust into a special fund 'for the boy's education'. Well, what use would Gerry have had for that?

She'd made a tragic error in revealing herself to Godfrey all those years ago. If she had only waited for Edgar's death she might have bagged the lot. But Godfrey was a real shyster at heart, and managed to fix everything so that only Edgar's legitimate heirs could inherit. Edgar must have got wind that something was going on because there was all that talk of taking Gerry to Ashdean. Too bad, but he died before it came to that. Mary still thinks she wouldn't put it past Godfrey to have speeded Edgar on his way, with a generous present of bad gear, or something along those lines.

Still, he kept his part of the bargain and she hers. She was the beneficiary in perpetuity of certain monies as long as she lay low and kept Gerry a secret. At times, she'd been tempted to break the agreement, write to Edgar's mother just to get even, or play a double game with the other brother Michael, but it wasn't worth the risk.

Patience paid off. How could she know way back then that Gerry would inherit fifty grand from some old bat? This too was in a trust that dissolved on Gerry's death. At first, it looked as if it was going to revert to the old girl's daughter, but it seemed that the will Gerry made, scrawled on prison letter paper, was valid after all. There was a nerve-wracking time for Mary, but worth it in the end. The prison chaplain and an officer called Gosforth confirmed that he'd intended to make his mum sole heir. Quite the gentleman, Gosforth, she thought. He'd even come to visit her.

Well, she's set up now and, for the first time in her life, a happy woman. This is just what she wanted for herself, independence, a few friends, and respectability. She's thinking of taking up bridge. It's been hard graft, her life, her father a violent drunk, her mother a doormat. She ran away from home at fifteen and slept rough until she found a protector who saw the potential. Mary scrubbed up nice, which is how she met Edgar Hythe, through one of her Johns who'd owned a casino in the West End. She never got round to telling Gerry it was love. Edgar was so handsome, so different, so fucked up.

How she ever survived Gerry, God alone knows, she thinks. From the moment he was born, she knew he'd be trouble. He wet the bed; he trashed the flat. He even smeared his shit on the walls and she never had a moment's peace with the Welfare breathing down her neck. Still, he was her son and sometimes even now she can get a bit weepy when she considers where he died. She's glad she doesn't have to look at Grisholme any longer. On a clear day, she'd catch sight of the prison from the window in her lounge and would have to draw the curtains so as not to think. But she's a survivor, and survivors put things behind them, treat each new day as a golden opportunity.

It was a bit of a job ferreting out Mary's address from old prison records, and Gosforth found the meeting a distasteful experience; but he is stuck with Grisholme for the moment, and cannot so easily dispense with memories of Gerry. He has passed his Principal Officer exams, and as soon as there's an opening he will be moving to an open prison, and up to become a sub-governor there. He is holding out for this job because of its two main advantages. There are no sex offenders in the Category D establishment of his dreams, and its location is good, not very far away from Cassie Hythe.

Gerry's death has turned Gosforth inward, and for some time afterwards he wobbled in his sense of vocation, wanting to find an alternative way of making a living. He finally shelved his novel. The resonating complexities of Gerry's case, and of prisons in general, have put him off thrillers, and he ponders deeper things these days. Surely, he thinks, there is a better way than prison to deal with men who feel compelled to prey on children. What way, he cannot imagine. Are their 'personality disorders' truly 'untreatable'? Perhaps they should be redefined as mentally ill. Could more effective therapies be sought and tried? Maybe paedophiles are simply wicked. Maybe they should just be punished. He knows they should repent. Faced with these imponderables, Gosforth feels weary. All the solutions mooted, humane or inhumane, would seem to start with the premise that men like Gerry should be viewed as specimens in jars and this feels wrong to him when he senses them as individuals.

Gosforth's personal life has taken an upturn recently. For some time he has been asking Cassie to marry him, and so far she has put him off. Is she in love with him or not? That's what he really wants to know. She tells him it isn't that simple, but he can't think why. In an ulterior way, he knows, though, that it has something to do with the questions Gerry raised between them. But there has been a breakthrough, and Gosforth lives in hope now. As a result of a week he spent on Naxos, where Cassie asked him so that he could meet her parents, Michael Hythe seems to be making some real progress towards a recovery from the blighting effects of the boy's death. And this has given Cassie food for thought.

Eleni Hythe has been almost too communicative lately, and she tells Cassie that her father has rallied since Gosforth's visit. It has been a while since she has come upon him secretly weeping and she knows he has not been out to see Vassilis's grave for some time. Eleni has made it clear to Cassie that she could do an awful lot worse than Gosforth. To Cassie's annoyance, she has even been dropping heavy hints about weddings and June and the cathedral. This is probably because after Gerry's death Cassie had her boys baptised, and Eleni hopes for the full set of sacraments.

Gosforth would like to think that he has helped Michael. Maybe it is by association with Cassie, but he is mightily taken with her parents. She tells him wryly that he is not only good with her children, with whom he will play interminable card games and whose jokes he always finds funny, he is also a model of patience with the elderly. He does not know exactly how to interpret this. It makes him sound appallingly dull. But there is something in her tone that tells him she knows she needs his stability.

The visit to Naxos promised to be sticky. Quite reasonably, Gosforth thought, the Hythes were cautious of a man who had heard Gerry draw his last breath, a prison officer to boot. Quickly, however, a mutual passion for archaeology provided a bond between him and Michael, and one thing led to another.

Gosforth was not looking for an opportunity to take things forward, only a way to survive the visit, but one came unexpectedly when Michael, more out of courtesy than enthusiasm, took his guest one late afternoon for an archaeological stroll through Naxos Town. First, they made the obligatory tour of the Palatia and Ariadne's gate. Their conversation, minimal and stilted, seemed a formality. As Cassie's avowed suitor, Gosforth felt rigid in her father's presence, and imagined that he felt the same. That afternoon, the sea was combed with gold and the rhythmic crash of waves sent spume flying from the rocks.

Soon Gosforth began to realise that he was not the principle cause of the old man's stiffness. 'You know about the child who died here?' Michael said, apropos of nothing, it seemed; they had been talking about Ariadne. 'Cassie has told you that, I presume.' Gosforth nodded and when they exchanged a glance, he saw it. It came by way of a resemblance he caught around Michael's eyes to Gerry or, to be more precise, the lack of it. It was a question of expression, perhaps. The old man looked out into the distance, and a look of such sorrow crossed his face that Gosforth's first impulse was to reach out a hand. Maybe it was this simple reflex of compassion that brought Gerry so fully to his mind . . . in regard to what was present in his uncle, absent in him. He shrugged and shook his head.

The two men made their way down the Palatia along the sea wall, then out to a short stretch of shore that lay beyond. Michael wanted to show Gosforth a newly built museum at Grotta, which preserves an entire Mycenaean cemetery that archaeologists have scrupulously excavated.

A glass walkway runs over the site, and Gosforth became a time traveller, flying weightless as he peered down into the complex of tombs. Within the ancient cemetery excavations have uncovered altars where, in the eighth century BC, families would gather to eat a sacred meal in honour of their dead. Gosforth forgot everything, even that Michael was Cassie's father, in a heady zeal for the deep past. He read the learned blurbs, absorbing them, and gazed upon the crockery that lay beneath his feet.

It seemed that the ancients used to hold their feasts upon ancestral tombs, using them as tables. They would eat and drink from consecrated vessels, pouring libations from pottery jars made with clay mixed with purifying sea water. At the end of the meal, these had to be destroyed to avoid spiritual contamination by the dead. Gosforth could see it all in his mind's eye, the solemn consummation of special foods, the ritual breaking of crocks, the quick march away.

Gosforth did not know quite how it happened, but by the time they left the museum, he and Michael had become the best of friends. He supposed it must have been the interest he took, and the informed judgements he was able to make. Michael became quite lively, exploring his own theories and expounding on the way that some of these ancient rites of purgation find echoes in present-day Greece. There was, for instance, a link between Mycenaean funerary customs and Orthodox memorial liturgies. And did Gosforth know that modern Greeks say, 'Let's throw a stone over our shoulder' when they are trying to put something unpleasant behind them? Gosforth did not. Michael pointed to a pile of stones by the gate to the ancient necropolis. When the sacred meal was finished, the crocks purged and honour done, the mourners would leave. And when they did so, the Mycenaeans, careful that their dead should not follow, would throw a ritual stone behind them. Gosforth was suitably impressed.

The sun was beginning to sink as they made their way down to the front in search of a drink. A crowd of tourists had gathered on the Palatia to watch the sunset. They could have been Mycenaeans, Gosforth thought. They could have been worshipping Apollo. But then he and Michael were embroiled in a discussion raised by one of the plastic placards on the museum wall. Gosforth had noted that, like many primitive societies, the Mycenaeans told and re-told the stories of their ancestors as part of the funerary rites. As these grew and became ritualised, the honoured dead became commemorated in statuary erected outside the city walls.

He wasn't sure that Michael's theory was very scientific, but he liked it all the same. Perhaps in the telling, the revision and embellishment of these tales, the House of Atreus took on the shape of fiction. Perhaps the sacrifice of Iphigenia, or the murder of Agamemnon, told and told again, grew and formed themselves into tragedy. Maybe western literature itself had come into being this way! Gosforth wasn't too sure about that, but he was willing to take the plunge for the birth of family psychology.

It could have been for the evocation of Sophocles that, when they found themselves at ease at Michael's favourite ouzerie, they began to talk of Gerry.

Gosforth did not know if they really should.

Soon enough, though, there was no choice but to listen. Maybe it was the ouzo, but Michael began to speak about the day Vassilis died. The morning Gerry and the boy set off on their hike he had been full of misgivings, nothing he could pinpoint, but his conversations with Gerry had taken an ominous turn the night before. Over and over he replayed the scene, how he had been in a state of shock over various revelations; how, for this reason, he had dismissed his nagging fear as overly suspicious. He had wanted to talk to someone. If only he had rung his wife! But they had quarrelled. Instead, he thought of telling Harriet.

'Surely you're not blaming yourself for the boy's death!' Gosforth cried, though from Cassie's account he knew the old man did. Perhaps he told everyone who would listen. Perhaps he had to exorcise it.

There was a moment, Michael continued, one moment in which the situation could have been wholly redeemed. That morning, he and Harriet had sat together, the two of them at breakfast, and he opened his mouth to speak. But she had looked up at him, then away, with an impersonal tranquillity, like someone waiting for a bus. It was as if she had caught the idle glance of a stranger. It was as if even his most casual remark might be an intrusion on a profound and unknowable solitude. If only he had foraged on, even with the slender evidence of intuition! Surely, if he had spoken she would have told him what she knew. And if she had done, he could have put a stop to it all. Vassilis would be alive, and they could have persuaded Gerry to get appropriate help. Not that he blamed Harriet. Gosforth was not to think that he blamed her. Not when he knew how Gerry had been using her. And not when he knew her agony of mind.

Gosforth listened with great care, still a little puzzled why he had been chosen for this confidence. But when it came time to speak, he found himself oddly articulate. His having known Gerry made a great difference and it pleased him to realise that his daily contact with men like him had not gone completely to waste. He wasn't sure he had a lot of insight to offer, but whatever he said it did seem to bring a kind of relief to Cassie's father. They sat without a word for quite a while, bouzouki thumping from the tannoy of the bar. Fairy lights went on as the sun finally set.

Gosforth is convinced that what came after was something of a gift, maybe in advance of a betrothal. After seeming to consider it for a while, Michael began to talk again, this time about his father and his brothers. It was an obscure story, obliquely put, but one from which Gosforth has derived some truths, implied not stated, that he will never tell Cassie. Someone needs to know, he can see that, but not Cassie, not ever. Gosforth hopes that Michael trusts the Hythe legacy is in safe hands. He is privileged to have it, and will not betray it.

The two men strolled down the quay to the other end of the harbour. They were to meet Eleni and Cassie for supper at a beach taverna, where the food is good, and the wine plentiful, cheap and local. The chat that night was relaxed, even cheerful, but at the end of the meal Gosforth had an urge, which he resisted, to linger behind the party as it ambled home.

What a good thing it would be, he thought, if he had the nerve to pour the end of the wine into the sand and smash the jug, for the sake of Vassilis, Harriet and Gerry.

For Cassie, himself, her parents and her boys, he surreptitiously picked up a stone from the beach and threw it over his shoulder, so that he could mark their separation from the dead and, thus cleansed, go forward in peace, at ease with the living.

ON BECOMING A FAIRY GODMOTHER
Sara Maitland

'Her reach is breathtaking, her prose as liquid and potent as a witch's brew'—*Publishers Weekly*

£7.99
ISBN 1 904559 00 X

Fifteen new 'fairy stories' breathe new life into old legends and bring the magic of myth back into modern women's lives. What became of Helen of Troy, of Guinevere and Maid Marion? And what happens to today's mature woman when her children have fled the nest? Here is an encounter with a mermaid, an erotic adventure with a mysterious stranger, the story of a woman who learns to fly and another who transforms herself into a fairy godmother.

LEAVING IMPRINTS
Henrietta Seredy

'Beautifully written . . . an unusual and memorable novel'— Charles Palliser, author of *The Quincunx*

£7.99
ISBN 1 904559 02 6

'At night when I can't sleep I imagine myself on the island.' But Jessica is alone in a flat by a park. She doesn't want to be there – she doesn't have anywhere else to go. As the story moves between present and past, gradually Jessica reveals the truth behind the compelling relationship that has dominated her life. 'With restrained lyricism, *Leaving Imprints* explores a destructive, passionate relationship between two damaged people. Its quiet intensity does indeed leave imprints. I shall not forget this novel'— Sue Gee, author of *The Hours of the Night*